# HARLEM BOYZ

## *ARMANI WILLIAMS*

A JERZEE BOY PUBLICATION
Bringing you only the best in urban chic fiction!

First edition printing: Fall 2013

Harlem Boyz a/k/a Boyz In The City

Published by Armani Williams for Jerzee Boy Publishing, LLC
Newark, NJ

Cover Design by Sudan Martin AKA Su Incredbl of Suincredbl.com & James A. Grant

ISBN: 978-0-9910736-0-3

Printed in the United States of America

Also from Armani Williams

# Acknowledgements

So here we are at book number two. This has been an incredible journey so far. I still want to thank everyone for all the love and support I got from my first book *Scandalicious*. I am so humbled and grateful for all the wonderful things that have happened as a result of it all.

So *Harlem Boyz* is finally here! It was truly a labor of love. I started writing this story back in the fall of 2008 and worked on it over the course of the next two years and completed its first draft in late 2010. It didn't come so easily but I enjoyed the challenge. When I decided to make New York City the backdrop of the story, I had to really research some key places in New York—more specifically Harlem. Being that I lived there briefly, I was able to do a better job at that. Most of the places you will find the characters in are real places. The streets they live on, the restaurants where they eat, the subway lines they catch, the parks and so on and so forth. I want you to be able to read this book and feel like you are watching a movie or even better, walking the streets of New York. Now I did take some creative license with some things but it all blends well. These characters deal with real situations that we all face. It is my hope that you will embrace them and appreciate their experiences. So much of my own life story went into this book. This isn't my autobiography but each of these four main characters represents a piece of who I am. And I'm very proud of the story I've created for the world to see. I hope you enjoy it as much as I enjoyed writing it.

First, I give thanks, honor, and praise to God whom I call my creator. I simply say thank you and I am glad that we still know each other. We've had our ups and downs but I'm still here and you're still there for me. I know no one has my back like you do. It took a while for me to see that but you showed me what the real deal is. Thank you for my life and this gift. A special rest in peace always goes to my father who is up in heaven, John Hemby AKA J Hassan El-Amin. I still feel your presence and hope I am making you proud. To my mother, Ms. Cassandra who is still here with me, loving you is like food to my soul. I thank you for pushing me to continue to write and always supporting my writing even when I thought of it as nothing more than a hobby. I hope you and Abu are proud of your "little son." All 6'3 of me! To my "big" sister Quiana, thank you for everything. My parents raised me into the man I am but it was my sister Quiana who gave me the wings to fly. And now I'm flying because she taught me how.

To my editor, Jessica Barrow-Smith AKA my second pair of eyes, what can I say? My book is all buffed, polished, and shining because of you. I feel like thank you isn't enough. You are a blessing to me. Thank you so very much! To my third pair of eyes, my homie from Willy P, Zellie Thomas, thank you for your last minute edits. You rock!

To all of my people who read this book before publication: Shawn, Mina, Jess J, Michael, Aunt Mauri, Taj, & Mommy, I thank you for all your feedback and for being my first audience. Special shout out to Seychelle & Khalil—you guys pulled me through and pulled me back from the edge at one of my darkest hours. I am eternally grateful to you both. I love you both for life. Thank you for teaching me how to fly *again.*

To all my folks who hold me down, y'all know I love y'all. If I sat here and named everyone I would forget someone, so I'm thanking everyone now. Y'all know who you are and you know what you mean to me. Where ever we know each other from, you know I got love for you. EO 4 Life! Sunnyside Terrace stand up! This tall Jerzee Boy is on the move!

To Uncle Phil & Aunt Audrey for all your love, wisdom, and support you have given me. You are both amazing! I will always love you both dearly. And Uncle Phil, you were there when I had to go pick up those copies of *Scandalicious* from the printer at the last minute. If you sell those copies I gave you on Ebay, we're gonna have to fight! (Chuckle)

Special shoutouts to my fellow authors who have given me words of wisdom and encouragement far and wide: Damon Darrell, Stanley Bennett Clay, Takerra Allen, Geoff McClanahan, K. Murray Johnson , Michael A. Lewis, James Earl Hardy, Jerrice Owens, Lee Hayes, Daryl T. Sturgis, and all the other authors I have waxed politics with, I thank you. I still consider myself a newbie as a publisher so all of your help has not gone unnoticed.

Shoutout to all the press and media outlets that showed me love: The staff of the East Orange Public Library, The Air it out girls Staxx Cordero & Lorene Martinique, J. Blair Brown, Glenys Colclough of Prominence Magazine, Tyler Johnson & Andrea LaTrell of Future Icons, Tamika

Newhouse of Kontrol magazine, Ro Jay of Middle Child Promotions, Phillip Esteem of Pride Index, Rashawn "The Professor" Chisolm, Kindle Reading Club, The Future Best Selling Authors club, Embellish book club, Black Debonair Reading Lounge, Fine Success magazine, Slyce book club, my applebuddy Leigh Darden and all of the outlets who have pumped up the Armani Williams/Jerzee Boy Publications brand. Y'all helped me get on the train and thankfully the wheels have not fallen off. A very special thanks goes to my Facebook mama Rosemary Leverson AKA Mama Rose who has a very special place in my heart and introduced me to several new readers.

To my oh so sexy, oh so fly, and oh so beautiful cover models who embody the characters you are about to read about, Khalil Muhammad, Jeremy Burnett, Khadish O. Franklin, and Shaun Willis Bentley—what can I say? I was honored that you all said yes without my having to twist any arms. I love you guys and thank you.

To my cover designers, James Grant AKA Jay Williams, you are one of the best visual artists I have ever seen. Please continue to do what you do because you are excellent at it. To the man, the visionary, and the legend, Sudan Martin AKA Su Incredbl, my brother you are still in-fucking-credible. Expect your phone to ring every time I publish a book cuz damn, you can certainly show up and show out! Love you bro! BK stand up!

And to my loyal readers, you are all Kings and Queens to me. Thank you and I love you all. Your support means everything to me. And now ladies and gentlemen, I want you to imagine yourself on the subway platform at New York City Penn station waiting for the next train uptown to Harlem via the Jerzee Boy Publications train line. We're going express so make sure you hold on tight. Stand clear of the closing doors. The next stop on this train is Harlem. Enjoy your time spent there.

Peace, Miracles, & Blessings,
Armani Williams

# Dedication

To my dear friend Michael, we go back to the playground of Washington Academy of Music in the fifth grade. (In my Whitney voice) And we're still friends. *GIRL!* And to gay black men worldwide, this one is for us! We are strong, beautiful, gifted, and talented! Be proud and be happy!

# 1

## SHAWN

### WINTERTIME

"Alright everyone, there will be a test on Monday on the first act of Macbeth. For those of you who slept through the in-class readings we had this week, you have your three day weekend to get all caught up. I hope you do," Shawn said to his class of twelfth grade English students.

"Mr. Jones, I ain't really understand none of that Shakespeare stuff. I was lost the whole time," said one of the male students.

"Terrell, when you weren't texting you were sound asleep while we were reading."

"Come on Mr. Jones, you know this stuff is wack. When are we gonna read something good?"

"We're reading Antwone Fisher's book after we're done with Macbeth."

"Well I know I can pass that test; I saw the movie."

"I'll be testing you on the book, not the movie. Now I suggest you get with one of your classmates on the first act of Macbeth so you don't fail the test on Monday. I'd hate to have to tell the basketball coach you're failing tests when he's working so hard to get you on to Syracuse's basketball team next fall. You're too sharp of a player to not be pulling your weight in the classroom. You're more than just a ball player; you have a great mind you can use."

Terrell hung his head and frowned.

"And while we're on the topic of college, those of you who want me to proofread your college essays, you have until the 25th of this month to get them to me for edits."

The school bell rung and everyone began to gather up their things.

"Have a good weekend everyone. Enjoy your day off tomorrow."

As he headed to his desk, everyone filtered out of the classroom, but his student Taneisha approached him. Sporting a long weave ponytail with blonde highlights, big gold hoop earrings with her name in them, airbrushing on each fingernail, and too much jewelry, she was as ghetto as they come. Not to mention her tight fitting outfit screamed video chick.

"Mr. Jones, I got my college essay right here. I'm applying to Duke, Spelman, and Columbia University," she said proudly in her New York B-girl voice.

"Those are good schools," Shawn said briefly looking over her essay.

"Didn't you go to Columbia?"

"I went there for grad school."

"Ooh, can you write me a letter of recommendation? I know you gotta know somebody down in the admissions department."

"I don't know anyone in admissions, but I can give you a letter of recommendation. What's your major gonna be?"

"Biology. I'm gonna be a doctor. I'm on my way to work at the hospital now. I do dietary. But it's this one nurse that sometimes lets me follow her around to see what she does with the patients."

"Okay, that's good. I'll remember that when I do your letter."

"Where did you go for undergrad?"

"I went to NYU."

She patted her weave and smacked her gum. "I thought about going there, but I wanna get out of New York. Especially out of the Butler projects. I mean, that's gon' always be my home but I want something better for myself. I'm the first girl in my building who ain't have no baby before graduation."

"Keep making those A's and you will do just that. I'm proud of you, Taneisha. You've been doing really well. No problems lately."

"It's only when people test me, Mr. Jones. I be having to show them I'm from Butler and we go for blood in my hood."

Shawn laughed and said, "Well, go easy when you get to school. They won't care where you grew up. They'll send you right back to the projects. So I want you to promise me you'll do your best to leave that hood mess in the hood when you leave."

"I will, Mr. Jones. Thank you so much. Have a good weekend!" She picked up her coat and knock-off Coach handbag then hurried out of the classroom.

Shawn chuckled at her as she left. He knew she had the brains it took to be a doctor. She was just so damn ghetto.

As he walked to the bathroom, his phone vibrated. It was a text from his boyfriend Jamon (pronounced Juh-mon) who was flying back from Atlanta.

Jamon: I just landed. Can we stop @ the deli? I'm starving.

Shawn: Sure.

Jamon: K. See u soon. Love u."

Anticipation caused butterflies to flap in his belly as he hurried in the bathroom, washed his hands, collected his things from the classroom, and nearly ran to his car in the parking lot.

He bumped into one of his best friends on his way out the door. Malcolm was not only one of his best friends, but one of the security guards for the high school.

"Got-damn, Shawn! You almost knocked me over!"

"Sorry, Malcolm," he apologized without slowing down. "My boo just texted and told me he landed, so you know it's on and popping."

Malcolm laughed, showing off a smile of beautiful white teeth that made plenty of women and men swoon. "Don't hurt him, Shawn!" he yelled out after him.

"Oh, you know I will!"

It had been two weeks since he'd last seen his boo, and even though they'd talked on the phone nearly every day, he missed seeing his face, being close to him, touching him. He jumped into his Dodge Charger and sped off with spinning wheels. He was still amazed at how he lucked out with landing such a nice catch as Jamon King. Not only was the man every bit of sexy—with oatmeal brown skin, a bald head, sexy lips, a fat ass, and a muscular frame that lingered well over Shawn's six feet, one inch of height—but he was also a rising R&B singer and successful songwriter. Many of the songs he had written for other artists had become chart-topping hits, so every three months, he received a rather hefty royalty check that he didn't mind showering on Shawn. With such a fulfilling relationship and a successful career of his own as a tenured teacher at James Weldon Johnson High School, Shawn was loving life with few reasons to complain. The closer he got to the airport, the more antsy the butterflies became in his belly.

Traffic wasn't as heavy yet, so he made it to the airport in good time. Jamon was standing outside waiting when Shawn pulled up. Shawn got all warm inside when he saw Jamon standing there. He always wore hats to compliment his outfit and his stunna shades made him look like a celebrity waiting on his man to pick him up. He had on the same black leather coat as Shawn and a gray scarf around his neck. He put his bags in the backseat and jumped up front with Shawn.

"Hey baby. You miss me?" Jamon asked.

"Nah not really," Shawn said trying to play coy. "You weren't gone long enough for me."

"Oh word? It's like that?"

"You know I missed you."

Jamon moved in and they kissed each other. Jamon's tongue ring always made their kisses sweet.

"I missed my Mookie too."

Mookie was a nickname Jamon gave Shawn because he thought Shawn was so cute and innocent looking. Shawn loved when Jamon called him that. He pulled off and held Jamon's hand as he drove.

"So how was your trip?"

"It was cool. I wrote two songs for this new girl group from LA. They're signed to Geffen Records. They were down there to work with Ne-Yo and Chuck Harmony. But they're gonna use the songs I submitted for their first two singles. According to their manager anyway. We'll see how that goes."

"That's wassup. Are you excited?"

"More excited about the stuff I recorded for my own project. I was in the studio with James Captcha, and he made these hot ass beats. Oh my God, these beats were so fucking crazy, baby. I wrote the songs in like ten minutes cuz they just came so easily. I got the unmixed versions on my iPod. You wanna hear?"

"Sure." Jamon hooked his iPod to the radio and turned the music up loud. Shawn loved the fact that Jamon always wanted to play his new music for him. Like a kid showing off a new toy, Jamon would always grin with excitement as he shared the exclusive tracks. As the sounds of his silky smooth baritone played over the catchy beats, Jamon mouthed the words to the song.

"Damn, baby! That beat is hot!" Shawn yelled over the music.

"Told you! They're gonna send me the mixed version tonight!" Jamon yelled back.

"Your voice sounds great on this!"

"Well, you know...I try!" he said with a smirk.

They listened to both songs and Shawn was impressed.

"Listen to this one. I did an all acapella track. It's all me on the lead and backgrounds. Took me all day cuz I had to layer the backgrounds really tight. But it's mixed down and everything. I'mma put it up on my YouTube channel tonight."

While Jamon played his acapella song, Shawn scrunched up his face.

"What? You don't like it?" Jamon sounded crushed.

"Are you crazy? You are sangin' the hell out of this song. And you did the backgrounds all by yourself?"

"Yeah, it's all me. You really like it?"

Shawn nodded and continued listening as the song played. By time the bridge played, Shawn was waving his hand back and forth like he was in church. He'd heard plenty of Jamon's songs, but never one that sounded this good. Jamon's voice was so captivating and relaxing.

"I want this on my iPod as soon as we get home. This sounds like a platinum hit. And I'm not just saying that cuz you're my man. You should make this one the single for your album."

"It's that good?"

"You know I wouldn't lie to you." Content, Jamon leaned back and smiled for the rest of the ride. Shawn pulled up in front of the deli around the corner from their building and they went inside and ordered sandwiches.

"These little delis are the best. I missed the hell out of them when I was in ATL."

"I missed the hell out of you," Shawn said so only Jamon could hear him. Jamon stepped closer to him and Shawn could feel his body heat, which excited him. They stood there watching their food cook and the man made their sandwiches just how they liked it, but the only thing Shawn could think about was how it would go down once they finally made it home. Jamon was an exquisite lover, the best he'd ever had.

On the way back to the car, Jamon said, "Man, that trip wore me out. I could go home and go to sleep."

"Yeah, you do look a little drained."

"I ain't goin' to sleep before I tear that ass up. I'm never too drained for that."

"You so nasty."

"You love it."

They drove up to their apartment building on W. 127th St and St. Nicholas Ave in a newly constructed building. Their two-bedroom ninth floor apartment had become their love nest and sanctuary since they moved into it a year before when the building first opened. There were no pest problems, the amenities still worked like new, and the neighbors were friendly. Shawn fell in love with the apartment from the first time he saw it. There were hardwood floors throughout, a nice sized kitchen, and a big master bedroom. Jamon smacked Shawn's ass as they walked into the bedroom.

"Don't you wanna wash off that flight?"

"I showered before I got on my plane. And my flight was only two hours."

"Well, I need to."

"Don't make me wait too long, Mook." Jamon palmed Shawn's ass and looked at him with desire. They pecked on the lips and Shawn went to shower. While Shawn was showering, Jamon ate and then lit candles, incense, and created a playlist of ballads to play on the computer while they were catching up on their lovemaking. Naked, Jamon sprawled across their big comfortable king sized bed as he waited for Shawn. He couldn't wait to be inside of Shawn and as cool as Shawn was being about it, he couldn't wait either. He felt like he couldn't shower and fleet fast enough. In almost perfect timing, "My Little Secret" and "Softest Place on Earth" by Xscape played one after the other as Shawn entered the room in a towel. Jamon licked his lips with anticipation when Shawn gave him that look that drove him crazy as he undid his towel. Shawn's days in the gym had definitely paid off and so had Jamon's. As Shawn lotioned himself, Jamon's dick got even harder watching him rub lotion into his caramel brown skin. He looked so good with that goatee framing his juicy pink lips.

"Come here, Mook." Shawn walked towards him and Jamon took him by the hand and looked up at him. "I love you."

"I love you too."

"I really did miss you."

"I missed you too."

"But I can't control myself for much longer watching you all hot and wet from the shower." Shawn chuckled.

"So have your way, papa."

He grabbed Shawn around the torso and kissed his stomach and licked inside his navel. Then he stood so he could pick him up and kiss him deeply. There was no better feeling to either of them than kissing. They each had big soft lips and long tongues that loved to touch. Their kisses became even more passionate as they lavished in each other while Xscape crooned in the background. Shawn's dick instantly became hard as Jamon held him close straddling him. He wrapped his legs around Jamon as they made their way to the bed where it was about to go down. Jamon broke their kiss only so he could suck hard on Shawn's neck and ears. A soft moan escaped Shawn and he closed his eyes. The sensation of pleasure and slight tickle made him squirm uncontrollably and Jamon loved it. He loved making Shawn feel helpless. They spent almost an entire fifteen minutes kissing and touching each other in the most sensitive places. They were both standing at attention and getting jabbed from each other's erections. But this was only their warm up. What Shawn loved most about Jamon's lovemaking was how he took his time. He inhaled the intoxicating scent of Jamon's cologne and let him do what he did best other than sing—fuck his natural brains out. Their fingers interlocked as they continued to kiss. Jamon caressed Shawn's nipples and swiveled his tongue in circles on Shawn's hard chest, and when Shawn flexed his six-pack in Jamon's face, it made his dick jump even more. His tongue was all over Shawn's torso as he reached down to Shawn's dick and caressed it.

"Just who I've been waiting on." Shawn made his hard dick jump and wave side to side, lightly hitting Jamon's face as if he were smacking him with it. Shawn had a freaky smile on his face as Jamon looked up at him. He chuckled and stroked Shawn's long dick as he inserted it in his mouth, opening wide so he could deep-throat it. Jamon's perfected technique and tongue ring made Shawn coo with pleasure. Jamon went on for a while and Shawn could feel his insides tightening as the coolness of Jamon's tongue ring and hot breath worked him over. All of a sudden, Jamon stopped and looked at him.

"What you doing, baby? I was bout to cum."

"Shut the fuck up. You gon' cum when I tell you to, lil' nigga." Shawn's dick jumped straight up. Even though he was a dominant force in his classroom on a daily basis, he was a poodle with Jamon and relished in Jamon's forceful nature in the bedroom. Not to mention Shawn hated the "N-word" with a passion but *loved* when Jamon called him that when they made love.

"Precumming ass nigga," Jamon said as he licked up Shawn's precum. He lifted Shawn's legs and bent them back as far as they would go. For a man, Shawn was extremely flexible and it always excited Jamon to see just how many different ways he could bend and stretch Shawn's limbs. It always came in handy for moments like this. Jamon buried his face in Shawn's ass as if it were his last supper. And boy did he get up in there. Shawn was beside himself and started to moan again. While in the throes of it all, Jamon masterminded his entry. He always slathered his thick brown dick with lube while eating Shawn out so he could go in while Shawn was still wet. And as soon as Shawn felt the tip coming in, he started to precum again. His body began to twist and turn as it welcomed Jamon with glee. And it felt so good. Especially because Jamon took a really long time to cum, so this would go on for a while. Whenever they spent time apart, their lovemaking was like the Bliss and Fourth of July fireworks Mariah Carey was singing about in the background. Only their fireworks were their massive cum explosions.

After a half hour, Shawn began to whimper like a puppy. Jamon became a ferocious beast as he verbally chastised him. Shawn liked when Jamon cursed at him while they were enveloped so tight. Jamon reached down and softly slapped Shawn's face. "You like this fucking dick nigga? You gon' ride this fucking dick nigga? Huh?" Shawn moaned loudly as his eyes rolled in the back of his head. "Answer me when I fuck-ing talk to you bitch. You bitch ass nigga you hear me fucking talking to you? You gon' ride my fucking dick or what?"

"Yeah."

"Yeah what? Who the fuck you talking to bitch?"

"You daddy. I'm talking to you."

"What's my name nigga?"

"Jamon."

"What's my fucking name nigga?"

"JJ."

"And who am I?"

"My daddy."

"Your what?"

"My daddy."

"That's right nigga; I'm your fucking daddy. Remember that shit." Shawn's moans turned into full-fledged screams as he once again felt his insides tightening. Shawn began to squirm and wiggle and Jamon pinned his arms back against the bed making it impossible for him to move them.

"Be still and take it like a fucking man." Shawn's eyes closed. "Open your fucking eyes and look at me bitch. I ain't fucking tell you to look at nothing else. Look me in my fucking eyes and tell me you love my dick nigga."

"I love it," Shawn said looking him in the eyes.

"Say it again," Jamon said with eyes piercing Shawn.

"I love it."

"What's my fucking name?"

"Daddy."

"Say my fucking name."

"Daddy."

"Say it with your chest nigga!"

"Daddy."

"That's right. You better not look at shit else neither. Look at me and only me." Shawn never took his eyes off of Jamon and could feel his sweat dripping on him. With every dominant word Jamon spoke, Shawn began to tingle. And he knew his body was preparing for a massive explosion. He could feel the tingling getting stronger. And stronger. And stronger.

"Give me that nut before I take that shit nigga."

"I'm about to cum."

"Give me that fucking nut, lil nigga."

"I'm about to cum."

"Bust that shit. Bust that fucking nut nigga. Come on nigga, bust that fucking nut. Give me that fucking nut, lil' nigga." Shawn could feel his body bracing itself.

"Come on nigga, bust that fucking nut. Bust that shit out nigga. I want you to fucking bust right now, nigga. Come on!" It was like a rocket launching inside of Shawn and as his breathing got heavier his body started to jerk with his wild cum shooting out of him, getting everywhere. The harder his body jerked and he heaved, the harder his hot cum shot out of him. It was all over the sheets, the headboard, Jamon's chest, and all over him.

Watching him cum like that not only made Jamon proud but made him weak. He pulled out of Shawn and rained his own cum all over Shawn's face and chest. And Shawn loved when Jamon came on him—especially on his face. Jamon cleaned them both up and he listened to SWV sing "Rain." That Jamon was something else. And he was so glad he was all his. Jamon came back to the bed ready for round two but that was easy for Shawn. Jamon had a very intense foot fetish so all he had to do was lay there and let Jamon play with his feet. He would wiggle and spread his toes and it would turn Jamon on in ways he had never seen before. He didn't quite understand where Jamon's foot fetish came from but since Jamon liked it, he did whatever he needed to do to make him happy. As Shawn spread his flexible toes around Jamon's hard dick and gave him a foot job, Jamon would be in a fit of ecstasy. Sometimes when Jamon would be on the road, Shawn would text him pictures of his feet and Jamon would always text back pictures of his cum explosion. It tickled Shawn every time. Round three was Shawn returning the favor and eating Jamon out and fucking him back. Before meeting Shawn, Jamon was an exclusive top, but Shawn taught him Kegel exercises so he would relax and now he loved bottoming.

After making him cum one last time, Shawn got up to blow out the candles and threw the incense in water. Jamon wrapped his arms around Shawn and they basked in the afterglow. As they drifted off to sleep with "Beauty" by Dru Hill playing in the background, they said a silent thank you to God because they had finally found the love of their lives in each other.

# 2

## MALCOLM

Malcolm sprayed on his Bvulgari BLV cologne for men and jumped into his jeans, white Rocawear hoodie, and Yankee's fitted. He checked his reflection in the mirror and smirked. At 6'6" with smooth sable skin, a movie star smile, piercing brown eyes, and connected sideburns to his goatee, he didn't need anyone to tell him he was bangin'. He just knew. Still staring at his reflection, he ran his hand over his super spinning waves, then flexed his chest and biceps and whistled at himself. Hitting the gym daily had definitely paid off, and he loved to show off his muscles and his many tattoos. Everywhere he went, women fucked him with their eyes—even the young girls at the high school never missed an opportunity to try and flirt with him. Though he could appreciate the attention he got from women, he loved making the men scream his name in ecstasy. And once they got a load of his rich, sexy baritone voice, he could get anyone to drop their drawls with the quickness by just saying what they wanted to hear.

After checking his reflection, he slipped some condoms and lube into his hoodie pocket and zipped it in there. He grabbed his iPhone and headed for the door. His mother, Nzingha (In-zing-uh) Brown sat at the dining room table reading the latest Essence magazine. When he walked past, she looked up at her son.

"Heading out?" she asked.

"Yeah. Don't wait up." He kissed her cheek.

"I know better than that, honey. I hope you got condoms."

"Never leave home without them."

"Alright now, you be careful out there. Don't come back with no extras cuz you didn't buckle up."

"Yes, ma'am," he said with a sheepish grin.

"You smile just like your father."

Malcolm glanced over at a picture of his dearly departed father on the mantel. His mother's eyes followed his and they stared at the photo for a few seconds, neither of them saying a word.

His mother cleared her throat. "So, is he anyone special?"

"Not really," he admitted. "I'm just trying to get in and make it do what it do."

"Is settling down anywhere in your near future?"

"Mama, I'm 26. Was that a joke or a serious question?"

His mother chuckled and shook her head. Malcolm was gonna be Malcolm. She could only hope that one day he grew out of his ways. "Have fun, baby."

"See ya later, Mama," he said walking out the door.

As soon as he left, Mama Nzingha stood up and went over to the phone and dialed a number. "Hey, Malcolm just left so you can come on by. You're down the street? Oh okay, well come on then. Okay. See you in a few."

She untied her cherry wood colored locks from the ponytail holder and shook them loose, letting them hang to her shoulders. In the bathroom, she freshened up and applied Victoria Secret perfume and light makeup. Well into her fifties, she had the body of a thirty-year-old. She was a curvy size six and kept herself up with yoga, palates, and cardio exercises at the same gym as her son. She ran her hands through her locks and made them lay the way she wanted them to. After shuffling through her lingerie drawer in indecision, she settled on a lace nightgown and draped herself in a satin robe then returned to the living room to wait for her evening companion. Within seconds of her sitting on the couch and sipping a glass of wine, he buzzed the door and she let him up. She opened the door for him and saw him holding a bouquet of roses.

"Oh! Well, aren't these beautiful?" she exclaimed.

"They pale in comparison to you," he said and she almost melted. She loved how he made her feel like pure gold. After kissing him on the lips, she took the flowers into the kitchen, knowing she wouldn't keep them long because if Malcolm saw them, he might start asking questions.

"I poured you a glass of wine, baby," she said from the kitchen.

When she came back, he lifted his glass and said, "Let's make a toast."

Simultaneously smiling and frowning, she lifted hers and said, "Okay. To what?"

"To us. And this evening. You look beautiful tonight."

"Well, thank you, sweetheart." They clinked glasses and sipped their champagne, but neither Randy nor she were able to keep their hands to themselves. Minutes later, they set the glasses aside and after she found a smooth jazz channel on digital cable that kept the mood mellow, Randy lowered her onto the couch cushions and devoured her as though he'd been thinking about this moment all day.

Meanwhile Malcolm was stepping off of the 2-train in the Bronx to do some late night creeping of his own. He'd met a hot Latino man named Pedro on *Jack'd* he'd been talking to for the past few days. He'd told Malcolm that he'd never had sex with a man before but wanted to be topped by a sexy chocolate black man like Malcolm. Malcolm looked back at his phone to double check the address and text Pedro, telling him he was there. He buzzed Malcolm in and told him to come up to apartment 32. When the door opened, Malcolm was pleasantly surprised at how handsome Pedro was in person. His light brown eyes, smooth butter pecan skin, shiny bald head, and neatly trimmed goatee aroused Malcolm.

"Wow, you're tall," Pedro said, his Hispanic accent caressing his words.

"Six-six," Malcolm replied licking his lips. Forget the small talk; he was ready to get things started.

"Yeah, you're tall. And just as hot as your pictures."

"Thanks."

"You smoke?"

"Bud."

"I got some sour. You want some?"

"Yeah, let's." Malcolm sat with him and watched him roll up a fat blunt. Pedro lit up and took a puff then passed it to Malcolm.

"You know, I never did anything like this before."

"Yeah, you told me."

"I'm a little nervous. You gonna be gentle, right?"

"I got you. Just relax once we get there."

Pedro nodded. "You drink?"

"Yeah, I drink."

"I got some homemade sangria. It's kinda strong though."

"I can rock."

"Okay, I'll bring you some." Pedro left Malcolm smoking alone to fix him a drink.

Malcolm watched him walking away and he rubbed his dick, which was already straining against his pants. He'd known Pedro would be sexy, but he was very impressed. And he couldn't wait to tear Pedro's ass up. Pedro brought them the sangria and Malcolm guzzled it quickly. They finished the L and Malcolm reached over to kiss Pedro. His lips were so soft and inviting.

"You ready?" Malcolm asked.

"*Si.*" They kissed again and Malcolm grabbed him tight lifting him up, straddling him. Immediately, Pedro's dick got hard. Malcolm carried them into the bedroom and laid him on the bed. Pedro's dick grew harder by the second as he watched Malcolm strip out of his clothes in front of him, flexing his muscles to entice his Latin lover. Watching Malcolm flex, Pedro's tongue lolled out of his mouth. Malcolm climbed on top of him and helped him out of his wife beater then he kissed him deeply and nibbled on his neck. Pedro moaned softly as Malcolm sucked his nipples and licked all over his stomach. The way Malcolm worked his tongue amazed and intimidated Pedro; Malcolm was definitely a pro and he could only hope that he'd be gentle with him. Everything was heightened because they were both high and tipsy, which made every touch feel even better.

Malcolm unbuckled Pedro's pants and slid them down along with his boxers. Thankfully, it smelled good. Plenty of times, Malcolm had left guys hard with blue balls when they didn't smell fresh downtown. He sucked Pedro's dick so good, he had him speaking Spanish and moaning. Pedro's eyes rolled in the back of his head and he bit his bottom lip, quivering in sheer ecstasy. He lifted Pedro's legs up and proceeded to eat him out. That was when Pedro started to get loud. He moaned and spoke Spanish so loud that Malcolm wondered if the neighbors could hear him. Malcolm made sure Pedro was wet, relaxed, and ready. He slipped on his condom and lubed Pedro up then leaned down to kiss him as the head of his dick slipped inside.

"Mmm," Pedro moaned. Malcolm kept kissing him while slowly inching himself inside further. Pedro was so tight and Malcolm liked it. He winced in pain slightly, but Malcolm kissed him even more until he was fully inside.

"Relax," Malcolm whispered.

"I can't."

"If you relax, I promise it'll feel so much better for both of us."

"Okay."

Though Pedro was still tense, he felt his anal muscles relax the slightest bit. At first, Malcolm went slowly and gently because he could tell that Pedro was still in pain. But the more Malcolm went on, the less Pedro frowned, the more he relaxed and the better it felt. He finally understood the phrase "pleasure and pain." And it felt great. He pulled Malcolm close and enjoyed the ride he was being taken on. He breathed heavy and could feel Malcolm's dick pulsating inside of him. Nothing had ever felt so good. Nothing had ever felt so sweet. And one thing was for sure. Pedro loved the way Malcolm fucked him—as did everyone Malcolm fucked. One thing Malcolm knew how to do was work it out in the bedroom. For this very reason, he had a lot of men at his beck and call whenever he was horny because everyone wanted another ride on the Malcolm-go-round. And now Pedro wanted him all to himself. For always. He took Pedro to a level of orgasm that he'd never known existed.

Malcolm smirked as he saw the way Pedro soaked the sheets and pillow cases with his cum. Some even got on him but he didn't mind. Malcolm liked when his subjects came on him. Especially like Pedro did. Malcolm slowly pulled out of Pedro and removed his condom, throwing it away. He lay down next to Pedro, stroking his still hard dick.

"You wanna cum?" Pedro asked.

"Yeah."

"Lemme help you out." Pedro took a hold of Malcolm's dick and sucked on it. For someone who never fucked a man before, he could sure suck a dick. Malcolm closed his eyes and let Pedro do his thing. And he was working it out. Until the front door opened and they heard keys jingling.

"Pedro, I'm home, papi," a woman with a strong Hispanic accent said, shutting the front door.

"Oh shit, that's my wife," Pedro said, rolling off of Malcolm.

*The fuck? Not another one of these DL muthafuckas!*

"Go in there." Pedro pointed to the closet. "Rapido, rapido!" Pedro threw Malcolm's clothes in the closet behind him. Thankfully, it was a walk-in closet so he could stand up inside. Hangers full of flowery dresses and extra-large blouses hung from the above rack, the scratchy material brushing against his face. He knocked the hangers away.

*Damn, I knew I shoulda asked this dumb ass nigga if he was married,* Malcolm thought while putting on his shirt and hoodie. From the inside of the closet, he could hear Pedro and his wife speaking Spanish to one another. Malcolm carefully stepped inside of his pants, realizing he had left his briefs and sneakers he paid $150 for on the floor of the bedroom.

"Fuck," Malcolm cursed under his breath. He could still hear them talking. He had no idea what they were saying, but he could see through the crack in the door that his wife was a short, fat, dumpy Hispanic woman with unkempt curly hair and dark circles under her eyes.

*Damn, this bitch is almost as bad as Big Ang. This is why he's fucking with dudes. She ugly as hell.*

She sat down on the bed to remove her heels; her feet looked like they were screaming from being stuffed into her too-tight shoes all day. Based on her plain blouse and long skirt that had clearly seen better days, Malcolm assumed she was some kind of office worker. Her poor swollen feet had red shoe marks embedded all over them. They continued their conversation while Malcolm tried to be still and quiet.

*I don't know what it is about Hispanic people but these muthafuckas talk loud as shit for no reason.* Soon, he realized they weren't just talking loud. There was definitely some tension here.

*Damn, I wish I knew what they were saying. Knew I shoulda paid more attention in Spanish class.* Whatever was happening made her get off the bed and get in his face. Their voices escalated until they were screaming at each other. Pedro pounded the wall with his fist and she jammed her finger in his face.

*Damn, they mad, huh?* Both of their faces turned bright red as they yelled at each other, one trying to outdo the other. She attempted to walk over to the closet, but Pedro stepped in front of it.

*Oh God, please don't let this ugly fat bitch open this door and see my black ass in here.*

Pedro and his wife continued to argue while Malcolm stood in the closet scared shitless that he was about to be caught in the middle of this lover's quarrel. And he didn't even know what the hell they were fighting about.

*Lord, please forgive me of my wayward dick. I will check next time to make sure whatever bastard I hook up with ain't married.* Malcolm could feel himself beginning to sweat. He didn't know if it was fear or if it was heat. He just wondered how the hell he'd get out of that closet. He could hear Pedro and his wife's footsteps retreating from the bedroom as they headed into the kitchen. Cautiously, he peered out of the door and looked at his sneakers in the middle of the floor, trying to think fast as to how he'd get out of there. The bedroom window lacked a fire escape route. As he stood there in indecision, he heard their voices and footsteps once again approaching the bedroom. Cursing his luck, he closed the closet door and returned to his dark cubby hole.

*Oh, for the love of God, please just slap this bitch in her mouth so I can get the fuck out of here.* His wife's voice seemed to travel closer and closer to the closet door, and just when it sounded like her voice was on the opposite side of the door, the arguing abruptly stopped. Malcolm reached for the closet door knob, hoping she wouldn't think to open the door. Now he was sweating profusely and it seemed as if Pedro had forgotten he was in there. As his fingers inched closer to the door, it opened and Pedro's wife looked up at the tall black man standing in her closet. Her raccoon eyes widened with fear and she let out a blood curdling scream. Malcolm's reflexes made him scream too.

"Pedroooooooo! Negro! Negro!" she screamed.

Malcolm rushed from the closet and she tried to make a run for it and fell flat on her ass, making a loud thud as she hit the floor. He kneeled over her to get his sneakers, which made her scream even louder. Her rancid breath caught Malcolm's nostrils and he gagged. Pedro came darting out of the kitchen as Malcolm went speeding by towards the front door with his sneakers in hand. Pedro's wife's hysterical screams could be heard all throughout the entire hallway of their floor as Malcolm made it out of the apartment. Quickly, he slipped into his sneakers and avoided the curious looks as people came to their doors to see what was going on.

Without warning, Pedro's apartment door flung open with his wife holding a gun. She fired off a shot in Malcolm's direction and the bullet whizzed past his right ear. He hauled ass out of the building, almost leaping down each flight of steps in a single bound. Once Malcolm made it out of the building, he ran all the way to the 2-train subway station to catch the next Harlem-bound train. As soon as he swiped his metrocard and sat down at the empty station to catch his breath, his phone rang. It was Pedro.

"What 'cho dumb ass want?" Malcolm yelled at him, completely out of breath.

"Where are you?"

"Far away from you and your fat crazy ass wife. Why the fuck you ain't tell me you was married, yo?"

"I'm sorry."

"That's all you got? Your wife almost fucking shot me and you sorry?"

"I didn't know she was coming home early. I would have had you come earlier."

"Had me come earlier? Nigga, do you know what the fuck you just pulled? I coulda died fucking around with you just now."

"I'm sorry. I'm really sorry. I was hoping we can finish what we started. Can you come back tomorrow?" Stunned Malcolm looked at his phone with his eyebrows furled.

"You out yo' beans-and-rice-eating ass mind. Fuck you and that fat stank breath bitch you married to. Lose my number you down-low ass nigga." Malcolm ended the call while Pedro was still pleading on the other end. He called back twice and Malcolm sent him to voicemail both times.

"All this shit for some dick? And I ain't even get to nut. Nigga almost got me shot and bout to have me catching blueballs out this mu'fucka."

Malcolm took out his phone and dialed a number. "Watup? What you doin? You cook? Aight, I'm coming by. I'm in the Bronx. I'll be there in a little while. Aight, see you then. One."

Malcolm ended the call, feeling a little better than before. As the train pulled into the station, he put on his headphones and chuckled to himself about what had just happened. He hadn't ran from a bullet since he was nineteen. Was a piece of ass really worth all of that? Maybe he needed to slow down on his sexcapades. Maybe Mama Nzingha was right; maybe he needed to find that one and settle down.

*Me settle down?* Malcolm thought as he stepped onto the train laughing to himself. *Nah, not in this lifetime.*

# 3

## DAMON

Teena Marie's soulful voice flooded Damon's living room as she cooed about that starry winter night in Portugal where the ocean kissed the southern shore.

"These girls are so tired this evening on this site. Ugh, everyone just wants to fuck. God, are there any real men left who just wanna get to know you? Where are they hiding?" Damon said aloud as he browsed the personal ads. He took a swig of his White Bordeaux wine and turned up his music. Teena Marie was taking him in.

"Girl! There ain't nothing but trollip on this site tonight."

He got up and danced and sang along to "Portugese Love" all the way to the kitchen where he was making curry chicken, roti, veggies, and cook-up rice. His dog Lucky followed him into the kitchen and drank water from his doggy bowl.

Damon took his chicken out of the oven and turned off the rice and vegetables cooking on top of the stove. His doorbell rang and Lucky started barking. He ran towards the door as Damon went to open it.

"You sure are happy to see your Uncle Malcolm, huh Lucky?" Damon said with a laugh.

He opened the door and Lucky jumped up on Malcolm's leg and sniffed him. Malcolm towered over Damon's 5'11" frame.

"Watup, Luck?" Malcolm said as he rubbed Lucky's head. "Big D, watup? Where the food at?" Malcolm asked giving Damon dap.

"In the kitchen."

"That's where I'll be," Malcolm said as he made a beeline for the kitchen. He washed his hands in the kitchen sink. "Man, every time I come in this house, I wish it was mine. I guess a nigga can dream can't he?"

"I thought you were gonna stop using that word."

"Nigga, I'm trying, but old habits die hard." He laughed and Damon rolled his eyes.

"Well please refrain from saying it in this house. We don't use language like that here. Show some respect muthafucka."

"Oh, so I can be a muthafucka but not a nigga?"

"That's right."

"D, you know you my muthafuckin' nigga," Malcolm said with a smirk, playfully jabbing Damon's arm.

"You're a mess."

As a multi-millionaire who sold real estate, Damon lives in a plush home on a quiet tree lined block full of million dollar brownstones. Though it was only him and Lucky, they lived in a beautiful three-story brownstone on Harlem's west side on W. 138th St that was paid for in full. A navy blue Range Rover that he paid cash for sat out front. His home boasted four large bedrooms, three and a half bathrooms, and a fully finished basement. Mahogany brown hardwood floors went throughout the house and the kitchen and bathrooms sported granite countertops and sinks. There was a red deck in the backyard surrounded by a garden that he planted vegetables in every spring.

With an eye for design and detail, Damon had decorated his whole house by himself and had it hooked up quite nicely. He had a sunset orange carpet put in the living room with two modern-style semi-circular groupings in black and white leather imported from Milan, Italy. The dining area sported a winter white and aubergine theme featuring a glass table with beveled edges and legs designed in France. Alternating white and aubergine chairs surrounded the table. On this chilly winter evening, his rustic tumbled stone façade fireplace was keeping his large living room toasty. Every clothing item that he owned came from a top-designer. Though he had money and had expensive tastes, he never let his wealth go to his head and he was not the kind of man who boasted.

"Where you coming from?" Damon asked.

"Man, you ain't gon' believe the ignorant shit that just happened to me."

"What happened?" Malcolm told him the whole story blow by blow and how he narrowly escaped being shot.

"That is crazy! You're lucky she missed."

"Hell, yeah, I'm lucky she missed. You know I ain't religious at all. I was making promises to God and everything while I was standing in that closet. And then once she shot at me, I was like, 'God, I'll never suck another dick again in my life if you just get me outta here alive.'"

"Only that would happen to you," Damon said as he fixed their plates. They ate and drank the wine with their food. The kitchen ceiling fan wafted the delicious flavors throughout the house.

"So what you getting into tonight?" Malcolm asked.

"Not a damn thing. I was sitting here bored."

"You know they opened a new club on W. 23rd? It's called Waves. We should roll through."

"Yeah, I heard about that spot. I heard it's real nice."

"We should go. Let's call Shawn and Kevin," Malcolm said with a mouth full of food.

"Chew your food nasty. You know Jamon just came back in town so Shawn ain't coming out. And Kevin has to work late tonight and gotta be in early tomorrow."

"So it'll just be us. Thursday nights are always fun at the club. The school district is closed tomorrow so I'm off."

"You gonna go like that?" Damon asked pointing to Malcolm's hoodie.

"Nah, we gon' have to swing by my house so I can change clothes."

"You might wanna shower Mr. Latin lover's dick-sweat off of you too."

"Yo, speaking of that shit, would you believe I ain't even get to nut?"

"Seriously?"

"Hell no! I woulda got blueballs if his wife ain't try to shoot my black ass. That bitch looked like Ursula the seawitch! I ain't even lying."

Damon fell out laughing at Malcolm. "You can't make your life up. At all."

"Sure can't."

They finished eating and Damon pulled out a fitted white shirt, jeans, and shoes for himself and they drove over to Malcolm's house. Damon sat on the living room sofa and flipped through the TV channels while Malcolm showered.

Inside of Mama Nzingha's room, she and Randy had gone to sleep but the sound of the TV in the living room turning on awakened her. That couldn't be Malcolm home already, could it? His nights were usually much longer than that, she thought.

She slipped into her robe and went into the living room. "Damon, is that you?"

"It's me. You just don't age do you, Mama?" Damon asked getting up to hug her.

"Oh stop it. How you been?" she asked, giving him a warm hug.

"I've been really good."

"What y'all doing tonight?"

"We're gonna hit this club on 23rd. It's new so we'll see how it is."

"Alright. Well y'all be safe out there."

Malcolm got out of the shower and saw his mother. "Hey Mama."

"Hey baby, let me use the bathroom," she said darting past him in hopes that he wouldn't notice the makeup on her face or the fact that it wasn't there when he left out earlier.

She quickly closed the bathroom door and went to wash her face.

Malcolm pulled out an outfit for himself to wear to the club, and Damon gave it the thumbs up. He had on jeans, hard bottom shoes, and a button up shirt that hugged his big muscles.

"Y'all have fun, okay? I'll see you in the morning, son," Mama Nzingha said kissing him on the cheek.

"Good night, Mama."

Damon and Malcolm walked to Damon's truck like they knew they were fly as hell. Sexy men on the prowl for fresh trade.

They hit the West Side Highway and drove down to 23rd St and found parking a block away.

The club was popping like they didn't expect. The DJ was spinning all the heat, the drinks at the bar were flowing, the men up on the tables dancing were twerking it out, and there was some of everyone up in there. The fems, the DL's, the girls, and the regulars. Damon and Malcolm went straight for the bar and ordered drinks.

A Beyonce song came on and the fems were going in, singing every word while they imitated her. Damon and Malcolm were killing it on the dance floor with each other and with other guys too. Everything was great until Damon mistakenly backed up into a guy on the dance floor who had his drink in his hand. The guy spilled his drink on himself and some of it spilled on Damon.

"Come on man, watch where the fuck you're going!" the guy yelled.

"Oh, my bad, man. I'll buy you another one."

The guy threw the glass to the floor and it shattered. "What the fuck, yo! I paid $14 for that shit! And you fucked up my shirt too, you fag ass muthafucka!"

Malcolm approached them both and stood next to Damon.

The man stepped forward, eyes glaring at Damon while his fists clenched and unclenched at his sides. "I should knock you the fuck out!"

"You could try that, but then I'd fuck *you* up!" Malcolm said, his face remaining cool and calm despite his words.

"Oh, so y'all niggas gon' try and jump me?"

"Yo, calm all that rah-rah shit down. Ain't nobody jumpin' nobody."

"I'mma fuck you up!" the guy yelled at Damon who stood perfectly still.

Just as the guy grabbed Damon by the collar, Malcolm's fist cracked against the man's jaw and he fell straight back and hit the floor. Malcolm always had a quick and powerful punch that knocked most people out in just one shot. As Malcolm began to kick the guy, security and a few cops moved in on them quickly; people were pointing at Malcolm and Damon, trying to yell to the officers and guards over the blaring music. Malcolm grabbed Damon by the arm and made a run for the emergency exit. They knocked a few people over running out of the club with security hot on their trail. Malcolm flung the doors open and they ran as fast as they could down the street from the four security guys chasing them. They ran down into the subway station down 23rd St and hopped over the MTA rail, then jumped onto the departing Queens-bound N-train.

"How is it I always manage to get into all types of wild shit just hanging out with you?" Damon asked out of breath.

"Cuz I'm fun and you love it," Malcolm said in between breaths. "Damn, I'm breaking my own record. Running for my life twice in the same night?"

"Yeah, well, thanks for having my back."

"You know I got you. You prolly ain't need me though, Mr. Golden Gloves."

"If I woulda hit that dude, I woulda went to jail."

"That's why I clocked his ass. The way you taught me to swing is exactly the way I hit him."

"I saw. Wow, I taught you that a long time ago."

"I still got it too," Malcolm said as he swung at the air. "We're heading to Queens."

"I know. We gotta get off at the next stop."

They got off at the next stop and walked back down to 23rd St to get Damon's truck. Damon dropped Malcolm off and headed home. As he picked up his phone to call Kevin and tell him all about the crazy shit Malcolm just got him into, he realized he had two missed calls and a voicemail message from Kenny, a ghost of his past.

"Hey Damon. It's Kenny. I was just reaching out to say I was thinking about you. I was hoping we could meet for coffee and talk. Get caught up. I'd love to see you. My number is still the same. Talk to you soon. Take care."

Damon rolled his eyes and pressed seven to delete the message.

"Kenny, when you get a divorce from your wife then we can talk," Damon said aloud.

Back at home, Damon hopped in the shower, soaping his body up with suds. Though he tried not to think about him, an image of Kenny lingered in the back of his mind. What they had shared had been amazing, and he had thought he was the one...that is until his wife called his phone wanting to know who he was and how he knew her husband. That was the end of him. Damn! And that had been some good sex too, some of the best he'd ever had. No matter how steamy the sex was or how intriguing the conversations had been, he wasn't about to share a man with his wife.

"It's all or nothing here," Damon said as he shut off the spray of hot water and stepped out of the shower into his master bedroom suite. It boasted a sleek, modern and stylish California king size bed, appointed with spa hotel quality bedding with gun metal gray pillows and taupe and cream hand-sewn comforters and sheets.

As he rolled back his bed covers, Lucky came into his room and nestled on the floor next to him. Damon curled his body into the fetal position and drifted off to sleep in his big bed all by himself with a pillow between his legs, clutching a teddy bear. Yes, he was lonely, but not so lonely that he'd get re-involved with Kenny. He would never put his heart out there again only to have it smashed in his face. So what if Kenny was only a phone call away? That was one phone call that he just wouldn't make.

# 4

## KEVIN

Holding his cup of hazelnut coffee and bag with two raisin bagels, Kevin left the bagel shop and made his way to work. He cranked up the volume on his mp3 player and listened to Shirley Strawberry of the Steve Harvey Morning Show reading the wild strawberry letter of the day. He was just waiting to hear Steve Harvey tell someone "What they ain't fin' to do" on his show.

In his pocket, his cell phone vibrated. It was his Aunt Mecca calling to check on him. He figured she'd be calling soon since he hadn't heard from her all week. She made it her mission to call him at least once or twice a week to check on him.

"We miss you down here, Kevin. When you gon' come check on us?"

He hadn't taken a trip to North Carolina in a while, so he knew he needed to work one into his schedule. "Aunt Mecca, I've been crazy busy, but I promise you I'll come check on you and Aunt Medina soon."

"We'll be looking forward to it."

Aunt Mecca and Aunt Medina were his mother's sisters. Ever since his mother passed from cancer almost ten years ago, his aunts had taken him under their wings and treated him as though he was their own son. He loved them both dearly.

After ending the call with his aunt, he walked one block over and he was on campus.

Thank God it's Friday. If these people up in here give me much today, someone is getting sent home because I am not in the mood, he thought as he hurried down the brick walkway.

Kevin looked across campus and saw students in pajama pants and flip flops. How he missed those carefree days of undergrad. Wear whatever you want and no one says a damned thing. He spotted out the metal bench near the water fountain that Damon, Shawn, and he used to meet at every morning before they walked to the one class they had together when Shawn took a course there as a visiting student. Damon and Kevin were undergrads here and met Shawn in the one class they took together. Since the time they spent here, they managed to forge a bond that had stood the test of time.

He entered the financial aid office and greeted his co-workers. "Good morning, everyone."

A chorus of "Good mornings" followed.

He entered the office with his name on the door and prepared to get set up for the day. He hung his coat, pressed play on his voicemail, and booted up his computer. His first voicemail was from a student who was clearly in tears.

"Hi, Mr. Malone. This is Christina Graham. This is my last year of school and I am being denied for my loan and have no other options. My family can't afford to send me here and I am so close to graduation. Any help you can give me will be greatly appreciated. I have worked really hard and want to get the degree I have been working for. It's just so…so hard for me," she said sobbing.

As she recited her phone number, Kevin wrote it down so his office would give her a call for an appointment. When students were in her predicament, they always made a concerted effort to help. Sometimes, Kevin wished he could pay these kids' tuition himself. He received another phone call from a student who fell two points below his scholarship requirement and couldn't his afford tuition either. Kevin heard some of the most heartbreaking stories but tried to help everyone he could.

He got a knock on the door from his assistant, Marcia (Mar-see-uh), a tall, attractive woman born in Jamaica, raised in London. Her accent would fluctuate depending upon whom she was talking to.

"Come in, Marcia. What's up?"

"Your first appointment is here. It's Ms. Thompson and her son, Duane," Marcia said with her British accent.

He rolled his eyes and said, "Okay, send them in."

She nodded and sent them inside. Kevin hated situations like this one. Parents who send their kids to school when clearly the kids don't want to be there annoyed him to no end.

The meeting was exactly the way Kevin anticipated and his head was spinning after it was over. As usual, she didn't listen and her son was an ignoramus with his pants sagging, hair half braided, and a very indifferent attitude about college and his future. He managed to maintain a professional demeanor and say all the right words when what he really wanted to say was, "Woman, I wish you would shut your big ass mouth and chill out with that ignorant ass attitude of yours. Doing all this fussing for nothing because your dumb ass son *don't* even want to be here."

He wasn't even mad when she walked out, slamming his door hard enough behind her to split his eardrum. He was just happy she was finally gone. Kevin grabbed his coat, needing another coffee after all of that.

"Marcia, I'm on my way to get coffee. Would you like some?"

"Please. And can you get me a cinnamon bun too?" she asked, delving through her purse for money.

"Your money is no good; I'll take care of you."

"Thanks, Kevin."

The walk across campus to the grease truck was just the break Kevin needed to clear his mind after talking to that lady and her son. On his way back to his office, he noticed a man looking around and holding a map of the campus with LOST clearly stamped to his forehead. He spotted Kevin and asked for help.

"Excuse me, but can you tell me where the North Academic Center is?"

Kevin said, "Actually, I'm walking in that direction."

"Thank God," he said, sighing his relief. "I'm new to this campus and my class is starting in ten minutes."

"I'm sure the professor will understand."

"I am the professor," the man said with a sheepish grin.

"Oh, are you? What do you teach?"

"I'll be teaching a grad-level business seminar here."

"Oh, that's cool. Is this your first time teaching a course?"

"No. I'm a full professor at Columbia. I teach political science there. Charles Wright by the way," he said extending his hand.

"Nice to meet you. I'm Kevin Malone, associate director of financial aid." Kevin shook his hand. They looked at each other for a brief moment, and Charles held on to his hand just a little longer than necessary. When he finally released Kevin's hand, they began to walk.

"So how long have you worked here?"

"Too long. I started as a student worker when I was actually an undergrad here."

"So you worked your way up, huh?"

"I did."

Kevin looked Charles up and down subtly. He looked like a model. He was tall, light skinned with curly hair and had a sharp beard line up. He looked more like a Wall Street banker than a college professor. From underneath Charles' nice winter coat, he could see his fine blue Italian suit and noticed his shiny brown Ferragamo shoes. He knew the shoes because Damon had a pair just like the ones Charles was wearing. His mother always told him you could tell a lot about a man by his shoes.

"Well, this is the North Academic Center on the right and I'm over in financial aid," Kevin said pointing to the building.

"Thank you, sir. I appreciate it. Here's my card."

"Thanks. Here's mine."

Charles smiled at him and went inside his building and Kevin floated back to the financial aid office. He gave Marcia her coffee and cinnamon bun and went into his next meeting. The whole meeting long, all he could think about was Charles' smile, how long he had held on to his hand, and how good he looked in that finely tailored suit. By the end of the meeting, he couldn't tell you a single thing that was said, argued, or discussed. Back in his office, he sifted through all the emails and paperwork he had to do, smiling to himself. His office phone rang.

"Yeah, Marcia?"

"Kevin, there is a Professor Wright here to see you."

More delighted than a young school girl, Kevin bridled his excitement and contained himself.

"You can send him in."

In walked a smiling Charles with his briefcase and coat draped over his arm.

You better wear that suit you sexy muthafucka! Kevin thought as he eyed him from the floor up.

"Hi," Charles said.

"Good afternoon."

He looked like he wasn't quite sure what to say, so he gestured at the room. "This is a nice office you have here."

"Thank you. What brings you here, Professor Wright?"

"I'm on my way to have a bite to eat for lunch. I was wondering if you wanted to join me."

"Lunch?" Kevin looked at the clock hanging on the wall behind him. It read: 1:30.

"Yeah, you know the meal between breakfast and dinner? Middle of the day?"

"Oh my goodness, I didn't even realize what time it was."

"I guess not, with all that work you have in front of you."

Kevin chuckled and thought, Gosh, he sure is familiar.

"Well, there are a lot of students who need financial aid and they want it as soon as possible," Kevin said pulling off his glasses.

"I like those glasses. Those frames are hot."

"Thanks." Kevin blushed and dropped his gaze to the pile of papers on his desk. *Is he flirting with me?*

Charles cleared his throat. "Well, I see you're quite busy. I can take a rain check."

"No, it's fine. I could eat something. What did you have in mind?"

"Do you like Food for Life on 116th?"

"I do."

"Alrighty then. I don't wanna take you away from your work too long, so maybe we should jet."

*He is really inviting me out on a lunch date. And he is talking to me like has known me for a lot longer than a few hours.*

"Maybe we should," Kevin said grabbing his coat.

Kevin stopped by Marcia's desk on his way out of the office.

"Hey Mar, what time are you going to lunch?"

"In about fifteen minutes. I'm waiting on Tangie to call me."

"Okay, I'm going now. I'll see you in an hour."

She looked at Charles and back at Kevin. "Oh, yes you will, and I want all the details on that fine ass professor over there. What GQ magazine did you find him in?" she asked, getting close so he could hear her.

"We'll talk, dahling."

"I want all of those details, honey. And I mean *all*." She said as her accent went straight Jamaican.

Kevin smiled and followed Charles to his car. He did a double-take when he saw Charles hit the alarm to unlock the white Bentley parked out front.

*There is no way he is just a college professor driving this car.*

As Charles turned the ignition, Jill Scott's decadent voice came bouncing through the speakers. Kevin spotted another business card in the console of the car.

"Charles C. Wright, Financial Investor and Banker, huh?" Kevin said reading the card aloud.

"That's what I was before. I worked on Wall Street for twelve years. Now I teach our future how to do it the right way so they can drive Bentleys too," Charles said with a wink and a smile.

"I've never been in a Bentley before. It feels like we're floating on air."

"Yup. That's why I love it."

"So how'd you find your way to Wall Street?"

Charles chuckled. "That's a long arduous story, Mr. Malone." He buckled his seat belt.

"We've got an hour."

Charles looked at him and smiled. "So we do." He pulled off to the restaurant for a tasty meal and a very flirty Q&A.

# 5

## FLASHBACK JOINT

A nineteen year old Malcolm sat defiantly with his arms folded across his chest as he sat with his counselor, Damon, who was growing more and more impatient with Malcolm's blatant disregard for life.

"You're angry. You're bitter. And your violent temper is going to eventually get you or somebody killed." Damon pulled his chair close to Malcolm and stared at him until he finally met his gaze. "So what makes you so angry, Malcolm?"

"A lot of stuff."

"Like what?"

"Things I go through."

"Like."

"Yo, why the fuck we gotta talk about this?"

"Because you're one snap away from going back to jail. So you can either talk to me or I'll let the board put your out-of-control ass back behind bars. Now your mother begged me not to let that happen because this time, they're gonna send you to the state pen. And you won't get out any time soon. This is the first step before you undergo psychiatric evaluation."

"What, am I some kind of study patient?"

"No, you're too smart for that. You scored a 1580 on your SATs, you made honor roll all through middle school, but you started robbing people, stealing cars, and fighting. Your mom put you out at sixteen for pistol whipping your uncle, and you've been arrested three times for assault. And you just did a year and a half in county jail. That spells temper issue. Why all the violence?"

"Why not? Everybody else did it where I'm from. Why not me too?"

"If everyone else jumps off of the Brooklyn Bridge, are you gonna go too?"

Malcolm looked at Damon and sucked his teeth. "Don't fucking insult my intelligence."

"Then fucking speak intelligently."

"I don't know why you're acting like you care anyway. They giving yo stuck-up ass a check either way."

"That doesn't mean I can't help you."

"I don't need your fucking help!"

"Fine. Sit there then. I'll let your mother know you'll be writing her from prison." Damon threw Malcolm's folder onto his desk. He turned around to the computer and acted as if Malcolm wasn't there.

Malcolm sat in silence and tried to stay angry. He remembered the way his mother cried the first time he went away to juvenile jail. He never wanted to see her cry like that again. The more he remembered what it felt like sleeping on that tiny cot in the cold concrete cell, not to mention eating that disgusting stuff that they called food, the more he realized how much he really didn't want to go back. He stayed quiet a whole ten minutes before saying another word.

"I miss my father."

Damon turned around and looked at him. Finally, they were makings some leeway.

"Why do you miss him?"

"Chu mean why? Cuz he was my father. I gotta have a reason to miss my dead father?"

"No, but I wanna know what it is you miss about him."

"Everything. Before he started getting high, anyway."

"What do you remember about him before he used drugs?"

Malcolm cracked a smile. "Him taking me to the park when I was a little boy. Walking me to school. Teaching me how to tie my shoes. Telling me how my mom was a queen and I better not ever let anyone disrespect her."

"So I'm guessing you and your father were really close, right?"

"Like this," he said, holding up a hand with his fingers crossed. Then his expression changed. "But he fucked everything up when he started doing drugs. I'll never forget when he started doing that shit." A faraway look filled his eyes. "We were living in the Astoria houses projects in Queens. Then all of a sudden, he started disappearing for long periods of time. He would come back rubbing his nose or sniffing real hard.

Scratching his arms. Mom would be in the house looking for stuff and he would have taken it somewhere and sold it. And then that's when he started beating on her."

"He hit her in front of you?"

"At first, no. But then he started getting careless with it. When Pop started getting high, he and Moms started fighting. She would fight back cuz she wasn't bout to let no man hit her. One time he blacked her eye and she cut him right across his face with a box cutter. Left a permanent mark. Supposedly he had got some woman pregnant, but I ain't never heard of my father having another child. So I don't know how true that was."

"Then what happened?" Damon asked, watching Malcolm's face as he struggled with the painful memories.

"One night, she packed up our things and we left. We went and stayed with my grandmother in Hollis. And Nana was cool, but I got sick of going to church with her every Sunday. I was missing my father, you feel me? But he wasn't worried about me; he was steady getting high. He would come over from time to time, but he was like a different person by that point. He wasn't my pop no more. He was just a fucking crackhead. And when I tried to tell him about Uncle Claude—" Malcolm stopped abruptly and jumped up from his seat. "Man, fuck this conversation," he said, headed toward the door.

"Malcolm."

He continued walking until his hand reached the door, and he twisted the brass knob.

"Malcolm, you've been holding it in for so long and you finally have a chance to let it out. And that's what you're gonna do? Walk away? Just like that."

Malcolm paused, his hand still holding on to the door knob like it was his lifesaver. Without turning around, he said, "Why you acting like you care?"

"Uncle Claude was the uncle you pistol-whipped, right?"

"Hell yeah. I beat the shit out of his ass."

"Why'd you do it?"

Malcolm was quiet.

"Malcolm."

Finally he turned around to face Damon, but he stayed close to the door. "Cuz."

"Cuz what?"

"Cuz. He tried to do it again."

"He tried to do what again?"

Malcolm leaned back against the door and put his hands on his head. He lifted his head and a single tear rolled down his cheek. "You ain't supposed to do that kinda shit to your nephew, you feel me? You ain't supposed to touch me like that. I was ten, yo. Who touches a ten-year-old like that?" More tears fell at his confession.

Damon's heart was racing. "Did your mom ever know?"

"He always said if I told my mother, she would never believe me because he was her brother. And he threatened me. Said he'd kill me and bury my body before my mother came home from work."

Damon was stunned.

"Just knew my pop could save me. I just knew that I'd be able to tell him and that he'd kill Uncle Claude. But all he cared about was his next fix. He kept overdosing, always in and out of the hospital. When I was fourteen, he ended up in a coma that he never woke up from." Once again, his entire demeanor changed from vulnerable to guarded. "But what the fuck I'm telling you all this for? Like you care."

"I care."

"Nah, I doubt it."

Damon stood and walked over to the door. "It's okay to cry, Malcolm."

"Man, fuck you," Malcolm yelled, his eyes brimming with tears. He slid down the door until he was seated on the floor and Damon sat on the floor beside him, grabbing a box of tissues off the nearby bookshelf.

Malcolm couldn't hold back any more tears. He bawled his eyes out, and Damon passed him tissues and comforted him by putting his arm around him. "It's okay Malcolm. It's okay to hurt."

Malcolm laid his head on Damon's chest and continued to cry. For a few minutes, neither of them said anything. As Malcolm's tears slowed down, Damon gave him a bottle of water.

"Did your mother ever find out about your uncle?"

"Yeah. He's in jail for life. I still wanna kill that nigga, yo. I swear to God if that gun was loaded, I wouldn't have pistol whipped him. I would've shot him between his eyes. I ever see him again, I just might.

He's the reason my head is all fucked up. It's all his bitch-ass fault that I'm like this. Now do you understand why I'm so angry? Now do you understand why I'm so bitter?"

Damon paused and nodded. "I do understand."

"I guess that means that I'm...like you."

"What do you mean, like me?"

Malcolm looked Damon in the eyes. "That I'm a fag. There. I said it."

Damon's eyes bugged. "You're gay?"

Malcolm nodded his head. "And it's all cuz of him. He turned me out. I just don't get how you could do that to a child. I just wanna fucking kill that nigga!" Malcolm grabbed a book off of the coffee table and threw it as hard as he could up against the wall, which knocked down a statue Damon had near the window. He pounded his fists on the coffee table with each word: "*I hate that muthafucka!*"

"Okay, come on. Let's go for a ride and get some air."

"Where we going?"

"Somewhere where you can't break up anything else in my office."

They jumped into Damon's car and Damon drove to a boxing gym in the Bronx. When he and Malcolm walked in the front door, the man behind the desk greeted him excitedly.

"Well, look who it is! What's up, Damon?" the man said.

"What's up, Bruce? This is my boy, Malcolm. Let me get room 125 for an hour."

Bruce turned around and grabbed the key off of the rack behind him and Damon slapped down a $20 bill.

"Thanks, man."

"You got it. Aye, Malcolm that's the golden-gloves champion you going in there with, so I hope you're ready," Bruce said grinning.

Malcolm looked at him confused.

"Why are we here?" Malcolm asked Damon as they headed down the steps to the basement.

"I'm gonna show you how I made it through my childhood and teenage years. I'mma show you how to box."

Malcolm sucked his teeth. "What you know about boxing? You mad soft."

When they entered the room, Damon turned on the light and put on a pair of gloves that were in the drawer. "This is what I know about boxing."

Damon turned to the bag and hit it with several fast and powerful combinations. All of a sudden, Damon didn't seem so soft anymore as Malcolm watched how intense his boxing skills were. Damon took off his shirt and tie and his muscles contracted as he took more swings at the bag. Malcolm was impressed and somewhat turned on.

"When you learn how to box?" Malcolm asked in awe.

"When I was a kid. Cuz I was a 'fag' as you said. So I had to know how to fight. And after fucking up a few big-mouthed muthafuckas, didn't nobody else fuck with me. Cuz they knew I would fuck them up."

Malcolm drew back as Damon's whole demeanor changed. Now his hood-side was beginning to come out. In the time Damon had been his counselor, he had never heard him use the MF-word on anybody.

"Take off your coat and put these on." Damon passed him a pair of gloves and Malcolm did as he was told.

Over the course of the next hour, Damon showed Malcolm how to properly swing and hit harder. Malcolm was already strong and could street fight, but now he was learning technique. He actually liked it.

The challenge came when Damon instructed him to act like the bag was his Uncle Claude and the drugs that killed his father.

"Come on, hit it hard! It killed your father!"

Malcolm hit the bag as hard as he could.

"Come on! Fuck it up! It's your uncle. You haven't seen him since he went away and now he's talking about how good you look. Like he wants a piece of your ass again," Damon instructed.

Malcolm hit the bag with several punch combinations. He started to yell at it. "Muthafucka! I hate you! You fucking bitch! You fucked up my life, you punk bitch ass muthafucka! I hate you! I fucking hate you bitch!"

He grunted and growled as he hit the bag. He turned into a tornado and punched, kicked, and took what seemed to be all of his anger, frustration, and pain out on the bag. His furious words became squeals of pain as he began to sob again. Damon watched him as he seemingly turned back into that innocent little boy he was before his father died and his uncle touched him. Malcolm's eyes looked like red raw sores, but that didn't stop him from crying. Damon grabbed him and hugged him tight.

"Don't let him do it again," Malcolm whispered. "Please don't let him do it again! It hurts," he said between sobs.

"He'll never hurt you again. I promise."

# 6

## THE BOYZ

Every Sunday morning the boys have a ritual. Damon sends Shawn, Malcolm, and Kevin a text telling them what time to be ready. He hops into his Range Rover and picks up Kevin first, then Shawn, and Malcolm last. They convene at their favorite brunch spot on W. 116th St. at Amy Ruth's Restaurant. They throw down on some good food, "kee kee", recap the past week, and have some of their most intimate and personal conversations. This week was no different as they made their way to what they considered the best breakfast spot in Harlem.

They entered the restaurant and were greeted by the host who escorted to them to the same table they got every week. Their normal server, GG, greeted them happily after they were seated comfortably. GG was a big girl who knew she was sexy and wore confidence on her sleeve. No matter what kind of hair style or outfit GG wore, she always walked like she was on a red carpet. She was their favorite server.

"Hey, my babies!" GG said.

"Hey, GG," Damon said with a twang.

"GG, you're looking real good. I like the hair," said Kevin, referring to her new honey blonde short cut.

"Thank you, boo. Y'all ready for your drinks?"

"I could use some coffee," Damon said.

"Me too," Shawn said.

"Me three," Kevin joined in.

"Y'all a bunch of old ass men. Let me have some milk, GG," Malcolm said.

GG laughed. "I got y'all. Half and half okay?"

"That's fine. And can we have a carafe of orange juice?"

"You know I got you, boo. Are y'all ordering the usual, or...?"

They scanned their menus.

"Why we looking at these menus like we don't know them?" Malcolm asked.

"Yeah, I pretty much know what I want," Shawn said.

Still flipping through the menu, Kevin said, "I think I want something different."

"I'll give y'all a minute to decide. Let me grab your drinks."

When she walked off, Damon said, "You want something different, huh, Kev? Like what the professor orders?"

"Oop oop oop. Get him," Shawn said with a laugh.

"What professor?" Malcolm asked.

"Kevin met a professor on campus this week."

"Whaaaat? Kev you getting some?"

"Don't listen to him."

"Well what happened?"

"Nothing. I met this professor the other day. He was lost and so I helped him find his building."

"Yeah, then he came by Kevin's office and invited him to a private lernch," Damon said.

"He took you to lernch? Where y'all go to lernch?" Malcolm asked.

"Food for Life."

"In his Bentley," Damon piped in.

"Bentley?!"

"We woulda got it *in* the Bentley if it was me!" Malcolm said.

"I'm sayin!" Shawn said giving Malcolm a hi-five, and Kevin blushed.

"So what's mystery-man's name?" Malcolm asked.

"Charles. Professor Charles Wright."

"Professor Wright drives a Bentley? What the hell is he professing? The secrets to eternal life?"

"He's a full professor at Columbia. He's teaching a business class at City College."

"You still haven't explained how he drives a Bentley. Inquiring minds wanna know."

"He worked on Wall Street for twelve years before becoming a professor. He made a lot of money there and some very smart investments so when he was ready to leave, he left. He wanted a change of pace so he became a college professor. Said he always wanted to teach at the university level."

GG came and brought their drinks and complimentary cornbread and took their orders. When she sashayed away, they continued their conversation.

"Sounds like this professor was pretty forward."

"He was. And I was kinda caught off guard but I liked it. It was actually turning me on."

"When you gon' see him again?"

"We're gonna go out on Tuesday night."

"Where?"

"Over to City Island to have seafood."

"Somebody's seafood salad is getting tossed that night!" Malcolm exclaimed.

They laughed.

"Shawn, how was you and Jamon's first night back together?"

"Awesome! He wore me out the first night. Chile, I ain't had an orgasm that good in so long. It was some of the best I've *ever* had."

"You ain't beat off while he was gone?"

"No. I don't really do that."

"Geeeeeet the fuck outta here. What you mean you don't beat off? What man don't beat off?" Malcolm exclaimed.

"I didn't say never. Just not that often. Plus I was saving it cuz I knew he was coming home and we were gonna get it in."

"That's some kind of self-control. I gotta nut at least twice a day," Malcolm said.

"I'm at the worst in the morning. I can fuck like ten dudes when I first wake up cuz my morning wood is insane," Damon said.

"I like to do it before I go to bed at night," Kevin admitted.

"I can do it any time of day cuz I'm eternally horny," Malcolm chimed in.

"Don't we know it? The consummate man whore," Kevin said and everyone laughed.

"Guess who called me the other night, y'all?" Damon posed the question after sipping on his coffee.

"Who?"

"Kenny."

Silence fell over the table. Malcolm and Shawn were tearing the complimentary cornbread up and they both stopped chewing. Kevin raised his eyebrows.

"Please say you told him to kick rocks."

"Or bricks for that matter."

"I haven't called him back. But I did listen to his voice message. He wants to meet for coffee and talk."

Shawn and Kevin sucked at their teeth.

"Meet for coffee and talk, huh?" Malcolm tilted his head and twisted his lips up like Ed Lover. "C'mon, son. Fuck outta here with that bullshit."

"Do you want to see him?" Shawn asked with his brows lifted high.

"Honestly? I kinda do. I mean, there is no harm in talking is there?"

"In this case, yes. You don't owe him anything. He's the one who deceived you. He led you on for eleven months before you found out he was married to a woman. And afterwards, the bastard just shook his head like, 'Oh my bad; yeah, I happen to be married.'" Shawn spoke with plenty of attitude.

Damon looked down. What could he say? Shawn was right.

Malcolm looked at him. "You gon' meet up with him, ain't you?"

"No. Of course not."

"I just saw that look on your face. You still want him."

"Are you crazy? I do not want him. He can go to hell."

"Who you think you talking to? You think we don't know you?"

"What? I'm not gonna meet him."

"Well at least if you do, let it be the last time. If he's good for nothing else but a nut, use him for that and kick his ass to the curb."

GG brought their food and they continued to discuss Damon's meeting up with Kenny over plates of Belgium waffles, honey dipped fried chicken, scrambled eggs, home fries, and sausage. They talked, laughed, joked, and shared the most personal details of their lives with each other as they often do. As Damon dropped them all off in the order in which they were picked up, they rejoiced in the fact that they shared a bond with each other that they had with no one else. They were more than friends. They were family to one another. The "Boyz of Harlem." And what a thing it was for them.

# 7

## MALCOLM & MAMA NZINGHA

As Malcolm and Mama Nzingha took an afternoon stroll through Central Park, she lit a cigarette. They walked across the Bow Bridge and looked at the bare trees that had melting snow on them from a recent snowfall. The temperatures were beginning to rise a bit as warm air tried to cut through the winter chill that still lingered over New York City.

Mama Nzingha looked fly in her black pants and leather boots that zipped up her legs. She wore a dark brown mink jacket, shades, and a brown fedora on her head. Her locks were in curls as they hung down past her shoulders. On her shoulder, a designer black leather bag hung at her side. Malcolm was stuntin' hard in his jeans, Timbs, and nice pea coat and shades.

"Hey, Mama you ever miss Dad?" Malcolm asked.

She glanced at him as though she was surprised he'd asked that Question. "Sure."

"How do you deal with it?"

"I just do."

"You ever get sad?"

"Sometimes. But not like I used to. Why you ask?"

"Just wondering. You don't be lonely?"

She thought about Randy who had just left her fully satisfied this morning before leaving for work. "Naaaa, not really."

"How though? I mean, you still fly. Ain't nobody creeping around you tryna get at you?"

"Bless your heart son. And yes I have my share of admirers but you know Mama ain't exactly a young little thang anymore. I don't have time for games men play. I raised the one son I gave birth to. I don't have any intention on raising any more boys. And that's the thing. When a man

41

comes to me with something, he's got to come correct. Cuz this lady here? She really ain't got time for that."

Malcolm laughed but quickly got serious again. "I just don't want you to be lonely for the rest of your life."

"What makes you think I'm lonely?"

"Cuz you're single."

"I may be. But I'm not lonely. I still manage to lead a very full life. And if God sees fit, I'll find love again. You know, even when your father died it took me a while to rebound. For the first five years, it was hard for me to even look at another man without feeling guilty. That's why for those first five years, I still wore my wedding rings because as far as I was concerned, I was still a married woman."

"And now?" She exhaled because she wanted to tell him about Randy but felt the time wasn't right.

"Now I'm open to the possibility of dating again. On my own terms though."

"I guess that's fair enough. You know when I go out, I be wondering why you not doing the same thing." She chuckled.

"Mama has lived. I had my heyday. But what I wanna know is when you gon' stop running around and get you a steady?"

"A steady what?"

"A steady boyfriend. You all up in my business so let me get in yours."

"Can't no one man handle all of this. I don't mind sharing my love cuz I got a lot to go around."

"Is that right?"

"That's right."

His mom eyed him as though she knew something about himself that he didn't know. But one thing he did know was that being in a steady relationship, like what Shawn and Jamon have, was not for everybody. He couldn't fathom the thought of being with one man for the rest of his life.

"Well, son, I believe we should have as much fun as we like. We only get one life to live. But—" She gave the word much emphasis and stared at him intensely, making sure that he was listening to her every word. "But don't you be so busy sharing all your love that you don't receive any. If you never remember anything your mother tells you, remember a life without experiencing love is a life wasted. You must be open to it though. And it'll catch you. And when it does, it can be the most beautiful thing to ever happen to you. So don't miss out cuz you like to share with everybody. You get where I'm going?"

Though he was rolling his eyes on the inside, for his mother's sake, he donned a serious expression and pretended like her words had truly affected him. "Yes ma'am," he said, nodding his head. "I get it."

"Good. Now enough serious talk for the day. Why don't you say we hit this hot dog cart over here, I'll sneak 'em in my purse and we go over to the movie theatre to see that new Denzel flick?"

"Let's."

"Alright now," she said as they walked to the hot dog cart with her arm looped in his.

Oddly enough, though his mother's words had not pierced through his promiscuous exterior, the phrase *"A life without love is a life wasted"* replayed in his head for the rest of the day.

# 8

## SHAWN & JAMON

"Jamon, man, so good to see you back in town," one of the club workers said as he approached the VIP booth and gave him dap.

"Good to see you too, man, and good to be back."

"Hey, look, anything you want to eat or drink, you know it's on the house. Y'all want some wings, more drinks?"

Jamon glanced over at Shawn who shook his head.

"Nah, we good with what we got. But if we need something else, I'll wave you over."

"Aight. No doubt." Shawn sat across from Jamon in a plush VIP booth of the New York Underground nightclub while they sipped Long Island Iced Teas. They were at what was becoming New York's most popular open mic spot. Record execs, celebrity guests, and much of the best talent in NYC came to this open mic regularly. Before Jamon became a songwriter and really began to tour as a background singer, he was a staple at this open mic and it was where he was first spotted. Since he has gone on to do things in the industry, he is somewhat of a celebrity there. Whenever he is in town, the owners always invite him down to perform, get him a VIP booth, and pay him a percentage of what they collect at the door for admission. One night, he walked out of there with $1,000.

This open mic was purely voluntary and no one ever got paid to sing. Much of the talent who performed was local talent trying to get put on. They all sign the list in hopes of performing and getting seen by someone who can advance their careers. Shawn always had to be on his best behavior because although he and Jamon were a couple, he had to help maintain Jamon's smooth crooner "ladies' man" image. And the ladies certainly loved him. They often approached him for pictures and autographs for his mix tape he had for sale. And some of the fellas would gawk at him. It always made Shawn uncomfortable, and he would have to take as many drinks as he could handle to help him keep his cool about it. He wished that he and Jamon could stroll up in there arm in arm and everyone know the deal. But he knew that was never gonna happen.

"So Rell wants you to go to LA next week?" Shawn asked.

"Yeah. He got me recording a duet with Lyndsay Belle for her next album."

"You just came back, though."

"I know, but I gotta keep hustling and making this money. I want us in a mansion in Connecticut or Jersey somewhere. Something more than Harlem for us."

"I like Harlem."

"I do too. But there are other places we can live," Jamon said taking a sip of his drink.

Shawn admired Jamon's passion, but he was feeling left out of the inner circle of Jamon's life. Since Jamon had been home, Shawn had barely seen him. He stayed holed up in the studio, and if he wasn't there, he was walking around in his own zone, headphones on his ears, pen and pad in his hands as he worked on writing more music. This was the longest time he had spent around him since that evening when they'd made love Jamon's first night back in town. Shawn felt like he was starving; not for sex, but for quality time with his lover. But it seemed like Jamon had time for everything except for that.

"In seven days, you'll be gone again and we hardly spent any time together."

"We're spending time together now."

Shawn rolled his eyes. "That's not what I mean."

"You know music is my life. Come on, don't act like that."

*Seriously dude?*

"I get that. But do I fall anywhere in there?"

Jamon frowned. "What is that supposed to mean?"

"It means you do everything you have to do to support your career. What about us? We've only spent time together once since you've been home. Do I fit into your schedule at all?"

"You're in my schedule. We're here aren't we?"

"This is your idea of us spending time together?"

"And now ladies and gentlemen, we wanna bring up one of our own stars. New York City, show your love for one of our very own, Jamon

King!" the host said, dragging out Jamon's last name to make a lasting effect.

"We'll finish this later," Jamon said rising from his seat.

*They would call his ass up there now.*

The crowd cheered as Jamon walked up. He gave dap to the host and sat behind the keyboard that one of the band members vacated for him. After he adjusted the microphone to his mouth, he turned his hat backwards.

"How's everybody doing?"

"Fine, just like you!" one of the women screamed out. Jamon grinned and winked at her. "You fine, too, baby."

*Why'd he have to say that?* The woman screamed like his words had actually caressed her body. Shawn couldn't roll his eyes any harder if he tried. Once the noise settled down, he continued.

"I'mma do an original piece I wrote. People always ask me why I don't perform my originals more often, so here's one of them."

Jamon began to play a ballad he wrote called "Destiny."

From the first note he sung into the microphone, people began to clap and cheer him on. His velvety smooth voice brought a certain mood that sent a feeling of calm and warmth over the audience. People stopped talking and just listened to him sing. He seduced the crowd with his melodic voice and undeniable charm. It never failed. He could do every vocal run, riff, and trick under the sun. And he never held back from using his beautiful falsetto. It always made his audience swoon. Equal parts soulful, jazzy, and endearing, Jamon's vocal talent was on a level that was almost unmatched. It seemed like he could do anything he wanted with it to captivate the audience's ear. They swooned, yelled out, and rocked back and forth as he played the keyboard and sang his song. At the sound of the last poignant chord as he ended the ballad, the crowd gave him a standing ovation with thunderous applause. He smiled, bowed, and thanked the audience before leaving the stage.

"Y'all like that?" the host asked.

They continued to cheer, yelling for more.

"Jamon, they love you. Come give us another one," the host said, waving him back to the stage.

Jamon returned to the stage and whispered to the band what he was going to sing. They began to play the opening chords of the song

"Cruising" by Smokey Robinson. The band played the old school tune and he took the audience right in. He had everyone up on their feet like they were at a party dancing, clapping, and singing with him. And he sung the hell out of it. Even through his funk, Shawn grooved alone in the booth, bobbing his head to the beat. Jamon finished the song to yet another standing ovation and stretched his arms out to the sides and bowed like he was at his own concert.

"Thank you. Show some love for the band too. Make sure y'all go to my website and cop my new mix tape. *From Jamon 2 U.*"

As he left the stage, people hugged him and shook his hand; some handed him money as he made his way through the crowd. And the women, they could not keep their little roving hands to themselves. They rubbed all over his head and face, pulled at his clothes, hugged him so tight, they might as well have been trying to fuck him. And Shawn lost count how many women kissed his cheeks; one woman had the audacity to put a kiss at the corner of Jamon's lips. Not wanting to see anymore, Shawn lowered his gaze to the ice cubes in his glass. To make matters worse, Jamon's manager Rell had made his way inside and approached him through the crowd. They dapped and Rell said something to Jamon, which made him let out a big laugh. They made their way back to the table. Shawn saw him coming back with Rell and rolled his eyes. Now he was really ready to go.

"Wassup, Shawn?" Rell said extending his hand.

Shawn extended his hand back and gave him dap. "Wassup, Rell?"

"I'mma run to the bathroom but think about what I just said," Rell said before disappearing into the dimly lit club to find the restroom.

"You were born for the stage," Shawn congratulated him once he sat down.

"Thanks. Rell just said I should remake 'Cruising' with the band up there and put it on iTunes for sale."

Shawn nodded. He was over it as soon as Jamon mentioned Rell's suggestion.

"You gonna kick it with Rell?"

"I guess. I didn't know he was coming."

"Alright, I'm gonna go," Shawn said grabbing his coat.

"Go where? What's up with all the attitude?"

"Home, J. I gotta go back to work tomorrow. I only came to hear you."

"So you're just gonna leave?"

"I'm tired."

"I thought you wanted to spend some time with me."

"Just you. Not you and all your fans and definitely not with your manager."

"Mook, why you acting like that? I'll be sitting here with you," Jamon said.

"With Rell while you discuss more business that will just take you away from home again. I don't wanna sit and listen to that."

Jamon shook his head. "Fine, if you wanna leave then go. I'll have Rell drop me off at home."

Shawn looked at him. He didn't want to leave like that, but he really didn't want to stay either. Jamon didn't want him to leave either, but he couldn't understand why Shawn was acting this way. Just a moment ago, he'd been fine.

"I'll see you at home."

Jamon flashed the peace sign and said nothing. Shawn grabbed his coat and made his way to the exit while Jamon watched him leave. When Shawn got outside, he pulled out his phone and called Kevin.

As soon as he answered the phone, he said, "Ugh! I am so over Jamon right now."

"What happened?"

"Remember I said I was tired of sharing Jamon with the music industry?"

"Yeah, I remember."

"Well, it's a little more than I thought. I was sitting there and I really didn't wanna be there. I always enjoy being with him, but it just feels like it's heightened security, ya know? Like, I can't sit too close, I can't really touch him, I have to watch what I say. I have to watch women fall all over him, other guys gawk at him, and I can't be his boyfriend. I have to play like I'm his friend. Or his assistant. Or some hanger on and I am so sick of it. Like, I am really fuming about that right now."

"He tells you not to sit too close?" Kevin asked.

"Not tonight but he has. I just have to remember it. I'm just so tired of playing this role and then in the end, I still get about an ounce of his time."

"I thought things were good," Kevin said and Shawn let out a *hmph*. "Have you shared any of this with him?"

"I have. He thinks if I wanted to spend time with him, I shoulda stayed at the open mic."

"That's not the same thing."

"Thank you! So I know I'm not crazy."

"So where are you now?"

Shawn started up the ignition and pulled off. "In the car, taking my black ass home. What about you? What are you doing?"

"Deciding what I'm gonna wear on my date tomorrow night with the professor."

"So, are y'all an item, or are y'all still in the dating phase?"

"We're still getting to know each other. I've known this man less than a week, don't try to marry me off so soon."

"Well, I'm happy for you. And I really wish I could sound a little more enthusiastic for your sake, but misery loves company so I need to get off this phone before I end up spoiling your night too."

"Honey, don't worry about Jamon. I'm sure you guys can work something out. Even if it takes designating certain days you will spend together, cuz it's not like you don't work too."

"Yeah, you're right. I'll let you go. Thanks for listening to me vent."

"Anytime, love. And stop stressing; everything will be fine."

They exchanged good-nights and ended the call. Shawn turned up the radio in the car. He was very unsettled about the way he left the club.

As Rell and Jamon discussed matters of business, Jamon spotted an old friend making his way through the crowd. They locked eyes for a few seconds and Jamon couldn't end his conversation with Rell fast enough. His old friend made sure not to wander too far away. For the moment, Jamon forgot about his issues with Shawn and dealt with what was in front of him.

# 9

## KEVIN'S JOURNAL

Dear Journal,

So I haven't confessed this to the boys. But I am so nervous about going out with this professor tomorrow night. I mean he seems wonderful. And I don't want to paint him with any types of negative brushes before we even get a chance to spend time. But after my last relationship with Ryan, it's so hard for me to trust men. He was so abusive. Not in a physical way—just emotionally. I'm not beat for any man to ever hit me but I just remember the way he used to talk to me when he was angry—which was every other day just about. And then you remember Cedric was the same way—only he did hit me once. I deaded that so fast. I just hope if things do get serious with Charles and me, that things are different. I swore I was off men but the way Charles looked in that suit, he was just way too good to pass up. Mama didn't raise no fool!

And when I think back to Cedric and Ryan, they both came from messed up family situations that probably made them that way. Charles seems to really have his head on straight. I can't wait to hear all about his time on Wall Street. I need to learn more about investing money anyway.

And I know he knows all about that. Not to mention he is drop dead gorgeous and I loves me a light skinned man. Not that I don't like chocolate brothas but I have always had a soft spot for the light and curly boys like Charles. So I'm making up in my mind that things will be different.

And the moment (if it ever comes) that Charles shows his ass or gets disrespectful, I'm out of the door. Because I refuse to deal with another disrespectful man. Even though I know I don't want to grow old alone—I'd rather be alone than be disrespected. That's for sure. But in the meantime I will hope for the best. After all, he did invite *me* out. I asked both Cedric and Ryan out. In fact, I courted both of them until they returned interest. A man who shows interest in me wouldn't be the one to disrespect me, would he? I don't think so. Yeah, it's probably just the fears of my past calling. But I won't answer that call. I'm just gonna go with the flow and not have any expectations and make it my business to have a great night.

Love,
Kevin

# 10

## SHAWN & JAMON

"I just want to spend some time with you!" Shawn said.

"Well you had the perfect chance to last night and you left!" Jamon reminded him.

Shawn followed him into the bedroom. "We were not spending time! You were networking for you career. Dammit, is it always gonna be about your career? What about me? What about us?"

"So what you want me to do? Give up music for you?"

"That's not what I said."

Jamon looked at him. "Then what are you saying?"

"I want you to remember that you're in a relationship with more than just your music. You're in a relationship with me too! Why am I always on the back burner? Huh? Why is that?"

"You are not! I'm doing all of this for us. I'm grinding my ass off so we can live better."

"There is nothing wrong with the way we are living."

"Well, maybe I want more."

"And maybe I need more of you. Would it kill you to spend more time with me for more than an hour at a time or when we're having sex?"

Jamon scrunched up his face. "I don't understand why you're being so selfish."

"How am I being selfish? Because I want my boyfriend to spend time with me?"

"You knew what it was when we got together. You knew music was my thing then."

"You're missing the point."

"What am I not seeing?"

"You're not seeing as your man, my needs aren't being met. I always make time for you and I have a full-time job!"

Jamon's eyebrows jumped. "Full-time job? What the fuck is that supposed to mean? That what you do is more important than what I do? You think cuz you went to college and teach these stupid little muthafuckas Shakespeare that it makes you better than me?"

"I didn't say that!"

"That's what you meant! I know what you're trying to say!"

"Jamon, I want you to live your dream. My dream is teaching and yours is music. Is there not a way we can mutually do what we love and still be a couple?"

"Not when you're trying to tell me that I need to put you before my music. Trying to get all bourgeois with me cuz you went to college."

Shawn frowned and shook his head. "What does my going to college have to do with your being a singer?"

"Cuz you act like it makes you better than me because I didn't finish!"

"Who said anything about that? Why are you so insecure about that?"

"I'm not insecure! It's not like it matters cuz I make more money than you anyway."

Shawn's eyes filled with hurt. "Why would you say something like that to me?"

"Cuz it's the truth. You hate the fact that I make more money than you and you spent all of that time going to college."

Tears formed in Shawn's eyes. "I think you need to go for a walk."

Jamon raised his eyebrows. "So you tryna put me out?"

Shawn just looked at him.

"Fuck it then. I'm out." Jamon walked out slamming the door behind him.

Shawn peered out of the window watching Jamon walk down the block after he got outside. He tried his best to hold back his tears but they flowed almost instantaneously.

# 11

## OLD FRIEND

Damon sniffled and blinked back tears as he eased up the volume of "Old Friend" by Phyllis Hyman. He took a sip of champagne and nodded his head to the easy piano melody of the song as Phyllis' haunting voice saturated his living room. His mother played a lot of Phyllis Hyman music while he was growing up, and this particular song always stirred his emotions. Happy memories of his childhood and the emotional vocal delivery of Phyllis Hyman always made him cry. Behind his computer chair, Lucky lay on the floor. Damon realized he missed his parents. As he began to think of the reason why he hadn't been to their house in over six years, the doorbell interrupted his thoughts. He wiped his tears as Lucky went to the door barking.

Damon checked himself in the mirror to make sure his face was straight before he went to the door. A glance through the peephole made him gasp and his stomach filled with butterflies. It was Kenny. Damon hadn't seen Kenny in over a year. He glanced through the peephole again, certain his eyes had deceived him. Nope, he hadn't been mistaken; it was Kenny in the flesh. He turned his back to the door and closed his eyes.

*Do I answer the door or not?* Damon wondered. *He knows I'm here; my truck is parked out front.*

The doorbell rang again.

Damon took a steadying breath, turned around and opened the door. "Kenny."

"Hey," Kenny said with a smile.

*Why the fuck do you look so good?* Damon thought as his eyes took in the full sight of this tall drink of water. Wearing a gray suit and a tie that was slightly unfastened, Kenny looked like he'd stepped off the cover of a modeling magazine: tall enough that he'd have to duck to walk through the door, dark brown skin, smooth and flawless, and chiseled dark bedroom eyes that always seemed to twinkle, even when he was mad.

They looked at each other briefly.

"Surprised?" Kenny asked.

"That's an understatement."

"How have you been?"

"I'm well. Very well. How about you?"

"I'm hanging in there. You look really good."

"Thanks. You too."

An awkward silence settled between them.

"So..." Kenny said, gesturing at the door, "...are you gonna invite me in?"

*Hell no! Take your sexy ass back where you came from!*

"I was just listening to some music and sipping champagne. Have some?"

"Certainly." The smile on his face could've been considered cocky as he followed Damon inside. Lucky kept his eyes locked on the man and a warning growl rolled in his throat.

"Lucky, be quiet." Kenny jumped back as Lucky growled and barked at him.

Damon took Lucky by the collar and made him go down into the basement, closing the door behind him. "Sorry about that. He's usually not like that. I don't know what's gotten into him."

Kenny's focus had already shifted to Damon's chic living room.

"You always kept a nice house."

"Thank you," Damon said pouring him a glass of champagne.

Damon didn't want to ogle him while he drank the wine. But the way he held the glass in his hand, the way his lips clung to the rim, the way his lips pouted when he sipped at the amber liquid commanded Damon's attention. He couldn't have looked away if he tried. While Kenny sipped the champagne, Damon gave him a look that screamed, "I want you!" It didn't help that the end of the song was playing where Phyllis sung the lyrics that welcomed her lover back into her life.

"So what brings you over this way this evening?"

"One of my clients had an art show at the Schomberg. So I went to check it out."

"Why didn't you call and say you were coming?"

"I wanted to surprise you."

"It worked."

"So how goes selling houses?"

"It's up and down but I'm hanging in there. How is the corporate world?"

"Rewarding. Always new money to be made."

"And your family? How's everyone?"

"The kids are good."

Damon paused. "And your wife?"

Kenny turned and looked at him then looked away. "She's okay. We're not, though."

"Really? Why?"

He was quiet as he toyed with his half empty glass. "Basically, we're only together for the kids. But things between us?" He gave the thumbs down sign. "Ever since she found out about you and me, things have never been the same. We tried to work it out but that's hard to do when the trust is broken. And every chance she gets, she has to throw in my face that I swing with men. I'm not happy; she's not happy."

"Then why are y'all still together?"

"We're trying to hang in there for the kids' sake. Both of us grew up in single-parent homes, so we're trying to give them a two-parent advantage, but..."

"I see. Having both parents is good. But only if they get along. When my parents were on the verge of divorce, it was tough to live through. Thankfully, they got it together."

"Then she's always telling our oldest son, don't be like your daddy."

"She told him?"

"I don't think she has yet, and I don't want him to know. I don't want him to think that this is the way to go. I'd be pissed if my son turned gay."

Damon walked over to the couch and sat. "You sound like my father. When I finally admitted it to him, he checked out of my life for good. Said he could never accept my being gay. It was too hard for him. He hasn't had a lot to do with me in recent years."

"I could see how it would be hard."

"For whom?"

"For your dad."

Damon raised one eyebrow. "Excuse me?"

"No, I didn't mean it like that. You just don't want your kids to have to go through any hardships you can't protect them from. And I know I can't protect him from the hardships he would have to endure as a gay man."

"Just pray he never falls in love with a married man if he winds up gay."

"Ouch." He rubbed at the back of his neck. "I guess I kinda deserve that one, huh?"

Damon sipped his champagne and looked the other way. Kenny walked over and sat beside him on the couch, still nursing the last few sips of his champagne.

"So what are you and Sheila gonna do? Is it over, or...?"

"I don't know. We really went through it after she found out about you and me. She took the kids and went to her mother's house in Jersey for an entire year. That was hell because I couldn't see my kids. I mean I missed her too, but I really missed my kids more than anything. Her whole family found out about it. Her brothers wanted to beat me up. My mom calling me to say how ashamed she is of me and she ain't raise me to be no faggot. It was the hardest thing I ever had to deal with. She wanted a divorce, but we agreed to file for legal separation. She finally brought the kids back about two months ago."

"Wow. So do you want a divorce?"

Kenny took a swig of his drink and stared off into space. "Our marriage has been over for a while. However, the divorce would make things even more strained, I think. I just don't want her to take my kids away again. If we go through with the divorce, she will take the kids. Not to mention all the money I'd have to pay in child support and alimony. I would do whatever for my kids, but she would get me for as much as she could if she had the chance to."

"So y'all are still together?"

Kenny frowned. "I told you. Yeah, for the kids' sake."

"I mean, are y'all still together, like intimately?"

"Of course. That's the only thing that has never been an issue for us."

That really stung Damon. "I see." Then what was the point for him being over here? He'd told him once and he still meant it: it was either all or nothing, and even after all of this time, he could still clearly see that Kenny was not ready to give him his all.

"But I've missed you." He touched Damon's leg and squeezed. "And you can't tell me that you haven't missed me too."

As Damon swallowed his champagne, a feeling of guilt came over him. He stopped fighting the fact that he had fallen in love with this married bisexual man he was sitting with on his couch. He accepted the fact that he still loved him. His mind wandered back to when he first fell for Kenny. Their affair was one of walks in the park, dinners at four and five star restaurants, visits to art galleries, deep conversation, and trips to Atlantic City. It broke Damon's heart when he found out Kenny was married. Yet he still couldn't resist him. And he felt so pathetic.

"I can't believe this shit."

"Can't believe what?"

"That after all of this, I still want you."

Kenny looked Damon in the eyes and kissed him. And as much as Damon wanted to push him away, he couldn't. And when he didn't, Kenny climbed on top of him and started taking off his clothes. Damon wrapped his legs around Kenny and prepared to do what his body screamed to let happen. Kenny made love to him and they christened every spot in the living room. Damon could feel Kenny's dick pulsate inside of him with every thrust and grind. The feeling of Kenny's warm breath on him made him get wetter each time he felt it. He looked Kenny in his eyes and felt every fiber of his being fall back in love with him. Even after all the elapsed time, Kenny still made Damon feel his fire. And Kenny was the perfect mix of gentle and rough. Damon melted like butter from his touch. He lifted Damon up while still inside of him and they maintained deep eye contact until they both exploded. As badly as Damon didn't want it to be there, he still had a deep connection with Kenny. He loved him.

After they were done, Kenny took his hand and led him upstairs to his bedroom and held him until he fell asleep. When Damon awoke the next morning, he realized Kenny had gone home to his wife. And it tore him up. How could their lovemaking be that good and he still want to stay with her? *As we lay.*

# 12

## MALCOLM

Malcolm walked down 125th St on what was an unseasonably warm winter day. And 125th St was crowded with people as usual. Guys were in flight jackets and fitted caps all over, girls were strutting in their jackets and matching hats with oversized handbags, and vendors lined the sidewalks selling incense, candles, shades, DVDs, CDS, wife beaters, and socks. The sun beamed brightly and fluffy white clouds lolled across the sky.

Malcolm had his model strut in full swing as he walked down the street to do some shopping. Drake blasted in his Beats by Dre headphones as he decided which store he wanted to go into. He could feel eyes on him as he walked. He smiled to himself because he loved the attention he was getting. His shades rested on his nose and when the light hit his earrings, they could blind somebody. In a store window, he saw an unbeatable sale for sneakers: two pair for $150.

*Aww, shit now.* The place was loaded with items that caught Malcolm's attention. Jeans, shirts, and sneakers alike, they had everything. He looked at the Asian man behind the register and saw what looked like a hundred different colored fitted caps. He made a beeline for the sneakers and began looking for what he liked.

"Wassup, bro? Can I help you with something?" Malcolm heard a voice say.

He turned his head to the left and looked at the vision that stood before him. He was just a few inches shorter with what looked like a nice body. He was light skinned with deep hazel brown eyes, a goatee, and long locks down his back.

*Got-dayum.* He took off his headphones. "Huh?"

"Can I help you with something?"

"Yeah, I like these Nikes right here," Malcolm said pointing to the ones he liked.

"These are a part of the sale we're running this week. Do you see any other ones you like? We have two pairs for $150."

Malcolm looked over at the wall and spotted another pair he could go for. He wasn't so in love with them but thought they were fly.

"I like those too," Malcolm said pointing to a blue and yellow pair.

"What size?"

Malcolm looked down at his feet and almost forgot how big they were. "Damn, y'all probably don't even have my size."

The man looked down at Malcolm's feet. "Thirteen?"

"Fourteen, actually."

"Let me see what I have. I have a few big sizes that came in last week," the man said before disappearing to the back room.

Malcolm took off his shades to look at the man walk away. *"Mmm, mmm, mmm."*

He looked at some other things before the man returned with two huge shoe boxes.

"Someone got the last few fourteens; can you wear a fifteen? It's the biggest one I got."

"I'll try them on." Malcolm tried them on and they fit. They were a little big but not so much that walking in them would be uncomfortable. "They're good. I'll take them."

The man smiled. "Is there anything else I can help you with today?"

"I like those jeans over there," Malcolm said pointing to the table of jeans while slipping his sneakers back on. He didn't really care much for the jeans. He just wanted to prolong his time with this sexy ass man standing before him.

"What size?"

"I'm a 34/36. I can do a 36/36, though."

"I got the perfect shirts for those jeans."

Malcolm licked his lips watching him walk away. *Damn, that nigga is bangin.*

He returned with three shirts that Malcolm gave his stamp of approval. He threw three pairs of jeans over his arm, along with the three shirts, and juggled the two shoe boxes. Hands loaded, Malcolm knew he couldn't grab another thing. Yet and still, he followed the guy around the store and looked at the different sale items that he pointed out. Malcolm forget about everything else. Every time the man looked him in the eyes, it made him feel naked. It was as if he could see through him. They shared a few laughs and had a nice conversation. This was new for Malcolm because he was always the one who had this effect on everyone else. He had such a sexy smile and confident demeanor and was usually the aggressor, but this handsome guy made Malcolm feel like a bottom. He was blushing and feeling butterflies in his stomach. And it was crazy, but he was entranced by this man.

At the checkout counter, the guy told the Asian man to step aside so he could take care of Malcolm. His purchase rang up to $375. The guy knocked off $50.

"Are you the assistant manager or something?"

"Nah, I'm the head manager and co-owner."

"Really? I don't see a lot of brothas stepping behind the register around here."

"Well, this one does."

"And you may as well call me a brotha too cuz I ain't no white man," the Asian man said sounding like he was from the streets of Harlem too.

"Oh shit! Let me find out you're really a brotha too!" Malcolm said laughing.

"Yeah man. Cheech and Chong my ass." The man gave Malcolm dap and the three of them laughed.

Malcolm passed him his bank card and as he swiped it, the guy behind the register passed him a handful of business cards. "Give these to your family, your friends. Let them know we have a crazy sale going on over here, but it's not going to last for long."

"I'll definitely do that," Malcolm said, taking the cards. He read one card out loud. "Malik Williams."

"That's me," Malik said.

"Store owner, DJ, and a masseuse," Malcolm said, still reading the card. "A jack of many trades, huh?"

"I'm a hustler. Got to make money some way."

"Hey, I never knock a hustle."

Malcolm was even more turned on as he watched Malik switch from pleasant guy into business mode when at the register waiting for the transaction to go through. Malcolm's dick hardened when Malik's tongue flicked out to wet his lips, all while donning that serious look on his face. Malcolm zoned out and had a vision of him flipping Malik over on a bed and beating that ass up. It would be some of the best sex ever. He could feel the intensity, see the sweat, imagine the feeling, and he smiled thinking about it.

"Malcolm!" Malik said snapping him back to reality.

"Huh?"

"Can you sign the receipt?" He passed him a pen and the receipt.

"Yeah. How'd you know my name?"

"Cuz you just gave me your bank card."

After he signed the receipt, Malik gave him the customer copy of the receipt and passed him his bag. "Thank you for shopping here. Make sure you come back and see us—" But in Malcolm's mind, he heard it as, "Make sure you come back and see *me.*"

"I definitely will. Thanks, man," he said as he took the bag from him. They shared a look. He didn't think it was physically possible for his dick to get harder, but somehow it did. Malcolm left the store two hundred dollars shorter than he wanted to be and hornier than he'd ever been.

*Got-damn, I wanna fuck right now. Nigga got my dick hard as a fucking brick. I gotta make me some phone calls cuz I gotta get me some ass now.* Malcolm adjusted his pants so his erection wouldn't be visible.

He stopped at the man selling shades and picked up a few pairs for him and his mom. As he was leaving the shades stand, he spotted a familiar face. A guy he used to mess with from Sugar Hill. Malcolm couldn't remember his name, but he knew that the dude gave the best head he had ever had and had a nice juicy ass. He spotted Malcolm and smiled at him as he gave him dap.

"What's good, Black?" the guy said.

"I'm chillin. Everything good?"

"Yeah man, everything is good."

"So what's good with the thing?"

That was their code for "Can we get it in?"

He chuckled. "You don't waste no time do you?"

"Hell nah. I ain't got no time to waste. Where you at now?"

"I still live in the same place."

"I'll be there in an hour."

Malcolm stayed true to his word. He showed up at the man's apartment and gave him one of the strongest orgasms he'd ever experienced. But even after sexing the guy down, Malcolm couldn't stop thinking about Malik.

*I definitely gotta get that.*

# 13

## SIGNS

"**O**MG, where has this man been my whole life?" Kevin asked himself as they sat on the living room couch of Charles swanky 37th floor apartment on W. 72nd St. His apartment granted a breathtaking panoramic view of the Empire State Building, the Chrysler Buildings, and much of Central Park down below. Since he had a corner apartment, he was also able to see the river from the bedroom. The ceilings were high with ceiling-to-floor windows, a sunken living room, and a state of the art kitchen with marble floors and granite countertops. The apartment was large for New York City but very cozy and welcoming. Charles and Kevin were talking and listening to all of Jill Scott's albums play straight through.

In the time Kevin had known Charles, he'd had more orgasms than he could count. Not sexual orgasms—yet—but loads of mental orgasms. Charles was so intelligent and could hold a conversation about almost anything. Kevin loved an educated black man. And he had great teeth; none of them were gold, they were all there, and he kept himself up. But what he loved about him the most was that he'd been holding back the cookie from Charles, yet Charles continued to pursue him. If the professor only wanted him for sex, Kevin was sure that he would've checked out by now. But the fact that he continued to court Kevin made Kevin realize that Charles was feeling him on a level much deeper than the sexual. It excited him to know that he could have a relationship of actual substance.

"So how often do you get back to Philly?" Kevin asked.

"At least once a month. I have a home in Wynnewod right outside of Philly so I go there when I have time off. I go check in on my family and see my old friends from when I was growing up, make sure my mom is still doing good, looking good." Charles' tone changed. "Baby, what's wrong with you?"

Kevin shook his head. "Nothing. Why do you ask?"

Charles shrugged. "These last few days, you've seemed very introverted. Like you have something on your mind. You wanna talk about it?"

Surprised that Charles had noticed that something was bothering him, but reluctant to talk about it, he shook his head again. "My mom's birthday is coming up. It's always a difficult time for me. But I really don't want to talk about it."

"I understand."

Kevin got up to look out the window at the bright lights of the Manhattan skyline. It looked like a picture out of a book. Charles got up and wrapped his arms around Kevin's small frame and kissed him on the neck.

"What you looking at over here?"

"Just the skyline. It's beautiful."

"Yeah, it is. I love the view from this place. That's why I picked it when my broker showed it to me."

Kevin loved how romantic Charles was. They had been out to eat several more times all over the city. And when they would kiss and touch each other, it always felt like they were making love. Their kisses were like fireworks between them. He felt so safe in Charles' arms. Like nothing or no one could ever hurt him. And he had fallen head over heels for this man.

"I'll have to take you with me to Philly one of these days. We got a different kind of vibe out there."

"I would love that."

"You know what I would love?"

"Yes?"

"To be inside of you." There was an undeniable longing in his voice.

He'd made him wait long enough, and Kevin was just as ready to cross that line as Charles was. Kevin turned around and kissed him. As they were kissing and coming out of their shirts, Charles' phone rang.

"Aren't you gonna answer that?" Kevin asked in between kisses.

He spun Kevin around and kissed down the length of his neck, making him tremble and moan.

"It could be...important," Kevin said between kisses.

He kissed Kevin on the lips and took his phone call. "Hello?" Charles answered in a soft voice, motioning for Kevin to not move a muscle.

Kevin looked at him and smiled.

"Yeah, I'm here."

He frowned and motioned to Kevin that he would be a second and headed to the bedroom. Kevin poured himself a glass of ice water to extinguish some of the flames that Charles had lit within him. He danced along to the melody of Jill Scott's song "Whatever." He spun around and did his arms like he was an Alvin Ailey dancer onstage at Radio City Music Hall. So he just let Jill's voice move him as he followed his instincts and danced. He danced all over the living room and zoned out, just letting the music move his body almost on its own.

But then his groove was interrupted by Charles yelling and cursing from the bedroom. Shocked, Kevin lowered the music a bit so he could hear better.

"What the fuck are you talking about? What did I tell you about that shit? If I have to come down there, it's gonna be a muthafuckin' problem!"

He didn't sound like the scholarly professor anymore. He sounded like a thug from Philly. And he got louder and more aggressive as the conversation progressed. Kevin was actually starting to get nervous. He thought Charles might do something crazy. Charles pounded the wall as he screamed into the phone, issuing some rather ugly threats to whoever was on the other side of the line.

"You know what? I'm on my way down there now and we'll see who's taking what when I get there!"

He stormed back into the living room, his face an unbecoming shade of red.

"I'm sorry, Kev. I gotta go handle some business. Can we take a rain check?"

"Umm, sure. I guess we can," Kevin said trying to make sense of what just happened.

"Thanks for understanding." He reached into his pocket and pulled out a $100 bill and handed it to Kevin. "This should cover your car fare home." He kissed Kevin's cheek before dashing out the door.

Kevin sat confused and afraid of what had just happened. He had just seen a side of Charles he could not have imagined having ever existed. And he didn't know what to make of it. The fact that Charles didn't attempt to explain what was going on made Kevin even more nervous. He turned off Jill Scott and the lights, grabbed his jacket and walked out the door to the elevator. The last ten minutes replayed in his head and the more he thought about it, the more it scared him. He needed to know what was going on. He took out his phone and called Charles. It rang and went to voicemail.

Outside, the cool night air caused him to pull the lapels of his jacket closer as he hailed a cab to go back uptown. During the ride home, he sat quietly. He thought about calling one of his friends but had no idea what he would say. So he stayed quiet. It disturbed him for the rest of the evening.

After showering at home, he got a text from Charles apologizing and promising to make it up to him. Instead of texting him back, Kevin called him. "Charles, talk to me. What the hell just happened? It's like you turned into another person."

"Someone was stealing from me."

Kevin frowned. "Stealing from you?"

"Someone was messing in my account; messing with my money. I'm sorry you had to see me get gangsta, but that's one thing that I don't play about: my money. But baby, I promise you'll never see that side of me again. Is it too late for you to come back over?" His voice dropped lower, tempting Kevin with his sexy baritone. "So we can finish what we started?"

As much as Kevin wanted some more of Charles' loving, he glanced at the time on his nightstand and shook his head. "It's getting late. And I've gotta get up early for work. I'll see you tomorrow."

After ending the call, Kevin still didn't feel reassured. A thousand thoughts crossed his mind, wondering if this was the first sign that things were going to get dramatic.

*I'm sure it was just a misunderstanding*, Kevin thought to himself as he drifted off to sleep.

# 14

## KEVIN'S JOURNAL

Dear Journal,

Today would have been my mother's 54th birthday. It's been ten years since she died. I miss her so much. I cried probably every day this week anticipating this day. But now that this day is here, I think I'm okay. These days when I think of her, I think about how much I miss dancing. Mom was a great dancer. I definitely got my dancing ability from her. I danced from the age of five until it was time for me to go to college and then I just stopped. It's one of those things I regret. I used to feel so free and happy when I danced. Mom used to love to see me dance. God I miss her. She had the sweetest spirit. The most contagious laugh I had ever heard. And she loved me like no one else has. I thank God for my aunties Mecca and Medina. But goodness knows there was only one Malika Malone. My beautiful mother. Times like this I wish I had a sibling to lean on. Yeah, the boys are definitely my brothers but all of their mothers are all still here, so I'm not sure they can relate. I suppose Malcolm can relate on some degree being that he lost his dad some years ago, but it's still different ya know? I hope she's my guardian angel. And I know I'm far from perfect but I hope she is proud of me—in spite of the terrible choices I have made in men.

I'm still hoping that the spazz out I witnessed at Charles' house last night was a one-time thing. The way he got so furious definitely made me nervous but he did say it was about money. And I guess when someone steals money from you when you have as much as he does, you tend to get a bit more stir crazy about it, huh? I wouldn't know. I've never made the kind of money he has. But I know the time I spend with him is always so sublime. Just look how easily he picked up on the fact that something was bothering me. That means he pays attention to me, even the little things. Could I be falling for him? I definitely think I am. And it was so unexpected. I've never had a man be so nice to me. That's definitely a first. And he wants me. I'm gonna stick to my original thoughts and not have any expectations but I can have desires right? There isn't anything wrong with that, is there?

I definitely desire him. And I don't know how Damon goes so long without sex but I am horny as hell and would love a taste of that rich man's dick. He caught a glimpse of mine and I got the normal reaction I always get from guys who see my dick. They think because I'm short I must not be packing. Well if I do say so myself, I'm carrying a concealed weapon that has been known to dowse many a flame. And I wouldn't mind taking Charles for a ride with it. Maybe next time I talk to you, I'll have some news to share about that. Because it's becoming harder and harder to hide my erections from him (LOL). So we shall see. Talk to you soon.

Love,
Kevin

# 15

## SOON AS I GET HOME

As Shawn turned his key in the door to get into his apartment, he was surprised to see Jamon sitting at the dining room table. He rolled his eyes at him as he walked into the kitchen and didn't say a thing.

"So you really gonna act like you don't see me sitting here?" Jamon asked.

Shawn started putting the food away and said nothing. Jamon came and leaned against the kitchen counter as he watched Shawn put away the groceries.

"You said you wanted to spend time so I cancelled the trip to LA to be with you."

Shawn looked at him and continued to put things away.

"Did you hear me?"

"I heard you," Shawn said without pausing in his task at hand.

"So here I am."

"Whoop-ti-fucking-do."

Jamon shook his head. "You worse than a female. Nothing I do is good enough for you. Maybe I shouldn't have canceled my trip. Maybe I should've went and made that money instead of wanting to spend more time with you."

"Yeah, well maybe you should have. It's not too late, you know. You need a ride to the airport?"

Jamon narrowed his eyes. "Why are you acting like this?"

"Why are you acting like you're doing me a favor?"

"Because I'm trying to make things right. You gotta respect the fact that I'm trying."

"I don't have to do shit! You have some nerve acting like you're doing me some favor by staying here. Ever since you came back you haven't wanted to spend time with me. What makes now so special? Because I had to bring it up to you?"

Jamon reached out to Shawn, making that face that usually made Shawn melt. "You were right. I was tripping, and I'm sorry."

"Don't touch me."

"Mook, I'm here. I'm not going nowhere. I stayed here for you. For us, like you wanted me to. You just gon' be mean to me the whole time?"

"Why didn't you come home for three days?"

"Because I had to finish that song. And I couldn't work with all the tension we have between us. I had to finish writing it and recording the whole thing so I can send it to Lyndsay's people to record her part of the duet. I'm trying to compromise with you but you're making this shit real difficult. I'm tryna show you it's not all about me and my music. I love you too. So are you gonna let me stand here alone or are you gon' meet me halfway on this?"

Shawn folded his arms and looked at Jamon. "Is there a reason why I should?"

"Because you want us to work."

"That's not enough." Shawn walked off to the bedroom.

Jamon followed him. "What else do you want from me?"

"I'm tired. I'm tired of feeling like I'm not as important to you as your career. The only reason you're here now is because you feel guilty. You wanna ease your own conscience and I am not falling for that shit today! You left me here and didn't even bother to come back." Shawn blinked back tears, determined not to let him see him cry.

"Are you forgetting that you put me out?"

"I didn't put out."

"Yes you did."

"I did not!"

"Yes you did! You said go take a walk."

"That didn't mean don't come home!"

Though he tried his best to hold them back, the tears spilled forward. "It was like you didn't even care. You just left me here. I'm always an afterthought with you. And you accused me of being jealous of you because of money? What is that about? Sometimes I feel like the only one you truly care about is yourself."

Jamon's expression saddened as he watched Shawn cry. Guilt made him feel like the most selfish prick in the world. Shawn fell back on to the loveseat in their bedroom covering his face, and Jamon sat next to him, placing an arm around his shoulders.

"I'm sorry, baby. I don't want you to feel that way. You know I love you. Only reason why I didn't come home was because I needed to get the song done. And that whole money situation was nothing but hot air; I said it cuz I was stressing. I never meant to hurt you, and you are import-ant to me. I'm not going nowhere. Come on, Mook, stop crying."

Jamon kissed his tears away. The kissing led to lovemaking and it was some of the sweetest, emotion-filled sex that they'd had in a while. Afterward, Shawn laid his head on Jamon's chest and fell asleep. Jamon lit a blunt while Shawn slept and flipped through the TV channels and found an episode of "House of Lies" in the DVR menu. His phone rang. It was his manager Rell. He looked at Shawn and just let it go to voice-mail. As soon as the voicemail notification went off, he checked the message.

"Yo J, watup? You know who this is. I got some good news and some bad news. The good news is that Lyndsay Belle and her people love the song and like what you did with it. They wanna make it a single. The bad news is the label wants Trey Songz or Drake to sing it with her. Someone who is already established. They wanna keep your backgrounds and they want to list her name as a songwriter. She wants to change a few words but you'll still be listed as the main songwriter. I'm not gonna let them take your name off of it cuz I think it will really be a hit. So we're definitely not gonna accept a ghostwriter fee. I don't wanna do it like this so you let me know what you think. I told them I would get back to them after I spoke with you. So hit me back. Peace."

Jamon felt a burn in his chest from the anger he felt and his mind raced. *I wrote that fucking song! I want to sing it! I sing better than both of them clowns!* But this was business. He had to make way for singers more popular than he was to shine even if he wrote a song he wanted to keep for himself. It was all about making money. He would most definitely re-ceive some hefty royalty checks for writing the song, but he wanted his voice to be heard by the masses. He responded to Rell via text.

Jamon: Got ur message. Tell Lyndsay's people it's ok.

Rell: Aight.

He took a big puff of his blunt and closed his eyes and tried not to focus on how he felt. He kissed Shawn's cheek and stroked his head and let his mind wander. It really hurt him to know he could be replaced so easily on something he created. It just didn't seem fair. Shawn woke up and finished the blunt with him while Jamon explained what had just happened.

"So why won't they let you sing the song? You wrote it."

"Because I'm still relatively unknown."

"That could get you known. That's stupid."

"It's just the fucked up business I'm in."

Shawn shook his head. "That's messed up. You created that song all by yourself."

Jamon nodded and was silent for a moment. He reached over and touched Shawn's chin. "Something's still bothering you. Talk to me, Shawn."

It surprised Shawn how well Jamon could read him. Sometimes he felt like Jamon knew him better than he knew himself. He paused and sighed heavily. "It is still bothering me. Because sometimes it's hard for me to watch you do this."

"Do my music? Why is that?"

"Because I don't like feeling like I'm being pushed to the side. I know how much your music career means to you. Believe me, I get it. And I wanna be there for you every step of the way. But sometimes I wish you could sing those love songs to me, not the women. It's so much, J. When we first met, there was some of you that you seemed to only share with me. Now it feels like you're sharing it with everyone else. Everyone else but me. It feels like the music pulls you away from me. And I don't like that feeling. Because I feel like I have to constantly compete with it for your attention. I don't mean to sound selfish but I want some of my boyfriend for myself too. That's why it was hard for me to stay at the open mic."

"I didn't know it bothered you that much."

"It does. And it's hard watching you leave all the time to go record here or there or go on a tour for a few weeks or months at a time. It's hard not having you around as often as I want. And watching the women hit on you and the fellas look at you like they want a piece is hard too. I want them all to know you're mine and they can't have you. I mean come on, how would you feel watching people try and get at me all the time? And you couldn't say anything."

Jamon pondered that for a moment. "I see what you're saying."

"I want you to win. I just wanna be there to share the victory with you. Don't forget about me."

Jamon took Shawn's hand. "I could never forget about you. You're my baby."

They kissed. "You hungry?"

"I can eat."

"Alright, I'm gonna start dinner."

Jamon nodded. "Wake me up when it's ready," he said, snuggling beneath the covers and plumping the pillow.

In the kitchen, Shawn put on a pot of water for the spaghetti noodles and sliced up some onions and peppers. He noticed that he had a missed call from Damon and called him back.

"Wassup, D?"

"Hey, Shawnie. You feeling better?"

"Yeah, I'm good. I'm making some spaghetti for dinner," he said as he took out the pasta sauce and ground turkey.

He peeked back into his bedroom. Jamon was sound asleep, so he gently closed the door.

"He was here waiting when I got back."

"And what did he have to say for himself?"

"That he had to finish the song for Lyndsay Belle's album and send it to her. Said he was gonna stay here in New York with me instead of going to LA. But his manager called and said the label wants to take his voice off the song and put an established artist on it with her instead of him. Someone like Trey Songz or Drake."

"Ooop, the shade."

"Yes. I could tell his feelings were hurt."

"At least now he knows how it feels to be letdown, to have your feelings hurt."

"Exactly. But we had a long talk and I explained my feelings to him and he actually listened. So it seems like Kevin was right; everything is working out." He stirred the pasta sauce to keep it from bubbling over. "So when we finished talking, we started doing you know what."

"Of course. That's how it always happens. Where is he now?"

"In bed sleeping."

"And now you're cooking his dinner like a good little wife."

"Well, you know, he put it on me, now I gotta feed him. And I'll kick yo ass; I ain't nobody's wife."

"Mmm hmm. Well, I'm glad you're feeling better and everything is okay."

"Yeah me too. What are you gonna do about Kenny?"

"I'm gonna break things off. I have to. I got my feelings in last time and they are still there. But I need to cut him off before my feelings take over while I still have some sort of rationale."

"I can dig it."

"Well, I'mma let you get back to your cooking. I'm gonna go hit the gym."

"Alright, I'll talk to you later."

They hung up and Shawn looked at Jamon lying in the bed sleeping. Something was gnawing at Shawn about this whole thing but he didn't know what it was. But since he didn't know, he was just glad that Jamon and he were home together at this very moment. He'd just deal with whatever was on his mind later.

# 16

## GOTTA GO, GOTTA LEAVE

Rain sloshed down the window in trickling torrents as Damon looked outside at the cars that zoomed past the restaurant. He sat in a booth at the Dinosaur BBQ drinking a Corona with a slice of lime. He ordered hot Wango Tango chicken wings to go because he wanted to make this a brief meeting. In walked Kenny whom was escorted to the table by the host. Kenny joined him smiled.

"Hey, D. Thanks for calling me," Kenny said.

"Thank you for agreeing to meet me. Especially at such a last-minute notice."

Kenny picked up the menu and scanned it. "I love the wings here."

"They are good," Damon said admiring Kenny's goatee. But immediately, he stopped himself from admiring him because he wanted to be strong enough to walk away from him tonight without having any attached feelings. Once again, he returned his attention to the rain flowing down the window.

"What are you looking at out there?"

"The raindrops."

"Yeah, kinda romantic isn't it?"

Damon nodded and Kenny said, "I'd much rather you look at me."

The way he said it forced Damon to look over at him, and the way Kenny gazed into his eyes took his breath away.

*Please, stop that!*

Their server approached and took Kenny's order of a Corona and a churrasco chicken steak with a side of mac and cheese and cole slaw.

"You're gonna eat, right?"

"I got something to go. I'm not that hungry right now."

Kenny smirked. "So why did you wanna meet here?"

"I knew I wanted some wings and I wanted us to meet in a public place."

"Why? You scared if I got you alone, I might ravish you?"

"I have something I need to say."

Kenny sat back and folded his arms. His teasing smile slowly faded. "Okay, what's up?"

"I really like you."

"I really like you too."

"But what we did the other night at my house? We can't do that again."

"Why not? Was it bad?"

"It's not that."

"So then what is it?"

"You're still married."

"I'm legally separated. Technically, that makes me single."

"With strings attached. Didn't you tell me your wife moved back home?"

"Yeah. She brought the kids back home and is planning on moving out sometime in the next few months. We don't even sleep in the same bed anymore," Kenny said leaning forward.

"How many times have you had sex with her since she's been back home?"

Kenny frowned. "What does that have to do with anything?"

"It has a lot to do with the fact that I'm not trying to be your side piece again."

"My side piece? Is that what you think you'd be?"

"As long as you're still married, yes."

"Divorce takes time. It never happens overnight."

"Well, maybe you should try and work things out with your wife. You said you want your kids to grow up with both of their parents in the house. And that is your responsibility right now."

"Where is all this coming from? You were down the other night."

"Yeah, I was. But I shouldn't have been. You're somebody else's husband for goodness sake."

"I was somebody else's husband when I had you bent over your couch the other night too. And when you sucked my dick. I mean, you were all in that night. What, you talk to that little bitch clique you call your friends since you and I met up last? You tell them about how you were screaming my fucking name the other night?"

"Fuck you, Kenny. You gon' be someone else's husband sitting here by yourself tonight having your dinner too."

"Damon, wait a minute. You really gonna leave like that? We're not gonna talk about it?" Kenny asked reaching out to him. Damon snatched away.

"Get off me! I'm walking out of here with my dignity and with my bitch ass friends' good advice. Leave his married ass alone and get a man that is all yours. One who is sure of who he really is and not someone who is lying to a woman he's supposed to be fucking married to!"

"I didn't mean that."

"You meant exactly what you said, Kenny. This is where the train stops and I move on with my life. I can't do this again. Get my feelings all in to get my heart broken again? No thanks. Especially not by some closeted DL dude who can't make up his fucking mind. Good night, Kenny. Thanks for the drink." Damon grabbed his bag and headed for the exit.

Kenny looked down at Damon's empty Corona bottle and realized what he meant by "Thanks for the drink."

Damon walked out of the restaurant in his navy blue Marc Jacobs jacket and popped open his oversized umbrella when he got outside. Kenny followed Damon outside into the pouring rain.

"Damon!" Damon turned around to him.

"Come on, Damon. I'm sorry. I didn't mean what I said about your friends. Can you just please have dinner with me? Maybe we can come up with a solution for this. I don't want this to be our last conversation. Especially not like this. I love you. You've gotta know that."

Damon pondered the thought. "I love you too. But I gotta do what I gotta do for me. Don't get sick out here in this rain. You take care of yourself."

"Damon! Damon!" Kenny called out behind him.

Damon kept walking and didn't look back. He was so thankful that not a single tear fell from his eyes during the whole altercation with Kenny. But the moment he got in his truck, it was a wrap. His heart aching with heaviness, he covered his face with his hands and bawled his eyes out. Who was he gonna love now?

# 17

# MALCOLM & MALIK

## SPRING TIME

For the past few months, Malcolm wondered if Malik was gay. He really couldn't tell the day they met in the store. And true to Malcolm's nature, he still sexed down as many guys as he wanted. Well, he got his answer when he finally got the gumption to call him and ask him about what sales were happening in the store that week. Malik was quite the flirt over the phone and Malcolm liked it. He thought he had Malik's number and he would be like all of the other guys he had at his beck and call. Not so the case. Whenever the conversation would get sexual, Malik would change the subject which more than threw Malcolm for a loop. He was a man used to getting what he wanted. It didn't take long to realize after their first few interactions that Malik wasn't giving it up unless he wanted to.

Malcolm thought Malik changed his mind when he asked him out. He had never been on a real date before. The thought of a date minus the option of sex had him uneasy. He was the hook up king and all of New York knew about it. But something about Malik had him willing to try. Why else would Malik be so flirtatious and send Malcolm all those shirtless pictures if he didn't want to fuck? At least that's what Malcolm tried to convince himself of.

"So where are y'all going?" Mama Nzingha asked standing in Malcolm's bedroom doorway as Malcolm got dressed.

"We gon' hit up Harbour Lights for dinner."

"He's taking you to the seaport? Alright now."

"Yeah. Figured maybe after a few glasses of wine or whatever we're gonna drink, he'll come down off that high horse and break a brotha off."

"Or maybe he's gonna make you work for it. Sounds like you may have met your match with this one."

"I don't know, Mama. After he gets a glimpse of how good I look tonight, he just may cave."

"We shall see. Behave yourself," she said as she closed his door so he could dress alone.

Malcolm turned on "So Fresh, So Clean" by Outkast and mouthed the lyrics to the song while doing the dance Andre 3000 did in the video. Once fully dressed, he looked good, smelled good, and popped a piece of Stride gum so his breath would be fresh. As he was admiring his nice reflection in the mirror, his phone started to ring. It was Malik.

"Hello?"

"I'm turning onto your block now so you can come outside."

"Okay, here I come. Ma how do I look?" Malcolm asked walking into the living room.

She looked up at him. "Turn around."

He did a slow model spin.

"You look good. Burgundy looks really good on you. You must really like him if you're getting dressed for him, huh?"

"Well, you know, I had to do a little something something."

"It's working."

Malcolm kissed her on the cheek. "He just called me and said he was here."

"Okay, well don't keep him waiting. Have fun." Mama Nzingha adjusted his collar before he could go out the door.

"I will. Love you."

"I love you too."

Once outside, Malcolm could feel the warm spring air hit him. He knew he was definitely gonna have to come out of this blazer before the night's end but for now, he was going to keep it on because he looked good in it.

He walked slowly to Malik's Chevy Trailblazer as if he were on a catwalk. Malik didn't even look at him until he got in the car.

"Wassup, man?"

"Chillin'. You can move the seat back further if you need to," Malik said barely making eye contact.

Malcolm slid the seat back as far as it would go and looked at Malik. He had on a fitted brown shirt and khakis with Air Force Ones. His long locks were flat twisted in the front and the rest hung down his back.

They headed for the FDR Drive to get down to the South Street Seaport downtown.

"Nice blazer," Malik said still watching the road.

"Thanks," Malcolm said, surprised Malik had even noticed his attire at all. Malik had hardly spared him a glance since he'd walked out the door. It kinda pissed him off, but he was certain that before the night was over, he'd make sure that Malik noticed everything about him—everything. "I like your hair like that. Who did it?"

"I did."

"You can do hair too?"

"A little bit. Started at cosmetology school and never finished. I can cut hair too but I got interested in other aspects of business."

"Cool." Malcolm didn't know what to say. Every attempt at beginning a conversation, Malik had a one word answer for. It was strange that now they were together, Malik was very stoic and quiet. Almost apathetic. This definitely was new to Malcolm. Usually he was the one to play it cool while he was the one being chatted up. *Basketball usually works for conversation.*

"What do you think about Teddy Bishop being traded to the Lakers?"

"I think now that they have him, they may have a decent season. They may even win a championship."

"I still think that whole scandal with him and LZ fucking was crazy. Who woulda thought the two of them were messing around?"

"I knew LZ from back in the day in the Bronx. He was actually a good friend."

"Yeah?"

"Yeah. I always knew he liked dudes, though. Still none of us expected any of what happened to go down the way it did. I was at the funeral. It was crazy."

"Do you know Teddy Bishop too?"

"Nah, never met him. Think it's fucked up he ain't show up to the funeral. Hell of a ball player, though. Can never take that from him."

"That he is." Silence.

After their twenty five minute drive downtown, Malik parked in a nearby lot and they walked over to the restaurant. The sky was darkening and the lights of the skyscrapers were beginning to illuminate the city skyline. After that awkward car ride down here, Malcolm figured with the romantic atmosphere, he could start putting the moves on Malik. That all changed once they were inside the restaurant. Malik asked if they could sit outside because they were meeting other people. They were escorted to a table outside which overlooked the New York Harbor and faced both the Manhattan and Brooklyn bridges with three of Malik's friends already seated.

"I didn't know we were meeting people." Malcolm said.

"Yeah, I told a few of my boys to meet me here tonight. We usually get together a few times a month and we're overdue. Hope you don't mind."

*Hell, yeah I mind! What the fuck, man? I thought this was a date!* "Nah it's cool."

Fighting hard to maintain a nonchalant attitude, Malcolm followed closely behind Malik. The warm breeze blew as they were seated. The bright lights of the bridge at dusk shined onto the harbor and they could see water taxis and boats going across the water. Malik introduced Malcolm to his friends as they sat and ordered.

To say Malcolm felt like a fifth wheel was an understatement. He felt totally out of place and didn't even know what to do with himself. Every time he tried to interject a thought, it was glossed over and or he was interrupted by one of Malik's friends. And what was worse? Malik didn't even seem to notice. Or care for that matter. A few times he contemplated leaving but stayed anyway, not saying anything. After all, he still enjoyed being in Malik's presence. One of Malik's friends suggested they go play pool after dinner and without even asking Malcolm, they agreed. That was it. Malcolm was ready to go.

"I'mma have to take a raincheck on pool. I gotta get up early," Malcolm said flatly.

"Well, fellas, I'll meet y'all there. I gotta take Malcolm back up town."

"It's aight man. I'll hop on the subway," Malcolm said rising from the table, reaching for his wallet.

"I got the meal. You sure you wanna take the train? I don't mind taking you back up town. Matter fact, we can play up there."

"Nah, man, it's cool. Have a good night guys. Nice meeting y'all." Malcolm tried to hide his attitude but he was incensed that Malik virtually ignored him the whole night.

"I'll walk you out." Malik followed him outside. "You okay, Malcolm?"

*Do I look like I'm fucking alright?* "Yeah, man, I just gotta get home."

"You sure?" *Stop fucking asking me that shit!*

"Yeah, I'm good." Malcolm turned around to hail a cab and one stopped right in front of him. As he turned around to say goodnight to Malik, Malik pulled him close and kissed him. He even slipped his tongue inside.

"Text me and let me know you got home safely." Malik opened the cab door for Malcolm.

"Aight." As the cab pulled away from the restaurant, Malik stood there and watched it pull away.

*What the fuck just happened?*

# 18

## TRUE COLORS

After Kevin's Sunday morning brunch with the fellas, he had Damon drop him off at Charles' house because according to Charles, he had a surprise for him.

As soon as he walked inside, Charles was sitting on the couch, butt naked, his long dick fully hard and pointing up at the ceiling. Oh, what a pleasant surprise! He crooked his finger at Kevin, nonverbally telling him to come here. There was no hesitation on Kevin's part. Each step towards his man made him grow wetter, and by the time he eased down on Charles' lap, there was no turning back. Kevin didn't even notice Charles pulling out any condoms or lube. He just saw him pull off the semen soaked condom afterwards. In the hours Kevin was there, they made love three times and Kevin couldn't seem to get enough of Charles' thick, long dick. The fact that they'd waited so long to consummate their relationship made the sex even more exquisite. Charles had worked him so good that he'd probably be limping in the morning, but he didn't mind.

As they lay in bed together, Charles got ready to apologize to Kevin once again for his embarrassing and inappropriate behavior the last time Kevin had visited him, but Kevin placed a finger against his lips. He didn't need to hear another apology; he was over it. Everyone has a button and when you push it, sometimes people lose it. Stealing money just happened to be Charles' button, and Kevin could understand that. So he forgave him.

They read each other's horoscopes, played chess naked at the dining room table, gave each other massages, and fed each other fruit.

"I really like you," Charles said, holding a strawberry to Kevin's lips for him to bite it.

"I really like you too."

"Sometimes I think I might even love you."

"You love me?"

"I'm beginning to."

Kevin glowed. "I'm growing to feel the same way about you."

They kissed and retired to the bedroom to relax and watch TV. Kevin found a Ginuwine video countdown on VH1 Soul.

"Oh, this was my boo back in the day," Kevin said. "You remember when he first came out with 'My Pony'? You remember that, Charles?"

"Yeah, I remember."

Charles got up to pee while Kevin sang along to "None of Your Friends' Business", which was blasting from the TV. Charles came back and saw Kevin all into the video. He muted the TV.

"Hey! Why'd you do that? Turn it back up."

"You're really into this, huh?"

"I've always had a crush on him. He is so fine."

"Figures."

"What does that mean?"

"Nothing at all. Carry on," Charles said, unmuting the TV and laying down. He turned on his side.

Kevin watched the videos and they all made him happily reminisce on different periods of his life. Charles turned and looked at him.

"You look like you would fuck him if you ever got the chance."

*Is he really sounding jealous right now?* He narrowed his eyes at Charles. *He can't possibly be over there brooding because I'm vibing to Ginuwine.* "I would. And you probably would too," Kevin said swaying back and forth to the song.

"I wouldn't fuck that nigga. What would I want to fuck him for?"

"Who wouldn't want to fuck him? Look at him. Look at that body. The way he grinds."

Charles shook his head. "That's disrespectful." In one swift movement, Charles got up and shrugged on a pair of briefs.

Kevin was so into the video that he didn't hear Charles say anything. Charles looked back at him and started grinding like a stripper next to the TV. Kevin laughed.

"Oh my God, what are you doing?"

"Doing the Ginuwine."

"Oh my goodness, you are embarrassing yourself. Stop it! I can't!"

Charles stopped and frowned while Kevin continued to laugh.

"Fucking disrespectful as hell, yo."

"Stripping is not your calling. Stick to teaching, boo."

"Whatever, man."

Kevin looked at him quizzically as he stormed out. He was confused. He slipped on a pair of shorts and went into the kitchen behind Charles. From behind, he wrapped his arms around Charles' broad back.

"Get off me."

"What's the matter with you?" Kevin asked letting him go.

"Nothing. Go watch your videos." Charles poured himself a glass of water.

"What is the problem?"

"I said nothing. Go watch your damn videos and leave me alone."

"What is all the attitude for?"

"Cuz that's some real disrespectful shit you just did. Word up."

"Why? Cuz I laughed at you? I mean damn, your dancing wasn't that bad. I was just making a j—"

"You talking about you wanna fuck some other dude."

Kevin paused. "I was watching a video. It's not like I know him or will ever have a chance. Hell, he ain't even gay."

"That's still disrespectful. You're in my house kicking it with me and you talking about wanting to fuck some other dude."

"You are overreacting."

"Am I?"

"Yes! It's just a video. Why are you getting so defensive? I mean, damn, when did we become exclusive?"

"I told you earlier that I'm starting to fall in love with you."

"And I feel that way too, but we've never made anything official."

"Yeah? You were just riding my dick like I was your man. Fuck you think this is? Free dick to go around? Huh?"

"First of all, watch your fucking tone when you're talking to me! I am not your—"

Charles slapped Kevin so hard across the face that spit flew from his mouth.

"Not your what? Huh?"

"Nigga, are you fucking crazy?" Kevin asked holding his face.

"Who the fuck you screaming at, boy? I'll kick your ass all over this muthafuckin' house." Charles yoked Kevin up by his throat.

Shell-shocked, Kevin didn't move. His mouth still twisted in a snarl, Charles glared at him then finally let him go.

Rubbing his throat in disbelief, tears shimmering in his eyes, Kevin whispered in a broken voice, "I'm gone."

"Gone?" Charles forcefully slapped the other cheek harder than the other one. The impact of the slap caused Kevin to sprawl across the floor. Charles' limber body towered over Kevin's small frame, and Kevin looked up at him with fear in his eyes. Scrambling to his feet, Kevin ran to the bedroom with Charles power-walking behind him. He tried to gather up his clothes, but Charles knocked them out of his hand as he pinned him to the wall.

"Don't you ever in your muthafuckin' life raise your voice at me. And I don't ever wanna hear about you wanting to fuck no other dudes either. You and this belong to me now. You understand?" Charles asked grabbing Kevin's crotch.

Kevin stood perfectly still and didn't even blink. Charles squeezed his balls even harder.

"I get it! I got it!" Kevin said with tears spilling from his eyes as he writhed in pain from Charles' vice grip on his balls. He let them go.

"You're not leaving either. I'm not ready for you to leave yet." He put Kevin's arms around his waist as he tongue-kissed Kevin's neck.

Kevin's body trembled, more from fear than pleasure.

"I want you to suck my dick again, okay, baby? Come on, give Daddy some head." Charles wore a psychotic smile on his face.

"Come on, baby. Suck it good. Suck it real good or I'mma black your fucking eye," Charles said just above a calm whisper. His smile slowly dropped and he had the most intimidating straight face Kevin had ever seen. Kevin couldn't even think straight. But he knew Charles wasn't kidding. The size difference between the two of them intimidated him and it was more apparent now than ever.

Obediently, he knelt down and pulled out Charles' dick. Everything in his mind screamed at him to try to bite the damn thing off. But Kevin was too scared. Doing it just the way that Charles wanted, Kevin went to work. Charles put his hand up against the wall and bit his bottom lip. He let out a moan.

"Yeah. That's what I'm talking about. Suck my shit, baby."

Tears fell from his eyes and dripped down to his mouth. The taste of his tears mingled with the musky taste of Charles' dick was making him sick. He was confused, scared, and humiliated. By far, this was the most degrading experience of his life. He became numb and just continued to give Charles head. It felt like an eternity.

"I'm bout to cum. I'm bout to cum."

Kevin started to taste Charles' cum seep into his mouth and he moved. The cum got all over the floor. Charles let out a loud moan and caught his breath. He took a hand towel that was lying on the dresser and cleaned himself up and wiped up the floor.

"Next time, I want you to lick it up off the floor," Charles said to Kevin, patting him on the head. Kevin touched the side of his face which was swollen and still stung. Charles lay down on the bed and began flipping through the channels as if nothing had happened.

Unsure of what to do, Kevin just stood there. He wanted to leave, but he wasn't sure if he was allowed to leave. It was unbelievable that he was now in fear of this big man who was just making love to him so gently just hours ago. He picked up his clothes from the floor and as he put on each item of clothing, Charles ice-grilled him.

"Take those fucking pants back off. You ain't going nowhere."

Kevin looked at him. Charles jumped up off the bed and approached Kevin. He quickly took his pants back off. Charles grabbed Kevin's chin, tilted his head to the side, and looked closely at Kevin's face.

"Go get some ice for your face. Bring me some for my hand."

Kevin walked out of the room and passed a hall mirror where he saw handprints on both sides of his stinging face. He ran into the bathroom and threw up in the toilet then clung to the commode as he burst into tears. He tried to make sense of what had just happened all in the last 20 minutes. He sobbed even harder. I can't believe he hit me, Kevin kept saying in his head over and over again. He felt like such a fool. The room felt like it was spinning. He kept replaying everything in his head over and over. How was he going to get out of there? He knew he couldn't go to the police. He was too ashamed to tell his friends. What should he do?

Charles walked into the bathroom with some ice in a sandwich bag. Kevin jumped up.

"I'm sorry, baby. Here, put this on your face."

Kevin backed up against the wall.

"I'm not gon' hurt you. Here, just put this on your face." Moving slowly, Kevin took the bag of ice and held it to his face.

For the first time, remorse and regret crossed Charles' handsome features. He stretched out his arms to Kevin. "I'm sorry, baby. Come here." Kevin went to him and cried again and Charles held him tight.

"I'm sorry, Kev. Please don't be mad at me. I was being stupid. Don't leave, okay? Stay here with me." Kevin continued to cry in Charles' arms. He felt like he was watching a movie. Like he was the tortured victim everyone thought was the dummy.

# 19

## THE SHAKE UP

"Places like this normally start at eight million but the owner is asking for $6.5."

"And if you don't mind my asking, why such a steep drop in the price?"

"With the recession and all, this place has been on the market longer than expected so they had to drop the price," Damon said to his clients.

Mr. Stergenhoff seemed satisfied by his answer. He looked at his wife and she nodded her head, giving her consent. The Stergenhoffs were a wealthy white couple with three children looking to purchase a new home on Long Island. Bob Stergenhoff co-owns a plastic surgery practice in Manhattan that was opening another office on Long Island. His wife Peggy is a cardiologist. To put it lightly, they are *loaded*.

Damon led them on a grand tour of the large luxurious mansion they were looking to buy. He loved cases like this. A wealthy couple with millions of dollars and no cap on their spending was his favorite kind of client. He was going to walk away with a nice six figure commission check when he sold this house. There were six bedrooms, seven bathrooms, a master suite with a balcony, a five acre yard, a pool, a jacuzzi, and a large finished basement in a serene gated community. At ten thousand square feet, the house was exactly what Peggy specifically requested: spacious. The Stergenhoffs loved it.

"Honey, this really is a steal," Peggy said to her husband as they walked down the long hallway on the second floor.

They entered the master bedroom suite. It had mahogany brown hard wood floors, a ceiling fan, and was so big their footsteps echoed when they walked in the room. The master bathroom was large as well, complete with his and her section, two toilets, and a huge shower separate from the bathtub.

"There is so much I can do with all this space in the master bedroom." Peggy said.

Bob nodded in agreement.

"How are the schools here, Damon?" he asked.

Damon knew that question was coming and he was prepared for it. He had already familiarized himself with the Stergenhoffs' children, who were headed to the ninth, sixth, and first grades respectively. "Well, the high school is a national magnet school. They have a college bound rate of ninety-five percent. The middle schools already have SAT prep courses with opportunities for the kids to take the test if you want them to and elementary schools have creative arts and after school programs."

"That would be perfect for our little one, Sam. He loves to paint. What do you think, honey?"

"I'm very impressed, Peg. This is the best place we've seen today. It really is grand. I love the yard and I like the peace around here. We've been in Manhattan for the last fifteen years since we first got together, so it will be good to get away from the hustle and bustle of the city. And we can get used to having more space. We can finally get a dog like the kids want."

"Are there other families here with children around our children's ages?" Peggy asked Damon.

"Well, there are quite a few families with children on this particular block, so I'm sure the children will make new friends quickly. And there's also a women's block association, a golf club, and a park just three blocks away. I think the adjustment could be quite smooth for the whole family."

"Did you say golf club?"

"Oh, you've really done it," Peggy said with a laugh.

"Yes, there is a golf club here."

"Where?" Bob asked excitedly running to the window. "I didn't see one."

"Well, the club meetings are held at the recreational facility in the park a few blocks away. The golf course is about a mile away."

"Do they have tournaments?"

"They do."

"Oh, this is definitely our number one contender."

"I agree. I wish we could sign the deed right now."

"We've got two offers so far. One wants to put one million down and the other wants to put down $1.2 million."

"We'll put down two million," Bob said. Peggy nodded and that was music to Damon's ears.

"That sounds awesome. Let me call my office and let them know. You all take another look around, okay?" Damon said making an exit to the hallway while dialing his office. They nodded and continued to look around. He placed the call to let the office know that his clients were ready to buy. Though he kept his cool, he was giddy inside about his success.

He returned to his clients and asked them if they could come in the following day to start the paper work and complete the credit check.

"We'll be there at 3pm sharp," Bob said with a grin.

"Thank you so much, Damon. We knew you would come through," his wife said, shaking Damon's hand enthusiastically.

"Yes, sir. You oughta be running your own office, pal."

Damon laughed. "Someday soon, Bob. Someday soon. So I'll see you two tomorrow."

He shook their hands once more and they went and got into their sleek Lexus truck and pulled off. Damon's phone vibrated in his pocket. He thought it was the office calling, but it was his mother.

"Hey, Mom."

"Damon?" his mother said in her heavy Jamaican accent.

The sound of her voice sent off a red flag alert. "Mom, what's going on?"

He could hear his mother sniffling as if she had been crying.

"Mom, are you okay?"

"Your father."

Damon's stomach dropped. "Wh—what about Dad?"

"Your father collapsed today. I had to call the ambulance to come and pick him up."

"Oh my God. What happened?"

"The doctor said he had a heart attack. They are going to keep him and run some tests. It doesn't help that he is a diabetic."

"What hospital did they take him to?"

"He's at Saint Barnabas Hospital in Livingston. Here in Jersey."

"Okay. How are you?"

"I'm gonna stay at the hospital tonight. I just want to be here. Will you come?"

Damon froze. He opened his mouth to respond to his mother, but no words came out. It had been six years since he'd spoken to or seen his father. He kept in contact with his mother via her cell phone, emails, and times when should would come and visit him in New York. In a matter of seconds, he remembered his last conversation with his father. It wasn't a good one. He'd brought his boyfriend at the time to meet his parents. He remembered the exact way his father screamed at him, "No son of mine is going to be a faggot! Get the hell out of my house and out of my life!" Damon had taken his boyfriend by the hand and left. His father had hurt him more than anyone else had. He had never cried quite so hard in his life. Even now, the thought of it made him well up with tears.

"Damon," Mrs. White said snapping her son out of his painful memory.

"Yeah?"

"I said I want you to come. Your brother and sister are coming too. I want you all here together. Please. Please, Damon."

He forced his mouth to move. "I'll come. I can't promise it will be today, though. How did the doctor say he was doing?"

"He's responding well. It was mild but his pressure was high so they need to bring it back down. The doctor said they're gonna keep him here for at least another week."

"Okay. Well, I'm on Long Island right now because I had a showing out here. It's gonna be at least two hours before I get back to the city. I wanna try and beat some of the rush hour traffic. I'll call you when I get home and get settled, okay?"

"Okay. I love you, son."

"I love you too."

He hung up and a rush of melancholy overcame him. He turned and looked at the house he was about to sell and went and sat in his truck. He didn't want to drive so shaken, so he just sat and thought. Amazing how many twists and turns that life held in store. He'd vowed never to speak to his father again—unless his father called first and apologized. Now his old man had had a brush with death and he didn't even know how to take it. As far as he was concerned, his father and he had etched each other out of their respective lives. He was definitely sad but the circumstances brought back so many conflicting feelings. He was both hurt and angry still.

The two hour drive did nothing to put him at ease. He turned on music to try to distract him, but even that didn't work. It didn't seem that long of a drive as he found himself crossing back into Manhattan while still thinking of when he visited his father what they would possibly say to each other. He looked at the clock and it read 4:30pm. He pulled up a block away from Sylvia's Soul Food restaurant and dialed Shawn.

"Hello?" Shawn answered.

"What's up, Shawnie?"

"Hey, D. What's going on?"

"Just coming back from Long Island. I had a showing out there."

"Wow, really? How long was that drive?"

"Bout two hours because of traffic."

"I hope you stand to make a lot of money driving all the way out there."

"I do. House is selling for $6.5 million."

"Oh, well that's worth traveling for."

"You already know. What are you doing?"

"I just put on my workout clothes. I'm gonna jog to the gym since it's nice outside. You make it back to the city yet?"

"Yeah, I'm starving too. Bout to go to Sylvia's and get some take out. I need to go to Food for Life but after the news I just got, I need some comfort food."

"I was just about to ask what's the matter? You sound like something is wrong."

"Is it that obvious?"

"Either that or I just know you. Wassup? Talk to me."

"My mother called today and said my father had a heart attack."

"Oh my God! Is he okay?"

"He is. It was mild but his pressure is too high so they're gonna keep him for about a week. My mother is so upset."

"I'll bet. Are you gonna go see him?"

"Mom asked me to. But I am really feeling some kind of way about it."

"Yeah?"

"Yes. I love my father, don't get me wrong. But I ain't spoke to this man in six years. Not a birthday wish, not a congratulations when I got my real estate license or sold my first house. Nothing on the holidays or anything. So now it's like, what do I say when I see him?"

"Wow."

"And I feel some kind of way about feeling some kind of way. That doesn't make me feel good either. He is my father and he did raise me. I know he had a hard time accepting me because I'm gay, but my last memory of him is what he said to me when I brought Jarvis home to meet my family."

"Yeah, I remember when that happened."

"That was the worst day of my life and I have never forgotten it. Jarvis was so embarrassed and I was just so overwhelmed. Now I gotta go up in this hospital. And I don't wanna say get well soon. What I wanna say is so inappropriate and will not be the time or place. Hell, my mother is the one who wants me to come. I'm not even sure if he wants me there."

"I understand what you're saying. And it's okay to feel that way. You're certainly justified. However, I think you have to put this into perspective. He is your father. He had a near death experience. I don't think he would be angry with you for coming to see him in the hospital. For one, it wouldn't be good for his heart. Two, I know your father loves you. And in his vulnerable state, he may welcome you with open arms. Besides, you know if you want us to come with you we will. I'll even drive if you want me to. Or even if it's just you and me that go together we can do that. But I think you need to make peace with the unfortunate incident with your past and think about today. Your father could have one foot in the grave and just listening to the sound in your voice and knowing your heart, you don't want him to leave this world and you not have made amends. You don't owe it to him. You owe it to yourself to at least attempt to make peace with him."

Damon felt himself getting emotional. "I don't know if I can man."

"Yes, you can. I know you can. You will."

"Will you come with me for real?"

"I'll come pick you up whenever you're ready. Just say the word. I'll gas up the Charger and we'll head over to Jersey."

"I think I need that. Thanks for keeping it real with me. I needed that too."

"Anytime. You know I got your back. But yeah, let me get on up outta here. I got my workout clothes on and I'm ready to hit the street. Call me when you're ready to go out there."

"I will and thanks, Shawn."

They hung up. Damon walked into Sylvia's and was thinking of what he would order for take-out. As he was eyeing the take-out menu, he looked over at people eating in the restaurant. What he saw made his mouth drop open and drop the menu on the floor. He saw Jamon all cozy with another guy in a booth. The guy was laughing at whatever Jamon was saying and they both seemed very touchy feely. Damon immediately moved out of their sight so he could see them but they couldn't see him. He watched them over the course of the next few minutes. He text messaged Malcolm.

Damon: OMG I see Jamon in Sylvia's all cozied up with some dude. They r yucking it up and Jamon's ass ain't even that funny. I'm so bout 2 call Shawn!

Malcolm: Get the fuck outta here!

Damon: If I am lying I am flying child I swear to God that is Jamon.

In a few seconds Malcolm's name appeared across Damon's phone as an incoming call.

"Hello?" Damon answered just above a whisper.

"You joking, right?"

"I wish I was. They are over there looking just like a couple. See, I knew when Shawn said Jamon was acting funny and not coming home, there was some shady shit going on."

"Can they see you?"

"No. But even if I was visible, they are so in each other's grill, I doubt they would even notice me."

"What are they doing now?"

"Dude got his fork on Jamon's plate. Ooh Jamon just scooped the food on his fork for him. And they are looking at each other like they could just eat each other up."

"Something always seemed foul to me about that dude. You gon' go over to the table?"

"Nope, I am calling Shawn right now. Hold on," Damon said turning to walk out of the restaurant. He dialed Shawn back once he was outside.

"Hello?" Shawn answered.

He could tell Shawn had already begun to jog.

"Hey where are you?"

"I just made it to 135th and Saint Nick. Why, wassup?"

"Shawn I gotta tell you something. You might wanna stop running for a second."

"Is it your father? What happened?" Shawn asked alarmed.

"No, it's not my father. Malcolm is on the phone too."

"Wassup, Black?"

"Yo."

"What's going on? You're making me nervous."

"Shawn I...I was just in Sylvia's and, um..."

Silence.

"You were in Sylvia's."

"And I, um. Maybe I should come pick you up and tell you."

"Tell me what?"

"I just saw Jamon."

"Okay, you saw Jamon. Eating in Sylvia's?"

"Yeah."

Silence.

"Did you call me to tell me he was in Sylvia's?"

"No I..." Damon tried to begin again.

"Shawn, he saw Jamon in Sylvia's with another dude. They were sitting at a table, dude was eating off of Jamon's plate, and he said they was looking real lovey dovey," Malcolm said.

Silence.

"Damon, is that what you're trying to tell me?"

"Yes."

"Malcolm, are you there too?"

"Nah, D sent me a text when he saw it."

"What, am I last to know? Did you call Kevin and tell him before me too?"

"No, I just sent a text to Malcolm and then he called. I'm sorry; I know I shoulda called you first."

"What does the guy look like?"

Damon went back into the restaurant and peeked from the same blind spot from before.

"He's brown skinned with a bald head. Big doofy smile. Really skinny too."

"Does he have dimples?"

"I can't tell. Oh yeah, he does. He is just kee-keeing it up like Jamon is on Def Comedy Jam."

"That sounds like his ex, Darnell. Does he have big eyes?"

"Uhh, yeah he does."

"Does he have a big gap in his teeth?"

"Yeah, I could kick a field goal."

"That's definitely Darnell."

"Excuse me sir, did you want a table for one?" the hostess asked Damon.

Damon put his index finger to his lips and shushed the hostess.

"Not right now," Damon whispered.

"Excuse me, excuse me," Shawn said to people around him.

They could hear Shawn's breathing get heavy.

"Are you running?"

"Hell yeah, I'm on my way to Sylvia's."

Damon turned and looked at Jamon and Darnell. They flagged the waiter down for their check.

"It looks like they are about to leave. The waiter looks like he is cashing them out. He is ringing them up."

Damon saw them stand up and put their jackets on and hurried out of the restaurant. They're leaving," Damon said.

"Okay, pick me up on the corner of Saint Nick and 134th. I know where Darnell lives in the Bronx. And if they don't go back to his house, I will find them before the evening is over if I gotta walk through all of the Bronx."

"Alright, stay there. I'll be right there."

They hung up and Damon headed to his car.

"Damon!" he heard someone yell.

He turned around and saw Malcolm come running up.

"Where were you?"

"Near Malik's store. Trying to see if I could see him without actually going inside."

"What the fuck? Are you a stalker now? You tryna crack a case, Nancy Grace?"

"Nah, but a nigga is definitely confused. Homeboy igged me the whole time we were at the restaurant and then when I bounced, gave me the kiss of life. I don't get it. Does he wanna fuck me or not?"

"Okay, we'll worry about that later. Right now, we gotta go get Shawn."

Malcolm turned around and saw Jamon and Darnell turn and walk in the direction of the 2-train. They ran out of sight so Jamon wouldn't see them.

"Look, there they go. They're going to the 2. They gotta be headed uptown to the Bronx."

"Fuck. Let's go get Shawn."

They rushed to the truck and drove up to W. 134th and saw Shawn standing there. He looked like he was ready for war. His eyes narrowed, his jaws clenched, and his nostrils flared; his hands were two tight fists at his sides.

They knew whenever Shawn looked like that, he was pissed.

"I have a feeling it's gonna be a long night."

"Son, it's about to go down."

# 20

## SHIT, DAMN, MUTHAFUCKA

"I can't believe this muthafucka had the audacity to come up in my house every day knowing he's been fucking around! And I fell for that bullshit. And with Darnell's beetle juice looking ass? Hell muthafuckin' no!" Shawn exclaimed.

When Shawn was angry like this, all of his Ivy League education and proper speech went out of the window. His temper made him shed his calm demeanor and he was straight hood.

Malcolm and Damon didn't say anything.

Shawn stared out of the window as they made their way up to the Bronx. Traffic slowed them down as they got crossed the bridge to the Bronx. Once deeper in the Bronx, their surroundings began to change. This was the hood for real. Tenement buildings, abandoned buildings, trash on the street, and groups of thugs on every corner, mean-mugging the occupants in every car that passed by. There was a tension in the atmosphere, like a drive-by waiting to happen.

"Make a left here." Damon turned onto Darnell's block. "It's this building here on the right. Second floor, apartment 2H." Damon pulled into a parking space and put the club on his brake pedal. Then put his navigation system and music all in his glove compartment.

"What the hell are you doing?"

"You act like you don't know where the fuck we are. I grew up in the Bronx. I know what it looks like around here."

Shawn got out of the backseat and made a beeline for the front entrance of Darnell's building. Someone was coming out of the building and Shawn caught the door. Malcolm and Damon ran behind him. Sprinting up the steps, Shawn raced to the second floor and found apartment 2H.

"Wait out here," he told Damon and Malcolm.

Shawn banged on the door and stood out of the peephole's eye view. Loud hip-hop music came from inside and Shawn knew his man was in there; Jamon's cologne lingered in the

hallway. Footsteps approached the door, and Darnell opened it, dressed only in a pair of loose shorts. As soon as he opened the door, Shawn pushed his way inside and immediately punched Darnell in the face. He headed for the living room where Jamon was sitting on the couch naked and rolling a blunt.

"So this is the new music you've been working on, huh?" Shawn said to Jamon. Jamon's eyes got as big as saucers. "You lyin' muthafucka!"

"Shawn, I..."

BOOP! Shawn punched him in the mouth before he could finish his sentence. Then he unleashed a series of body blows that made Jamon cover himself. Darnell made his way over and grabbed Shawn by the hood of his hoodie and spun him around and punched him in the face. Pain reverberated through Shawn's cheekbone and the pain pissed him off even more. Shawn lost it and went for blood. Clenching his fists, he proceeded to beat the hell out of Darnell's ass, throwing one blow after the other. Darnell wasn't a punk, so he fought Shawn back with everything in him. But Shawn was winning and both of them were knocking things over. They fell over the rectangular coffee table and knocked the lamp off the end table; it crashed against the floor. But that still didn't stop them or slow them down. Jamon tried to break them up but it didn't work. Shawn pushed Jamon to the side and continued fighting Darnell. Darnell was quick, but Shawn was quicker; he was finally able to pin him to the floor.

"Think I'mma let you take my man? Huh, you bitch ass muthafucka?" Shawn punched him in the nose and the mouth. Blood oozed out one nostril and poured from his cracked lip.

"Shawn, chill out," Jamon yelled and pulled Shawn off of Darnell again. Shawn turned around and cracked his fist against Jamon's jaw so hard that he was certain he'd sprung his hand or cracked one of his knuckles. The pain was intense but not enough to stop his fury from raging.

"Get the fuck off me!" Darnell grabbed Shawn by the waist and threw all of his weight onto him, knocking him to the floor. He hit him twice in the jaw. Shawn grabbed him by the ear as if he was going to pull it off and Darnell loosened his grip.

Malcolm and Damon busted in and pulled Shawn and Darnell off of each other. Jamon snatched up his briefs and put them on while still trying to grab at Shawn.

"Shawn, calm down!" Jamon said.

"Come on, man; come on, let's go," Damon said grabbing a hold of Shawn.

Darnell raced at Shawn and head-butted him in the chest. The blow was supposed to do serious damage, but Shawn saw it coming, so he steadied himself for it. He followed up Darnell's weak attempt by back-handing him to the floor. He tried to kick Shawn, but Malcolm and Damon were pulling him away.

"Fuck you, Jamon! Fuck you, bitch! I gave yo ass everything I had. Whatever you needed, I gave you even when you didn't have shit!" Shawn yelled. "Even when you *weren't* shit!"

Jamon reached out for him.

"Don't touch me! Stay here with his ass. Y'all muthafuckas deserve each other!"

Unwilling to give up the fight, Darnell lunged at Shawn and swung. Jamon held him back.

"I'mma fuck you up, nigga!" Darnell yelled.

"You ain't want it today so you ain't gon' want it next time either!"

Darnell broke free and went swinging at Shawn. Malcolm stepped forward and threw a blow at his chest, and he went down like a crashing plane.

"Fuck outta here, lil' nigga," Malcolm said.

Jamon helped Darnell up.

In spite of all his anger, watching Jamon help Darnell up to his feet saddened Shawn. "You better not come back to my house neither! It's over! Stay here with this muthafucka. I hate you! I *fucking hate you!*"

Jamon watched Malcolm and Damon carry Shawn out, and he wanted to follow after them, to try to talk to Shawn, explain the situation. But he knew it was pointless. Shawn was past the point of reasoning

"I'mma fuck him up! I'mma fuck him up!" Darnell yelled trying to break free from Jamon. He clutched at his chest, the spot where Malcolm had hit him, but he still wanted to go get at Shawn.

Meanwhile, Malcolm and Damon were pulling Shawn down the steps.

"Muthafucka hit me in my mouth!" Shawn said trying to go back up the steps.

"Let's go, Shawn!" Damon said pulling him back down the steps.

"I hope he knows it's over. It's fucking over now. You hear me?! It's over! It's fucking over Jamon! It's over!" Shawn yelled up at the second floor.

People turned around and looked at Shawn.

"Get in the car, Shawn," Damon said noticing all of the unwanted attention that they had gathered.

Shawn climbed into the backseat while Damon and Malcolm got up front.

Damon pulled off and they rode in silence back to Shawn's place. He took a detour to swing by Kevin's and pick him up, even though he had yet to answer a single one of his calls or texts. He was surprised when Kevin answered the door.

"Damn, you don't know how to answer your phone?" Damon snapped.

"I, uh...I was busy getting caught up with some paperwork."

"Yeah, yeah, yeah. Grab your stuff and come on."

"Come on where?"

"Just come. We'll catch you up in the truck."

The whole ride was them taking turns recounting to Kevin what had just transpired at Darnell's apartment. Kevin couldn't believe his ears. He never thought Jamon would cheat on Shawn, and he never thought Shawn would go ham like that. They parked near Shawn's building and followed him inside. Once inside, Shawn went straight into the bedroom and started pulling all of Jamon's clothes out of the closets and throwing them into the middle of the floor. He grabbed all of his fitted caps, hats, shirts, and everything else he could and threw them all in the middle of the floor. Damon walked into his bedroom and saw him.

"What are you doing?"

"I'm getting all of this shit out of my house. I don't want any of it here anymore."

"Shawn, are you sure? I mean this is some pretty nice stuff. Can't you wear some of these shoes or give the clothes away? Hell, sell it."

"Yeah, we both wear a size twelve shoe. But I got my own and I want all of his shit out of here. Can someone go grab the box of trash bags from under the kitchen sink?"

"You really gonna put all his shit in the dumpster?"

"The dumpster? Who said anything about the trash? I'm dumping this shit in the Hudson River."

"Oh, bet. I'm down for that," Malcolm said gleefully.

"Is he sure he wants to do that?" Kevin asked entering the room.

"I'm positive. Kev, all the stuff in that hall closet is Jamon's dress clothes and shoes. Pull them all out and start filling one of those bags with it."

"Shawn. I don't think we should..."

"Fill up the fucking bag, Kevin! You know what? Fuck it! I'll do it." Shawn walked past Kevin into the hallway. He flung the closet door open and started pulling everything out.

"Y'all go ahead and get started in here. I'm gonna help him out there."

Malcolm and Kevin started filling up the bags as they were instructed to do. Damon joined Shawn in the hallway and started filling up the bag with everything Shawn was pulling out of the closet. Shawn was pulling so many things out so quickly that he had to stop to catch his breath. Damon filled his bag.

"I'm gonna get another bag. This one is full," Damon said. He turned to look at Shawn who by now had tears streaming down his face. Damon dropped his bag and hugged Shawn. Shawn began to sob loudly as the tears continued to come from his eyes.

"How could he do this to me? I love him."

"It's okay. It's okay. We're here for you."

"I love him, D. And he hurt me. He hurt me so bad."

"Shhh. Come on, let's go sit down."

Damon walked him over to the couch with his arm around him. Malcolm and Kevin brought bags out into the living room.

"I am so tired of him making me cry. I am so tired of feeling like I don't matter to him as much as he matters to me. I can't believe he fucking cheated on me. I just wanna know why. I don't understand. What did I do to make him cheat on me?"

"Just a selfish ass dude. That's all. And he doesn't deserve you."

"I gave a good one in the chest to that muthafucka Jamon was with," Malcolm said throwing a punch.

"I wanna get this stuff out of here. It's making me sick."

"Well, let's load it up," Malcolm said, hoisting the two biggest bags to the door.

Shawn hurried to the bedroom to make sure everything of his was gone. Clothes hangers laid all over the floor. But Jamon's side of the bedroom closet was empty.

By the time they finished loading up Damon's truck with all the bags, there wasn't any room left in the truck for anyone to sit. "I'll take Shawn," Damon said. "Y'all clean up and order some food."

"Do I look like my name is Geoffrey?"

"I'll clean up. Malcolm, can you at least call and order the food?" Kevin asked.

"Yeah, I can do that."

"Yeah, just some pizza and wings. We'll be right back."

Damon drove Shawn over to West Piers Park and put on his hazard lights. They dragged the big heavy bags over to the edge of the platform and dropped them over into the water, one by one.

"It's about to be some fly ass fish in that river with those clothes."

"I hope they eat them," Shawn said.

All of Jamon's designer clothing, suits, sneakers, and everything was soon going to be on its way to the bottom of the river. And Shawn didn't feel the least bit guilty about it. Just hurt.

"We better get going before the cops see us."

They hurried back to the truck and sped off.

# 21

## SLEEP IN THE MIDDLE

Shawn, Malcolm, Damon, and Kevin sat around Shawn's dining room table eating pizza and wings, drinking beer, and smoking weed.

"I knew this day would come eventually," Shawn said blowing smoke.

"How?"

"Just something kept gnawing at me. I felt it but I just ignored it and thought I'd deal with it when the time came."

"How are you feeling?"

"Numb. Kevin, I owe you an apology for yelling at you earlier. I just wanted to get his shit outta here."

"It's okay. I know you were just upset."

Shawn nodded and they bumped fists.

"You going to work tomorrow?" Damon asked.

"Yeah, the year is winding down. One month left so yeah I'll be there. He ain't fin' to have me missing days from work."

"I know that's right."

"How long had you been feeling like something wasn't right?" Kevin asked.

"Probably like the last six months. I couldn't put my finger on what was wrong, though. It was just something different going on with him. But I would be so happy to have him around, most times I would just ignore it."

"You think it's really over?"

"I don't know. I know I need to take care of myself now, though. I just feel lost," Shawn said.

"Why?"

"A lot of my life in these last three years has been enraptured in my being his boyfriend. I feel like he protected me. Now I'm not his—" Shawn choked up. "I'm not his boyfriend anymore. And now I gotta live with that. And I don't know how I will get through this."

"What do you mean? You know we got you. Just like you told me earlier."

Damon got up and walked over to Shawn with his arms extended. "Come here."

Shawn stood up and hugged him. Then Malcolm and Kevin came and surrounded him in a group hug.

"I don't even know what to do with myself now. Where do I begin?"

"You start with yourself. Everyday when you wake up in the morning. You start with you."

"I'm scared y'all."

"It's okay to be scared. But you won't be alone. We're not going anywhere."

They hugged him as he sobbed.

Silence. "I swear if I cry one more time about this dude, I'm gonna fucking break something," Shawn said as they let go and he wiped his eyes with tissue.

"Get it out. It's okay to cry. It's okay for you to feel exactly how you do. You love him. And he was a big part of you. But don't discount yourself. There is so much more to you than your being with him. You got a lot of people who depend on you. And hello, you have two college degrees and a thriving career. Those kids at that school need you. We need you. And most importantly, you need you. You're our brother. And we're gonna help you get through this together."

"And if you feel like you lost yourself in your relationship then find yourself now. School is about to be out. Get back to finding out what makes you happy."

"And don't forget about how much fun we're gonna have in Miami when we go to Pride in a few weeks," Kevin said gyrating.

"We gon' be doing it big!"

"You already know!"

Shawn smiled. Malcolm went over to the stereo where Shawn's iPod was hooked up. He turned on "Take This Ring" by Toni Braxton.

"Come on, Shawn, let's dance," Malcolm said.

"Oh no, y'all. I'm not in the mood to dance."

"Well, you gon' dance now. Come on!" Malcolm said taking him by the hand and pulling him up.

Malcolm started dancing on Shawn from behind.

"Come on, Shawnie; drop it like it's hot."

Kevin and Damon found their way over and they all danced around him. He looked at them and slowly started to move to the rhythm of the song. As his friends danced around him, he began to smile and laugh. And the four of them danced hard to the music like they were in the club. They really starting getting it at the part where she repeats "That's what Imma do, that's what I'mma do, that's what I'mma do" after the second verse.

As the first lady of LaFace Records was fading out, the bouncy beat of "Didn't You Know" by Tha Rayne featuring Joe Budden and Lupe Fiasco came on full blast.

"Oh, now this is the shit! Owwww!" Kevin said.

They continued to dance. "Break it down, Shawnie!"

Shawn started to dip it low and allowed himself to be seduced by the moment. The other three dipped it low with him and all were cheering him on.

"Owww! Get it, Shawnie. Break it down!"

"Get it, boy!"

Damon, Kevin, and Malcolm did their best to lift their friend's spirits. And it worked. Before the night was over they had danced, made him laugh and smile, and reassured him that they would be there for him every step of the way. He went from feeling like shit to feeling like he could win all from the support from his friends. They all gave him warm hugs on their way out.

"I love y'all so much," Shawn said to them.

Shawn took a long bubble bath and as he ventured into his empty bedroom alone. His house never seemed so quiet. But now the silence was deafening. The one thing he knew he had to do was go through the motions of feeling the pain of this break-up alone. No matter how much his friends promised they would be there for him, they couldn't feel his pain for him. He realized he may never feel Jamon's arms wrapped around him in their bed ever again. Or wake up to one of their morning lovemaking sessions. Or sit at the kitchen table in the morning listening to the radio over breakfast on Shawn's way to work and Jamon's way to the studio. The thought of it made him sad. But instead of crying, he closed his eyes and took a deep swallow. For the first time ever, he laid down in the middle of the bed instead of what was normally his side.

*This bed is all mine now. Might as well sleep in the middle.* The Blu Cantell song of the same name rolled him to sleep as he played it on repeat.

# 22

## TOO LITTLE AND TOO LATE

"Let's clear out of this hallway people!" Malcolm said in a big booming voice to the students who crowded the hallway of Johnson High after the bell rung.

"Hey, Mr. Brown," said a female student undressing him with her eyes.

"Wassup, Deena?" Deena and her girls stopped in the hallway and talked amongst each other while looking at him.

"Wassup, Mr. Brown," another student called out as he passed by.

"Hey, wassup man." A chorus of "Hey Mr. Browns" happened as he stood watching all the hallway activity. He politely responded with a "Wassup, y'all."

Students were getting books out of lockers, laughing, popping gum, and talking loud as they made their way to class.

"Girl you crazy!" one girl yelled out.

"You know how I do," another answered back.

"Alright now, don't be late to your next class."

Students were walking out of the side door Malcolm was near. Seniors were going home for the day, some students were leaving for lunch, and others were going up the steps. Malcolm turned around and looked out the open door. A man with shades walked in and approached him.

"You're either in or you're out, man. Next time you gotta come in the front," Malcolm said, not really looking closely at him.

"Malcolm."

Malcolm turned and looked at the man. It was Jamon.

"Where is Shawn?"

"You gotta sign in at the main office. Go around the front."

"Come on, Black. I know you know where he is."

"I know you need to go to the office and ask for him. And the name is Mr. Brown."

"Can you just tell me where he is? It's important."

"Then take your important ass to the office."

Jamon looked at him as the late bell rung.

"You better hurry up. He closes his door at the late bell."

Jamon walked back out of the side door and Malcolm hurried to Shawn's classroom.

"Mr. Jones," Malcolm said.

Shawn looked up at him. "Yes?"

"Can I talk to you for a minute?"

"Sure. Everyone take out your essays and pass them up to the front. I will collect them when I get back."

He stepped outside of his classroom. "Wassup?"

"Jamon is here."

"Where?"

"On his way to the main office. He tried to come in the side and I made him go to the office."

"Did he say what he wanted?"

"Nah, just that it was important."

"Like I really need this fucking drama at work today."

The telephone in Shawn's classroom began to ring.

"Damn, that's probably the office." Shawn went inside and answered. "Hello? Yes. Okay, here I come." He closed his classroom door on his way out.

"Is he up there?" Malcolm asked.

"I think so."

"You want me to watch your class?"

"No, they'll be fine. Come with me to the office."

"Okay."

They walked down the much quieter hallway. Shawn took a deep breath and the closer he got to the front, the more his temperature rose. Malcolm saw the panicked look on his face.

"Hey, hey. Relax, okay? Stay cool."

Shawn nodded. They walked to the main office and Shawn went in. He saw Jamon standing there; he could barely look at his face.

"Mr. Jones, your brother said he needed to talk to you," one of the office secretaries said. *Brother my ass!*

"Thank you." They walked out of the office and walked around to the front entrance steps outside. Malcolm followed them.

"Can I speak to you in private please?" Jamon asked looking at Malcolm.

Malcolm stood in front of the doors with his arms folded as if he were Shawn's bodyguard.

"This is private enough. Why the fuck are you at my job?"

"Because I need to talk to you."

"You have one minute."

"I'm sorry."

"Time's up."

"I am sorry, Mook. I know what I did was foul. But I love you."

"My name is Shawn." He snatched his arm away as Jamon reached out for it.

"I went to the house today. Where is my stuff?"

"Oh, that's why you're here."

"I got a show tonight and I need something to wear. But all my stuff is gone."

"Well, maybe you should have Darnell buy you some more shit."

"Come on, what you do with my stuff?"

"West Piers Park."

"You took my stuff to the park?"

"Mmm hmm."

"You just left my stuff there? That's like 20 G's worth of clothes. Half that shit I ain't even pay for. It's exclusive shit that was given to me."

"Well, when you go buy yourself some more, make sure you get yourself a swimsuit."

"A swimsuit?"

"Yeah. Maybe a boat too."

Malcolm chuckled. Jamon looked at him quizzically.

"Oh, did I forget to mention it's in the Hudson River?"

"You threw my shit in the river?"

"Yup."

"What the fuck? You know how much that shit cost, man?!"

Shawn shrugged his shoulders. "Frankly, my dear, I don't give a fuck."

"You lucky that's all he did," Malcolm said.

Shawn looked at Malcolm and shook his head.

"So that's my payback, huh? What about this?" Jamon asked removing his shades. He revealed his swollen black eye. "I gotta sing tonight with this!"

Shawn jumped at the sight of it. His first instinct was to apologize but he stuck to his guns. "Well, that's what happens when you cheat on me."

"So it's like that?"

"Don't you dare act like you're the fucking victim. You created all of this."

"And I said I was sorry. What else do you want?"

"I want you to stop making a fool of yourself. Get from in front of my job and go on about your business. And leave me the hell alone."

"I'm sorry."

"I know you're sorry. Now get your sorry ass from in front of my building and go on about your business. Comprende?"

Jamon looked at him with sadness in his eyes. He reached out for Shawn's arm.

Malcolm snatched Jamon's hand off of Shawn's arm. "Come on man, get the fuck outta here. He don't wanna talk to you."

"Shawn."

Malcolm grabbed Jamon and pushed him off the front steps. "Get the fuck out of here," Malcolm said again.

"Shawn, you just gon' let him push me away?"

Shawn looked at him and began to walk back inside.

"Yo, I'll black your other eye if you don't get the fuck out of here," Malcolm said.

"Man, fuck you! Mind your fucking business!"

As Malcolm approached Jamon, Shawn called after him. "Malcolm! Let's go."

Malcolm gave him a final look. "You ain't even worth the beat down. But if you bring yo ass back around, I'mma fuck you up."

"Whatever," Jamon said putting his shades back on and walking away.

Malcolm watched him walk off and went back inside the building with Shawn.

"You okay?"

Shawn took a deep breath and closed his eyes. "Yeah, I am. Let me get back to class."

Shawn walked back to the classroom and Malcolm returned to his hallway post.

# 23

## MS. UNDERSTANDING

While making chicken parmesan for dinner, Kevin dipped his hands into the hot suds and began washing the dishes that he had dirtied. He wanted everything clean and ready by time Charles came over for dinner. And he was making it in good time. The oven kept the chicken warm and pasta boiled on the stovetop. He hadn't told the guys about the day Charles put his hands on him. Or the second time either. Both times Charles had apologized profusely and promised to never do it again. But Kevin had apologized to him too. Maybe he shouldn't have been drooling over Ginuwine like that. It was pretty disrespectful if you thought about it. And the second time? Well, maybe he should've kept his thoughts to himself about no one needing to have an upper-hand in a relationship. Kevin said relationships should be an equal partnership. Charles had argued that someone needed to dominate and it was usually the man.

"But we're both men," Kevin had said confused.

"Yeah, but someone has to play the woman or be the submissive one."

"And so I'm guessing you're the dominant one, huh?"

"Isn't it pretty obvious?"

They went back and forth about it, and what had started off as a deep conversation soon turned into a full-blown argument. Charles ordered Kevin to stop yelling at him, but Kevin was caught up in the moment and determined to get his point across. That is until Charles' hands tightened around his throat until Kevin's face literally turned blue. He didn't let go until Kevin was on the brink of passing out. Of course he apologized for that incident as well. And Kevin figured if he had just shut up when Charles asked him to, he could have prevented that from happening. That happened Saturday night, so when he woke up that next morning barely able to talk and noticed a huge bruise across his neck, he knew he wouldn't be going to Sunday brunch with the boys. It was the first Sunday brunch he had ever missed and the boys had a thousand questions, but he avoided them. He wasn't ready to let them know about his situation just yet.

He finished the dishes and lit two candles at the already set table. A knock at the door made him stand up straight. He answered the door and saw Malcolm standing there.

"Malcolm. What are you doing here?"

"Nice to see you too."

"Hey."

Silence. "You gon' invite me in?"

"Oh yeah, sure."

Kevin stepped aside and let Malcolm in. "What you got going on? Candles and shit."

Kevin looked nervously at the door. "Oh, I'm just waiting on Charles. He's coming over for dinner."

"Oh good. I wanna meet him."

"Tonight?"

"Yeah. Is there a reason why I can't? He is real isn't he?"

"He's real." Kevin began to wonder if Malcolm knew what was going on.

"Okay, so then I can meet him? Why is he like your best kept secret?"

"Well..."

"Damn, it smells good in here. What you cook?"

"I made some chicken parm."

"Word? You know that's my favorite. Let me get a plate!" Malcolm said going into the kitchen. Malcolm washed his hands in the kitchen sink and pulled a plate off of the shelf. Kevin got him a smaller plate.

"Who gon' eat off that?"

"This is for you."

"Yeah, aight." Kevin sucked his teeth and took the chicken out of the oven. "I don't know who you think is eating off of that little ass plate." Kevin fixed him a plate and they sat at the center island. "So you got the candles happening and gourmet food. What's good with you and this professor dude? And why haven't we met him?"

"I'm just waiting for the right time."

"Yeah? Well, I figured I should just let you know Shawn and Damon ain't too happy about you missing brunch on Sunday. What was that about?"

"Nothing. I was just tired," Kevin said trying to avoid eye contact.

"Tired?"

"Yeah, I was tired. Last week was really hectic."

"Work seems to be real hectic for you lately. Is everything aight?"

Kevin frowned. "Yeah, it's just busy this time of year."

"You sure that's it?"

"I'm sure. What's with all the questions?"

"I just came to check on you, man. I wanted to make sure everything was okay. Relax. I come in peace," Malcolm said putting his hands up.

"I'm fine."

"We just miss you, that's all. At least I do. Shawn and Damon wanna beat your ass. And I wanted to come see you in person to see how you were in case something was wrong." Malcolm continued eating and Kevin tried to do something to calm his nerves. He really didn't want Malcolm to meet Charles.

"Well, thanks for your concern, but I really am fine. One of my staff members is on vacation this week and another is out sick, so they have me doing all these financial aid workshops. So this weekend, I was just so tired. And Charles wanted to spend time on Saturday. I really wasn't up to it, but he insisted."

"Too busy for us, huh? What does he even look like cuz as far as I'm concerned, he's a ghost."

Kevin picked up a framed picture that Charles had given him. He held it out to Malcolm. "Does he look like a ghost to you?"

"Damn, he's fine. You like him?"

"I do. I really do."

"So tell me all about Professor Clay."

"It's Charles. He's a really good guy."

"Word? Why? What makes him such a good guy?"

"He just caters to all of my needs, ya know? Like I don't even have to say anything, he just knows what to do. He anticipates everything perfectly."

"Yeah? So how come we haven't met him?"

"I'm just...waiting for the right time. And why are you in such a rush to meet Charles? Hell, no one has met Malik yet."

"For your information, Shawn and Damon already met him."

Kevin drew back.

"I'm playing. They ain't meet him yet. I don't even know what the hell we're doing honestly. It's hot and cold with him. One minute he acts like he don't care and the next minute he's asking me about my day. So I don't know."

"Are you still really messing with other guys?"

"Lately, just Stefon."

"Who the hell is that?"

"Puerto Rican dude I used to fuck with from the Bronx. We get up when I get that itch."

Kevin shook his head.

"Damn, you put your foot in this one boy," Malcolm said eating.

"Thanks."

A key turned in the door and Charles walked in. Malcolm turned around and looked at him.

"Hey, baby," Kevin said running to Charles. They kissed as Kevin threw his arms around him.

"Hey," Charles said not taking his eyes off of Malcolm.

"This is one of my best friends, Malcolm."

"Oh, Malcolm. How you doing, bruh?" Charles asked with his hand extended.

They shook hands.

"I'm good man; nice to meet you. Heard a lot about you."

"Nice to meet you too. Kevin is always talking about his friends and how close you guys are. I hope I can meet the other two. Shawn and Damon, right?"

"Yeah. That's us. The Harlem Boyz."

They both looked at Kevin. "What?" Kevin asked.

"I wanna meet the rest of your friends."

"Yeah, set it up, Kev. You the hold out."

"Okay, fine. We'll set something up soon."

Kevin had some apprehension about introducing them all but since he was now under pressure to set it up, he knew he would have to do it.

"We'll see about this weekend."

"Good deal. You gonna stay for dinner?"

"Oh nah, I just stopped by for a few. I'mma let y'all have your couple's night."

"You sure? It's okay; we don't mind."

Malcolm looked at Kevin who gave him an awkward smile.

"I'mma bounce, man. It was good meeting you."

"Alright. Well, it was nice meeting you. I'mma go to the little boy's room. Come back and have dinner with us soon and bring the fellas." Charles shook Malcolm's hand again.

Charles took off his jacket before heading to the bathroom. Malcolm admired Charles' physique as he left the room.

"Damn, he got a nice ass body. He look like he can pick your little ass up with one hand."

Kevin sucked his teeth. "Well, thanks for coming by to check on me. You can tell the fellas I am fine."

"Oh, you gon' put me out? He did invite me to stay."

"Yeah and I'm telling you get out."

"Aww, das fucked up. And um, he has a key?"

"He does."

Malcolm raised his eyebrow. "You've known this dude like five minutes and he has a key to your place? I mean he seems nice and all but a key?"

"I have one to his place too."

"You wildin' my dude."

"I know we haven't been together that long but we feel really close to each other and I trust him." In all actuality, Charles had demanded a key to his place and to avoid a physical altercation, he had made one for him. And the truth was, he really didn't have a key to Charles' place. But there was no way he could tell Malcolm that.

Malcolm shook his head. "Just seems like y'all are moving a little fast to me."

"Thanks for your input Malcolm, but we're good."

Malcolm looked at him like he was full of it. "Cool. I'm out."

"Good night."

Malcolm saw himself out while Kevin watched him. He took Malcolm's empty plate and cup and washed them out. Charles came back in the room and hugged Kevin from behind and kissed his cheek.

"I'm so glad you cooked, babe. I love parmesan."

"Well, then sit down and let me fix you a plate."

"I can do it." He moved over to the stove and fixed his own plate. "So how long have you and Malcolm been friends?"

"Oh, a few years. Damon introduced him to us and he became like a younger brother to us all. It's funny that he's the youngest one but he's the most protective one, like he's the older brother."

"He seems cool. How tall is he? He's a big guy."

"I think he's about 6'6. Yeah he works out like every day. He's the free-spirited one."

"What do you mean by free-spirited?"

"Malcolm does whatever Malcolm wants. He's very...sexually liberated."

"So basically he's a ho."

"More or less."

Charles chuckled and sat down at the table. "You not gonna eat?"

"I'm not really hungry. I munched on some salad earlier."

Charles nodded. "So be honest. Did you and Malcolm ever fuck?"

"What?"

"Did you and Malcolm ever fuck? You can tell me the truth. I won't get mad."

"No, we never fucked. We're just friends."

"You sure?"

"Yes. Why are you asking me this?"

"I just wanted to know. I can tell the brother is a flirt and he was flirting with you."

"Flirting with me? When? How?"

"Just the look in his eyes. I can tell he wanted a piece of you. Good thing I walked in when I did."

"Are you suggesting I would have done something with him?"

"Are you admitting to the fact that he was flirting with you?"

"No. Malcolm doesn't want me. Our relationship is like brothers. I don't even look at him like that."

"You said yourself that he was a ho."

"He is, but I don't want him."

"So you're admitting that he was flirting with you?"

"No, I am not saying that."

"But he was, though. I know he was. What were y'all talking about before I came in?"

"We were just shooting the breeze. I showed him your picture."

"So he was flirting with you while looking at my picture?"

"He just wanted to see what you looked like."

"Okay, now we're getting somewhere. He wanted to flirt with you while looking at my face as if I was sitting there. He's one of them types. You know what? I don't want him in this house anymore."

Kevin felt stunned. The moment he thought Charles couldn't get any crazier, he went completely left field. "This is my house, Charles. You can't ban my friend from my house."

"I can ban his ho ass from seeing my man if I want to." Kevin exhaled and rolled his eyes. "What am I supposed to do when I see some muscle-bound negro drooling over my man? You're my man, not his. Let him go drool over some other dude. You know, cats kill me with that shit. He smiled all up in my face like everything was cool knowing he wanted to fuck you. That's pretty low isn't it? And you call him a friend too? A friend wouldn't be trying to poach you from a relationship. Don't you agree?"

"Charles, I can't do this. I'm tired and I really don't feel like arguing tonight. I just wanna lay down. You come in the bedroom when you're done," Kevin said rising from the table.

"You just let him know he's not welcome back in this house."

Kevin walked into his bedroom and turned on the TV. His mind was racing after that conversation. He lay across the bed while his thoughts continued to race. He turned onto his side and stared at a picture of Malcolm, Shawn, and Damon and him that was on his nightstand. These were his brothers; none of them saw the other in a sexual way. Once again, Charles was overreacting, but he didn't want to rile him up any.

He could feel Charles walk into the room and lay down on the bed. Charles took Kevin's face into his hands and turned it towards him. "Kiss me."

A kiss turned into a blow-out love session that had Kevin purring like a kitten. They lay in the bed naked while the ceiling fan blew cool air on them.

"I don't mean to come off like the jealous boyfriend. But I know a dog when I see one. You can still be friends with him but I'd rather him not be here when I'm not here. Can you do me that one favor?" Charles gave him a passionate kiss. "Please?"

Kevin nodded but knew he wouldn't saying anything to Malcolm about it. Charles smiled and went down and gave Kevin head. After the explosion, Charles cleaned him up.

"I need one more favor."

"What?"

"Can you make me a bacon, egg, and cheese sandwich?"

"There's more parmesan in there."

"I know but that's what I have a taste for."

Kevin looked up at the spinning fan. "Okay."

"Thanks, baby."

Kevin put on a pair of shorts and went into the kitchen. As soon as he left out the room, Charles grabbed Kevin's charging cell phone and found Malcolm's number. He sent him a text, pretending as though he were Kevin. They texted back and forth until he heard Kevin's footsteps approaching; he held down the 'end' button, shutting the phone down. Kevin came back in with the sandwich.

"Thanks, babe, you're the best. Can you get me a glass of OJ?"

Kevin looked at him like he was crazy but he went to the kitchen and returned with a tall glass of orange juice. By the time he returned, Charles had gulfed down the sandwich. He drank the juice, then pulled Kevin into his arms, holding him tight. Kevin fell asleep in Charles' embrace. He awoke that morning to Charles kissing him on the cheek, saying, "Have a good day, babe."

He reached for his cell phone to check the time and realized that it was off. He turned it on. When the phone finished loading, it alerted him that he had four missed calls from Malcolm and fifteen text messages dissing Charles, calling him a fool, and questioning their friendship. Kevin was puzzled and confused. Immediately, he dialed Malcolm's number.

"Look, I ain't got time for no bullshit," Malcolm answered.

"Well, good morning to you too. Malcolm what's the matter? I just woke up. What are all these text messages? Why are you so angry at me?"

"It's too early in the morning for you to be playing dumb."

"What are you talking about?"

"I gotta get ready for work. I said everything I had to say in the messages." Malcolm hung up on him.

Kevin read through the last of Malcolm's text messages. He seemed really upset. But Kevin didn't have the slightest clue as to why. He called Malcolm back.

"Da fuck you want now?"

"Malcolm, I don't understand why you're so upset. What is the problem?"

"I can't come over but you're allowed to talk to me on the phone?"

"Who said you can't come over? What are you talking about?"

"The text you sent me last night. I'm no longer allowed at your home cuz your bitch ass boyfriend is uncomfortable with it? What kind of bullshit is that? I thought we were friends. And after all the years we've known each other, you really think I want you like that? I've *never* looked at you like that."

"I know you don't like me like that—"

"Then why'd you text me that dumb shit?"

"I didn't text you anything."

"So what, am I just seeing shit now? I was just texting myself last night, right?"

"Wait! Just hold on for a minute." Kevin scrolled through his sent text messages. His mouth dropped open as he read all the things that Charles had sent to Malcolm, pretending to be him. He was even more shocked by the rude, hateful things that Charles had said.

"No, the hell he didn't." Kevin shook his head in disbelief. "Malcolm, I didn't send you these messages."

"Well, unless Casper the friendly fucking ghost was at your house, you musta been drunk or sleep texting."

"No, I...wait a minute. I got up to make Charles a sandwich last night and this was sent at 11:34pm. That's when he must've did this. Charles sent you these texts, not me."

"Why would he send me that?"

"Cuz he...we...never mind. It's a long story. Look, I gotta start getting ready for work too. I'm gonna call you back."

"Aight."

Kevin hung up with him. He was officially pissed. He showered and planned on going to Charles' office before he got to work. That mutha-fucka had crossed the line.

# 24

## SAY YES

Kevin got out of a cab and marched onto the campus of Columbia University to Charles' office. He knocked on the closed door and Charles answered with a smile.

"Hey, baby," Charles said moving in for a kiss. Kevin moved back and turned his head. "What's the matter?"

Kevin walked into the office and closed the door. He took out his phone and scrolled to the messages Charles had sent to Malcolm.

"What the hell is this?" Charles looked at the phone. "Do you know I woke up to four missed calls and fifteen unread messages from him this morning? Because someone decided to play me and send him messages saying I'm banning him from my house because you're uncomfortable." Charles looked at him. "Say something."

"I sent them. I don't want him in your house anymore. I don't trust him. And I knew you wouldn't say anything."

"He has been my friend longer than you have been my boyfriend. You do not have the right to ban any of my friends from my house."

"Are you trying to tell me that he's more important to you than I am?"

"It is not about that and you know it."

"Oh yeah? Then tell me what is it about?"

"This is about you not respecting boundaries. I don't have to choose between you and my friends. I am not supposed to wake up and see messages from one of my friends who is like a brother to me asking me about some messages I didn't send."

"So I guess I'm just supposed to let him yuck yuck and smile all up in your face. Even you said he was a ho."

"Not with me! Are you gonna act like this with all of my friends? Or with every man you see me talk to?"

"Just the hoes."

Kevin rolled his eyes. "You are overreacting."

"You know what? If you really cared about me and our relationship, you would respect the fact that I have reservations about you being around him."

"Respect it? It's not respectable! You are being ridiculous!"

"It is not ridiculous! It's how I feel and if you loved me you would take it into consideration."

Kevin shook his head. "You have no *right* to go through my phone or ban any of my friends from my house. My name was on the lease last time I checked."

"I have a right to protect what's mine."

"Protect what's yours? I am not your property!"

"You're my boyfriend. That means we belong to each other."

"You are doing the absolute most right now."

"Why, because I want some appreciation?"

"Appre—are you kidding me? You want me to knock off my friendship with Malcolm to show *you* some appreciation? That's crazy."

"I have to get to class in five minutes. I've said all I need to say about this. You can go now."

Kevin stood defiantly. Charles gathered up his things and walked out the door leaving Kevin standing there confused and angry.

"So that's it?" Kevin called down the hall after Charles.

"We'll finish this later. Get yourself to work before you're late," Charles said still walking away without turning around.

Infuriated, Kevin watched Charles walk down the long hallway with a confident stride. He slammed the door and sat on the couch in Charles' office.

"I can't believe him. I'm not breaking up with Malcolm or barring him from my house. I refuse." He sent Malcolm a text.

Kevin: I'm sorry about the texts Charles sent you. He and I just had a big argument about it. I will never ban you from my house. You are always welcome. I'll call you to discuss it later.

Malcolm: I don't like that dude. Something about him doesn't sit right with me.

Kevin: We'll talk later.

The nerve of that man! Beating on Kevin was one thing; but when you began to harm his friends and get them involved in this mayhem, that was a whole other story. And Charles had been so flippant about it, like he really didn't care one way or the other. Anger painted Kevin's thoughts and he clenched his fists and closed his eyes tight. After a few minutes of simmering in his anger, he sent Charles a two-word text: It's over.

He went back out the way he'd came, hailed a cab, and went to work. All day long, Kevin thought about how he would cope without Charles in his life. It wasn't going to be easy to let him go, but he had to do what was right for him. And obviously, Charles was okay with it because despite the two-word text he'd sent him, Charles hadn't texted or called him back. Kevin felt like he was easily irreplaceable, and the thought hurt.

On his lunch break, he called Malcolm. "I broke things off with Charles."

"You did what?"

"I had to. Charles is just too much, Malcolm."

"I mean, yeah he overreacted and took things a little too far, but you don't have to end things just like that. Unless there is something you're not telling me."

An image of the rape and the choke out flashed before his eyes.

"Malcolm, do me a favor and please just keep this between you and me. I don't want Damon and Shawn knowing this just yet."

While they were on the phone, Charles beeped in.

"That's him beeping in. I'll call you later."

"Aight." The conversation between Charles and he was short and sweet. Basically, Charles asked him to come over to his place so they could talk. Kevin let him know that it didn't matter what he had to say, the relationship was done.

"Okay, and that's understandable. But I'm requesting that you please show up at seven. Please. And if you wanna leave after that, I swear I won't do anything to stop you."

They hung up and Kevin finished up his paperwork. The whole way home he practiced what he would say to Charles that evening when he went to his house. He wasn't planning on spending the night or staying very long. He went home, showered, changed his clothes, and made himself look good so when he confronted Charles, he would be reminded of everything he just lost.

He arrived at Charles' apartment and could smell something savory coming from inside. He knocked on the door and was greeted by a white man dressed in a butler tux.

"Mr. Malone, I presume?" the butler asked.

"Yes," Kevin replied looking at the man quizzically.

"Right this way. Dr. Wright has been waiting for you."

Kevin walked into the apartment which had been totally redecorated. The lights were dim but very romantic. There was a string quartet playing, a baby grand piano with a pianist who was playing, a harpist, and a guitarist. Red and white flower petals lined the floor and a suited up catering staff stood behind tables of food they prepared for the evening. In the center of the floor was a circle table set for two draped with a white table cloth and two lit candles. Standing next to the piano was Charles dressed in a tux as if he were about to walk down the aisle. Kevin was impressed but puzzled at the same time.

"Kevin. Thank you for coming," Charles said approaching him.

"What's going on, Charles?"

"This is my apology. I owe you an apology for how I acted and for what I did. I was wrong for sending those messages. And I was wrong for asking you not to have your friend over. I know how much your friends mean to you. Can you please forgive me? I was being a jealous asshole and you didn't deserve that. I love you and I hope you can forgive me."

"I'm not gonna lie, I am impressed. And I do forgive you, but...I'm still done with this."

Charles held out his hand to him. "Come have dinner with me."

After the slightest moment of hesitation, Kevin took his hand and allowed him to lead him to the table. The small ensemble began to play "Say Yes" by Floetry. The butlers pulled out their chairs and served them a full three-course meal with a fresh Caesar salad, sorbet to cleanse the palate, and a main course of a 14 oz. grilled steak seasoned to perfection with spinach and garlic and parsley mashed potatoes. The fact that Charles went through all of this to say he was sorry melted Kevin's resolve to end things. Malcolm was probably right. He didn't have to take things to this extent.

Kevin breathed in deeply. "Charles, if we're gonna work, you have got to stop putting your hands on me."

Charles held up both hands and said sincerely, "Done. I've already enrolled myself in anger management classes, so I'm one step ahead of you."

A smile tugged at Kevin's lips. "And you have to respect my friends and respect my privacy. You have to know your boundaries and limitations in this relationship."

"I can respect that. And I still wanna meet your friends," Charles said holding his glass of champagne to his lips.

Kevin nodded, knowing in his mind by now Malcolm had probably told Shawn and Damon what had happened. He knew they would want to meet him but also throw him a massive amount of shade.

"We'll see how soon we can make that happen."

Charles had fallen back into Kevin's good graces. And Charles had Kevin right where he wanted him.

# 25

## THE TEA

Malcolm tried to rid his mind of Malik as best he could. But it was virtually impossible. The more he made advances, Malik continued to send mixed messages. He figured if he started doing his hook up thing again that would solve his problems. His mother's warnings of not letting love pass him by occupied his thoughts more and more. He was falling in love with Malik. The hook ups began to mean less and less. In talking about it with Damon, he had to ask "What in the world about Malik is so special that you want to be with him?" Malcolm couldn't quite put his finger on it but it was somewhere between his swag, his conversation, and those sexy dreadlocks. Malik wasn't just a piece of ass he wanted. He liked and respected the way Malik carried himself. But his hot and cold reaction puzzled Malcolm on a daily. So after insisting they talk in person, Malik invited Malcolm to the store so they could speak privately in his back office.

"What's going on?" Malik asked sitting behind his desk with his hand on his chin.

"Yo. I don't really know how to beat around the bush but I gotta confess something to you."

"Okay, what's up?"

Malcolm paused. "I like you."

"Okay. I like you too."

"Nah, man, I don't think you get it. I mean, I like you like...a lot. Like on some relationship type shit. I don't wanna just be ya friend." Malik had a stoic look that once again Malcolm couldn't gage. "And I don't know how you feel about me but I actually wanna be with you. And it's like, every time I try to holla at you, you blow me off. So basically, I just wanna know where we stand. Cuz I'm mad confused."

Malik nodded and averted his gaze. Malcolm sat back and tried to be cool but he had no idea what Malik was going to say.

"If I told you that I think you're cool and I just wanna be friends cuz I don't see you that way, would you be able to handle that?" Everything inside of Malcolm screamed hell muthafuckin' no and it was hard for him to hide the disappointment on his face.

"I would just have to respect it."

"Would you still wanna be my friend? Cuz I think you're mad cool."

"Yeah," he lied.

"Can I be honest about something?"

Malcolm sighed. "Yeah sure."

"I know all about your history. I mentioned your name to a few people I know, and a few of them are definitely familiar with you."

Malcolm hung his hand and he could hear his mother saying "Don't miss out on love because you're out there sharing yours with everybody."

"And honestly, it worried me. I felt like because of your past, you may try to run game on me."

"I wouldn't though."

"Let me finish. I heard you're the dude that says whatever he needs to say so dudes give you what you want and then you disappear. Don't return phone calls. Walk right by them in the street and not speak til you wanna fuck again. And I don't wanna be on the receiving end of that. I love hard. I ask if I let myself fall in love with you, would you be the one to break my heart?"

Malcolm had no words.

"But I like you too. And if you can prove to me and promise me that you will never break my heart then I may take you up on your offer."

Were his ears deceiving him? Was Malik telling him he was willing to give him a chance? "You, uh, you wanna shake on it?"

"No. I want you to look me in my eyes and tell me you'll never break my heart and you won't cheat on me. Cuz I don't wanna know Black. I wanna keep getting to know Malcolm. Black is a ho. Malcolm is the sweet guy with the tough exterior who deep down inside wants to be loved. That's who I'd like to get to know."

Malcolm exhaled. *Damn, he just got me together.* Malcolm stood up and stood directly in front of Malik. He raised his right hand and Malik stood to look at him.

"I, Malcolm Brown, promise you that if you give me a chance, I won't break your heart or cheat on you. And I'mma hold you down."

Malik smiled. "Come here."

Malcolm stepped close and Malik wrapped his arms around him and kissed him deeply.

"Was that a welcome kiss?"

"No, it was me kissing Black good bye. Now I wanna say hello to my new boyfriend, Malcolm." Malcolm kissed him deeply once more, glad he got what he wanted. But was he going to make good on his promise?

* * *

Unbeknownst to his friends, Shawn struggled every day to get through his breakup with Jamon. But it seemed like nothing would give. Until one day after class, Taneisha and Terrell showed up in his classroom, begging for him to tutor them in college essay writing. It was just the distraction he needed. He threw himself into tutoring Taneisha and Terrell and teaching them how to correctly write college essays and papers using proper formatting and language formats. Taneisha's hood chick demeanor and Terrell's constant jokes served as constant laughter whenever the two of them were around. And it was great for Shawn because it gave him something work-related to do to get his mind off of Jamon. Jamon, on the other hand, refused to believe Shawn had really broken up with him and constantly text messaged and called him daily, which made it even harder for Shawn to shake himself loose. But he was far too emotional to forgive him so quickly. Sometimes he wondered if he ever would.

* * *

Damon put off visiting his father as long as he could but his mother broke down in tears and begged him to please come to the hospital. So he called Shawn and said he was ready to go. Shawn pulled up outside of Damon's house and they drove to St. Barnabas Hospital in Livingston, New Jersey. Shawn pulled into an empty parking space but made no move to get out the car. In Damon's head, a full replay of what happened the day his father said he never wanted to see him again played out like a movie. His insides trembled. He had never been so nervous in his life.

Shawn put his hand on his shoulder. "We can sit here all day, man. But I know you didn't come all this way for that."

Damon nodded. "You're right. But I'm so scared, man. What if he doesn't wanna see me?"

"You'll never know until you try." Damon took a deep breath and closed his eyes.

"We gotta go in there. I'll be with you."

Damon opened his door and got out. Shawn walked with him inside the hospital to the front desk.

"Hi, we're here for Cecil White," Damon said to the woman seated at the front desk.

She directed them to his room and gave them passes. Damon got a nauseous feeling as they stepped onto the elevator. As they got off the elevator, Damon felt like his feet were in blocks of cement. His heartbeat accelerated and beads of sweat covered the top of his head. He was breathing hard like he was running a marathon. Shawn noticed Damon's panicked state.

"Sit down." Damon sat and tried to collect himself. He felt like he was having a panic attack. "Breathe. Don't try and fight it, just breathe." Damon did his best to do that and took a few minutes to get himself together.

"I'm ready." They got back up and walked down the hall to the room his father was in. He saw his mother before anything else. She jumped up and ran to him.

"Damon! I'm so glad you came!" she exclaimed. She immediately burst into tears of joy as she hugged him tight.

"Hey, Ma."

She moved over to give Shawn a hug too. "How are you, Shawn? It's been a long time."

"It's nice to see you, Mrs. White."

Damon's mother took him by the hand and led him over to his father's bed. He had really put on some weight since Damon last saw him. He was always a big guy but now he was fat.

"Cecil, wake up. Cecil, honey, wake up." His eyes opened and he looked at her. "Look who is here."

Mr. White turned and saw his son. "Damon?"

"Hey Dad."

He immediately turned and frowned at his wife. "Lauren, I wish you would have told me about this."

"He needed to know."

"And so did I."

"Well, he's here now. And I think it's time you settle this. You said you miss him. Now here he is."

"Lauren!"

"Cecil, I'm tired of this. And you should be too. It's been six years. It's time you talk to your son once and for all. All of this stubborn behavior is why you're sick now. Come Shawn, let's go to the vending machine." She grabbed his arm and they left the room.

Damon turned to his father and put his thumbs in his pockets the same way he did whenever he got in trouble as a child. Mr. White turned the opposite direction and said nothing.

"So Dad, what happened?"

"I had a heart attack."

"I know that. But why? What happened?"

"Doctor said my pressure was too high. I haven't been watching what I eat. Not getting enough exercise. And I let things stress me out."

"You ever try meditation?"

"No."

"A lot of times that does the trick for me."

"How do you, uh..." He finally turned to face his son. "How do you meditate?"

"Well, it's really simple. You sit in a comfortable position, close your eyes, and focus on inhaling and exhaling. And you relinquish control of your thoughts. Just let them run wild. Whatever you're really thinking about or whatever is bothering you will pop up and just let it play. No matter what the visions are, you just let them play out and as long as you breathe deeply, you will calm down and gain clarity. I find myself sometimes locking myself in my office when I'm working to do that."

"And it works, huh?"

"It does."

"How is work going? Judging by that cashmere jacket and those nice shoes you're wearing, it looks like it's treating you well."

"It's going good. Thanks for asking."

"So how is big city life?"

"It's good. I love it."

"Your mother showed me pictures of your house. It looks like something straight out of a magazine. "

"I'd love for you to come visit some time. You and mom can come spend the night and I'll give you the whole Harlem experience."

"You want *me* to visit?"

"If you'd like to."

A long silence stretched between them. Damon realized he was holding his breath while he awaited his father's response. He released the pent up breath in small bouts until he'd emptied his lungs. His father still hadn't responded to his offer.

"I would like that sometime," Mr. White finally said and smiled.

Slowly but surely they began to reconnect over the course of the next few hours. By the day's end they had shared some laughs and had many wonderful memories to reminisce about.

\* \* \*

For a while, Charles remained true to his promise to Kevin. The abuse stopped. Charles still had his moments when his temper would get ugly, but he managed to keep his hands to himself. Kevin still had some reserves about him, but Charles wooed him in. He was sweet, loving, kind, and gentle, so thoughtful and attentive to Kevin's needs. And the sex was bananas. Charles lavished him with expensive gifts. He gave him diamond earrings, a diamond Cartier watch, bought him new furniture for his apartment, and would give him wads of cash at a time. Somehow, Kevin convinced himself that Charles had changed and had become his Prince Charming. Things couldn't possibly get any better. That is, until Charles hit him so hard that he cracked two of his ribs the day Charles wanted to hang out and Kevin had to work late. When Malcolm, Shawn, and Damon showed up at the hospital, they wanted to know what had happened. Charles explained that Kevin had fallen down a flight of steps. His story was actually quite convincing. It was Shawn and Damon's first time meeting Charles. Malcolm still thought he was a shady character so when Charles reached for a handshake, he just gave him a head nod. Malcolm sent a text to Shawn and Damon.

Malcolm: Something seems off about this muthafucka doesn't it? Look at his eyes.

Shawn: He does look a little special. But I'm glad he at least brought him here.

Damon: Yeah that says a lot.

Malcolm didn't tell Shawn and Damon about those text messages so they were clueless as to why Malcolm had concrete proof as to why he thought Charles was "special." But the thought of Charles doing something to Kevin hadn't crossed any of their minds, not even Malcolm's. And Kevin kept his mouth shut and once again found a way to blame himself for the reason why Charles had hit him.

A few days later, Kevin returned to work. His ribs were tender and he moved a little slower than normal; the doctor had ordered him to stay home for about two weeks, but he didn't want to fall too behind in his work. Besides, it took his mind off of his personal problems. He was torn. When things with Charles were good, they were great. He couldn't be happier. But when times were bad, they were awful. At the moment, Charles was an angel. He cared for Kevin as though he were Kevin's personal nurse and Kevin was his patient. His assistance came in handy, but Kevin needed to take a break from him. He needed some time to clear his head. But it wasn't easy. Charles suffocated him with phone calls and text messages, always showing up at his office or at his apartment.

To get a break from Charles, Kevin asked Damon if he could stay with him for a couple of days because they'd "repainted his walls in his apartment and the fumes were making him nauseous." He set his phone up so that all of Charles' calls would immediately go to voicemail. He ignored all of Charles' texts and left instructions with Marcia to tell Professor Wright he was busy and not taking visitors if he happened to come by.

But then one day, Charles walked into the financial aid department at the same time that Kevin was walking into his office.

"Can I talk to you?" Charles asked.

"I have an appointment in five minutes so it will have to be quick."

Kevin looked at Marcia. "I'm sorry," she mouthed.

"It's okay," he mouthed back.

Charles sat in the chair in front of Kevin's desk. He looked sad. "Why are you avoiding me?"

He opened up his calendar and began going through everything with a pen as if he were updating things.

"Kevin." Kevin looked up at him and saw the tears rolling down Charles' face. "I'm an asshole, okay? I'm sorry I hurt you. You're right for not wanting to be bothered. I'm a coward. I had no right to put my hands on you. But these past few days have been killing me. I've been thinking suicidal thoughts and everything."

More tears plummeted from his face and plopped on Kevin's desk. Kevin got up to close the door. Charles grabbed him around the waist and pulled him close, soaking the front of his shirt with his tears.

"Charles, you're hurting me."

Realizing that Kevin was still sore, Charles loosened his hold on him but kept his arms wrapped around him.

"Please don't leave me. I promise I'll get help. I'll never hit you again. Never. I swear on my life."

"How many times have I heard that?"

"You've gotta admit, I was doing good for a while. I thought I was rehabilitated, so I stopped going to the anger management classes. I'll go back. I'll start taking them again. I swear I will. I can't lose you."

Kevin put his hand on Charles' back. "It's okay. Just get a hold of yourself."

Charles sniffed and wiped his face.

"Can you just give me some time, please?" Kevin asked.

"How much time do you need?"

"I don't know. This is a lot for me to deal with."

"Do your friends know?"

"No."

"Thanks for not telling them." Charles touched his face. "Come over today when you get off."

Kevin shook his head. "I'm not coming over. And I have a meeting in less than a minute, so you need to go. When I'm ready to talk about this, I will call you."

"Okay. I love you."

"I love you too."

Charles nodded his head and walked out. Kevin exhaled out loud and looked out his office window, staring at the cloud-filled blue sky.

"God. How in the world did I get into this mess?"

Marcia knocked on his door.

"Kevin is everything okay?"

"Yes. I'm just waiting for my 11:30 to show up."

"Okay. You know I once dealt with the same thing." Kevin looked at her quizzically.

"You dealt with what?"

"Never mind. I shouldn't be in your business."

Kevin's eyes popped and he started to shake his head. She quickly closed the door and walked close to his desk, looking compassionately at him.

"You mean you...you know?"

She nodded. Kevin's eyes welled up with tears.

"I, um...overheard your conversation. I wasn't eavesdropping; I just wanted to tell you that your 11:30 appointment is running late."

"Does anyone else know?"

"No. No one. And they won't."

"Thank you."

"I'll let you know when your appointment gets here."

"Mar."

"Yes?"

"How did you make it stop?"

"I took a self-defense class. And the last time my ex-boyfriend hit me, he got a very rude awakening. And I never saw him again."

"Did your family ever find out?"

"Well, you know my family is Jamaican. They would have killed him. I didn't exactly want that to happen, but he knew to leave me alone."

"My family doesn't know."

"They'll find out if you continue to let it happen. But when you get tired, it'll stop. But you have to make it stop. I still have my teacher's number if you need it."

"Thanks. I think I'll be okay though."

# 26

## I'M DOIN' ME

### THE FIRST DAY OF SUMMER

Shawn walked into his apartment after completing his final day of work. Graduation was over with, his classroom was all cleaned out, boards were covered, and he had an email inbox full of messages from now former students. Summer was officially here. He cranked up the central AC to combat the one hundred plus degree weather outside.

He took off his shades and swung his imaginary long hair. He went into his bedroom to find an outfit to wear for his date that evening. Robert, a guy whom he went to grad school with who liked him back when they were in school, had asked him out and he said yes. Now that Jamon was a thing of the past, he could date as he wanted. He was tired of being sad in the house about the breakup. Robert had invited him to a DL party that Robert's friend was promoting at a club in the Bronx. Shawn figured why not? Shawn was even gonna let Robert hit it if the feeling was right. He just wanted to be held. He had a bite to eat, checked and returned some of his emails, and proceeded to shower. After getting out of the shower he turned on "I'm Doin' Me" by Fantasia and turned it all the way up and sang along. This was a "getting over Jamon" song and tonight he truly was gonna just do him. In this moment and with this song playing he stripped away the layers of Mr. Jones, the studious English teacher, and morphed into sexy Shawn on the prowl looking to embrace his newly single lifestyle. He stood in the full length mirror naked and admired what he saw looking back at him. He flexed his arm muscles and liked the way they contracted. Then he flexed his six pack and his chest muscles, making them jump. As Fantasia sang about her independence, he danced around his bedroom naked. He felt empowered.

"Yup, daddy still got it. Being Jamon's boyfriend didn't make me lose my sexy. Shout out to the gym."

He applied his deodorant and cologne and put on a pair of ripped jeans that showed off his apple bottom he'd developed and a fitted tee so he could flaunt his arms and chest. He kept all the expensive jewelry Jamon had bought him over the years and put some of it on. He put on a pair of diamond stud earrings, a Concord watch, and a chain around his neck.

As he decided which shoes to put on, "Bittersweet" by Fantasia came blasting through the speakers. He froze as the song played because it embodied all the hurt related to his breakup and the bittersweet memories. Every lyric was true to his life as of late. He still had a framed picture of Jamon on the dresser that immediately caught his eye. Everything she said from the box of things Jamon gave him, wondering if it was a big mistake, and how it was all so bittersweet was all true. By the time she reached the chorus, Shawn realized he was crying. It was eerie the way this song described all of his feelings.

"Can't listen to that again," Shawn said aloud as the song faded out.

Once he was fully dressed with his fresh pair of blue and white sneakers, he cocked his fitted cap to the side and looked at himself in the mirror. He felt so sexy. He did a few spins to look at his outfit in the mirror and smiled.

"Jamon ain't got no idea what he is missing. And that punk ass bitch Darnell can suck my dick. I'll beat his ass down again."

Robert came to pick him up and they went to the party in the Bronx. It was jumping. The classic club anthem "Follow Me" was playing and all of the homo thugs in New York were up in there. And they were giving Shawn some serious eyes; he loved the attention. But Robert made up for lost time flirting with him on the dance floor and buying him drinks. Shawn was nice and tipsy mid-way through the party. And Robert loved how the liquor was loosening Shawn up. They partied hard and took off their shirts as they rocked out. Robert was all over him and didn't even want to dance with anyone else. He wanted Shawn all to himself and he had him. All was good until Shawn saw Jamon walk in with a group of his friends.

"Oh fuck," Shawn said.

"What's the matter?" Robert asked.

"There's Jamon."

Robert looked closer and saw Jamon coming into the entrance. "You gonna speak to him?"

"Nah, if I see him, I see him. If not, whatever." Shawn knew he was lying. He did want Jamon to see him. He wanted Jamon to see how good he looked and how he was still living in spite of their breakup. Especially if Darnell was with him. He couldn't clearly see the faces of the guys Jamon was with, but he was ready for whatever if Darnell wanted to get it in again.

Jamon and his boys posted up against the wall just checking out the scene. Shawn continued to dance with Robert to the music. Shawn and Robert worked up a sweat and headed to the bar. Jamon was in the midst of laughing and then Shawn caught his eye. To see Shawn walking around a crowded party shirtless sent a burning sensation through his body. Shawn knew Jamon could see him but was acting like he didn't see him. Every time he looked away, he could feel Jamon's eyes burning a hole through him. He even flexed his chest muscles and made them jump while Jamon stared at him while waiting for his drink. He and Robert clinked glasses, drank their drinks and went back to the dance floor. Shawn stole a few glances at Jamon who was still staring at him. He put his shirt back on and went to the bathroom. Within seconds, Jamon followed him into the bathroom. As Shawn came out of the stall and went to wash his hands, Jamon was standing there looking at him.

"You not gon' speak?"

"Hi," Shawn said not making eye contact.

"Oh, that's how you gon' do it?"

Shawn looked him up and down. "What do you want me to say? I said hi."

"So you rolling up in here with this square-ass nigga Rob, huh?"

Shawn sucked his teeth. "At least he's not a liar. Or a cheater. And you know what else? He has a date tonight."

Jamon squinted his eyes. Shawn looked him up and down and added, "Since you can do whatever you want, so can I."

He returned to the dance floor where Robert had two drinks in his hand and gave one to Shawn. Shawn threw his head back in laughter, and Robert escorted him up to a higher level of the floor. All night long, they danced together to every hot song that came on. Shawn took off his shirt again and just turned up for the rest of the night. He was singing along to all the songs and danced with a few different guys, but Robert always came back and snatched him up. They left the club around 4am and went back to Shawn's place. Shawn was drunk, but he still wanted to fuck. They showered and headed straight for Shawn's bed. Robert was elated that he was finally getting to sex Shawn down.

"Damn your ass is juicy, baby. I've been wanting to fuck you ever since I first laid eyes on you," Robert said in his ear.

"Fuck me then, daddy. Fuck me good."

Robert took Shawn for a hair-raising screamtastic ride and it was exactly what he needed. It even made him forget about Jamon. Robert slept in Jamon's old spot and Shawn cozied up to him as they fell asleep.

Shawn woke up in the morning to an empty bed. His cell phone flashed, indicating he had a message. He read it.

Robert: Had a great time with u last night. Didn't wanna wake u cuz u looked so peaceful. Def need 2 get up again soon. Talk 2 u lata.

Shawn tried to get up but realized he was hung over; his head began to pound when he sat up. Unwilling to wrestle his way through a hangover, he fell back asleep and woke up slightly disoriented a few hours later.

"Jamon!" he called out. "Can you bring me a..."

Then he remembered Jamon was gone.

He sat up and his head was still pounding. Stumbling to the bathroom, he relieved his bladder and took the Excedrin out of the medicine cabinet. In the mirror, he stared at his reflection. He looked bad. Face ashy gray, eyes full of bloodshot veins, and dark circles forming under his eyes. He could still smell the alcohol on his breath. He made his way into the kitchen and grabbed a few slices of raisin bread and a bottle of water. Back in his room, he lay back across the bed and realized that after sleeping with another man and getting drunk, he still missed Jamon. He was ashamed but too hung over to agonize over it, so he turned on the TV, flipped to the channel showing a marathon of *The Game* and tried his best to sober up.

# 27

## COULD THIS BE LOVE?

Malcolm was falling deeper and deeper into a spell of Malik every day. They would play one on one basketball, have deep conversations about their inner most desires, and started going to see different movies on Saturday mornings. Malik confessed to Malcolm that he intentionally invited his friends to their first date to see if Malcolm was really into him. He said he could always tell Malcolm was bothered by that, but he had to test Malcolm's intentions. So once he opened up to him, he promised their dates would just be the two of them.

A very cultured guy, Malik was a stark contrast to Malcolm's round-the-way hood mentality. But Malik opened him up. One date night, Malcolm showed up at Malik's place giddy with excitement because Malik had promised him over the phone that they were going to "get it in" tonight. However, when Malcolm showed up at his doorstep with a pocket full of lube, he found out that the only thing they were "getting in" were books. Malik wanted him to read books with him; certain that this was another of Malik's tests, Malcolm decided to go with the flow. And after that night, thanks to Malik's influence, Malcolm found himself avidly reading books like "Afrocentricity" by Molefi Kete Asante and "The Miseducation of the Negro" by Carter G. Woodson. And Malcolm was really taken by "The Autobiography of Malcolm X." He never realized how much he had in common with Malcolm X and really liked what he was learning.

Slowly, Malcolm started to upgrade his mentality and become more conscientious of numerous things. For one, he stopped sagging his pants and finally stopped dropping so many N-words. It all came to an exciting head when Malik came to pick him up without telling him where they were going.

"We're gonna *really* get it in tonight," he said with a smile in his voice.

"What exactly do you mean by get in?" Malcolm asked, recalling the books. Malik's voice took on a naughty tone that instantly made Malcolm get hard. "I mean I want you to get in. All the way in."

That night, Malcolm spent the night with Malik for the first time. They made love like Malcolm had never experienced. He had never kissed anyone he was in love with in a fit of ecstasy. While Malik introduced Malcolm to the art of lovemaking, he learned Malcolm's reputation was very well deserved. Malcolm was a beast in the bedroom. And for the first time it felt great for Malcolm to lay there and cuddle with the man he loved after making love. Nothing ever felt better.

The next day, Malcolm and Mama Nzingha had their monthly appointment of eating crabs and drinking cold Heinekens.

"So Mama, I saw Mr. Henry checking you out this morning when we were coming in from Fairway."

"Was he?"

"Yeah. I think he likes you. He's always checking you out."

"That's cute. He's a nice guy."

"You should go out with him."

"Oh, here you go. Go out with him where?"

"I'ono. Go see a movie."

"I don't think he's my type."

"Yeah? What's your type?"

"Definitely more swag than Henry. Besides, I knew his wife before she died. It would feel weird."

"I bet I know what your type is."

"You think so?"

"Yup. A man by the name of Randy who works at the Board of Ed as a chief custodian."

Mama Nzingha gasped. "How did you know about that?"

"Cuz he called today when you were in the bathroom. You shoulda heard him tripping over his words trying to make it seem like he was calling you for some business."

"But how did you know he was..."

"Cuz his number was on the caller ID like five times. Why didn't you tell me you had a man?"

"Because for a while, I wasn't sure what we were doing."

"How long has it been?"

"About six months."

"You've been seeing him for six months?"

"Yeah. And I've known him for about fifteen years now. But you know, at that time I was still married to your father." Malcolm nodded. "And I still haven't told him my son is gay."

"Think it'll make a difference? He ain't dating me."

"I know. But if he has a problem with it, you know he's a thing of the past."

"He ain't gotta like it. As long as you're happy with him. He ain't gotta worry about me."

"That's very mature of you. But I don't know how I could be with a man who doesn't love my son. Even though you're an adult now."

"We don't know that he won't. You know I don't care if you tell him, but I'm more concerned with how he treats you."

"He treats me well. He really does."

"Invite him over to dinner. I wanna meet him."

"Do you?"

"Yup."

"I'll invite him if you invite Malik." Malcolm's eyes popped.

"Oh word?"

"Word."

"Deal. You know the boys are gonna wanna come too."

"Invite them too. May ease the tension."

"Yup, and if he is a big old homophobe, we'll be real gay in front of him."

"Lawd, have mercy."

# 28

## THE BOYZ

Damon called Shawn, who conference called Malcolm, who then called Kevin on his three-way. Rain pounded the ground outside and each of them were lying cozy in their beds on the phone with each other. It was an unseasonably cool 65 degrees outside during this monsoon summer rainstorm.

"Everyone here?" Damon asked.

"Yeah," the remaining three all said in unison.

"The Mac man is here. Kick it! See y'all gotta understand. I ain't scared of you muthafuckas!" Malcolm said imitating Bernie Mac. They laughed at his spot-on imitation.

"*Poetic Justice* is on HBO two," Damon said.

"Oh that's my shit!" Malcolm said. "What part is it on?"

"Where she meets Lucky in the salon."

They each tuned in and caught it, and everyone got quiet as they watched the scene.

"Are you all in love? What would you know about love? And I know das right!" Malcolm said, imitating Maya Angelou's scene in the movie.

"Malcolm, you need to make a You Tube video of your celebrity impressions. You can make a lot of money doing that."

"Fuck outta here with that. I'm just fooling around."

"I gotta tell y'all something," Damon said.

"Wassup?" Malcolm asked.

"I went out on a couple of dates."

"What's a couple of dates?" Shawn asked.

"Three."

"And you just now telling us?" Kevin asked.

"I had to let them happen first," Damon replied.

"We should kill you. Were any of them good?"

"Men are crazy. This is why I'm single!" Damon yelled.

"What the hell happened?"

"Okay, so I met these guys online. The first one was Rodney. We had a few phone conversations and I thought he was cool. He asked me out to B. Smith's and I agreed. We decided to meet there and so I thought that was okay. Well, I get there and he's not there. So I call twice and he finally hits me back saying he was running a little late and if I could go inside and get a table. He said he would pay for our dinner himself. I go in and forty-five minutes later, he came in. I was hungry, so I'd already ordered by then."

"What did he have to say for himself?"

"First of all, homeboy didn't look shit like his pictures. In his pictures, he was slim. In person, I felt like Ruben Studdard came and sat at my table. Just big, fat, greasy, and nasty for no damn reason."

"You got something against fat guys? I think Ruben is cute."

"No, but I got a problem with liars. Don't have me thinking you're slim when your ass needs to be on a diet and doing Insanity."

"Das cold, D."

"Why? I ain't got nothing against big guys but if you're big, then say you're big. You know I had to ask him about that shit."

"You didn't!"

"Why didn't I? Honey, I needed to know if he was still in high school when those pictures were taken."

"What did he say?"

"He said they were a year old. But he gained weight cuz he had been sick. It would be his last night eating out because he was about to do the master cleanse."

"Was he really that big?"

"In his pictures, his stomach was completely flat. In person, he had two chins, a beer gut, and thunder thighs. There was no way in hell those pictures were only a year old. The only sickness I could tell he had was full of shit disease. His fat ass gon' order a salad like he eats those on the regular. He claimed he needed a ride back up to the Bronx so I took him. Then we pull up to the projects he lives in, but before he could invite me in, he had to make sure his mother was asleep."

"Oh, hell no."

"Hey, I live with my mother," Malcolm reminded him.

"You're also not thirty-six years old, bragging about having a master's degree making six figures. I don't know why these girls need to lie."

"Touché," Malcolm said.

"Talking about, 'Oh, I really wanted some head.' I said, 'If you don't get your humpty dumpty fat ass out of my car, we gon' have some problems.'"

"That's crazy."

"So then I went out with Fernando. His mom is Filipino and his dad is Puerto Rican. He's from Brooklyn but he wanted to come uptown to Harlem. Now he was fine as hell. But he has a pet issue."

"Excuse me?"

"So get this. Homeboy tells me that his cat isn't feeling too well. I asked if he wanted to reschedule. He said no he'd be fine. Okay but why did he brought the cat *on* the fucking date? And had the audacity, the unmitigated fucking gall to ask me if I could take him by the vet."

"No, he didn't!"

"I swear to God he did."

"You lyin' on that boy."

"I wish I was. He's all petting the cat like, 'It's gonna be okay; Daddy is gonna take care of you.'"

"So you took him to the vet?"

"I did. And I left his ass there too when I said I needed to find a place to park. He musta called me ten times afterwards. Had I known he was bringing a pet, I woulda took Lucky."

"Did you get it in with any of these dudes?"

"I did with the last one, but that was a disaster too."

"How come?"

"Okay, so this last dude named Jay wanted me to come over."

"Jay what? Why is it that every dude whose name starts with the letter J wants to be called Jay?"

"His name was Jared," Damon said.

"Where does he live?" Malcolm asked.

"Jamaica."

"What does he look like?" Malcolm asked.

"Caramel complexion, kinda thick, nice smile. Got a tattoo of the letter J on his neck."

"I know that dude," Malcolm said.

"Oh, God no. Please don't tell me y'all fucked."

"We did."

"Did you top him?"

"Of course I did."

"Well, I bet what happened to me didn't happen to you."

"Curiosity is killing me," Kevin said. "What happened?"

Damon exhaled. "I topped him. But when I pulled out, the condom was painted brown."

"*What the fuck?*" Kevin exclaimed.

"Ewwwwwww," Shawn said.

"That's some nasty ass shit. But that's what happens when you go digging for oil and you don't fleet before you meet," Malcolm said.

"Did that happen to you?" Damon asked.

"Nah. I mighta punched him in the face if that shit happened. I made him douche first."

"Well, I pulled off the condom and he was so embarrassed. I said good night and left. And I damn near scrubbed the skin off of my dick when I got home."

"Damn, Dame. Fat bitches, cats on dates, and niggas with swamp ass? Guess who's not having the best week ever."

"Tell me about it! But I'm sick of that. And now that I done kicked Kenny to the curb, I'm shit out of luck."

"You mean you don't have *any* jump-offs on reserve?"

"Nope."

"*Girl!*" Shawn and Kevin said in unison.

"You gotta do something about that. I don't know how you deal with not getting none on the regular."

When Damon paused for a second, Shawn jumped in and admitted, "I had sex with Robert the other night. Y'all remember him?"

Damon gasped. "Did you really now?"

"Yes I did. We went out to a DL party in Bronx. It Guess who showed up."

Shawn smacked his lips.

"Jamon?"

"Sure did. And I looked good as hell. I mean I was *snatched* honey! Beating the boys off of the whole time. He watched me and Rob dance all night."

"He ain't say nothing to you?" Malcolm asked.

"We had a little run-in in the bathroom. He was *not* happy to see me there with Rob. And I gave him the *only* shade."

"I wish I coulda seen Jamon's face. He probably looked swole as hell."

"That's an understatement. He didn't even stay the whole time. And me and Rob went home, and he fucked me like there was no tomorrow."

"Well good bye Jamon and hello Robert!"

"Speaking of differences," Damon said, "how are you holding up, Kevin?"

"What do you mean how am I holding up?'"

"I thought you broke up with Charles after he sent Malcolm that crazy ass text."

Kevin's heart skipped a beat. "Malcolm, *I'm gonna kill you.*"

"Hey, man, it slipped."

"Yeah, I bet it did."

"What's the tea with that situation?" Shawn asked, sounding a bit impatient.

"It was nothing. Charles just had a little moment of jealousy when he met Malcolm. I was gonna break things off, but I couldn't, not after he apologized and got me this big catered dinner with a mini orchestra to show how sorry he was. But we aren't really speaking at the moment."

"Hold up. Back up. Mini-orchestra? Dinner? Where?"

"At his place. It was quite impressive."

"So if that was so great then why aren't you speaking to him?"

"And I damn sure ain't get no apology," Malcolm said.

"We just don't see eye to eye on everything. And I just needed a break. I was starting to feel a little smothered by him."

"You gonna get back with him?"

"I mean, yeah. I didn't exactly break up with him. I'm just taking a moment to breathe."

"I don't like that muthafucka," Malcolm said.

"Who could blame you?" Kevin said before catching himself.

An awkward silence stretched between the four. Malcolm sensed that Kevin was very uncomfortable talking about this subject and he felt guilty for putting his boy on blast anyway. Changing the flow of the conversation, he said, "Guess what, guys?"

"What?" they asked in unison.

"I'm introducing Malik to my moms next Sunday. And y'all are invited too."

"Oh shit now!"

"You're introducing him to Mama already?"

"Get this. She got a man for me to meet too."

"You're lying!"

"Oh my God, look at the both of y'all dating. And keeping secrets at that!"

"Does your mother's boyfriend know that you're bringing a man to meet your mom?"

"She's gonna tell him. And then he'll meet my queeny bitch ass friends."

"Who the fuck you calling a queen?" Shawn shrieked in a high voice.

"And I know you ain't calling me no bitch!" Kevin said in a high voice like Shawn's.

"And if I'm a bitch, yo mama's a bitch. Bitch!" Damon said.

"Save that black woman shit. You bleed once a month just like the rest of the hoes," Malcolm said, quoting Tupac in *Poetic Justice.*

"You want us to bring anything?" Damon asked.

"Just yourselves and leave the fag shit at home."

"You tried that."

"What time Sunday?"

"About 5:00."

"It's a bet. It's about to be real interesting."

They switched the topic to their upcoming trip to Miami. As they each relaxed in their beds while the rain poured outside their windows, they all sounded excited about what the future might hold.

# 29

## SNAPPED

Shawn came in the house from a workout with Damon and hopped right into the shower. He put on a pair of boxers and lay across his bed watching episodes of *Martin* on TV. He was cracking up and recalled how he and Jamon would watch episodes of this show together and just laugh. Thinking about him must have made Jamon text him because Shawn's eye caught the flashing light on his phone letting him know he had a message. He picked up his phone and saw it was a text from Jamon.

Jamon: Can I come back home? I miss u.

Shawn: You don't live here anymore.

Jamon: Wat u mean by dat?

Shawn: What do you think?

Jamon: U already got rid of my clothes. Now u kickin me out?

Shawn: You'll be alright. You've got people and your mailbox key will still allow you to get your royalty checks.

Jamon: Das foul. U gon break up wit me thru text?

Shawn paused but then called him.

"Yeah?" Jamon answered.

"It's over."

"Just like that?"

"Don't act like this is sudden."

He swallowed hard and his heartbeat increased but he tried to play it cool.

"After everything we been through?"

"Conversation is over. Text me if you have any more questions," Shawn said before hanging up.

Jamon called him back three times and Shawn sent him to voicemail each time.

"God, I miss him." He closed his eyes and saw a series of flashbacks as if he were watching a movie of Jamon and him rolling on a reel. He remembered watching him sing live on stage, kissing him, making love to him, holding him while they would watch TV, his smile, his cologne, and how affectionate Jamon was. The sound of the door slamming woke him up out of his flashback. He jumped up and went into the living room and saw Jamon. His heart skipped a beat when they made eye contact.

"I coulda been a killer and you just walking out here in your boxers. Looking all good and shit," Jamon said trying to move in for a kiss. Shawn moved back. "Why you acting like that? You still mad?"

"What part of 'over' don't you get?"

"I let you black my eye and you threw my clothes in the river. Ain't we even?" Jamon asked reaching out, touching him.

"Don't touch me."

"Come on, how long are you gon' punish me? I know you still love me. I love you too."

"Then why are you fucking other dudes? Why do you keep shitting on me? I'm tired of your shit!"

"I know, baby, and I'm sorry. I fucked up. I know I did but you gotta believe me. I really am sorry."

"You think your weak ass apology is enough? Get the fuck out of my house!"

Jamon pulled him close and Shawn pushed him away. "I told you not to touch me."

"You so cute when you get mad." Jamon smacked Shawn's ass and squeezed it.

Before he realized what he was doing, Shawn spun around and punched Jamon in the face. Shocked registered in his features as he grabbed his aching face. Shawn glared at him; he stared back at Shawn, and then with lightning quickness, his fist jabbed out and caught Shawn in the eye. Shawn fell to the floor.

"Gotdammit I'm tired of you fucking hitting me! What the fuck is wrong with you?! Shit!" Jamon held his jaw. Shawn crawled into a fetal position and held his eye. Immediately, Jamon felt guilty and got on his knees to help Shawn up.

"I'm sorry, baby. Get up. I'm sorry. You know I ain't mean to hit you."

Shawn snatched away from him and got up. He rammed his body into Jamon's and started swinging on him wildly, making Jamon's hat fly off of his head. Shawn landed a few hits but Jamon wrapped his arms around him and restrained him.

"Calm down!"

"Get off me!" Shawn said with his teeth clenched, trying to kick himself loose.

Jamon wrestled him to the floor. "Calm your ass down!"

Shawn continued to try to break free.

"Get off me!"

"Calm down!"

"Get off of me!" Shawn said and angry tears blurred his vision.

"Are you calm?"

"Get off me," Shawn said softly trying to stop his tears.

Jamon let him up and Shawn ran into the bathroom. Jamon picked up his hat and adjusted his clothes. Shawn returned to the living room enraged after looking at his eye in the mirror.

"Get the fuck out."

"Let me at least get you some ice for your eye."

"Get out, Jamon."

"Shawn—"

"*Get the fuck out of my house!*" Shawn screamed at the top of his lungs.

"Just let me—"

"Don't touch me! Don't *fucking* touch me!"

Shawn's face turned bright red and his eyes filled with rage.

"Why you screaming?"

"*Get the fuck out before I kill you!*" Shawn screamed at him as loudly as he could with his voice jumping to a high octave that startled Jamon. His voice ricocheted throughout the house and made the pictures on the wall shake. He had never seen Shawn so furious. He looked and sounded possessed, as if a demon had taken over him. In that moment, Shawn unplugged the lamp and threw it at Jamon's head. Jamon ducked and the lamp shattered against the wall.

"Get out!" He picked up a pair of his dress shoes and flung them at him.

"What the fuck?"

Shawn flung the remote at him and it cracked against his shoulder. "Ahh!" Jamon cried out, grabbing his shoulder.

"Get out!"

Shawn went into the kitchen and grabbed a big butcher knife and charged into the living room with it. "I'mma tell your bitch ass to get the fuck out of my house one more time!"

Jamon ran for the door when he saw the knife.

"Get the fuck outta my house, you muthafucka," Shawn screamed at him in the same high-possessed voice. He pulled the knife back, then released it. It soared toward Jamon's head and had he moved a second later, it would've went through his eye. Instead, it implanted into the closet door behind him.

Scared for his life, Jamon threw open the front door and fled. Shawn chased him out of the apartment and down the hall to the staircase. "And stay the fuck out! I fucking hate your ass! I hate you!"

Jamon quickly disappeared from sight down the steps, and Shawn walked back to his apartment. Neighbors were peeking out of the doors.

"Go the fuck back in your house and mind your business!" Shawn snapped at them. He went back in the house and slammed the door. His chest was burning from the anger that rolled through his body. He poured himself a big glass of wine and sat on the living room couch in silence and in the dark for over an hour crying in while Vivian Green sang "No Sittin' by the Phone" on repeat. He kept replaying the whole exchange in his head over and over. His cell phone vibrated. It was Damon sending a text.

Damon: Hey you want some company? I'm a block away.

Shawn: Sure.

Within minutes, Damon was knocking. He took one look at Shawn's face and said, "What happened to your eye?"

"Jamon came by. It got ugly. It got really ugly."

"Oh my God, did he hit you?"

"I hit him first. It was bad. And now I feel..." Shawn burst into tears and cried in Damon's arms as he tried to comfort him.

"It's okay; it's okay. Just let it out." Damon rubbed Shawn's back and hugged him.

"Now, Damon, be honest," Malcolm said between laughs, "didn't Kevin lose that bet that time when—" Malcolm's words faded and his smile became a frown as he walked into the house and looked over at Damon and Shawn. "Yo, what's up? Why Shawn crying?"

"What's going on?" Kevin asked as he entered the house behind Malcolm, his eyes searching Shawn's face.

Damon motioned for them to come in, and they walked into the living room and sat next to Shawn. Shawn laid his head on Damon's shoulder.

"What's going on?" Malcolm asked.

"Jamon came over and they got into it," Damon explained.

"Yeah, but why did that muthafucka hit you, though?"

"I hit him first. I told him not to touch me and he smacked me on my ass. So I snuffed him and he hit me back"

"Damn, Shawn. When did you turn into Mike Tyson?"

"I just lost it. I was out of control. I was throwing shit at him. I tried to kill him," he said, gesturing at the door. All four heads turned in the direction of the door and when they saw the huge butcher knife stuck deep in wooden closet the door, they gasped.

"Oh my God. You really did try to kill him," Kevin said, his eyes opened wide.

Malcolm walked over to the door, and it took quite a few hard yanks before the knife came free. "Damn, yo. You was trying to make that nigga leave in a body bag, huh? You really was going for blood."

"I told you I lost control."

Kevin looked like he had a lot on his mind as his eyes darted back and forth from the knife, to the ugly bruising around Shawn's eye that was gradually getting worse. "I'mma get you some ice," Kevin said as he disappeared into the kitchen.

"Thanks for coming over and everything, but I really need a minute. I'll call you guys later."

"What are you about to do?"

He held up the bottle of wine. "Nothing really. Just finish this off and do some serious thinking."

"Oh, no you don't. You're coming out with us." Damon took the glass from Shawn.

"I don't feel like going out."

"Too bad. You are not gonna sit up in here crying and wasting perfectly good wine over some dude who doesn't appreciate you. And Malcolm please turn off this depressing ass music."

"Hell yeah. Fuck that soft ass nigga," Malcolm said cutting off Vivian in mid-note.

Kevin returned with an ice pack for Shawn to put on his eye.

"You know we are not about to let you sit up in this house alone after what you just dealt with. Just cuz Jamon doesn't know what he's missing doesn't mean you will sit up in this house moping."

Malcolm pulled Shawn up. "Let's go out and have a good time. We gon' treat you so all you gotta do is get fly and come with us, aight?"

"But my eye—"

"Rock some shades. Now come on and get yourself ready cuz we gon' hit up Club Magic."

"I haven't washed clothes in weeks. I have nothing to wear."

"I'll find you something," Malcolm said escorting Shawn to the bathroom.

Damon looked over at Kevin. "You alright, Kevin?"

He was in a zone. He hadn't heard a word Damon said. Damon shook his shoulder, shaking him out of his thoughts. "What? Wassup?"

"You alright?"

"Yeah, I'm fine." He painted on a smile, but Damon had known him too long to believe that that smile was actually real.

# 30

## BOYZ NIGHT OUT

Kevin hurried out of the room because Damon was making him feel uncomfortable. He peeked at Shawn who was looking at himself in the bathroom mirror. He touched his eye and whispered softly, "I can't believe he hit me."

Those words hit home with Kevin. He had spoken the exact same phrase the first time Charles had hit him.

"You gonna be okay?" Kevin asked.

"Yeah, lemme get myself together," Shawn said closing the door and turning on the shower water.

Malcolm pulled out an outfit for Shawn to wear and started ironing it for him.

"Y'all know I never particularly cared for Jamon right?" Damon asked.

"I never liked that punk muthafucka either. I was glad when Shawn threw his shit in the water."

"He was kinda arrogant but I see why Shawn liked him. He is very handsome and once he started hitting the gym his body was pretty nice. But once them royalty checks started coming, he liked to lose his damn mind," Kevin said. "Something about money changes folks."

"Personally, I always thought Shawn was too good for him, but he was in love. Wasn't nothing nobody coulda said about that."

"Shawn is one of the coolest dudes I know man. Like when you got him in your corner, he is really down for you. That's one dude that will give you the shirt off of his back. He's a sweetheart, so to see Jamon play him makes me wanna fuck him up. I knew he wasn't shit from the jump."

"So if you two had such strong feelings about him, how come y'all never said anything?"

"I didn't wanna rain on his parade. He was so happy and so sprung."

"Yeah, I ain't want him to think I wasn't happy for him cuz I was, but I ain't wanna see him get done dirty either."

Malcolm finished ironing Shawn's clothes and laid them across the couch. Shawn got out of the shower and got dressed. Even though he didn't feel like going, it felt good to know his boys had his back and didn't want him to sit in the house and be sad. They got on the elevator and followed Damon back to his truck. There was barely any traffic going down so Damon floored it. They got down to Brooklyn and stood in line outside the club.

"What time does it start?"

"I think ten."

"They serve food here? I'm hungry as hell," Malcolm said rubbing his stomach.

"They do. Their wings are amazing," Kevin said. Malcolm turned and looked at a cute guy walking pass and smiled at him.

"Behave yourself, Black," Damon said.

"Why would I do that? We at the strip club. I'm goin' in!" Malcolm said watching the smiling guy walk by while licking his lips and giving the guy a nod.

"Watup, Black?" said a white guy with a fitted cap on passing by.

"What's good, man?" Malcolm replied giving him dap as he walked by.

"One of your victims?"

"Yeah. He's from down here. I can't remember his name for the life of me but we definitely fucked. In a bathroom at the mall too. Yeah, I remember that. He came quicker than anyone I ever fucked with."

"You crossing over to white guys?"

"I don't discriminate."

Shawn, Damon, and Kevin all shook their heads. The line began to move and they were escorted to a set of seats off to the right of the stage. They each ordered wings and their drinks were all extra strong. The lights went down and "Rock with You" by Janet Jackson came on and the curtain went up. The crowd went wild as a team of ten men stood on stage with shades and trench coats. They started grinding to the music and opened their coats to reveal their muscular bodies. With the precision of a Broadway cast of dancers, they moved in unison. For every song the DJ spun, the lights changed colors, from fuchsia pink to highlighter green. They slowly stripped down until they were all nude.

They made their way around the audience and waved their big dicks in everyone's faces.

"Damn, how are all their dicks so big? Everyone is ten plus inches," Shawn said to Kevin.

"I don't know, but I loves me a big old dick. He just ain't coming inside with all that," Damon said and Shawn hi-fived him. They watched the men as they made their way around to each table, dancing on all the club members.

Malcolm approached one of the strippers as he got close to their table. "Yo, my boy over there just got his heart broken by his dude. Hook him up," he whispered and slipped the stripper a $20 bill.

"Where is he?"

"Right there. His name is Shawn."

"You got it."

He was a sexy brown skinned man with chinky brown eyes and braids. Malcolm gave him a slap on the ass as he turned to walk away. He slapped Malcolm back on the ass and followed him back to the table. Within seconds, the stripper was grinding all over Shawn and he was blushing like he was a little boy living out a fantasy. Malcolm recorded Shawn with his phone and Damon snapped pictures with his. By the time the stripper finished the lap dance, Shawn's face was the same shade of a Red Delicious apple. He was laughing and his dick was visibly hard to anyone who looked at it. The stripper kissed his cheek and disappeared into the crowd. Shawn slid out of his chair and onto the floor.

Malcolm, Damon, and Kevin started laughing.

"I tink I love heeeee!" Shawn said in a faux Jamaican accent.

"You no love he, him a nasty strippuh, ya bumbaclatt!" Damon said in a real Jamaican accent.

"That just made my night." Shawn got back up into his seat, fanning his heated face.

They ordered a few more rounds of drinks and everyone got twisted except Damon who had to drive back home. Malcolm kept his promise and got fucked up more than everyone else. However, Shawn and Kevin weren't far behind. They all danced with the strippers and made it rain. Once the revue was over, the boys danced with each other and enjoyed the DJ playing the music. On the way back to the car, Malcolm vomited on the street.

"Drunk bitch," Shawn said stumbling to help him up.

"Fuck you. That just means I had a good ass time. So did you, frisking that stripper."

"Just as long as y'all get that shit out before y'all get in my car," Damon said continuing to walk.

"Aww, damn I gotta pee."

Shawn stood behind Damon's truck and went. Meanwhile Kevin threw up on the sidewalk too.

"Like I said, y'all messy bitches better get all your bodily fluids out before y'all get in my got-damn truck."

They all piled into the truck and were drunk and disorderly all the way back up to Harlem. Malcolm was loud, Shawn was silly, and Kevin laughed at everything he saw. Damon laughed at them too. Malcolm and Shawn were hilarious drunkards. The four of them had a fabulous night out on the town, and Shawn forgot all about his earlier run in with Jamon and that was exactly what his friends wanted. They had a ball and things were only about to get more interesting.

# 31

## GUESS WHO'S COMING TO DINNER

M alcolm lay stretched out across his bed still slightly hung over from the night before. He knew that part of his overdrinking had a lot to do with the fact that he was still nervous about his mom and friends meeting Malik. After all, this was his first relationship and although things were going good so far, he was still uncertain about how long Malik could keep his attention. Malcolm had grown accustomed to getting ass from a variety of men whenever he wanted. Even though Malik was very appealing at the moment, he wondered how long it would be before he began to want something new.

However, there was something about Malik that fascinated him. The way Malik made the most of life and maximized his opportunities. And how he was such a successful entrepreneur all at the age of 32 seemed like such a cool thing. Malcolm did his best not to stress over it but he knew himself and knew that even though he was no longer single, his wild oats had been spread out all over the five boroughs and he still had folks trying to get a piece of him. Was he destined to be a single man filling the fantasies of those who desired big strong black men to make love to them or was he destined to be a family man?

He had slept with so many men because they filled the void that his father left. Malik was filling that void now...but how long would it last?

While processing all of these thoughts, his phone rang. It was Malik. "Yo?"

"Yo, what's good? I'm about to leave the store now. I'm gonna go to my boy's crib in Harlem to change and shower. I brought my clothes with me to work, so I should be there in about an hour."

"Aight, das cool. I'll see you then."

"You okay?"

"Yeah, I'm good. A lil' hung over but I'm good. We took Shawn out last night and we all got drunk."

"I can't wait to meet them today. But let me get going. I'mma see you in an hour."

"Aight."

They hung up and Malcolm could smell the food coming from the kitchen. He got up and was glad the room wasn't spinning anymore, but he still had to walk slowly into the kitchen.

"Hey, Mama, you need some help?"

"I could have about an hour ago while you were sleeping, but I'm pretty much done with everything. I just gotta get in the tub and get dressed now."

"We got anything to drink?"

"Some water and some lemonade."

"Nah, I mean real drinks."

"There's some wine on the shelf."

"I'll be back. I'mma go to the liquor store."

"Well, if you're going then get me some Absolut. When you get back, if I'm still in the tub, start setting the stuff on the table in the dining room."

"Okay. Hey, Mama, did you tell Randy about me?"

"I did. His brother is gay. And he said it was hard to accept at first, but he loves him."

"See. No problems."

"Good for him right?"

"Better for you. I'll be back," Malcolm said slipping out the door.

On his way to the liquor store, he saw Marco, a cute Dominican guy he used to mess with.

"What's good, Black?"

"What up, Marco?" Malcolm responded giving him dap.

"How you been?"

"I'm chillin', man."

"Word on the street is you're off the market now. Is that true?"

"Rumors are rumors, man. Can't believe everything you hear."

"Everyone was hoping it wasn't true. Especially me."

"You crazy, man. Your number still the same?"

"Yup. Use it whenever."

"Aight man. Stay up."

Marco stood there and watched him walk away. Malcolm turned up the music in his headphones and walked to the liquor store. He tried to shake off what Marco had said to him but he couldn't. How did people know about that?

When he returned home, he showered after his mother got out of the tub. One thing the both of them could do was get fly when the time came. She put on a little makeup, a sexy long black tube top dress with black heels, and tied her locks into a ponytail. Malcolm put on a black button up with blue jeans and black hard bottom shoes. Malcolm helped her set up the food on a table in the dining room so everyone could serve themselves. There was a pan of fried chicken, a pan of BBQ chicken, a pan of macaroni and cheese, yellow rice, string beans, collard greens, cornbread, and a pan of turkey meatballs. The doorbell buzzed.

"That's probably Randy. I'll get it," she said.

Randy stood at the door dressed in a black suit holding a bouquet of flowers. She was a little nervous but greeted him with a smile.

"Hey, baby. Don't you look handsome?"

They kissed. "Hey, pretty lady."

"Malcolm!" she called out.

Malcolm walked into the room and Randy looked up at him.

"Wow, you're tall. It's nice to finally meet you, Malcolm," Randy said extending his hand.

"You too," Malcolm said shaking his hand.

Malcolm looked him up and down, feeling him out. "Any history of crazy in your family? Crazy ex-wives? Kids?"

Mama Nzingha smirked.

"No mental illnesses but everyone's got a little crazy in their family, right?" He laughed but Malcolm didn't laugh with him. "I've been married and divorced. My ex-wife is remarried with more kids now; we only have a daughter together. She's fifteen."

"I guess that's fair enough."

Malcolm put his arm around his mother. "This is my most precious jewel here. So if she approves of you, I'mma give you a shot."

"I appreciate that, brotha."

Malcolm's face got serious. "But this is my mama. She means everything to me, so it would be in your best interest to take care of her. Or I'mma have to take care of you, ya heard?"

"Yes sir."

"Is the interrogation over?" she asked trying to break the ice.

Malcolm didn't take his eyes off of Randy.

"Malcolm?"

He looked at his mother and smiled. He kissed her cheek and nodded his head. "Do your thing, man."

"Here, Malcolm. Put these flowers in some water for me." Malcolm took the flowers into the kitchen. In his absence, she said in a low voice, "He's only joking around."

"He must have a hell of a sense of humor."

She hugged and kissed him until the doorbell rang.

"I'll get that," Malcolm said from the kitchen.

"Come help me in the kitchen, hun," she said to Randy taking him by the hand.

Malcolm went to answer the door and there stood Malik in all of his sexiness. He had on a brown top and khakis with brown hard bottom shoes. His long locks were tied into a ponytail that hung down his back. He was holding a gift bag. His muscular frame filled his shirt and made Malcolm smile.

"Damn, you gotta be that sexy?" Malcolm asked.

Malik smirked. "Only for you."

Malik stepped inside and they kissed. "It smells good in here."

"Moms threw down. What's this?" Malcolm asked taking the bag.

"That's for you and your mom."

Malik peeked inside the bag and saw a Bvlgari Omnia Crystaline perfume gift set for her and a men's Bvlgari cologne gift set for him.

"Well, hello there," Mama Nzingha said as she entered the room with Randy behind her. "Are you the one who has my son reading all those wonderful books?"

"That would be me. It's nice to meet you, Ms. Brown."

"Oh, honey, call me Mama. All of his friends do."

He wrapped his arms around her and gave her a big bear hug.

"Well, you sure give great hugs. This is my boyfriend Randy."

"I'm Malik. I'm Malcolm's boyfriend."

"Randy. Nice to meet you," Randy responded, shaking Malik's outstretched hand.

"Ma, look what he brought us."

She looked inside the bag. "Oh, wow, I love this fragrance. Thank you." She kissed him on the cheek. "You hungry?"

"Starving."

"Well, you fellas meet me in the dining room. Everything is all set up so you can serve yourselves." Everyone went and fixed their own plates and sat at the dining room table and dinner was off without a hitch.

"Malcolm was right. You sure can cook," Malik said.

"Thank you, baby. Have as much as you like."

"Yeah, you threw down on this one. So Malik, I hear you run a business," Randy said.

"Yeah, my business partner and I have a store on 125th St. We sell urban apparel and sneakers. Just got some dress clothes in too. I deejay parties as well."

"And he's a masseuse," Malcolm said.

"Yeah, I do that too."

"Oh, that's great. I used to deejay too. I was thinking of getting back into it."

"There's room for everyone. What do you do now?"

"I'm a chief janitor for the school district. I've been doing that for twenty years. Worked my way up and I met this beautiful lady when I was at the Board of Ed. I did a stint in the service for four years—"

"Really? What branch?"

"Navy."

"I was in the Air Force for two years."

"You shoulda did the Navy."

"Nah, *you* shoulda came to the Air Force," Malik said playfully.

The three men discussed sports and that went on while Mama Nzingha cleared the plates from the table. When the conversation switched to the politics of the New York City school district, they all could join in the conversation then.

As the night went on, Malcolm warmed up to Randy and thought he was a good match for his mother. He was old enough to make her happy but young enough to wax poetic with him on almost any subject. Mama Nzingha liked Malik's genuine personality. She could tell by the way he spoke that he was a well-versed individual and she liked the positive impact he was having on her son. Malcolm was so relaxed around him and she had never seen him be that way with anyone except her and the boys. As they were talking, the doorbell buzzed again. Malcolm got up to answer the door and it was Damon, Shawn, and Kevin. Damon and Shawn were both holding boxes in their hands.

"Hey, hey, hey," Malcolm said in a spot-on impersonation of Fat Albert. They held out the boxes. "We brought cheesecake from Junior's."

"Did I just hear Junior's?" Mama Nzingha asked.

"You sure did. Hey Mama!" Damon said.

"Hey. What kind did you get baby?

"I got marble and strawberry."

"Oh, let's crack that open now cuz I wasn't too sure about the dessert. I made brownies but I left them in the oven just a little too long."

The boys each hugged her tight and they shook hands with Malik and Randy.

The boys ate dinner while Mama Nzingha cut everyone fairly large slices of cheesecake. The boys were mass texting each other about Malik and Randy.

Shawn: Damn, Malik is fine!

Damon: He sho is! I approve!

Kevin: Look at those eyes and that hair. Black, u betta not fuck this up!

Malcolm: Yeah my baby got it goin on.

Shawn: Your baby, huh? Owwwww.

Kevin: You heard him das his baby.

Damon: Randy ain't too bad either.

Shawn: Not at all.

Kevin: I'd hit it if he wasn't str8.

Malcolm: HE AIIGHT!

"Are y'all texting each other at my dinner table? Put them phones away. I'm sitting here like what the hell is everybody snickering at?" Mama Nzingha said.

They all looked at each other with guilty faces and put their phones away.

"They tell each other everything," she explained to Randy and Malik. "So y'all two will definitely be the topic of conversation later on."

Malik and Randy looked at all four of them.

"Best friends huh?" Randy asked.

"We stopped being friends a long time ago," Damon said.

Randy looked at him confused.

"What he means is, we're past the point of friends. These are my brothers," Malcolm said.

Shawn, Damon, and Kevin nodded.

"And I'm the mama. These boys are all my children."

"The phenomenal woman," Malcolm said imitating Maya Angelou.

They laughed at his immaculate imitation. The night continued when Malcolm mixed up the drinks and brought them out.

"Let's have a toast. To Malcolm and his beautiful mother Nzingha who have invited us into their home and made us a part of their family dynasty this evening. And to Nzingha, who came into my life when I was just a lonely man in his forties. You brought me light, love, and peace. I love you."

"I love you too, Randy." They shared a sweet kiss.

"Here, here," Malik said.

They all raised their glasses and toasted to them both.

The verdict was in. The boys loved Malik for Malcolm and were thrilled to see him be in a relationship. And boy did they talk about it when they returned home that night.

# 32

## PHILLY, PHILLY

Charles had been calling Kevin trying to make it up to him and had finally gotten his wish. He begged Kevin if he could see him before he went to Miami with the boys. Their trip was only four days away. He offered to take Kevin to Philly to meet his family for his Great Aunt's 90th birthday party. Kevin obliged and said he would go down for the weekend. He took a half-day at work and met up with Charles so they could beat the rush-hour traffic. Charles picked Kevin up in the Bentley and they drove down to his home in Wynnewood, a suburb of Philadelphia.

Kevin had never seen such a beautiful home. This was like one of those houses Damon told him he sold for a living. It had a nicely tended front yard with bright green grass with neatly trimmed bushes and shrubs. Charles parked in the driveway and led Kevin inside. The house was golden yellow with a large semi-circular window in the center above the front entrance. It boasted cathedral high ceilings, five bedrooms, four and a half bathrooms, hard cherry wood floors and black marble kitchen and bathroom floors. The bedrooms were all large but his master bedroom suite was probably the size of Kevin's whole apartment back in Harlem. Charles had the place fully decorated by interior decorators to really hook things up. The basement was set up like a big living room. The yard had a deck and in-ground swimming pool. A large grill was up against the white picket fence that enclosed the yard.

After leading Kevin on the grand tour of his beautiful mansion, he took him to dinner at the famed Geno's Steaks where they ate authentic Philly cheesesteaks outside underneath the canopy umbrellas.

"I'm going to Miami in four days. I'm not supposed to be eating this... deliciously fabulous sandwich," Kevin said taking another bite.

"It's good for you. There's nothing like a Philly cheesesteak from here. You ain't gonna get this in New York."

Kevin savored the flavor of the delicious authentic cheesesteak. "I feel like such a fat ass. I never drink soda."

"You feel good though, don't you?"

"It's one of the best things I've ever eaten in my life. And these fries are orgasmic."

Charles smiled. "Welcome to Philly, baby."

They left the restaurant and Charles drove Kevin to his old west Philly neighborhood where he grew up. "Do you feel comfortable driving your Bentley in this part of town?"

"I still know people in this neighborhood. My car will be fine."

They got out and walked down Charles' old block. He pointed out his old house, which was a small, two-story apartment house.

"My two brothers and I shared a bedroom until I went to college. My mom raised us on public assistance and then she worked as teacher's aide at my elementary school. My father left when I was five. He told my mom he was going out for a pack of cigarettes and he never came back. Never saw him again."

"I never knew my father either."

"Yeah, it sucks."

They stood and looked at the green and white house.

"What do you remember most about living here?" Kevin asked.

Charles broke into a big smile. "We were poor little ghetto kids but we had so much fun. Mom always let us watch TV at night after we finished our homework. We had to take turns cuz you know, boys always wanna be in charge. Saturday morning cartoons were always the hardest. But summertime around here was the best. We used to play with water from this fire hydrant right here," Charles said pointing to a yellow hydrant a few feet away.

"This was and still is a real working-class neighborhood, so there were a lot of families with a lot of kids. So we had plenty of friends."

They continued walking the neighborhood and Charles showed Kevin the park he and his friends used to play in. He was the oldest so he usually had to take his younger brothers there and watch them. Then he showed Kevin his former elementary school.

"When I come back here, it makes me grateful because most of us weren't expected to make it out of here. I busted my ass to get a perfect GPA in high school and went to three Ivy League schools and got my PhD. I was never expected to do anything like that coming from this neighborhood. Raised by a single mother on welfare, especially. But I got everything I ever wanted and more. How about you? Is your life exactly the way you want it to be?"

"I'm content, I guess. But I always wanted to dance. Never got around to it though."

"You always wanted to dance—like, what kind of dance?"

"Ballet."

"Really? How come you never did it?"

"No good reason."

"There is still time."

"And so there is. I just need to carve out some time I guess."

Charles' phone rang. "Hang on, let me take this call."

Kevin's mind drifted to what it would feel like to be on stage at Radio City Music Hall dancing his heart out. The vision made him feel elated, anxious, so ready that he could already feel the burn in his arms and legs. He smiled as his imagination painted this clear vision of himself doing something he loved.

"Kev," Charles said snapping him out of his fantasy.

"Huh?"

"That was my mom. She wants me to bring you over."

"Oh, wow. I thought I wouldn't see her until the party."

"She wants to meet you tonight."

"Okay then. Lead the way."

They walked back to Charles' car and drove to his mother's house in Upper Roxborough. She lived in a modest home on a nice tree lined-block. They smelled barbecue coming from the yard and saw the smoke as they got out of the car.

"She cooking out?"

"She just said dinner. I didn't know there was gonna be a party too. I really didn't know that."

"It's okay. We're here now."

"I don't even know who all is here. I think my brothers are though cuz there is a truck with a Maryland license plate, so my brother Elijah is here."

They made their way to the backyard and there was Charles' mother, Mary Wright, manning the grill. She was a big boned light skinned woman with glasses and silver gray hair. Her other two sons were there with their wives and children, who were all playing in the yard.

"Wassup y'all?" Charles said in loud voice. Everyone came over to greet Charles and Kevin. Charles' family was very nice and inviting. Especially his mother. Everything she said was followed by "Sugar" and "Honey." Kevin felt like part of the family immediately, but he still felt some kind of way. He was not fully convinced that Charles had no idea that his whole family was here; it was almost as though Charles was passively forcing him to meet his whole family. And honestly, Kevin wasn't ready to meet them as he still wasn't sure what the future held for them. But they were all very nice to him.

Back at Charles' house, Kevin took a bubble bath in the jacuzzi tub in the master bathroom while Charles showered in another bathroom. Charles lit candles in the bedroom so he and Kevin could make the best of their weekend getaway. Charles helped Kevin out of the bathtub and ushered him into the bedroom and they made love on his big California king bed. That's one thing Kevin missed about Charles during their break. His tenderness while they made love made Charles the best in bed he had ever had. They cuddled under covers watching movies afterwards. It made the physical attacks Kevin suffered at Charles' hands all seem like a distant memory. Until Charles looked at the mark on Kevin's torso near his ribcage.

"What's that mark?"

Kevin looked at him. "It's from when I had to go to the hospital. When you cracked my ribs."

Charles' face got sad and he kissed the mark.

"I'll never hurt you again, baby."

Kevin shifted uncomfortably. Bringing it up changed his whole mood. "I'm sleepy." Charles nodded. He blew out the candles and turned off the lights and spooned Kevin as they fell asleep.

"I love you, Kev."

"Love you too." Charles wrapped his arm around Kevin and they drifted off to sleep.

They woke up around 11am the next morning and went to the London Grill for breakfast. Charles took him shopping on Main Street and they visited the Museum of Art. Kevin still felt guilty about the food he was eating so he insisted they do some exercises. They went to Charles' local gym and used a guest pass for Kevin and they worked out until they were both sweaty and funky. Charles' big body covered in sweat made Kevin horny so after they showered, they had sex in Charles' bed again when they got home. It felt so good.

They dressed in suits for Charles' Great-Aunt Maxine's 90th birthday party, which was happening at the Marriott Hotel in downtown Philadelphia. The affair was upscale with great music and food. His Aunt Maxine was a beautiful older woman who was aging very gracefully. She had long gray braids in her hair and a beautiful white evening gown. She was on a cane and moved a little slow, but when she stood up to give her speech, she was very alert and spry.

"I wanna thank everyone for coming out tonight. Y'all have made an old lady feel very loved. I look around and I see my family looking all good. We sure are some good looking folks ain't we?" she asked.

Everyone clapped.

"You know, I'm really not ninety; I'm only fifty-five."

Everyone laughed while she did a sexy pose.

"I love you all so much and I thank God for waking me up this morning and every morning for the last ninety years. He is merciful and great. To my husband Maynor of seventy years who left us seven years ago, I love you still. To my six children, seventeen grandchildren, fifteen greatgrands, and four great-great-grands, you know Mama loves you. It just feels good to get to my age and still have family that cares about me. I have friends whose families could give a rat's ass about them and put them in homes. I still live in the same house Maynor and I bought years ago and I ain't goin' nowhere. You've all made me so happy today," she said beginning to get teary.

"Whether I go tomorrow or next year or years from now, I want y'all to stay together as a family. That's my one birthday wish today. That my family stays together and that when I'm gone, you all gather together in my name. I love all of you. This food is outstanding, y'all lookin' real good, and I wanna thank you all for coming here this evening. God bless you." She gave the microphone back to a staffer. Everyone applauded as she made her way back to her seat.

The night continued on and Kevin was introduced to Charles' cousin Michael who was also from Brooklyn.

"What part of Brooklyn are you from?" Kevin asked.

"Brownsville. You?"

"I'm from Flatbush."

"Alright, where are you now?"

"I'm in Harlem."

"I'm in Bed-Stuy now."

They hit it off and laughed about all the great things about New York. Charles was all over the room talking to various family members but spotted Kevin laughing with Michael. He sent Kevin a text.

Charles: U having fun?

Kevin: Yeah I'm having a great time.

Charles: U gon come kick it with me or yuck it up wit Mike all nite?

Kevin: We're having a good time over here. Just come on over when ur done.

Kevin and Michael talked about New York radio and all the great places to eat in their native Brooklyn. Charles came over and said he was ready to go and Kevin bid him good night.

"Here's my card, man. Give me a call when you get back to New York; we can have lunch or something. Nice meeting you," Michael said.

"Definitely, man. I'll do that."

The valet brought Charles his car after they said good night to everyone.

"That was a lot of fun."

"Yup."

"Your aunt is beautiful."

"Yeah, she is."

"You tired?"

"Yeah."

Kevin sensed Charles had an attitude as they got into the car. "What's the matter?"

"Nothing."

"You sure?"

"I said I'm fine."

They rode in silence back to the house. When Kevin turned on the radio, Charles turned it off. A sour feeling began to spread through Kevin's belly. He had a feeling that things were about to get very ugly. When they got into the house, Kevin took off his jacket, sat on the couch, and turned on the TV. Charles went to use the bathroom and then came into the living room with Kevin. He took the remote and turned off the TV.

"Charles, what is wrong with you?"

"You really enjoyed yucking it up with Michael, didn't you?"

Kevin rolled his eyes heavenward. "Are you kidding me?"

"Am I laughing?"

"You went off talking to everyone. Mike and I were just talking."

"I saw how you were looking at him. He's not gay, so there's no chance of you sleeping with him."

What the...? Not this shit again. "Just the slightest little thing makes you so jealous, Charles. Did they teach you that in your anger management classes?"

"This isn't about anger, this is about respect. You and I both know that you spent more time with him than you did me. And you didn't even try to hide the fact that you were flirting."

"I did not spend more time with him, and I wasn't flirting either."

"Yes, you were!"

"No, I wasn't!"

"*Yes, you were!*"

"*No the fuck I wasn't!*"

"So are you calling me blind or are you calling me a liar?"

"I'm sick of you trying to insinuate that I'm some kind of whore who sleeps with every man who smiles at me. First Malcolm and now you think I'm gonna fuck your cousin?"

"You woulda fucked me the day we met. The same way you looked at me was the same way you looked at him. Ready and willing. So hell yeah I think you're a fucking smut!"

"Take me home!" Kevin said as he pulled on his jacket.

"Where are you going?" Charles asked grabbing him.

"Get off me!"

Charles shoved him hard and he fell to the floor.

"I see you done forget who the fuck I am. But I'mma remind your bitch ass right the fuck now!"

Kevin backed up, scrambled to his feet and punched Charles in the face with all of his strength. "What you gon' do? Hit me? I'm sick of you thinking I'm your punching bag!"

Charles grabbed Kevin and pounded him in the face and he pushed him into the wall. As Kevin slid down the wall, his eyes focused on the large bulge between Charles' legs. He bent his knee for leverage and kicked him in the dick as hard as he could.

"Muthafucka," Charles squeaked out as he crumbled to the floor, holding his precious jewels.

Kevin tried to jump over him, but Charles grabbed his leg and he fell scrambling to get away. Once he got away, Charles chased him through the dining room and through the kitchen. Kevin threw things at him the whole way and Charles trailed behind him as if he were Jason Voorhees. Kevin ran into the laundry room and locked the door behind him. He frantically searched for something to defend himself with. Laundry detergent? No. Fabric softener sheets? No.

"Open this fucking door!"

His eyes zoomed in on the bottle of bleach and he sighed his relief. "Come on in here and I got something for you!"

"Open this door!"

"No!"

"Don't make me break this fucking door down. You better open this door and I'll let you live. If I open this door, I'm gonna fucking kill you!"

Hairs on the back of his neck raised on end. He believed Charles' threat wholeheartedly.

"Open this door, Kevin!"

No answer.

"Come on, Kevin; just let me talk to you."

No answer.

"I just wanna talk. I know you hear me. I'm not gonna hurt you. Just let me talk to you."

Kevin tiptoed over to the dryer and grabbed the bottle of bleach, untwisting the top.

"Aight, fine. Stay in there. We can talk when you're ready to come out."

Kevin could hear Charles' footsteps walk away from the door. He stood still and clenched the bleach handle tight.

Suddenly the door came off its hinges as Charles threw his full weight against it. The rage in his eyes made him look like a monster.

"What the hell is wrong with you? Hitting me like you done lost your fucking mind! I'll kill you, muthafucka."

Kevin aimed at his eyes and threw the bleach. He was too tall; instead of it hitting his eyes, it him in the nose. He must've inhaled some of the bleach because he grabbed his nose with both hands and screamed like it was burning him. Kevin didn't waste time to see if he would recover. He ran out the laundry room and raced out the front door, taking the steps three at a time. Charles was right behind him, still clutching his nose. He chased him around the car but couldn't catch him.

"When I get my hands on you, it's on!"

*"Fuck your life, bitch!"*

"Fuck me? Fuck me?" He punched out his own car window, cutting his hand on the glass. Neither the pain nor the injury hindered his rage. Charles jumped on top of his car to grab Kevin.

"I'mma call the cops!" Kevin said running away.

"I don't give a fuck!" Charles said chasing him.

Kevin ran as fast as he could in his dress shoes but Charles was on his ass. Charles finally caught him and tackled him, punching him in the face twice. Kevin took his head and head-butted Kevin's hard abdomen. When it didn't do anything, Kevin sunk his teeth into Charles' leg and bit until he tasted blood. Charles let out a bloodcurdling scream and released Kevin.

"I'm gonna kill you, muthafucka! You hear me? I'm gonna kill yo ass."

Free once again, he ran for blocks until he saw a taxi cab parked outside of a convenience store. He jumped in the backseat of the cab and beat the driver seat. "Go, go, go!" he yelled.

The driver was stuffing his mouth with a loaded hotdog that had plenty of onions on it. "I'm off duty pal," the driver said.

"He's trying to kill me! Drive!" Kevin yelled.

"What? Who's killing who?"

"Him! Go!"

The driver looked out the window and saw Charles running towards the car with blood streaming down his arm and a flower of blood staining his pant leg. The driver started up the engine and attempted to drive off. Charles reached through the passenger seat window, trying to grab at Kevin as the driver was speeding off.

"Oh my God! Go! Drive man!" Kevin screamed to the driver while moving to the other side of the backseat. Charles held onto the handle of the passenger door tightly and opened it. The driver came to a sudden stop and Charles went flying to the side. The driver shut the door and locked them, then sped off. All the running and adrenaline had Kevin exhausted.

"Jesus Christ, man. What the hell did you do to that guy?" the driver asked in a thick New York accent.

"He's...he's crazy," Kevin said out of breath.

"You're telling me. He almost broke my got-damn door."

He turned around to look at Kevin at the red light.

"Oh my God. Look at your face man. Do you want me to get you to a hospital? Your eyes are both black."

"Just take me to the train station. I wanna get the hell out of Philadelphia."

"If you say so, but I really think you oughta let someone look at your face. It's gonna look horrible in the morning."

"Just take me to the fucking train station, man! Shit!"

The driver took him downtown to the 30th Street Train Station where he we bought an Amtrak ticket back to New York. He only had a $20 bill on him so he bought a cheap pair of shades to cover up his eyes from inside the station. The train boarded and his mind raced the entire time on the ride back to New York. He couldn't believe what had just happened. It didn't make sense. One thing was for sure. He had to officially end everything with Charles.

# 33

## MIAMI BOUND

The guys packed into Damon's truck and Mama Nzingha took her place in the driver's seat and they were off to John F. Kennedy International Airport. It was five after 6am but the sun was already up and shining over New York City. Damon was entrusting his beloved Range Rover to Mama Nzingha while he was in Miami.

Even though they were all going to Miami to have fun, they didn't seem excited. No one asked any questions though. All of the boys' heads were in different places and deep in thought. Damon was thinking about his father and was afraid to admit to his friends that he missed Kenny being around. Shawn was officially depressed as a result of his breakup with Jamon. And now he felt bad about spazzing on him the way he did when he came over. Malcolm had spent every evening of the last week with Malik and now he was going to miss him. He was also wondering if he could fight the temptation in Miami and remain true to his boo.

Kevin was the most sullen of them all. After being chased through the streets of Philadelphia by Charles who was threatening to kill him, he was all shaken up. He was glad to be leaving town but knew Charles had a lot of money and could use his resources to track him down in Miami. He'd had the super change his locks, but he still felt vulnerable and feared for his life. What if Charles caught him and he couldn't do anything to protect himself? What if he showed up with a gun? How would he protect himself then? Since he was taking his laptop with him on the trip, he was going to finally check into the self-defense classes Marcia had suggested. He even toyed with the idea of purchasing a gun.

"Well, y'all sure are quiet. Y'all excited about leaving or what?" Mama Nzingha asked.

"I just know I need a vacation," Damon said.

"Me too," Shawn said.

"You ain't said nothing but a word," Kevin said.

Silence.

"Malcolm."

"Yes, ma'am?"

"You excited, baby?"

"Yeah, I am. It's just early."

"You thinking about Malik? He'll be here when you get back. You better smile; you're going to beautiful Miami Beach with your brothers."

Malcolm cracked a half smile. Mama Nzingha turned on the radio and the boys continued to think deeply about their own situations and looked out the window at the things they were passing. Traffic hadn't picked up yet so they made it to the airport in no time. They each kissed Mama Nzingha good-bye and went to check in the bags and get screened before getting on the plane. Their Delta flight was forty-five minutes late leaving the runway but the guys were each zoned out. They started to perk up when the plane was beginning to land in Miami and they saw the ocean and how beautiful their sunny surroundings were. Almost instantaneously, they each pulled their minds out of their respective funks and got excited.

"And ladies and gentlemen, we are about to make our landing at the Miami International Airport. Please turn off all electronic devices and have all seat belts fastened as we prepare to make our landing in the next few minutes. Thank you for flying with us today and let us be the first to say, welcome to Miami," the handsome flight attendant, Michael said over the intercom.

The flight landed and everyone gathered up their carry-on luggage and made their way off of the plane. While getting their luggage, Damon called the car rental office to tell them he had arrived and to bring their rental.

"Look at this airport!" Malcolm said.

"Makes JFK seem like the projects," Shawn said.

The guys looked at the tropical-inspired airport and were in awe as they walked outside into the sunny Miami heat.

"Now I see why their basketball team is called the Heat."

"You ain't lying. It's hot as balls out here."

They looked around at the people hustling and bustling to get where they were going.

"So we ready to take over Miami, fellas?"

"Hell fucking yeah!"

"I'm ready to set it off."

Even Kevin somewhat came out of his sullen mood and nodded his head. Minutes later, the rental car driver pulled up with their rental. The boys settled on a fully loaded black Cadillac Escalade ESV. It had a V8 engine, sunroof, touchscreen navigation, a 5.1 Bose sound system, 22" chrome spinner wheels, headrest TV/DVD players, and leather interior.

"Awww shit! It's on and poppin'!" Malcolm said.

The driver hopped out. "Damon White?"

"That's me."

"We just need your signature on a few documents back at the office, so we'll go by and you can be on your way."

"No problem. Let's just load up the truck."

The boys loaded their things and were off to the car rental office. Damon signed the papers and got all the info he needed and punched in the address of the hotel into the navigation system. He turned on the AC and they were off to their hotel. They were staying at the Acqualina Hotel, Resort, & Spa on Miami Beach in a luxurious two-bedroom suite. They took in the beautiful sights as they traveled the freeway to the hotel, bumping the thumping bass of the surround-sound stereo. It was suddenly as if they weren't all stressing over their individual situations less than a half hour before.

"Look at that beach," Kevin said as they passed the beautiful sky blue waters of the Atlantic Ocean. They were all so excited. They were seeing why people loved Miami. Damon pulled up in the parking lot of the hotel and they went to check in at the front desk. They were even amazed at how nice the lobby was.

"Can I help you gentlemen?" asked the attractive white woman at the front desk.

"Hi. We have a two-bedroom suite reserved for check-in today," Damon said.

"May I have your names?"

He gave their names and she scanned the list and found them. "Yes, I have you here. You're in room 1110 on the eleventh floor."

She gave them all key cards and called out to the nearby bellhop to load their bags on a cart and escort them to their room. The young black man had a thick southern accent but was pleasant.

"Where y'all from?" he asked.

"New York," Shawn said.

"Oh, like Jay-Z."

"Yeah. He's actually from Brooklyn like Jay-Z," Shawn said pointing to Kevin.

"Das my favorite rapper. I knew y'all wasn't from down here by the way y'all was dressed. Y'all whole swag is different."

They looked at each other and tried not to laugh as the elevator doors opened. "Y'all room is right down here," he said pulling the cart down the hallway. He led them to the end of the hall and there was the room. When the bellhop opened the door, the boys gasped at how beautiful the suite was.

"This here is one of our best suites. Y'all must be rich cuz only people with money book this room."

"We're not rich but we thought if we were gonna vacation, why not do it up?"

"Fa sho." They unloaded their bags and each tipped the bellhop before he left. The sun shined brightly into the room and they got a look around. There was a spacious common area with a couch and loveseat, a big screen TV, a kitchenette, two large bathrooms with jacuzzi tubs able to comfortably seat two people, and a luxurious shower with a stained-glass door. Damon and Malcolm decided to share one room while Kevin and Shawn would have the other. Shawn took off his shoes and started jumping on his bed.

"I see the teacher has become one of the students," Damon said.

"I haven't jumped on a bed in years."

Malcolm slid the balcony door open and stepped outside on the terrace. He looked up at the beautiful cloudless blue sky, the blue ocean, and the white sand.

"I love you, Miami!" Malcolm screamed as loud as he could.

The boys joined him out on the balcony. "Fellas, we are in Miami. Let's leave all of our troubles in New York and enjoy this beautiful place," Damon said.

"I agree," Shawn said.

"I wanna go swimming," Kevin said.

"You wanna hit the pool or the beach?" Malcolm asked.

"I wanna hit the beach."

"I'm down with that. Y'all know I plan on being shirtless the whole week anyway," Malcolm said snatching off his shirt. They each went rifling through their bags to pull out swimwear. Kevin went into the bathroom, shut the door, and made sure it was locked tight. He wiped off the foundation and put on a new layer of waterproof foundation to make sure the rings around his eyes were completely covered. Yes, the makeup boasted of 24-hour wear, but he didn't want to take any chances with the foundation wearing off. So far, the boys hadn't asked any questions and he wanted to keep it that way.

The boys walked down to the beach and set up spots on the sand and splashed around in the clear blue water. It was so clean and pretty blue that you could literally see your feet walking along the bottom.

"I'll never do the beach in Brooklyn again!" Kevin said.

"This puts it to shame."

They played in the water and then decided they wanted to go jet-skiing when they saw people going by on jet skis. They walked down to the other side of the beach and signed up. It was more fun than they could have imagined. Gliding in the water and high speeds gave them an exhilarating sense of freedom. Afterward they chilled on the beach in the sun for a while underneath their umbrellas.

"I'm getting hungry," Shawn said.

"Me too."

"What are we doing for dinner?"

"You wanna go to Emeril's?" Damon asked.

"You mean the guy from TV?"

"Yeah."

"We could eat at a damn truck stop for all I care. Let's go," Shawn said rising.

The boys got up and followed Shawn back into the hotel. They each showered and got dressed. Kevin applied a new coat of makeup and shades to match his outfit. NYC swag was all up and through as the boys made their way downstairs to the Escalade. They looked good, smelled good, and were ready to live it up. Climbing into the Escalade made them feel like rock stars. Damon turned on their theme song: Jay-Z and Alicia Key's "Empire State of Mind." They made sure to roll down the windows and open the sunroof as they drove along the beachside roadway to Emeril's restaurant. They wanted everyone to know where they were from. They pulled up in the parking lot of the nice restaurant and were seated at a square table in the center of the dining room.

"Let the debauchery begin," Malcolm said.

"Indeed," Damon said.

"Pride celebrations don't begin for another two days, so til then it's just us."

"And I am not on a diet anymore now that we're here. Let's get it in!"

"You gon' keep your shades on at the table?" Shawn asked Kevin.

"My allergies are still bothering me."

"Are you wearing makeup?" Shawn asked.

Damon and Malcolm looked at him. His heart began to beat quickly. "My allergies caused me to have an allergic reaction and my skin broke out. And there's no way that I'm coming to Miami looking like I got rosacea."

Shawn laughed and slapped hands with him across the table. "I know that's right, honey!"

"Excuse me," Kevin said getting up. "My bladder is about to explode."

He went to the bathroom and leaned as close to the mirror as he could. With his fingers, he blended the makeup well enough that the lines underneath his eyes were invisible to the eye. But he looked closely and could see them. He closed his eyes and exhaled. "I gotta tell them eventually."

When he returned to the table, the server had already come to take their orders.

"We ordered for you," Shawn told him. "Hope you have a taste for chicken."

"I never even knew this was a real restaurant. Moms be watching this dude on TV," Malcolm said.

"How's your dad, Damon?"

"He's coming along. They're taking him home tomorrow."

"How are you feeling about him?"

Damon shrugged. "I'm just taking it one day at a time. I know at some point I'm gonna have to address the issue because I'm still gay and I still date men. Be they married or single."

"What's the deal with that? Have you heard from Kenny at all?"

"He stopped calling some time ago. Since that day I left him at the restaurant, he's reached out but I've managed to dodge him since then."

"You miss him?"

Damon nodded. "Sadly, yes."

"You believe he was really getting a divorce, though?"

"Who knows? Maybe. But I ain't messing with him no more. I'm done."

"Yo, Shawn, you hear from Jamon?"

"He sent me an email."

"Saying what?"

"I didn't read it yet. I saw it and just left it there."

"Why?"

"Even though I told him it was over, I don't know if I wanna hear him say it too. And I still feel bad about going crazy last time I saw him."

"Is it still in your mailbox?"

"Yeah."

"Well, why don't you read it now on your phone?"

"Why, so y'all nosy bitches know what he said?"

"I wanna know what he said."

"Me too. I mean, you did throw a knife at his head last time he came over."

They all looked at Shawn.

"What?"

"Read the damn letter, man."

Shawn rolled his eyes and took out his phone to pull up his email.

The rest of the boys sipped their drinks. "He sent this last week." In Shawn's mind, he couldn't help but hear Jamon's voice reading the letter to him:

*Dear Shawn,*

*I see that I have really hurt you. I'm sorry for the pain I have caused you. I know it sounds cliché but I never meant to hurt you. I never thought I would see the day you would be chasing me with a knife out of the home we built together. And I never thought I would hear you say that you hate me. I broke down in tears when you said that to me. When did we get here? When did we get to a place where you dump my clothes in the river? When did we get to a place where we are punching each other in the face like we're strangers? That's pretty serious, Mook. We need to talk. But without all the anger. I'm going to give you some time. But I think we've been through too much to just let our relationship go. I know I cheated but do I get any forgiveness at all? I really am sorry. I admitted my part in all of this. I know I'm the one who fucked things up. You're the best thing that ever happened to me. I went to see my mom and she asked about you. I told her about our breakup and she called me stupid. And she was right. I fucked up the best thing that I ever had. I know it was wrong. I still love my Mookie. I always will. Please give us a chance to work out our problems and start over. I will never cheat on you or break your heart again. I don't ever wanna hear you say you hate me again either. The pain on your face made me feel like I wasn't shit. As if I was worthless. That's how I feel without you. You really are the wind beneath my wings. And I hope one day soon you can forgive me. And we can get back to being together. I love you. Remember that. I love you.*

*Love,*
*Jamon*

Shawn put his phone down and rolled his eyes.

Silence.

"What do you think, Mook?"

Shawn's leg shook and his nostrils flared. "Why is he acting like he's the victim? As if I just started wilding out on him for no reason. I still wanna know why he cheated on me."

"I think he has a lot of nerve," Kevin said.

"How do you feel after reading that?"

"Angry. Like how dare he think that just because he sends me an email, I'm just supposed to be ready to talk. I'm not ready to talk. I'm still pissed and right now he can kick rocks." Damon shook his head. "Why are you shaking your head?"

"Because this isn't you."

"What does that mean?"

"It means this isn't how you are. I know you miss him. It's okay to say you miss him."

"I can't just forgive him that easily."

"Why? Do you want to? What are you trying to do? Make him suffer by being mad at him?"

"Maybe I am. I want him to know that what he did isn't okay."

"See, that's not you Shawn. You know better than that. That's not gonna do anything but eat at you while he goes on with his life. If you love him then fight for your relationship. But only you know if it's worth it."

"I don't want it to seem like I'm running back to him or forgetting what he did to me."

"Do you think you possibly played a part in the reason why he cheated?"

Shawn frowned. "Are you trying to insinuate that it's my fault?"

"I didn't say that and no I don't think that. But when someone cheats in a relationship, it's usually because they feel like something is lacking from it."

"Oh, I beg to differ," Kevin said.

"Why?"

"Because some of these men are just fucking greedy and wanna have their cake and eat it too. I honestly don't think it's anything Shawn did. I think Jamon just started feeling himself and wanted to have some cake. Come on! Shawn bent over backwards for him. What more could he have done?"

"And I'm surprised any of you think I should get back with him. I know y'all don't like him."

"I ain't say you should get back with him. I think you could do better. Much better," Malcolm said.

"Regardless of how you think we feel about him, we are not the ones who have to date him. You are."

"It still hurts." Shawn's eyes teared up.

"It's gonna hurt as long as it's supposed to. But you being mad at him is gonna make the pain worse. Now if he still wants to get back with you after you could have really hurt him or killed him, that is definitely something to take into consideration," Damon added.

"I think you need to give yourself some time," Kevin said. "Sometimes, you lose yourself in a relationship. Take this time to figure out who Shawn is. Smell the roses, live your life as a single man for a while and if the desire is still there, give him a call and see what happens. But I would totally use this time to rediscover myself and do things I like doing. It's summertime, so you don't have any students to worry about. Take yourself out to dinner sometime. Go see a Broadway play. The good thing about New York is there is always something to get into."

"You're right, Kev."

Shawn looked at Malcolm. "Malcolm, what you think?"

"I'mma support whatever decision you make. If you wanna get back with him, I'mma support you. If you don't, I'mma support that too. You could listen to what we think all day but the decision is yours. It's about you and your happiness, man. I agree with, Kev. I think you should take some time for yourself."

Shawn nodded. "Thanks for your honesty."

Silence. "I miss Malik," Malcolm said.

"Aww," Shawn, Damon, and Kevin said.

"That's so cute."

"Can I keep it real with y'all about something?" Malcolm asked.

"What's up?"

"Y'all know this is my first relationship. I am freaking the fuck out. On one hand, I really like him. I care about him a lot but y'all know me. I'm used to getting some new ass all the time. Or at least rotating. I ain't never had sex with one person consecutively like I'm doing now on no relationship shit. I'm scared."

"Why?"

"Cuz I'm wondering how long he can keep my attention before I want something else."

"How do you know you'll want something else?"

"Because I always do. I fucked a lot of dudes. I mean *a lot* of dudes; y'all know how I get down. Even when I would fuck them, I would be thinking about my next hook up."

"You mean you're a nymphomaniac?"

"Probably. I just love sex man."

"But you weren't connected to the guys you hooked up with. It was just sex. This time you might actually not wanna fuck with anyone else," Kevin said.

"Oh, I disagree," Shawn said.

"Why?"

"I was in love with Jamon. I never connected with any man like I did with him, but that didn't mean I didn't wanna fuck anybody else. I just didn't do it. That's just the challenge of being in a relationship, Black. You gotta decide if you're gonna commit to him and everything you've built together or be available to men outside of your relationship. I'm not gonna bullshit you; it's a tough thing to do, but it's a decision you gotta make."

"And don't stress over whether or not you will cheat. You could actually have the desire to be faithful but because cheating is on your mind, you'll attract it to the situation and get yourself caught in an okie doke," Damon said.

"Yeah, just take it one day at a time."

"And how was your trip to Philly, Mr. Malone?" Damon asked.

Flashbacks of the scariest event in his life flashed through his mind.

"Philly is nice. I had a real Philly cheesesteak and met his family."

"He introduced you to his family?"

"What, you bout to be his wife?" Malcolm asked.

"Uh, definitely won't happen."

"Think you're gonna get back with him?"

An image of the laundry room flashed through his mind, him clutching the bleach, Charles barging through the door.

"I don't know. We'll see what the future holds."

Kevin couldn't even look at them while he was telling that lie. Thankfully, their food came and the conversation shifted. They left the restaurant full, happy, with doggy bags and went back to the hotel and chilled until they fell asleep in their beautiful hotel room. And this was just the beginning.

# 34

## PARADISE DREAMS

The bright Miami sunrise filtered through the blinds, waking the boys the next morning. They wanted to take a swim in the big pool in the back of the hotel before breakfast. They decided this would be a day of relaxation. After swimming in the pool, they dined on fresh fruit, omelets, Belgium waffles, and chicken apple sausage for breakfast at the hotel restaurant.

"It ain't Amy Ruth's but it'll do," Malcolm said.

"I don't know what you're talking about. These waffles are the shit," Shawn said.

They left the restaurant and showered then went to the spa at the hotel. While getting manicures, pedicures, facials, and full body massages, they sipped champagne and munched on light refreshments. On their way back to the room, they saw a man in the lobby advertising parasailing and Shawn got his card.

"I'm so down. I wanna do this."

"Hell, yeah."

"I'm scared of heights, but I will go and watch y'all," Kevin said.

"Bet. Let's go."

They went upstairs to get dressed then hopped in the truck and used the navigation to find the place. They climbed aboard a boat with a gentleman named Jim who hoisted them up to the sky and took off. Malcolm went up first and they could hear him scream from all the way up. They all laughed at him.

"Black thinks he is so damn tough, but he is screaming like a girl," Shawn said laughing.

"That's what they all do," Jim said.

Shawn went up next but didn't scream. He actually enjoyed being up there. He could see birds flying past him. He opened his arms as if he were a bird spreading its wings and acted like he was flying. He felt free.

Damon went up last and he let out a high-pitched girly scream. Kevin took pictures of them all getting on and going up. The hours of the day seemed to fly by as they enjoyed the beauty of Miami. They went on a city tour after parasailing and learned the history of Miami and the tour guide showed them many places of interest. They were starved after the city tour and went to eat dinner at the hotel's restaurant. Back up at the room, Malcolm plugged up his video game and played with Damon.

Shawn had eaten something that wasn't agreeing with him. He hurried to the bathroom and threw open the door.

"Wait! Wait," Kevin called out, trying to close the door, but it was too late. Kevin looked at Shawn without his makeup on. Quickly, he unfolded his shades and put them on, but Shawn had already seen it all.

"Kev, what's going on?"

"Nothing. I'm just experimenting with some foundation."

"That didn't look like a rash on your face."

"It is. It's a rash. I told you it looks pretty bad," he said gathering everything up and putting it in a makeup bag.

Shawn got closer. "Take your shades off."

"I'd rather not. It looks really bad. So I'm just gonna let you do your thing in here and go to the other bathroom."

He tried to walk out the bathroom but Shawn stood in front of the door, blocking his exit. He crossed his arms over his chest. "Last night, you didn't wanna take your shades off at the restaurant. Today, I walk in here and you're rushing to put them on. You're all jumpy and secretive. So I'm gonna ask you again. What's going on?"

"Nothing."

"Then why won't you let me see your face?"

Kevin breathed deeply. Shawn looked him dead in the face and waited for an answer.

"It's...contagious."

Shawn raised his eyebrows. "Oh, really? So when did allergies become contagious?"

Realizing Shawn wasn't going to let him pass, Kevin took off his shades and looked down at the floor. Shawn lifted Kevin's chin so he could get a full view of his face. He gasped as his eyes roamed over the purplish-black marks circling both of Kevin's eyes.

"Who did this to you?!"

"Keep your voice down." Shawn's eyes narrowed. "I had a fight." Shawn immediately put two and two together. "Did he hit you?"

"Who?"

"You know who. He beat you up?"

"We had a fight."

"Does his face look like yours?"

He couldn't bear to tell Shawn the whole story. "Probably. I left after it happened."

"When did it happen?"

"Saturday."

"Weren't you still in Philly on Saturday?"

"Yeah, that's when it happened."

"So he beat you up, then took you home?"

"I took the train."

That answer pissed Shawn off even more. "That muthafucka beat you up and let you take the train home? Why didn't you tell us?"

"I just wanted to get out of there."

Shawn shook his head. "Now it all makes sense."

"What?"

"Why you haven't been acting like yourself. You've been distant. It's because he's been—" Shawn gasped again and took a deep breath, looking at Kevin incredulously. His voice was a stage whisper. "That muthafucka pushed you down the stairs, didn't he?"

"No, no," Kevin said, shaking his head repeatedly.

"For some reason, I don't believe you."

"I swear it to you that he didn't push me down the stairs."

"If you don't tell me what happened right now, I'm going in there and I'm telling them. And you already know that Malcolm is going to go off the deep end."

"Okay, okay," Kevin said and cracked the door to make sure none of the boys were in close proximity. He closed and locked the door then made Shawn sit down on the toilet. Kevin took a seat on the edge of the tub. After a few steadying breaths, he told Shawn everything from beginning to end.

When he finished, Shawn stood up shaking his head, his jaw clenching and unclenching with anger. "I can't believe you kept this from us. They need to know," he said walking toward the door.

Kevin grabbed his arm. "See, this is why I didn't wanna tell you because I knew you would go there."

"Where? To the truth?"

"If you tell them, they're gonna seriously hurt Charles."

"And who the fuck cares?"

"*I* care. And can you please lower your voice? I need to deal with this on my own without any added drama, so please keep your mouth shut."

"It looks like you're having enough drama dealing with it by yourself."

"Well, you should know that better than anyone. You hit Jamon enough times to make him not wanna deal with you."

Shawn gave him a look like 'no, you didn't go there.' "We're not talking about me and Jamon. We're talking about you and the punk ass faggot who's been beating your ass."

"Why is he all of that? Oh, I know what this is. You're jealous cuz I have a man and you don't."

"I see getting your ass beat on the regular has given you a fierce tongue. Tell me something. Where is all of that fierceness when he's slapping your ass around?"

"I don't have to listen to this." Kevin started walking to the door.

"I'm telling the guys."

"You can tell who you want. I don't even give a fuck. This is my life and I'll date who I want. And deal with my own problems before I go dumping my man's shit in the river."

"You got one more time to come for me about Jamon before I'm knocking you the fuck out. Who are you trying to impress with all that attitude?"

"I'm not trying to impress anyone. I'm just letting you know."

"And I'm letting you know that you need help, Kevin. This thing is bigger than you."

"What if I don't want y'all to help?"

"Fine then. Go get yourself killed. We'll be at your funeral."

"Kiss my ass," Kevin said walking out.

Shawn watched him walk out.

*I knew something wasn't right with him.*

# 35

## PRIDE BEGINS

The boys woke up to another sunny morning at the hotel. Today was officially the first day of the Black Pride celebration. Malcolm wanted to go do some cardio so Damon and Shawn went with him. Kevin wanted to sleep in a little more. He hadn't said a word to Shawn since their conversation in the bathroom. Malcolm and Damon had noticed the tension and the ugly looks that Shawn and Kevin passed each other, but they hadn't addressed it yet.

Down at the gym while on the elliptical machines, Damon and Malcolm decided to figure out what was going on between their two friends.

"It's nothing really," Shawn assured them. "Kevin's been acting weird lately, and when I addressed him about it, he flipped on me. We got into a little argument, exchanged a few choice words, and now we just have to let the smoke settle."

"What do you think is wrong with him?" Damon asked.

"It's that fag, Charles," Malcolm said nodding. "I know it is. I got this feeling about this dude that he just ain't right."

"Did he say anything to you, Shawn?" Damon asked.

"Just that I should mind my fucking business."

He wanted to tell them the truth, but things were already strained between him and Kevin. He didn't want to make things worse. So he lied and felt bad about it. The boys went for four miles and went back upstairs to shower. Shawn walked into the bedroom to find something to wear for the day. While he was flipping through the clothes in the closet, Kevin walked into the room fully dressed.

"The guys know something is up with you," Shawn said.

"Did you tell them before or after you worked out?"

"I didn't say anything. Just know that you can't keep it a secret forever. They're gonna ask eventually."

"Well then, let them ask away."

Shawn shook his head. "Why are you acting like this?"

"Because Damon is gonna have something to say. You know he thinks he knows everything already. And Malcolm is gonna try to make Charles physically disabled for the rest of his life."

"What is wrong with that?"

"I need to handle this on my own."

"Why are you trying to protect him?"

"Because this is my problem and I'm handling it. Y'all don't know what's going on in my relationship."

"The fact that you're covering up black eyes speaks louder than anything you could ever say. But if you don't say something before we leave Miami, I'm dropping the dime."

"You just said you wouldn't do my dirty work for me."

"I changed my mind."

"I don't believe you. If you were gonna say something, you'd have said it by now."

"Humph. You keep thinking that." Shawn left to shower and Kevin sat on his bed and looked at his cell phone. The light was flashing indicating he had a message. He picked it up to see he had four voicemail messages all from Charles. Rolling his eyes, he dialed his voicemail to see what he had to say.

"I know you're in Miami. Enjoy your vacation. We need to talk when you get back. Make sure you call me when you get back."

He listened to the next message.

"On second thought, call me when you get this. I need to talk to you before you get back."

He listened to the next message.

"Kevin, this is Charles. It's my third time calling. Please call me back as soon as you get this message. I need to speak with you as soon as possible. It's very urgent that we speak."

And the final message was just another weak plea for him to call him. Kevin deleted all of the messages and lay across the bed. He got a nauseous feeling and closed his eyes. It didn't matter that he was 1,500 miles away from New York. His problems with Charles filled up his consciousness.

"I gotta tell the boys." Kevin pulled the pillow over his head and moaned into it, still agonizing over how he would break the news.

"Y'all ready?" Malcolm called from the other room.

"Yeah," Shawn said.

They went downstairs to eat breakfast and decided they would hit the vendors for the street fair. They got all kinds of key rings, T-shirts, souvenirs, and Malcolm got a tarot card reading.

"Yo ass gon' turn into a frog at midnight if you fuck around with that," Damon said.

"It's all in fun," Malcolm laughed.

Damon bought a woman's handmade jewelry, Shawn got a henna tattoo, and Kevin bought a T-shirt that said "Black, Gay, and Proud."

"Y'all wanna go to that bike show? It's supposed to be starting in like fifteen minutes," Kevin asked looking at an itinerary.

"Lead the way," Damon said.

They headed to the block where the motorcycle bike show was and Malcolm went crazy over how hot the bikes were.

"Yo, I'm saving some cash to buy one of them!" he said pointing to a green and white Nissan motorcycle.

"The world will be a dangerous place," Shawn said.

They gawked at the bodies of the men on these motorcycles. Malcolm took off his shirt to flaunt his body too.

"Oh boy, here he goes," Shawn said.

Immediately, guys in the crowd started to stare at Malcolm. He flexed his abs and chest muscles making them jump to titillate the on-lookers. A few of them even reached out to touch him and he let them.

Damon, Kevin, and Shawn rolled their eyes at him.

"Oh, give me a fucking break," Kevin said.

"Don't hate. I got love for everybody," Malcolm said.

"How do you think Malik would feel if he knew you were out here letting dudes feel you up?" Shawn asked.

Surprisingly, Malcolm didn't have a quick comeback for that one. After a few more minutes of walking around shirtless, they noticed that he eased his shirt back on. But no one called him out on it.

They spent a few hours out there perusing the vendors, taking pictures with each other and the bikers. Two drag queens were having a yelling match and then they went at it, fighting like wild beasts. And they were going for blood!

"Beat he-she's ass! Beat that bitch's ass!" Malcolm yelled out as they all watched.

Some cops came and broke up the fight and the crowd let out a disappointed, "Awwww," in unison.

"Y'all smell that?" Damon asked.

"You talking about that barbecue?" Shawn asked.

"Yeah, that shit smelling real good right about now," Malcolm said rubbing his stomach.

"Let's get some," Damon said.

"Wassup, Black?" said a feminine guy walking past him. He was hands down one of the prettiest males that any of the boys had ever seen.

Malcolm turned around and looked at him.

"Wassup, yo?"

"So you tryna act like you don't remember me?" the guy asked putting his hand on his hip and batting his lashes.

The boys each looked over their shades at the guy and Malcolm.

"Nah, I remember you."

"What's my name?"

"Brooklyn."

"No, I'm from Brooklyn but that's not my name."

"Das all I ever called you."

"Oh, aight. I see how you do."

"What you want me to do? I'm sorry," Malcolm said imitating Jay-Z.

"It's Kejuan."

"Right. Yeah, I remember you though." He definitely remembered those succulent lips.

"So what's good? You here and so am I."

"Yeah, I know. Lemme get your number."

Kejuan gave him his number.

"I'mma hit you later on."

"I'll be waiting."

Kejuan went to catch up with his friends and the boys all stared at Malcolm.

"What?"

"You forget about Malik that quick?"

"I'm not really gonna call him."

Shawn, Damon, and Kevin sucked their teeth and rolled their eyes.

"I swear to God. I'm not calling him."

"Yeah, not now."

"No self-control."

"Such a slore you are."

"Man, fuck y'all. Let's get this barbecue."

They ordered their food from a BBQ stand whose line was long.

"What time is the play?" Shawn asked.

"Four," Damon said.

Shawn looked at his watch and saw it was ten minutes to three. "Y'all wanna make it?"

"I do," Kevin said.

"Me too," Damon added.

"I guess I'm outnumbered. I don't wanna see no damn play."

"We can drop you off at the hotel, Malcolm."

"That would be the perfect set-up for him to call old boy. We are re-forming his ho ass for his relationship before this week is over."

"I was not gon' call him!"

"We know you ain't cuz you're coming to the play."

Malcolm sucked his teeth and continued to eat. They made their way through the crowd and got back to the truck.

"Dame, I wanna drive."

"Knock yourself out," Damon said throwing Shawn the keys.

Shawn drove downtown to the theatre. It was a black box theatre already crowded with wise-cracking gay folks expecting to see a good show.

"Oh, the shade up in here," Kevin said.

The four of them put on their shades and tooted their lips up and busted out laughing at how they all did the same thing at the same time.

"What's the name of this show?" Malcolm asked.

"Look at the program they gave you on the way in."

Malcolm looked down at the program he didn't even realize he had. He had a lot on his mind, and the play wasn't a part of his immediate thoughts.

"B-Boy Blues. Wasn't this a book back in the day?" Malcolm asked.

"Yeah, it was a whole series," Damon said.

"They got some fine muthafuckas in this cast," Malcolm said flipping through his program.

"You ain't never lied about that."

The lights went down and for the next two hours the audience screamed with laughter and was thoroughly entertained throughout.

"I gotta admit, that was pretty hot," Malcolm said.

"Yeah, it was good."

"Y'all wanna hit the DBQ magazine fashion show at the convention center?" Damon asked.

"Why not? The night is still young."

"I'm down too."

"If we goin' to a fashion show, I wanna get fly," Malcolm said.

"Yeah, it starts at eight so we can go change now."

Shawn drove back to the hotel where they showered and changed their clothes. At the fashion show, the audience was packing in and the front row was reserved for the industry elite and VIPS. But the guys managed to get decent seats. DBQ magazine logos were on display everywhere and they were signing up subscribers and selling copies of the most recent issue. The hilarious comedian Sampson McCormick hosted the fashion show and had everyone in stitches during his opening set. Not to mention his muscular chocolate pecs and arms were popping out of his tight shirt. It had all the men in the house ready to pounce as he told his jokes.

"Alright little gay boys and fag hags and the straight boys who snuck up in here, start clapping cuz here she comes. Show your love for the Southern Hummingbird of R&B, Tweet!" he shouted.

The crowd went wild as Tweet took the stage looking fly. She wore a beige dress, a cinch waist belt, big silver hoop earrings and her trademark long black hair. She got the crowd hyped up and ready for the show with her set of hits and a few new songs that the crowd all sang along to.

"I love her," Kevin said.

"Yeah, she's so underrated," Damon said.

She bowed graciously to thunderous applause and the fashion show started immediately after she left the stage. The boys enjoyed seeing the models strut their stuff on the catwalk. Especially during the swimsuit and pajama segment. The women had fierce walks and the men had ripped bodies and strutted with such confidence. Damon wanted to make a detour after the show so after picking up Popeye's for dinner, they made a stop in downtown Miami. It was an office building he pulled up to.

"I'll be right back," he said hopping out.

"Where the hell is he going?"

"Who the hell knows?"

"He better hurry up cuz I'm hungry."

Damon was swift in coming back. He jumped in the driver's seat and rolled out.

"Where'd you go?"

Damon pulled a bag of weed out of his pocket. "Shlack-a-dack," he said.

"Oh shit! Who you get that from?" Kevin asked.

"You know I get around."

"Lemme smell it." He passed it to Malcolm and he pressed it close to his nose. Impressed, he nodded his head and passed it back to Damon.

"We just need to hit the LQ and we can settle in for the night."

"Hell yeah! We getting it *in* tonight! This shit is potent and fresh!"

At the liquor store, Damon and Shawn went inside and stocked up on all the good stuff. They happily skipped up to their hotel suite, got comfortable, and put wet towels under the front door to keep the weed smell in the room. Malcolm finished eating first and commenced to rolling up the weed and mixing the drinks.

"You're just turning into a bartender, huh?" Kevin asked.

"I gets it in," he said.

The boys finished eating and each picked up the cups Malcolm poured them. Each one held up his drink and they toasted to living it up in Miami. They sparked up the bud in the hotel room and took chairs outside to the terrace and commenced to more drinking. A great breeze rolled off of the Atlantic Ocean under the clear night sky, making the extra-warm night tolerable. The conversation got more interesting the more intoxicated they got.

"I got one. What's the weakest line a man has thrown at you?" Shawn asked.

"'Yeah shorty, I got a girl. But I like a little dick on the side too.'"

"Is that what Kenny said to you?" Shawn asked.

"No. Kenny's ass ain't even tell me he was married. His wife called my phone, remember?"

"Oh yeah, that's right."

"What about this one," Malcolm said. "'Let's do it raw cuz I don't like how the condom feels.' I be like, 'I just met you. Get ya dangerous ass outta here.' And I ain't gon' stunt; doing it raw does feel good, but not when I don't know you."

"Why does everyone just wanna fuck?! Like where are the guys that wanna get to know you? I swear I get on these phone chat lines and what I hear more than anything is, 'Yo, I'm riding around in the whip looking to get it in or get my dick sucked. Hit me up.' I mean, what the fuck? Am I missing something?" Damon asked.

"Hell no. These muthafuckas out here ain't shit. Then they wanna act like they're all sweet and romantic, get your feelings in, and then when you give them some, they wanna disappear and act like they never liked you," Kevin said.

"I just wanna know why they lie so much," Shawn said.

Everyone turned and looked at Malcolm.

"Fuck y'all looking at me for?" Malcolm asked.

"You're one of them."

"I ain't never led nobody on thinking we was doing more than fucking. Niggas would just be wanting to be with me. Blowing up my phone and shit like I got a problem hitting ignore every time they call. I had to start telling them straight up, I ain't looking for no relationship. But niggas always think they can change you."

"What's wrong with a relationship?"

"Nothing, if it's what you want. But I didn't want that. I just wanted to fuck. They would be wanting to be with me. That's when I cut shit off. 'Til now."

"Dudes need to be up front," Kevin said.

"Dudes need to listen from the get-go. Bend over, touch your toes, let me do what I do so we can get on with this shit. Don't even take your pants all the way off cuz I ain't fin' to be in this muthafucka all night! Spread them cheeks and let's get this show on the road."

"You are so fucking nasty!" Shawn said laughing.

"That's why my name is Black. Cuz I don't give a fuck."

They stayed out on the terrace talking and laughing until the sun came up.

# 36

## BOOM BOOM BANG

The next day, the boys didn't wake up until the afternoon. They all got up tired and very sluggish but wanted to continue their fun. It was another beautiful day. They showered, dressed, and went down to the beach for the fish fry and ate lunch. Then they went to the Bayfront Park for the concert series that was beginning today in celebration of Black Pride. The crowded park was full of gay men and lesbians holding rainbow flags and wearing pride T-shirts. There were AG lesbians with lipstick girlfriends, drag queens, flamboyant gay men, and straight-looking gay men. The energy was electric as excitement about the concert buzzed in the air.

CeCe Peniston took the stage first looking gorgeous in a cream-colored outfit that showed off her curvy figure. Her hair was pulled back into a long jet black curly ponytail, showing off her big gold hoop earrings. She came out and got the crowd rocking with the party anthems she was best known for. And she worked it out. The crowd showed her a lot of love and her voice sounded as clear and strong as ever.

When the host introduced Monifah as the next performer, the entire audience leaped to their feet to give her a screaming standing ovation. She came out smiling and looked stunning in a form-fitting dress with fly shoes, purple streaked hair, and long chandelier earrings. She kept the crowd on their feet as they danced while she sang. Especially during "I miss you (Come back home)" and "Touch it." She was just as sassy and soulful as she wanted to be. And the audience showed her so much love.

"I'm so proud to be a part of this community, y'all. Stay strong in what you believe in. Love one another and thank you all for your support. Keep supporting the R&B divas!" she said.

The crowd cheered as Monifah's wife, Terez, came and brought her a bouquet of flowers, kissed her cheek, and escorted her off the stage at the end of her set.

The crowd went wild when the headliners of the day, En Vogue, took the stage. During their hour-long set, they sang all of their hits and looked and sounded as good as they ever did. Everything about them was immaculate: their hair, their outfits, the way they moved with such precision, and their harmonies were still tight like glue. The ladies seemed to be in rare form as they sent the crowd into a soulful harmonious heaven with all of their classic hits. They received a rousing standing ovation and plenty of cheers.

The boys made their way out of the crowded park and headed back to the hotel to get ready for the all-white party. It was going to be on the rooftop of a fancy hotel that none of them could pronounce the name of in South Beach. Shawn watched Kevin walk into the bathroom with his foundation and concealer. He followed him in and looked at him.

"What?"

"I'm worried about you, Kev. You were talking about him in your sleep last night."

"What was I saying?"

"It was like he was chasing you and you were saying, 'Stop! Leave me alone!'" Kevin looked at his reflection in the mirror. "That's not okay, Kev. This man has hurt you more than I think you even realize."

Unable to hold it in for a second longer, Kevin cracked. He leaned against the sink counter and his body shook as he cried. Shawn passed him a towel and he pressed his face into it and cried harder. Shawn turned on the water in the sink so Damon and Malcolm wouldn't hear.

"I'm so sorry about yesterday. I shouldn't have snapped at you the way I did. I'm just so scared. I don't know what to do."

"It's okay. And I'm sorry for catching such an attitude with you too." He reached out and hugged Shawn him. "Thank you so much for not telling the guys. That really means a lot to me."

"You're gonna tell them, right?"

He nodded. "I will. I swear I will. And I love you, Shawn."

"I love you too. Now beat that face for these kids so we can show them how we New York City boys do it."

He stood up to wash his face and saw the dark marks were fading. He reapplied his foundation and hit the dark spots with concealer. They all finished getting dressed in their all-white and topped it off with diamond stud earrings that sparkled brightly. Once again, NYC swag was all up and through and they felt like rock stars.

"Damn, we look good," Malcolm said.

They piled into their truck and headed to the party. They let the valets park their truck and took the elevator up to the roof. When the elevator doors opened, all they could see was a sea of people dressed in all-white through the big glass doors. There were big pictures of the actors Jensen Atwood and Darryl Stephens on display who were the hosts for the all-white affair at this swanky hotel.

The DJ was playing "Fine" by Mary J. Blige. A photographer was snapping pictures as they walked in.

"Would you gentlemen like pictures?" he asked.

Then the boys posed for a picture of the four of them. The photographer gave them his business card and told them they could buy the pictures from his website. The warm summer breeze blew onto the nicely decorated rooftop. The huge blue pool was covered with a sturdy non-glass cover; there were trees and shrubs, big plush couches, and a breathtaking view of the Miami skyline and the beach. The boys hit the bar to get shots of liquor in them.

"Alright, y'all. Your hosts for the evening have arrived. Y'all seen them on TV and on the big screen as Noah and Wade. Give it up for the stars of Noah's Arc! Mr. Darryl Stephens and Mr. Jensen Atwooooooooood!" the DJ said.

The DJ cranked up "Remember the Love" by Adrianna Evans which was the *Noah's Arc* theme song. The main entrance doors opened and in walked Darryl Stephens and Jensen Atwood looking dapper in their all-white. The crowd went wild cheering and clapping. Flash bulbs went off like crazy as people snapped pictures of them making their grand entrance. Security accompanied them walking the long red carpet to the stage. People showed them so much love. They smiled, waved, shook hands and gave hugs as they made their way to the stage. Darryl and Jensen were just as sexy and handsome in person as they were on screen. People were still applauding and snapping pictures when they got to the stage. After a little bantering, Jensen let everyone know that he had

213

copies of his new calendar for sale and where they could purchase them. Darryl told everyone to check out two new films he had coming to theatres in the fall. As they left the stage and began to mingle with party goers, the boys hit the dance floor. The DJ was going in and making everyone dance with his great playlist.

A picture of Michael Jackson popped on the DJ's screen and he played a Michael Jackson play list that included "Billie Jean", "Blame it on the Boogie", "This Place Hotel", "Off the Wall", "Rock with You", "Don't Stop Til You Get Enough", "I Wanna be Where You Are", "Bad", "Remember the Time", "PYT", and "I Can't Help It."

"Rest in peace Michael Jackson! Let's swing through back in the day y'all!" the DJ announced. He took it back to 70s' disco, 80s' and 90s' R&B and hip-hop that had the gays losing their minds. Everyone became covered in sweat and slowly started to shed layers. Men were walking around shirtless and beginning to flaunt. Ladies with hair were pinning it up and still partying. They were on the floor non-stop for almost two hours, just dancing and having a great time.

"Oh my God, I ain't partied this hard in a long time," Damon said.

"Yo. that DJ is rocking the shit out this party," Malcolm said.

"I wanna get a calendar from Jensen Atwood before they're all sold out," Shawn said.

"Oh my God, he is *beautiful* in person! I want one too!" Kevin said.

They wiped the sweat from their faces and went to the line where Jensen was selling his calendars. When they got closer, they could see him and began to talk about him.

"Look at that smile," Shawn said looking at Jensen smiling to pose for a picture with a fan.

"Look at that skin," Damon said.

"Look at that body," Kevin said.

When they got up to him, Jensen signed their calendars and posed for pictures with each of them. He was so polite and handsome. They found Darryl Stephens mingling in the crowd and snapped pictures with him too.

"We got any Whitney Houston fans in the house? Let's get it going for her tonight!" He put a picture of her smiling face with angel wings on her back on his jumbo screen. The crowd went wild when they saw it and danced to her hits.

He played the popular club versions of "It's Not Right But it's Okay" and "Queen of the Night." Then "I Wanna Dance With Somebody", "How will I Know", "I'm Every Woman", "One of Those Days", "Step by Step", "I'm your Baby Tonight", "So Emotional", and "Celebrate." They boys sang along while the songs played but took a break from the dance floor and enjoyed the beautiful view of Miami. The opening chords of "Million Dollar Bill" by Whitney Houston came on.

"Is that our jam?" Damon asked.

"That's our jam!"

"Oh, let's get it! Come on Black!" Kevin said.

Damon led the way back to the middle of the dance floor and they all followed. They sang every lyric and were extra loud on all the "Oh-oh, oh-oh's" and danced really hard to this song. It felt like they were on the dance floor all by themselves and they didn't care who was watching. They loved this song and let everyone know it.

While catching his breath, Malcolm felt someone tap him on back. He turned around and there was Kejuan looking quite pretty in all white. Kejuan wasn't a drag queen, but he happened to be a stunningly beautiful man with somewhat androgynous looks and it caught Malcolm off guard.

"Hey, Black."

"Wassup, Brooklyn?"

"You wanna dance?"

"Uh, yeah, sure."

Kejuan took him back to the dance floor and started grinding up against him. He bent over and stuck his ass on Malcolm's crotch as he purposely tried to make Malcolm hard. And it worked.

"Happy to see me, huh?"

Malcolm smiled and continued to dance with him. The more they danced, the harder Malcolm's dick got until all he could think about was fucking. Thoughts of Malik crossed his mind, but he shook them away.

Damn, he smells good, Malcolm thought. Kejuan grinded himself closer to Malcolm and put Malcolm's big muscular arms around his small torso as they danced to more Whitney. Malcolm's dick grew harder and harder. Suddenly without warning, Kejuan turned around and kissed Malcolm. He reached down and grabbed Malcolm's hard dick and looked him deep in the eye. Malcolm eyed him like he was a juicy piece of steak.

"Come on. I know you want this and I want you too," Kejuan said.

Malcolm bit his bottom lip and looked at Kejuan. He wanted to tear him up. And he was feeling mannish. What Malik didn't know wouldn't hurt him. Just this one time, and from here on out, he'd be faithful.

With that promise egging him on, he followed Kejuan to the exit without saying anything to his boys who were at the bar having more drinks.

*I'll send them a text.* He turned to look at them one final time and slipped out the door. The elevator couldn't move fast enough to the ground floor. As soon as the elevator doors closed, Kejuan was all over him and Malcolm welcomed his touches. Once the doors opened, they darted into the lobby. While Kejuan went to flag down a cab, Malcolm felt his hard penis deflate as he thought about Malik. He tried to shake off his guilty feelings but couldn't. He was thinking about Malik so much that he could literally hear his voice in his head. It sounded like Malik was calling his name.

Then he turned around and realized that Malik's voice wasn't in his head. Malik was walking into the all-white party with the same three friends from his first date. Malcolm's stomach did a back-flip.

"Wassup, Malik? What you doing here?" Malcolm asked as Malik hugged and kissed him.

"They talked me into coming down here and I knew I would surprise you."

"Well, I'm surprised."

"Come on, walk in with me." Malik extended his arm. As Malcolm looped his arm with Malik's, Kejuan reached out and grabbed Malcolm's free arm.

"I'm ready, Black. You still coming with me?" Kejuan said pressing his body against Malcolm's.

Malik froze and looked at Kejuan. "Who is this?"

"This is, uhm...uh..."

Kejaun smiled at Malik. "Oh, is this one of your friends, Black?"

"No. He's my, uhm...uh..."

"Boyfriend," Malik supplied the word for him.

"Boyfriend?"

"Yes, his *boyfriend*." Malik eyed Kejuan.

"Black, you have a boyfriend?"

Malcolm cast his eyes to the ground. "Yeah."

"Then why was you just about to fuck me?" Kejuan said turning into a complete girl.

"What? I wasn't bout to fuck you."

"Yes, you was."

"Malik, he's lying."

"Why the fuck you tryna play me, Black?" Kejuan said getting loud, pushing Malcolm.

"Calm down, man."

"No! You was just bout to fuck me and now all of a sudden you got a man. It's alright. Cuz he need to know how you done ran through half of the dudes in New York anyway cuz you's a nasty ass ho!"

"Yo, shut the fuck up, man."

"No! Why don't you tell him how you just had me bent over and was kissing me?"

Malcolm mushed Kejuan.

"Don't you put your fucking hands on me, nigga! Fuck you! Old lying ass nigga stay tryna front and you know we was bout to fuck!" People were beginning to watch the developing fight. Malcolm looked at Malik's face, which was extremely tight. Malcolm wanted to lay Kejuan out. "Go ahead; tell him! Tell him you were about to fuck me."

"Get the fuck outta here, man!" Malcolm screamed.

"Yeah, whatever, nigga. You know what was up. He probably don't even suck dick like I do," Kejuan said getting into his cab. Malik asked his friends to give him a minute to speak to Malcolm alone. They ice-grilled Malcolm and went into the lobby of the hotel watching through the glass doors.

"Is any of that true?" Malcolm didn't say anything. "I asked you a question."

"Malik—"

"Just tell me the truth."

"He was..."

"It's a yes or no question."

"I..."

"Yes. Or no."

"Yes."

Immediately Malik's eyes filled with tears. "So you were gonna cheat on me. After you promised that you wouldn't."

"Just let me explain. I..." Malik's right hook landed in Malcolm's jaw. Malcolm's body stumbled backwards.

"I didn't do anything," Malcolm said as blood spilled from his mouth onto his white shirt.

"But you were going to!"

"But I didn't."

"Because I showed up! I knew yo' ass wasn't shit! I swear to God, I fucking knew it! Just a dirty ass ho that thinks he can do what he wants. Look at me, y'all! I'm Black, the biggest fucking whore in New York. Were you even gonna use a condom? You know what? I can't even believe I trusted your stupid ass. Actually let me take that back. I'm stupid for thinking I could trust a piece of shit ass nigga like you to be faithful."

"You can trust me. I'm sorry."

"I know you're sorry. You fucking sorry ass bastard. You go to fucking hell." Malik turned to walk into the hotel with tears of anger streaming down his face. As hard as Malcolm tried to fight them, tears began to pour from his eyes as well. And he couldn't stop them.

Back on the roof, the guys were beginning to wonder where Malcolm had disappeared to. As they began to look for him, he came through the elevator doors scanning the roof for Malik. When he spotted him, he approached but Malik's friends pushed him away.

"He don't wanna talk to you." It was like déjà vu of when he pushed Jamon away to get away from Shawn. Now he understood Jamon's plight.

"Malik, come on; let me just talk to you," Malcolm pleaded.

"Leave me the fuck alone!" Malik screamed. Malik's scream made people's heads turn. Suddenly Kevin spotted Malcolm and pointed to him so the boys could see him.

"Just give me a chance." One of Malik's friends grabbed Malcolm by the collar and pushed him away. Malcolm punched him in the face and he fell to the ground. Malik's other friends rushed Malcolm and then Malcolm's boys came over to intervene. Before things got too out of hand, security approached and threw them all out. Malik's friends whisked him away while the boys all but ripped Malcolm's shirt off of his back to get him to go with them before the cops arrested them all.

While Malcolm tried to explain everything to the boys on the way back to the hotel, he kept saying, "It's not over!"

But even he couldn't convince himself of that.

# 37

## THE SAGA CONTINUES

M alcolm spent the better part of the night calling Malik to try to explain himself. But he wouldn't answer his phone. He left voicemails and sent text messages convincing himself that if Malik didn't answer him, he must not have gotten the calls or text messages. So he doubled and tripled up his calls and text messages. He did go on facebook and see that Malik had blocked him though. That wasn't a good sign.

"Just leave him alone. He'll reach out if he wants to talk." Damon said.

"I fucked up D."

"Were you gonna actually do anything with Kejuan?" Malcolm nodded.

"Damn. Why, though?"

"I wasn't thinking. I just wanted to fuck. I was horny and he looked good. I just wanna tell him I'm sorry."

"Well, come on; let's get you outta here. Maurice Jamal is premiering his new movie today. And it will be over just in time for us to hit the concert again." Malcolm didn't much feel like it but the boys insisted. As entertaining as the movie was, Malcolm was sullen the entire time.

Back at the Bayfront park, the concert crowd was even bigger today and braved the intense heat. Deborah Cox opened the show. Her seemingly effortless powerhouse vocals and stunning beauty took the crowd by storm and got them very excited. Fantasia brought her down-home soul and electrifying stage presence to the stage and slayed like she always does. Jennifer Hudson took the stage last and brought the crowd to its knees and blew them away with her voice. The three talented ladies closed the show with a rousing rendition of "I'm Every Woman." Malcolm did manage to enjoy the concert and temporarily forget about his situation. They truly sang their hearts out. As they were leaving Malcolm received a text from Malik.

Malik: Stop fucking calling and texting me. You filled up my voicemail you jackass.

Malcolm: I'm sorry.

Malik: Yes, you are. You showed me exactly how sorry you are.

Malcolm: What can I do to make it up to u?

Malik: Lose my number.

Malcolm: I don't want it to end like this.

Malik: I can't believe you were gonna go fuck him.

Malcolm: But I didn't fuck him.

Malik: You were going to.

Malcolm: But I didn't. U gotta give me another chance. I really love u.

Malik: You don't love nobody but yourself and that ashy ass dick of yours. I hope that shit falls off.

Malcolm: I deserve that.

Malik: I haven't given you what you deserve yet.

Malcolm: What is that supposed to mean?

Malik: It means leave me the fuck alone.

Malcolm: I still love u.

Malik: I fucking hate you. How many dudes have you cheated on me with?

Malcolm: I never cheated on u.

Malik: I don't believe you. You probably gave me something with your whorish ass.

Malcolm: I swear to God on my father's grave I never cheated on u. And I'm clean. I ain't got nothing to give u but my heart.

Malik: Fuck you, your heart, and your father's grave. If you ever see me again, you better cross the street.

Malcolm: Damn why you gotta go off on my pops?

Malik: Because I hate his bitch ass son.

Malcolm: U told me u loved me.

Malik: And you promised to never cheat on me. Guess we both said things we didn't really mean.

Malcolm: U still love me and u know you do.

Malik did not respond to the text so Malcolm text messaged him again. Still, no response. Finally, Malcolm called Malik, but Malik ignored all his calls. Malcolm called him so many times that Malik finally turned off his phone. A tear fell down his face from behind his shades. The boys were too busy discussing the concert to notice the tear.

*Me and my wayward dick strike again. Fuck!*

# 38

## I'M STILL HERE

Their last day in Miami, the boys awoke to a rising sunshine that was bittersweet. Poor Malcolm's heart was broken and they all noticed. Damon wanted to go to the Sunday morning inspirational service being held at the convention center. Shawn was curious as to what it was, and Kevin enjoyed church growing up. Malcolm was none too pleased about the idea. He wasn't a fan of religion and abhorred the idea of going to church. They showered, got dressed and piled into the truck. When they got to the convention center, there was barely any place to park.

"Damn, it's mad people here. This better not feel like church," Malcolm said.

"I thought you believed in God," Damon said.

"I do, but I still hate church."

"This isn't exactly church. It's just something to get a little inspiration. Besides, it's in honor of Pride," Shawn said.

"Well, all I know is I ain't fin' to pay no tithes."

"Get your heathen ass out of the car and let's go," Damon said.

They followed the crowd inside the convention center and found seats up towards the front. The place was filling up quickly. For it to not actually be church, it sure felt like Sunday morning service. There was a band seated ready to play, a podium for the speaker which resembled a pulpit, and a big sign that said "GOD LOVES YOU TOO!"

"There are more queens up in here than the village on a Saturday night," Malcolm said looking around at all the gay people.

"Well, it looks like you're one of them today," Damon said.

Kevin and Shawn snapped their fingers and went, "*He-ey!*"

A pretty lady with a short haircut dressed in all white took the stage and stood behind the podium. "Good morning, everyone. Can we all please take our seats?"

Everyone found seats and those who couldn't stood up.

"Thank you. Good morning again and welcome to the Miami Convention Center. Happy Pride to all of you beautiful brothers and sisters. My name is Pastor Kenya Dobson and I pastor an SGL church in Atlanta. I know many of you are used to being in church at this time on Sundays. I know I am and look forward to it every Sunday. What we wanted to do is have a spiritual rejuvenation service here today in honor of Pride. We wanted to go where the need for love was and thought this would be a perfect place to come. Let me start by letting you all know today is brought to us all by nothing but love. God loves you all the way he created you. I love you all the way he created you, and I hope you all love yourselves the way he created you."

The crowd applauded.

"With all the gay suicides and beatings and everything going on in the world, I want to make it known that I stand here today in the name of love. And I hope you all share it with each other. I'm not a same-gender loving person myself, but I love you all just the same. My husband is back at home in Atlanta conducting service today and he sends his love as well. We as a couple of the cloth decided to reach out to the LGBT community simply because there was a need to. We know about all of the bigotry and hatred aimed at gay people and it's not of God. So what we're gonna do today is give some praise and honor to our Creator. We are going to thank him for each other, life, love, liberty, and the freedom to live in a way that makes us all happy. At this time, I'd like to bring forth Pastor Raymond Redgrave of the United Methodist Church in Detroit, Michigan."

Pastor Redgrave led everyone in a prayer and told his own story of hope and redemption as a gay man. He'd been disowned by his family but taken in off the street by another family who didn't know him but they raised him as their own. They took him to church and taught him to love himself for who he was. By the end of his sermon, he was in tears but thanking God for the gift of ministry and using him to inspire other gay people. He got a standing ovation.

Pastor Dobson came back to the stage and preached about the importance of love, tolerance, and forgiveness for everyone.

"It is so important you forgive people. Whether it's a lover who cheated on you and broke your heart, whether you've been raped by someone who was supposed to protect you, whether you've been hurt by someone who had no business hurting you, or whether you got yourself caught in a compromising situation you had no business being in—you forgive yourself. And you forgive that other person so you can continue to get your blessings. You have everything inside of you to be the best you that you can be."

Damon glanced over at the boys and noticed that Pastor Dobson had their full attention. Even Malcolm was looking at her and nodding, fully engaged in the service.

"At this time, I want to call forth the Agape Anointed Voices Choir who hail from Houston, Texas under the direction of the world renowned choir director, Mrs. Sandra Barnhardt. So we want to give them a warm welcome this morning. Put your hands together for them."

The audience clapped. Sandra Barnhardt, an attractive brown skinned woman with a short haircut rose up a choir of 60 men and women all dressed in black and white. As they made their way to the stage, the choir director took the microphone.

"Good morning everyone. I'd like to thank Pastor Dobson for that wonderful introduction. As she said, we are the Agape Anointed Voices Choir from Houston, Texas. We're very happy to be here with you all today and thank you for welcoming us. We held open auditions for all of our singers, we get together and practice twice a week, and we hope to move you today with our music and bless you in your spirits. Thank you for being here today and God bless you. We're going to start off with Roland Carter's arrangement of 'Lift Every Voice and Sing.' We're going to follow that up with the acapella spiritual, 'In Bright Mansions,' and the Kurt Carr classic, 'For Every Mountain.' Joining us on 'For Every Mountain' will be internationally acclaimed opera singer Mrs. Nicole Barrow White. Enjoy," Sandra said putting the microphone back.

She took her place in front of the choir and raised her arms. She gave the tempo to the band and they began to play. It was clear that from the first note, this was no ordinary choir. They were truly anointed. As they sang, there were hands in the air and tears flowing all around. And the soloist Nicole Barrow White didn't disappoint.

She was a beautiful chocolate brown woman with sparkling eyes and a bright smile. With her lush and crystal clear soprano, she brought the audience to its feet. Her diction and high notes were flawless and the audience was beside itself. The choir followed that up with the songs "Glorious" and "Revelations."

"For our next selection, we would like to welcome a twin brother dance duo also from Houston. Please welcome Dean and Craig Smith and our special guest soloist, Ms. Seychelle Elise on Richard Smallwood's 'Angels Watching Over Me.'"

The handsome, muscular twin-brother dance duo took center stage as Seychelle made her way to the mic. Seychelle was a full-figured chocolate woman with long braids and had the look of a singer who was going to kill. And did she ever! Sweet as honey, her anointed impassioned vocal ability sent the audience into praise and worship mode. Hands flew up in the air and people stood to their feet, caught up in the spirit. The Smith brothers' liturgical dance made the song even more powerful with their flexibility and grace and great passion in their faces as they danced to the words. After a standing ovation, the choir sat and six female dancers joined the twins and danced to "I Am" by CeCe Winans and "Serenade" by Sheri Jones Moffet.

Pastor Dobson came back on stage and asked if anyone wanted to share their testimonies. A few people came to the microphone to share their stories. One man shared his testimony of how as a kid he and his father didn't get along. His father feared he would grow up and be gay. But since he'd become an adult, his father had a change of heart and now they were rebuilding their relationship since the death of his mother. That really struck a chord with Damon. A woman told a story of how she recently lost her grandmother, but it was her Nana who told her to be proud of who she was and not ashamed.

An AG lesbian with a man's haircut and spinning waves held the hand of her exquisitely gorgeous girlfriend and took the microphone next.

"I ain't even wanna come here today but she insisted upon it. I ain't never felt this much love before in my life that I feel right now. It's all because of this woman I'm standing up here with right now. I just wanna say thank you to her and to all of you. I'm a better person today because of what's happening around me right now in this place. So thank you. I love you, babe," she said to her girlfriend before leaving the stage.

"I wanna go up," Kevin whispered to Shawn.

Shawn looked at him. "You sure?"

He nodded and rose from his seat, making his way up to the microphone.

"What is he doing?" Malcolm asked Damon.

"I don't know. Shawn, what's he doing?" Damon asked looking just as confused as Malcolm.

"Telling the truth." Shawn looked up at his friend and smiled his encouragement.

Kevin took the microphone and sighed heavily. He was nervous but needed to talk.

"Hi. My name is Kevin Malone." He looked around at the thousands of faces that stared at him. For a moment, nerves overtook him, but he looked at Shawn's nod, took a steadying breath and continued. "I'm in town from New York City with my three best friends." He pointed to them in the crowd. "There's something that I need to say. Only one of them knows about it and I'm gonna ask him to stand next to me while I do this."

Shawn came and stood next to him and put his hand on his back.

"For the past few months, I've been in a relationship. With a man whom I thought was perfect. He's Ivy League educated, very successful, a multi-millionaire who drives a Bentley. He owns a condo on the Upper West Side of Manhattan and a mansion in his hometown of Philadelphia. He wined me, dined me, treated me like I was a king. I thought, wow, I've really hit the jackpot on this one. But he had a secret."

Damon and Malcolm sat in shocked silence.

"He has a very volatile temper. At first I thought, maybe he just has a bit of a temper. We all get angry sometimes. But then it turned on me. I realized he didn't just have a temper. He had a problem. I became his punching bag. And I took it because I thought like most domestic violence victims that maybe it was my fault. Maybe I did something to make him react that way. Maybe I should have kept my mouth shut about certain things. Maybe I should have let him have his way on certain things. But when you get to the point where you're running down the street for your life with the person who claims to love you chasing you and screaming 'I'm gonna kill you' then you know it's not you. For months I've been holding this secret from my friends until a few days ago, my friend Shawn here saw me putting on makeup trying to cover my bruises. And he reminded me that what I was going through was wrong and I needed to tell someone. I wanna say to everyone here that no man is worth him putting his hands on you." Emotions choked Kevin and he struggled to speak as tears filled his eyes.

The audience clapped, encouraging him to go on.

"No matter what, don't ever let anyone put their hands on you. Whether they claim to love you or not. I didn't love myself enough. Or know my self-worth. I've been in quite a few abusive relationships. The past two relationships were emotionally abusive, which is just as bad as physical abuse. With this guy, I thought if I leave, who will love me? But not anymore. I have the courage to walk away and be by myself if I need to. And I wanna thank my brother next to me, Shawn, for telling me what I needed to hear and not what I wanted to hear. Love yourselves unconditionally. And if you're in a bad situation, please don't suffer in silence. Walk away and tell someone. It may save your life. Thank you."

Shawn pulled him close and hugged him tight. They walked off the stage hugging and crying, and a nearby woman pressed tissues into their hands as they passed by.

Pastor Dobson took the stage. "Kevin, come back." Kevin stopped in the aisle and turned around. "Come back and bring your friends with you."

All the boys went up to the stage and stood near Pastor Dobson. Kevin stood closest and she reached out and hugged him tight. The audience clapped.

"Thank you for sharing that. I hope you all were listening to what he had to say because it's real. Domestic violence is a rising issue in the LGBT community as well as the heterosexual community. And there is a place for you to go. You can call the domestic violence hotline or go online to www.thehotline.org. They will help you and there is a safe place you can go. Our brother Kevin is absolutely right. Don't ever devalue yourself and allow yourself to be mistreated. You are worth being loved and cherished. I'll see you gentlemen after service."

They turned to walk off of the stage. "The choir is going to close us out, so let's welcome them back."

The choir came back up and took their places.

"God bless you all for sharing your stories of triumph. We have the perfect song to minister to you right now." She motioned for Seychelle Elise to come back to the mic.

The pianist began to play "I'm Still Here" by Dorinda Clark Cole and they tore the place up! As the song reached its peak, Kevin walked up to the front of the room and threw himself onto the altar in tears. The boys followed him and got on their knees next to him, each shedding tears for their own individual pain and clinging to one another. Kevin cried every tear of every bit of stress he had been carrying around. And everyone in the place was moved for him. Seychelle walked over to each of them and took each one of them by hand and kept singing the words, "You're still here." Their tears continued to fall and they lifted their hands in praise.

When the song ended, she hugged them and she led them all in a special prayer.

The boys returned to their seats filled with hope and euphoria. The choir kept everyone on their feet with the energetic choir selections: "We Sing the Praises to our King", "Ride up in the Chariot", "Ride on King Jesus" and closed with the popular Richard Smallwood classic "Total Praise." The dancers, the band, and the choir brought the house down with that one.

"Thank you all for coming out today! We love you all and remember, do everything with love and keep God first! He's an awesome God and will love you when you're up and when you are down. Have a blessed day everyone! And you can purchase the Agape Anointed Choir's CD out in the hallway right now."

People swarmed Kevin and thanked him for his honesty. Pastor Dobson found him in the crowd and said a prayer for him and the boys, putting her hands on Kevin. She prayed for strength, courage, and love in his time of turmoil. None of them anticipated being moved like this.

"I want you boys to come and visit me in Atlanta. Here is my card. I expect to hear from you soon. God bless you," she said hugging them all.

"That was the most spiritually transcendent moment I have ever had in my life," Shawn said as they walked back to the truck.

"Me too. I love y'all," Damon said as he put his arm around Kevin.

"Love y'all too," Shawn said.

"Me too," Malcolm said.

"Me three," Kevin said.

Even though Damon, Malcolm, and Shawn were filled with joy from the service, they were pissed about Charles hurting their friend. And they were not about to take this lightly or turn the other cheek.

# 39

## REAL TALK

The flight back to New York was a smooth and a quick one. Although it didn't feel that way for any of the boys. There was much to discuss once they returned. They all agreed to meet up the next day at Kevin's house to discuss what their next steps would be. As they all showed up at Kevin's house, they noticed they were all wearing black and hadn't even discussed it with each other.

"How is it that we're all wearing black?" Damon asked.

"Because a war is starting."

"Well, fellas, Miami was something. Where do we start?"

"I'll start," Kevin said. He took a deep swallow. "I got a restraining order against Charles." He held it up.

"That's good. But the big question here is why didn't you tell us what was going on?"

"I didn't realize what was happening. Until it was too late. But my assistant Marcia gave me some information about a self-defense class to attend."

"You told your assistant and you didn't tell us?"

"I didn't tell her. She overheard me and Charles talking in my office one day."

"Did he ever assault you at your job?"

"No."

"Threaten to?"

"No."

"Well, I'm not gonna mince words here. I for one am a little more than pissed that you didn't think you could come to us."

"It's not that I didn't think I couldn't come to you. I just had to try and get a grip on the situation."

"And now?"

"Excuse me Damon for not being as perfect as you and not always knowing what to do in times of crisis," Kevin snapped.

"It's not about that. He could have killed you. And no one would have known."

"He didn't."

"But he could have."

"He's not going to."

"Hey guys listen. At least now he's got a restraining order. Now Charles will know the consequences if he comes back around," Shawn piped in.

"That restraining order ain't gon' do shit. A muthafucka like Charles needs to get the shit beat out of him so he knows what the fuck is really up."

"I'm agreeing with Malcolm."

"Well I'm not," Shawn said.

"Neither am I."

"Aight. Let's kill his ass then."

"What?! And then what? Run off to Mexico afterwards?" Shawn exclaimed.

"I'm just saying, yo. We need to eighty-six this character before some more shit happens. That could be our insurance to make sure he doesn't come back."

"Malcolm, please come off of level ten," Shawn said.

"You was on level ten when it was you and Jamon."

"And you're only on level ten because of what's happening with you and Malik. So *you* calm down!"

"Don't try to turn this shit around on me!"

"Easy you guys! Nobody is killing anybody." Kevin said.

"I ain't suggesting we do. Y'all know I know goons that'll handle that shit for me."

"Malcolm. Come back. Focus please."

Malcolm sucked his teeth.

"I'm not saying we should kill him like Malcolm says, but I damn sure think we should let him know this isn't gonna continue."

"Are y'all hearing yourselves right now? Y'all sat next to me in Miami at that service crying your eyes out and now y'all are talking about killing and beating him up? We need to go to the police and handle this like mature adults instead of trying to be vigilantes."

"Shawn, stop being a punk man! This nigga been fucking your boy up and all you wanna do is go to the cops? And say what? My gay best friend has been getting his ass beat by his boyfriend? They'll laugh your ass right out that precinct. We need to fuck that nigga up. And if y'all don't want to then I'll make one phone call and it'll be a done deal."

"Everybody just hold up!" Kevin said. "Now I appreciate everyone's input but remember this is *my* situation to handle. Malcolm, I don't want you making any phone calls. I'm going to do this the right way. I am going to file this restraining order and let the police know what's been going on. And y'all better than anyone should know I am not ashamed of being gay so I will tell whoever I need to in order to protect myself."

"Are you gonna look into the self-defense classes?"

"Yes."

"You sure this is how you wanna do this?"

"Positive."

"Okay. But if he hits you again, we're doing this Malcolm's way."

"Kevin, I'll go with you to make the report."

"Thank you, Shawn."

"Malcolm, have you heard from Malik?"

"Nah."

"Are you gonna reach out to him?"

"Nah, I'm off it. I'mma prolly just get up with Kejuan now that I'm back home."

"And what do you think that will solve?"

"Nothing. But shit, it ain't like Malik is gon' come back anyway so I may as well go back to Black."

"Don't you think you should take some time for yourself since all of this just blew up in your face the way that it did? You need to slow down."

"Dame. I don't how you always got the most shit to say about other niggas' relationships and you ain't got no man. And ain't had one in forever."

Shawn and Kevin both looked away almost as if they wanted to suppress laughter.

"Excuse me?"

"You heard what I said."

"You know what? I'm done. Manless old hag Damon is just gonna go home."

"Yeah? Well on your way why don't you club some random nigga over his head and take him back home with you so you don't go by yourself."

"Fuck you, Malcolm!"

"No, fuck you, D! I'mma say it for all three of us. Yo ass always tryna go in on our shit when you ain't got shit to go home to except a dog and a fucking vibrator. So you ain't got shit to say about how we handling ours cuz at least we had something to cozy up to recently that wasn't on the DL and was really ours."

"Well, at least I have my—"

"Don't you mention that fucking house or that Range Rover cuz yo' ass still ain't had no man with all them accessories you got!"

"Is that how you all feel?" Damon asked glaring at them. Shawn and Kevin were tight lipped and looked at each other. "Okay. Fine. I'll go. At least now I know how you all really feel about me." Damon stormed out and slammed the door. Silence.

"That needed to be said." Kevin said.

"It did. But somebody shoulda at least went after him." Shawn quipped.

"Yet here we are. Sitting."

"And sitting."

"Still sittin'." They looked at each other and bust out laughing.

"Aww, man, I needed that laugh."

"Me too."

"But wait did you see the way he whipped that invisible weave over his shoulder? *Is that how you all feel?* (Big gasp) Well then I'm just gonna *leave!* Bitch went pumping outta here with that dramatic turn like he was Angela Bassett in "Waiting to Exhale."

*"What am I supposed to do for money?!"* They yelled in unison in a fit of laughter that had tears streaming down their faces and could barely breathe.

"Lawd y'all stupid!"

"Malcolm, are you really okay?"

"Yeah, man, I'm good. But look fellas, I'mma roll. Kev, let me know if you change your mind about making that call."

"I don't think I will but thank you."

"Aight, see y'all later," Malcolm said as he left. Once outside of Kevin's front door he looked at a picture of him and Malik on his phone in happier times. He sighed and put on his headphones and shades as he contemplated how he could possibly fix the mess he'd made of his broken relationship.

# 40

## I'M MOVIN' ON

In one of the best moods he had been in months, Shawn woke up to a beautiful sunny morning. He looked out the window in the distance at the sun shining over the fabulous Manhattan skyline. He turned on some upbeat music, made himself breakfast, and began to clean up his house. It was a new day indeed. He could now think of Jamon without becoming emotional and accepted his newly single status. Now that his mind was clear again, it was really time to start doing Shawn.

He made himself a list of things he wanted to do and hopped on his laptop to start googling things. That very day, he took a ride up to the Pelham Bay golf course in the Bronx to sign up for lessons. He was surprised at how relaxing and fun it was. He took up yoga on Saturday mornings, would treat himself to a movie once a week, and finally put together ideas for the book he had always wanted to write. He may have been on summer vacation from work but his calendar was quickly filling up with new hobbies and research on the book he was beginning to write. He even created an online profile on a dating website. He got a lot of sexual favor requests from guys asking for oral because they thought his full pink lips were sexy.

After a day on there, he got a message from a cute guy named Derrick who actually seemed interested in more than just sex. He only lived across the water in Newark, NJ. He took a quick liking to Shawn and Shawn was beginning to like him too. Derrick showed himself to be a laid back and easygoing kind of guy. As far away from the entertainment industry as could be. They would talk on the phone for hours and even managed to share some laughs. It wasn't long before he was inviting Shawn out to Jersey to spend some time. He wanted to show Shawn the notorious Brick City. Derrick assured him he would be safe and could drive his car over and be fine, so Shawn agreed.

He put Derrick's address in his navigation system and it led him to Ellery Avenue in the Vailsburg section of Newark. Derrick met him outside of his three-story apartment house and told him he could park in the driveway. Shawn couldn't help but notice how smooth Derrick's skin was and how deep his brown eyes were. He stood eye to eye with Shawn and had a beautiful set of teeth in his mouth.

"So this is the infamous Brick City, huh?" Shawn asked walking up to him.

"This is my hood. Welcome," Derrick said putting his arms up.

They hugged each other and Shawn looked around. The seemingly quiet tree-lined block seemed safe. The lawns were well-manicured and tended to.

"I don't hear any gun shots, and I see that people's cars are still safely parked on the street. No one is breaking into them."

"We get a bad rep here. It's not suburbia by any means, but where I live ain't so bad. We're not all muggers and gang-bangers." Derrick led Shawn up to his second-floor apartment.

"Nice place you have here," Shawn said as they walked into the apartment.

"Thanks. My roommate and I tried to make it as cozy as possible. He's visiting his brother in DC this weekend."

"So is your roommate your best friend?" Shawn asked looking at the pictures on the mantel and walls.

"Yep. Steve and I have been best friends for almost ten years."

"Oh that's cool." Derrick kept smiling at Shawn. He thought Shawn was so fine in person.

"So what are we doing today?" Shawn asked.

"I got a few errands to run. And I'd like to show you around my hometown a little bit."

"Sounds like fun."

"Aight, let me put my clothes on and we'll go. Can I get you something to drink?" Derrick asked.

"Water is fine."

Derrick gave him a bottle of water and went to get dressed. They went to pick up Derrick's mother to take her to work, picked up Derrick's dry cleaning, and he showed Shawn downtown Newark where he was shopping for some new clothes.

"Wow, this like Harlem."

"There is nothing like downtown Newark. You can buy any and everything you want down here," Derrick said. Shawn looked around Broad and Market Streets and thought it looked similar to 125th Street in Harlem with street vendors selling T-shirts, shades, hats, and music was blasting. There were buses making frequent stops, traffic moving slowly, and tons of people shopping. There were FOI Muslims selling bean pies and Final Call newspapers. Every store had sneaker sales and fly clothes that even had Shawn taking a second look. Shawn helped Derrick pick out some nice clothes and sneakers and got a few things for himself.

"You ready to eat?"

"Yeah, I can eat."

They took their bags back to Derrick's car and he treated Shawn to lunch at Nubian Flavor restaurant on Springfield Avenue.

They ate and continued to talk. Shawn could feel that Derrick really liked him but he had to be honest with him. He thought Derrick was handsome and nice but after being around him, he realized he just wasn't ready yet.

"Listen, Derrick. I have to be honest about something."

Derrick turned to face him with a serious expression, giving Shawn his full attention.

Shawn hesitated then said, "I just came out of a relationship. A long one. I don't wanna lead you on into thinking that more could happen between us right now. I just don't think I am ready. And you're a nice guy. The last thing I wanna do is hurt you. I am in the market for friends, though."

"I mean, we can be friends and see where it leads to. What you think about that?"

"I'm still setting into my independence. And I like this feeling. I'm just doing my own thing these days."

"I can dig it."

They finished eating and went to the supermarket to do Derrick's grocery shopping. Shawn helped him in the house with all of his bags and helped him put the food away.

"So, what is it you do again?" Shawn asked.

"I work for a pharmaceutical company in Central Jersey."

"Do you like it?"

"It's okay. Pays my bills."

Derrick turned on a movie for them to watch and snuggled with Shawn on the loveseat. Derrick tried to focus on the movie but he couldn't. He was too focused on Shawn. He started kissing him on the neck. It felt good. And the kiss on the lips was magnetic. And while Shawn had enough sexual energy to devour Derrick, he knew he didn't want to take it further than friendship.

"So just friends, huh?" Derrick asked with sad eyes.

Shawn gazed into Derrick's eyes. "I'm sorry."

"Me too. We would be great together. You're just my type."

"You're so handsome."

"You too."

He leaned in and kissed his cheek. "I guess you gotta get on your way, huh?"

"You kicking me out cuz I won't give you none?" Shawn said with a smile.

"No, no, not at all; you can stay as long as you like."

"Nah, it's okay, man. I really do need to be getting back anyway."

"You want me to lead you back to the highway?"

"That would be nice. What's it called? Route 280?"

"That's it."

They got dressed, exchanged goodbyes, and Shawn followed Derrick to the highway and he was back in Harlem in less than a half hour. When he walked in the house, there was a manila envelope on the table with his name on it. He could tell it was Jamon's handwriting. He opened it and took out a wad of hundred dollar bills. The handwritten note inside of it read:

*I know you don't really want me around but I know you're not working this summer. So here is enough money for the rent and the bills until you get back to work and a little bit extra. I'm not taking the money back so just use it and consider it as a gift from me to you. Love you Mook.*

*Love,*
*Jamon*

Also inside of the envelope was a flier that had Jamon's picture on it. It said "NEW YORK'S PRINCE OF R&B JAMON KING LIVE IN CONCERT." The date was for the beginning of September. On it was a post-it that read:

*This is probably going to be the most important event of my career thus far. Please come. I need you to be there.*

Shawn looked at the picture and noticed he'd bought Jamon the shirt he was wearing in the picture. He kissed the picture and put it back down on the table. He counted out the money and saw there was ten thousand dollars' worth of one hundred dollar bills inside.

*Well, I'll just be damned.*

# 41

## RIGHTING OLD WRONGS

After stewing in his anger for a while, Damon called each one of the boys to apologize for being so judgmental to them in their times of need. Of course they forgave him. That was the easy part. Now he trembled as he sat outside of his parents' home in New Jersey. This time he was all by himself. The last time he was in front of this house, he was an emotional wreck over his father's banishment from his house and his life. But today, he was invited. His father had just arrived home from the hospital. A pacemaker had been put it his chest and he was slowly beginning to recover.

Once he got up the nerve to walk inside, Damon greeted his parents. His mother was in the kitchen cooking dinner and his father was in the reclining chair. Damon sat next to him on the couch. His father was watching his favorite movie, *The Five Heartbeats.* Even though they were having a nice time watching the movie and his father welcomed him to the house, he still needed to say what he had wanted to say ever since his relationship with his father soured.

"Dad."

"Yeah, son?"

"I need to ask you something."

"Okay." Mr. White put the movie on pause.

"Years ago when I came here with the guy I was dating and you told me you never wanted to see me again, did you mean it?"

Mr. White sighed deeply and turned off the TV. Damon's heart began to race like it did the day he visited the hospital. It took his father a long while to speak. When he finally spoke, his voice sounded different, lower, strained, and he looked at the floor instead of at his son.

"I said some pretty bad things to you that day. And I owe you more than an apology. I always feared that you might be gay. I pretty much knew it. But when you came here with that guy and the way you two looked at each other..." His father shook his head at the memory. "I just couldn't deal. I didn't think it was natural. Or possible. I thought true love could only exist between a man and a woman."

Damon sat straight up, every muscle in his body tightening.

"This is hard for me to say, but please just hear me out, son." He finally pulled his eyes from the floor and looked at Damon. "The hardest thing I ever had to do was watch you walk out of my life after I pushed you out. I couldn't believe I did that. My own child. My own flesh and blood. I want you to know I never stopped loving you, son. I was wrong for treating you that way. You're my firstborn. I also want you to know I am proud of everything you have accomplished. You have made me very proud in spite of our differences." His eyes and voice had grown teary.

Damon was beginning to get emotional himself.

"When I laid in that hospital bed, I realized I'd had a near death experience. And I looked around and saw your brother, your sister, and your mother. And it dawned on me that it was my fault why you weren't there to begin with. But I couldn't ask your mother to call you because I remembered what I'd said to you and thought you'd moved on with your life and were comfortable without my being in it. I'd pushed you away and I shouldn't have done that. My children are my greatest accomplishment and that includes you. I wished I could have leaped out of my bed when you walked into my hospital room. I was so happy to see you. And I realized that it didn't matter what you are. You are my son and it was by far the happiest day of my life when you walked back into it."

By this point, Damon had a face full of tears.

"You are amazing son. And I am very proud of the man you have become. I accept you for who you are. It's not for me to like or dislike. It's for me to love you unconditionally in spite of it."

On the verge of sobs, Damon managed to choke out, "Can I hug you?"

His father held out his arms and Damon fell into them. Though he wanted to hug him tight, he knew he couldn't because of the surgery. "I love you so much and I'm so glad I'm back in your life."

Mrs. White had been listening and she came into the room in tears and hugged her son and husband.

"I know you all weren't talking to me, but I have been dreaming of this day for the last six years. I am so happy it has come. Thank you God for bringing our family back together." She sat on the couch and held her son's hand while she wiped her tears with tissue.

"Now for the truth," Mr. White said.

"Truth?"

"Yes."

Mr. White exhaled and Damon looked at his mother. She didn't know what her husband was going to say.

"I knew you were gay as a child. That's why I insisted you learn how to box. I figured if you were around some other boys, you wouldn't be so soft. And even though you learned how to kick some ass and you were winning up all of those tournaments, you were still gay. It didn't change anything. I blamed myself for that. I kept asking myself if maybe I spent more time with you. Or wondering if maybe I should have taken you to church more. I knew no one had touched you because I would be in someone's jail cell right now."

"I knew too. But it never bothered me. I was just glad we weren't living in Jamaica. I would have slept with a machete under my pillow," Mrs. White said.

Damon smiled.

"I want you to be patient with me, son. I don't understand everything about your being gay. But I'm willing to learn if you're open to my being back in your life."

"I'd like that," Damon said.

"So I just wanna know. When you're in a relationship, are you the man or the woman?"

"Oh Dad, we've got a lot to talk about."

# 42

## MY FIRST LOVE

Atop the hill on Saint Nicholas Terrace that overlooked Saint Nicholas Park and many of the high rise buildings in Central Harlem, Malcolm stood with his face tilted upward. The warm sunshine and lush green trees that surrounded him did nothing to lift his depression-induced mood. For the fifth time, Faith Evans sang "My First Love" into his headphones. Every lyric of this song hit home with him. He replayed his time with Malik as he stood there staring at the Yankee stadium in the distance. He recalled the day they met, Malik's warm smile, the way he kissed him, and the first time they exchanged I love you's. Their first lovemaking session brought a temporary smile to his face but it was short-lived. That awful moment in Miami when he pissed it all away with Kejuan popped in his mind. He couldn't believe the amount of pain he was in. He felt like he'd been hit by a car.

*How could I fuck that up? Why did I do that? Ain't no ass worth what I had with Malik.* He looked to the right and could see the top of Shawn's building which was only on the other side of the park. He dialed Shawn.

"Hey, Malcolm, what's up?" Shawn answered.

"Aye."

"What's going on?"

"I been meaning to ask. You spoke to Jamon lately?"

"No, I haven't. Why do you ask?"

"Was just curious."

"That was random. Why'd you ask me that?" Silence. "Malcolm?" Once he saw people coming, he walked down the long stairs that led to the lower part of the park. "Are you there?"

"Yeah, I'm here."

"Are you alright?"

"Yeah."

"Are you sure?"

"I'm okay."

"Why did you ask about Jamon?"

"I just been doing some thinking."

"Are you crying?"

"Nah, man, I'm not crying. I got allergies," Malcolm said taking a big sniff.

Shawn rolled his eyes, knowing the truth. "What were you thinking about?"

"Wondering if you were gonna take Jamon back."

"I don't know. I haven't really thought about it."

"If he were to come to you and tell you how sorry he was, do you ever think you could ever trust him again? Even if he promised to never hurt you again?"

"A few months ago I didn't think I could."

"Do you still love him?"

"I do."

"Did you ever stop? Like when you were mad at him?"

"No. That's why I was so mad. Because in spite of how hurt I was and how much I wanted him to hurt back, I still loved him. And if anything ever happened to him, I'd be pretty devastated."

"But could you truly forgive him?"

"Maybe. You miss Malik, huh?"

"I'm good on, Malik."

"This is me you're talking to, Black. Keep it real and talk to me instead of cross-examining me like I'm on some witness stand."

"Yo. I just feel—like mad helpless. Like I fucked up the best thing I ever had. And I don't know what to do to even make it right. Or make it better."

"Have you spoken to him?"

"He told me to stop calling him. He said he hates me."

"I told Jamon I hated him too. When you get cheated on, it makes you kind of vengeful. To know Jamon cheated on me made me feel inadequate. Like he wanted something I couldn't give him. Is that how you felt with Malik? Was there something that young dude could give you that you couldn't get with Malik?"

"Nah. Kejuan was just there at the moment. Just selfishness on my part."

"Well since some time has passed, maybe you should tell him that. And apologize."

Malcolm chuckled. "You make it sound so easy."

"Well, I don't know how easy it will be. But I think you should try."

"You mean, you don't think he'll throw a knife at my head?"

"Not if you don't go by his house."

"And you know what I think?"

"What?"

"I think you should give Jamon another chance." Silence. "Oh, now you don't have nothing to say?"

"We'll see."

"I'm just sayin' man. If he feels anything like I do, he really does love you and is sorry he hurt you."

"Hmm."

"I'm actually about to walk past your building."

"You are?"

"Yup. I'm coming through the park now." Shawn looked out of the window and could see Malcolm's tall muscular frame coming down the street. As usual Malcolm, was walking like he was on somebody's runway.

"I see you." Shawn opened up his window and waved.

Malcolm put his arms up and screamed, "Shaaaaaaaaawn! Watup, Shawn?!"

"You're so hood," Shawn said laughing.

"You know how I do."

"Now the neighbors all know my name if they didn't before."

"That's usually what I make happen. But this is the first time I did it without fucking somebody."

"I bet."

"Aight, yo. Lemme figure out what I'mma say to Malik. I'mma swing by the store."

"Now?"

"Yeah."

"Okay. Well let me know how it goes."

"Aight. Talk to you later." They hung up and Malcolm looked up and waved at Shawn once more who was still looking at him through the window. As he inched closer to 125th St, he could feel his hands get clammy and his heart begin to beat quickly. *Here goes nothing. Time to man up.*

He made a left on to 125th Street and walked down to Malik's store. He walked inside and scanned the store for Malik. He was nowhere to be found.

"You need some help with something?" A worker asked him.

"Nah, man I'm just looking. Thanks." He kept looking around to see if he saw Malik and he didn't look like he was there. The store had quite a few people inside shopping. He took off his shades to see if he could see a little better. And boom. There was Malik carrying a box of sneakers to a waiting customer. Malcolm's body caught a chill and his stomach flipped twice. He had cut off his dreadlocks and sported a short curly fro. He looked good though. Malcolm paused a moment and just looked at him. Before he knew it, his feet were taking him in Malik's direction. He had no idea what he would say when Malik saw him.

"Malik?" Malik looked up. He didn't seem too happy to see him. Instead of addressing him, Malik turned to the customer he was helping. "Um, ma'am, do the shoes fit?" She nodded.

He said to one of his associates, "Andrea, do me a favor and get this lady checked out for me please?" Finally, he turned to face Malcolm.

"Surprise," Malcolm said.

"I'll say. What brings you by?"

"I was hoping I could talk to you for a second." Malik looked around.

"Yeah. Let's step outside." Malik led them outside as Malcolm admired how the arch in his back looked in his shirt. "What's going on?"

"I just wanted to come see you. I like the cut by the way."

"Thanks. I needed a change."

"It works."

"Thanks. Was there something you wanted to say since you needed to talk to me?"

"Yeah...um...you know, I ain't really good with words."

"Well, I don't have a lot of time. You wanna make it quick?"

"Yeah. I just wanted to say that...I...apologize for what I did. It was wrong." Malik nodded. "And I just, um...I wish I could take it back. And even more than that, I was hoping we could at least be friends. And then maybe one day pick back up where we left off."

Malik had his trademark stoic look on his face.

"I mean, I was just getting used to being in a relationship. But I was hoping you would give me another chance. I really wanna make it up to you cuz you deserve the best. And I wanna be that for you. So basically, I'm asking you to take me back. Cuz I can show you better than I can tell you."

"Wow. I know it probably took a lot for you to say that. You don't seem like the type to be so—forthcoming about your feelings."

"Right now, man, I don't even care. I love you. And I'm willing to do whatever I need to do."

"You know, before I say anything about that, I wanna apologize to you too. I take back what I said about your dad. That wasn't right."

"It's okay. I know you were just mad."

"I was hurt."

"I know."

"And I respect you for coming to say what you said." Malcolm smiled. "But I'm seeing somebody."

"Seeing somebody? But we just broke up a little over a month ago."

"I know. But he's a really great guy and I really like him."

"You made me wait for a few months before we made things official."

"We talked about why too. Come on, man, you know your rep."

Malcolm nodded. "So it's no chance of us ever gettin' back together?"

He shook his head. "Sorry, Malcolm. I'm in love with another man."

Those words hit him like concrete. "Can I at least get a kiss goodbye?"

"I only kiss my man. But we can shake on it." He put out his hand for a shake. Malcolm apprehensively shook it. While Malcolm tried to keep his face from hitting the ground, he heard a familiar voice say, "Hey babe." He looked and couldn't believe it. It was Kejuan hugging and kissing Malik on the lips. Kejuan turned to see Malcolm and his smile quickly faded.

"What the hell is he doing here?" Kejuan asked Malik.

"He just came by to say hello."

"Mmm, well tell him to get the fuck outta here unless he's buying something. We are both done with his black dusty rusty ass."

"Let me talk to him, okay? Go inside and wait for me. I'll just be a second."

Kejuan gave Malik a deep kiss and glared angrily at Malcolm as he walked away. Malcolm was stunned.

"So yeah, like I was saying, maybe we can be friends. You never know."

"Brooklyn—I mean, Kejuan is your man?"

"He is. And he's a real sweetheart."

"I didn't think you went for—fems."

"I'll go for anybody that respect boundaries. And you know I like nice guys."

Malcolm shook his head. He wanted to scream. "Yeah. Aight, man, well I'll get up. Congratulations."

"Take care of yourself." Malik extended his hand for another shake but Malcolm turned and walked away acting as if he didn't see it. He hauled ass down 125th and back around to Shawn's building. He rang the bell and Shawn buzzed him up. When he got upstairs to Shawn's apartment, he didn't need to say anything. In seconds, he came completely unhinged and cried in Shawn's arms. He had never seen Malcolm so distraught but he knew exactly how Malcolm felt. So he just stayed silent and let his friend cry the same way he'd done in the past.

# 43

## SOON AS I GET HOME II

**FALL**

Summer had gone by and it was time for Shawn to return to work. He was filling out his paperwork, making lesson plans, and had started decorating his classroom. He'd spoken to Malcolm who had put his security uniforms in the dry cleaners and was gearing up to suit back up as Mr. Brown. Shawn decided he was going to move. The feeling in the apartment wasn't the same without Jamon being there. Since he didn't know what the future held for them, he wanted to get his own place alone. In the midst of his paperwork and lesson plans, he text messaged Jamon.

Shawn: I'm moving so if you can come by and do a sweep to make sure you have everything I would really appreciate it. Thx.

Jamon: Moving? When? Why?

Shawn: Soon. I just need a change.

Jamon: Ok.

Shawn continued with his work and didn't think much else of the text conversation. Hours passed by and he never even lifted his head from what he was doing. Until he heard a key turn in the door. He looked up from the table and watched Jamon walk in the door. Jamon stopped where he was and Shawn froze. It had been months since they had seen each other face to face. They only kept in contact via email and text messages since the day Shawn chased him out of the apartment with the butcher knife. Both of their hearts started beating fast. For a moment, they just looked at each other and said nothing. Shawn didn't intend to be home whenever Jamon came. But then it dawned on him that they'd never discussed a time when he would come.

"Hey," Jamon said.

"Hey."

Their eyes locked.

"Lesson plans?"

"Yeah. I'm about to start back."

"I'm not sure what I have left so I'll just take a look in the bedroom and see what I still have here."

Shawn nodded. "Okay. All of your studio equipment is still here."

Jamon nodded and went into the bedroom. It felt good to be back in the home he once shared with Shawn. It still smelled good to him and felt like home. He took a moment and sat on the bed and looked around. Memories of the good times he and Shawn shared there flooded his mind. The day they moved in, the first time they made love in the bed, deciding which side of the closet would belong to whom, and how the apartment became their love nest. Jamon shook his head at how he'd messed things up between them. He looked in the closet and didn't see anything that belonged to him. He picked up one of Shawn's fitted caps and smelled it. It smelled like the hair grease he wore.

After looking around at other rooms, he went into the spare bedroom he'd converted into his home studio. Everything was the way he'd left it. He began unplugging things and decided he would come back with someone to help him with the heavy stuff. He packed a few smaller items into a box and walked out into the dining room where Shawn was still sitting doing his paperwork. He looked at him silently and Shawn looked up.

"Looks like you found something."

"Yeah, this came out of the studio. I'm gonna come back for the bigger things."

"Okay. I wanted to say thank you for the money you gave me. It helped out. I still have some left. As a matter of fact, I'll give you what's left of it," Shawn said rising from the table.

"You don't have to. Just keep it."

"But I don't need it."

"Save it for your deposit on your new place."

"Right. My new place. Thanks."

"It would really mean a lot to me if you came to my show. It's next Friday."

"I got the flier. I'm gonna try and make it."

"I hope you can. You look really good."

"Thanks. So do you."

"Well, I'm gonna take this and go. I'll come by sometime this week-end and get the rest of the stuff out of the studio."

"Why?"

"Cuz you wanted me to get my stuff."

"No. I mean, why? Why did you cheat on me?" Jamon hung his head and put the box down. "Did I do something wrong? Did I not do something you needed me to do?" Jamon shook his head. "I feel like I did everything I was supposed to do. I did my best to be supportive. I held things down but you still tipped out on me. And I just wanna know why."

"I'm sorry. It kills me to know that I hurt you."

Shawn smacked his lips. "No, it just kills you that you got caught."

"I don't have a good reason why I did it. But it's done. I can't take it back. I would if I could because I know I fucked up. I'm sorry."

"So you want me to come to your show but you can't give me a reason as to why you cheated on me? You broke my heart. And you can't even give me a reason. Maybe you should go."

"Come on, let's not do this. We've been together too long to just let it go without trying to work things out. We need to talk about this."

"You wanna talk? I just asked you a question that you won't answer. But you wanna talk?" Jamon was silent. "Just get your shit and get the fuck out."

"You think it's that easy? You think it's easy for me to walk around knowing you don't want nothing to do with me? Huh? You think it's easy for me to look at myself in the mirror or walk in this house and have to walk back out by myself? I'm sorry! I don't know what else to say. Tell me what you want from me and I swear to God on everything I love, I'll do it. Please, just tell me that you won't turn your back on me and give up on everything we've built together. I love you; can't you see that?"

Shawn shook his head. "I don't know."

Jamon frowned. "You know! You just don't wanna admit it. Sometimes people do stupid shit. They don't always need a reason; they just do it. I just did something stupid. That's all."

Shawn momentarily flashed back to Malcolm but his emotions took over. "That's not enough, J."

"Do you still love me?"

"What?"

"You heard me. Do you still love me?" Jamon asked getting closer.

"It's not about that," Shawn said backing up.

"Answer me. Do you still love me?"

"Back up."

"Not until you answer me. If you tell me you don't love me anymore then I'll leave and you'll never see me again. Look me in my eye and tell me you don't have no feelings for me at all, and I'll get gone. I swear to God."

Shawn looked at him and attempted to walk to the front door to let him out only to be grabbed by Jamon who pulled him close and kissed him. Shawn tried to fight it but the moment they kissed, all of the feelings came rushing back. Jamon wrapped his arms around him and kissed him passionately. And once he got him, he wouldn't stop.

"I love you, Mook."

"I love you too, JJ."

Jamon picked Shawn up and straddled him and they kissed again. They went to the bedroom and made love like old times. Their bodies were still familiar to each other. But the passion in their kisses seemed to be more intense than ever before. Shawn licked all of Jamon's spots, Jamon did everything Shawn liked, and held him close while he was inside of him. He kept whispering "I love you" in Shawn's ear every time he could. Tears streamed down both of their faces from the passion they felt. Jamon went down to the foot of the bed and lay at Shawn's bare feet.

"I missed these beautiful toes. I'mma eat 'em up today," he said and devoured Shawn's toes. Shawn let out a soft moan and enjoyed it. When he was done, they lay in their respective spots like they used to.

"I missed you, Mook."

"I missed you too."

They gazed into each other's eyes and smiled.

"I missed that smile too." Shawn's smile got bigger and Jamon saw all of his teeth as he blushed. He touched Shawn's smooth face.

"I just wanna come back home. Even if I gotta sleep on the couch, I just wanna come back and be here with you. Just so I can see you smile everyday."

Shawn continued to gaze into his eyes. "You can come back. You don't have to sleep on the couch. You can sleep in here with me."

"For real?"

"For real."

Jamon's face lit up. "I love you."

"I love you too."

Jamon climbed on top of Shawn and kissed him. Shawn wrapped his arms around Jamon and pulled him close.

"I promise I'll never hurt you again. It's just you and me. Nobody else."

Shawn smiled. As they lay there, Jamon shared all the new things he was doing with his music and how excited he was about his upcoming show. Especially now since he knew Shawn would be there. Shawn told Jamon about his eventful summer—minus hanging with Robert and Derrick. Even though Jamon saw him out with Robert, he never asked about it. Shawn was glad because he didn't want to tell him he slept with someone else in this very bed. But it felt good for them to just talk and pick up where they left off before things went bad. And it felt especially good for them to start rebuilding the friendship they shared as lovers. It was official. Jamon was coming back home.

# 44

# A RAGE IN HARLEM

Kevin tossed and turned in his bed. He opened his eyes and looked at the clock which read 3:47 am. It was pouring rain, thundering, and lightning. The windows were open and the wind was blowing the curtains. He'd fallen asleep with them open because the night air had been crisp and refreshing. Damn, he really didn't feel like getting out of the bed, but he didn't want the moisture to cause mold in the house. As he flipped back the cover, he was startled to see Charles standing over his bed with a black slicker on. He jumped back and screamed.

"Wake up, sleeping beauty," Charles said as he pulled the hood off of his head.

"How'd you get in here? What are you doing here?"

"You didn't think I was just gonna go away did you? You know me better than that." Charles lunged at Kevin who rolled himself off of the bed and stood on the opposite side.

"Oh, so you wanna play chase again? I'm down for that. But the only way you're getting out of here is through that open window over there. And that's a lot of floors to jump, baby."

He leaped across Kevin's bed and Kevin ran into the dark living room.

"Your boys ain't here to protect you now, huh? What you gon' do, Kev? Running ain't gon' help cuz you know I'mma get you." Charles walked into the dark living room looking for Kevin, calling his name in a creepy sing-song voice.

*A place to hide. A place to hide. He's gonna kill me. Where should I hide?* Then Kevin paused and wondered why he was running and hiding. It was time for him to fight back once and for all. He'd begun attending self-defense classes and now it was time to make use of what he had learned.

Charles left the room and Kevin got up to tip-toe to the kitchen. As he was entering, Charles hit him in the back of the head with something

261

hard and he fell to the floor. He grabbed Charles' leg and turned his foot upward in a quick move that was supposed to twist his ankle; Charles lost his balance and fell to the floor. He quickly got up and grabbed Kevin by his ankles and dragged him backwards.

"Let me go!" Kevin kicked himself loose and got up. He jabbed Charles twice in the face and disappeared into the dark kitchen.

"Soft hitting muthafucka!"

The light switch was on the other side of the room so as Charles fumbled around looking for it in the dark, he couldn't find it. Since Kevin knew his kitchen layout, he had the advantage over Charles' goliath size. He could see Charles' profile in the darkness, so he snuck up on him and hit him across the face with a ceramic casserole dish. Charles immediately hit the floor and Kevin made a run for his bedroom. He closed the door behind him and grabbed his house phone to dial 911.

"Yes, I'd like to report an intruder. Kevin Malone," Kevin said.

He gave the operator his exact address.

"Yes, that's 142nd and Lenox apartment 3C. Third floor. Please tell them to hurry. He is armed and dangerous."

After he hung up with the 911 operator, he frantically searched for clothes to put on. As he found something, he heard what sounded like Charles' stumbling footsteps in the living room. His bedroom door swung open. Kevin jumped at him and they brawled, knocking everything in their path over. Charles realized Kevin had learned how to fight and was much stronger than he thought. Kevin hit him in between the eyes and nose as hard as he could. Charles stumbled backwards as Kevin tried to make a dash for the front door. Charles caught him and pounded him in the face several times and pushed him to the floor.

"Told you I could get you if I wanted you. And I got your bitch made ass didn't I? Huh? I don't hear you talking shit now, muthafucka. You bout to be sorry you ever fucked with me bitch! Put this shit in your journal from the grave, muthafucka!"

As a disoriented Kevin tried to sit up, Charles took a bottle of lighter fluid from his pocket and dowsed the couch with it. He threw a match on it and in seconds it was engulfed in flames. Charles went into the bedroom and set Kevin's bed on fire next. As Kevin struggled up to his feet, Charles threw lighter fluid on Kevin. Kevin covered his face backing away. Charles lit a match and threw it but missed Kevin. Kevin managed to get the door open and as Charles attempted to chase him, he tripped over the end table. Kevin made a run for it without even looking back.

* * *

Outside, the rain eased to a drizzle. Fire engines and police cars lined the streets. People were outside under umbrellas and in pajamas. Neighbors from surrounding buildings were outside watching; a news crew was there filming footage, doing a live report and taking pictures. Kevin stood across the street with his arms folded in disbelief as his mind raced. Damon, Shawn, and Malcolm surrounded him trying to keep him away from the news crew who had been trying to get a statement from him. The EMTs had brought Charles out on a stretcher and drove away in an ambulance. Believe it or not, Kevin wanted to follow the ambulance to see if Charles was okay. A female police officer approached him and snapped him out of his desire.

"Mr. Malone. They're ready to let you all back into the building. I'm gonna need you to come down to the station after you've spoken to the firefighters, okay? This is my card. I'm Detective Sheila Perry."

Kevin nodded. People began to filter back into the building slowly.

"You ready, Kev?" Damon asked.

Kevin shook his head and looked at the commotion surrounding him all because of his relationship with Charles.

"Come on. We'll be with you." Damon put his arm around Kevin.

Shawn and Damon stood on both sides of him and Malcolm led them inside. The closer they got up to the third floor, the stronger the smell of smoke became. Fire fighters were coming out of Kevin's apartment.

"Sorry, guys. We saved as much as we could but the fire was pretty bad when we got here," one of the firefighters said.

They walked into Kevin's apartment and it was a mess. The fire had burned the walls and parts of the ceiling were now missing. All of the furniture was destroyed. There were puddles all over the floor throughout the place. There was still quite a bit of smoke in the apartment. Kevin and the boys went from room to room. The bathroom was the only thing that didn't have any damage. They went into the bedroom, which had the most damage. They could see straight through to the brick foundation of the building walls. The windows were now covered with wood covers. When Kevin saw all of the damage to his bedroom, his knees gave out and he fell onto the wet floor and cried hysterically. He curled into the fetal position and cried out in anguish. Damon and Malcolm lifted him up and he clung tightly to Malcolm.

"What am I gonna do? When is it gonna end?"

Shawn put his hand on Kevin's back and Damon wrapped his arm around him too. They let him get all of his tears out.

"It's okay, man. We're here," Damon said hugging him tight.

"Oh my God. I should have never showed him where that building was on campus."

"There was no way you could have known," Shawn said. They each called out of work for the day and went with Kevin to the police station.

Once there, Detective Perry explained that they had found Charles' car and inside of his trunk, they found rope, duct tape, a shovel, and paperwork for a cemetery plot Charles had purchased.

"It looks as if he was going to kill you and bury you," she said.

A chill reverberated through Kevin's spine. "Wh-where is he now?"

"He's in the burn unit at New York Presbyterian."

"Was he burned badly?"

"We're not really too sure of his injuries but he is being treated there. Can you tell me everything that happened?"

"How much time do you have?"

"I'm here until about 6pm this evening."

"That's about all the time I'll need."

# 45

## HE CAN'T LOVE U

Jamon stood at the microphone with his band and back-up singers on the stage of Club Soul where his show would be taking place. This was the last full rehearsal before the show tomorrow night. Things were going smoothly and everything was according to plan, but Jamon decided to change things up a bit.

"Bring the house lights down please. I want the spotlight on me when I do this song," Jamon said to the lighting guy.

The house lights went down and the spotlight came up.

"What's going on, J?" asked the musical director seated at one of the keyboards.

"This is a new joint I just wrote that I'm putting in the show. Just follow me."

"Alright."

Jamon closed his eyes and began to sing a song he wrote called "I'm sorry." Seamlessly, the band and singers picked up the melody of the song and followed him. He poured himself into the lyrics of the song so much that his eyes were full of tears when he was done.

His manager Rell approached the stage as Jamon wiped his face of falling tears.

"You okay, J?"

"Yeah, I'm okay. Take five y'all," Jamon said walking off the stage.

Jamon walked off of the stage and into the lobby of the club and Darnell was walking in.

"Hey. Why are you crying? You okay?"

"I'm fine."

"What's the matter?"

"Just got caught up in that last song I was singing."

Darnell passed him some tissues off of the coat check stand.

"Thanks. What are you doing here?"

"I came to see if you needed a ride. Maybe if you wanted to go get something to eat."

"No, I'm okay," Jamon said not really making eye contact.

"What's the matter? Why are you acting like that?"

"You shouldn't be here, man."

"What you mean I shouldn't be here?"

"I told you I'm working things out with Shawn. Me and him are back together."

Darnell's face saddened. "You serious?"

"Yeah. I gotta take care of my house. I love him."

"So you're just kicking us to the curb?"

"Us? There is no us."

"So why you been kicking it with me? When he put you out, you came to stay with me. Slept in my bed, watched my TV, ate my food and now you're telling me there's no us? That's how you gon' do it?"

"I tried to pay you."

"And I told you I didn't want your money."

"Then what do you want?"

"You gotta ask me that?"

"Help me understand."

"You. That's all I ever wanted." Darnell teared up. "You say you love him. But I had you first. I guess what we had wasn't good enough though, huh?"

Jamon looked away. "It's not about that."

"You know he can't love you like I can. Nobody can."

"We weren't a couple this time around. It was just sex between us."

Darnell's face showed even more hurt. "Just sex? That's all I mean to you?"

"No, that's not all you mean to me. But I'm not in love with you. I'm in love with him."

Jamon's words hit Darnell like a ton of bricks. His feelings were so hurt, he wanted to burst out into tears but did his best to hold them in.

"So this is how it ends?"

"We can still be friends."

Darnell felt insulted. "Friends? You think I wanna stand by and watch you date somebody else and be your friend? You fucking bastard. You got a lot of balls yo."

"We don't have to end on bad terms."

"How can we not? You know what? Don't answer that. Next time he kicks you out, don't come knocking on my door."

"Come on, Darnell. Don't be like that."

"What you mean don't be like that? You want it all and you can't have it like that. What do you want from me? Huh? What?"

"Can you keep your voice down?"

"Go to hell, yo! Go to fucking hell."

As Darnell walked towards the exit, Shawn walked in. They stopped to look each other up and down. Darnell sucked his teeth at Shawn and flung the door open angrily and walked out. Shawn looked at Jamon who had a solemn look on his face.

"You won't see him around anymore."

Jamon held his arms open for a hug and Shawn hugged him. "Come inside with me; we're about to be done with rehearsal." Shawn walked back inside with him and waited as he watched the rest of the rehearsal and tried to forget about seeing Darnell.

# 46

## ONE NIGHT ONLY

The line outside of Club Soul in the meatpacking district was down the street and around the corner as people waited to be let in. People who knew Jamon from the New York Underground made up the majority of people waiting. There was a huge promo shot of Jamon's face on the door. Inside the club there were pictures of him all over. As people began to be let in they commented on how sexy the ambiance of the club was. The club filled up quickly with people and the energy buzzed all around. Industry guests were seated in the VIP section off to the right at a table, his mother and family were in VIP on the left at another table, and Shawn was front row center with the boys at a third VIP table. When Shawn told the boys he and Jamon were back together, they couldn't have been happier for them. And they promised to be at his big show. The VIP tables all had complimentary bottles of champagne.

As the crowd filtered inside, Malcolm noticed someone.

"Hey, ain't that old boy we pulled you off of right there?" Malcolm asked looking to the right. Shawn looked up and saw Darnell with two other guys.

"Yeah, that's him."

"Fuck is he doing here?"

Darnell came walking past Shawn and his boys. He gave Shawn a mean look and Shawn gave it back, flaring his nostrils.

"Yo say the word and we will roll them muthafuckas out after the show."

"I don't wanna ruin Jamon's big night."

"He looked like he wanted to get it there."

"Yeah, but who is in VIP? Side bitches go where?" Shawn asked.

"Back there!" They all said in unison pointing their thumbs to the back.

"I'm not trying to have any problems tonight. But he better not walk his ass back over here looking at me like that or I'mma crack him over the head with this bottle."

Backstage, Jamon sipped tea as his barber finished giving him a haircut. He rubbed alcohol on his bald head and shaved parts of his face.

Jamon paid him and finished putting his clothes on and looked at himself in the mirror. A black blazer with a black and white button up, blue jeans, and a comfy pair of white Nike sneakers completed his outfit. The band and singers took their places on the stage and the lights dimmed.

"New York City. Show some love for New York's prince of R&B, Jamon King!" the offstage announcer said.

A heavyset drummer counted off the band and they started playing the opening song. On cue, the singers started to sway and sing their parts. As Jamon came out rocking to the beat in a pair of stunna shades, the crowd cheered. Shawn blushed looking at him and Malcolm gave Shawn a look.

"What?"

Malcolm shook his head.

Jamon started off with an up tempo song and glided through his set with ease. He was sangin' like nobody's business and the audience was eating him up. His presence electrified the stage, and he looked like fame. His runs were clean, fast, and intricate, his voice as smooth and clear as a bell. Not a single note was out of place. He smiled at the applauding audience as he took off his shades.

"Thank you. What's happening New York City? Y'all feeling good? Y'all coulda been anywhere in the world tonight, but you're here with me and I appreciate you. We all appreciate you. Y'all like the band? They're killing it, right? And how about my singers? Y'all gon' hear from them in a little while. I wanna keep it mellow right here for a minute. Is that okay?"

The audience clapped.

"You can sing anything, baby!" a woman yelled out.

"Haha, thanks." He went and sat behind a keyboard.

"I wanna do this song as a dedication right here. This is a Chrisette Michele joint." He looked directly at Shawn and began to play his favorite Chrisette Michele song, "Love is you." Shawn sat straight up in his chair.

"Isn't this your song?" Damon asked.

Shawn nodded his head. His eyes lit up and he smiled as Jamon sang this beautiful song with the same ease he sung everything else with. And he sounded amazing while making the song sound original. He maintained eye contact with Shawn the whole time. And the boys definitely noticed. After he was done, he stood up to the mic and took off his blazer.

"I wanna say something before I get started with this next joint. It's a real personal song that I just wrote. I do my best to write songs from my own experiences and this may be the most personal song I've ever written. Relationships are funny. And sometimes in those relationships, you mess up. Sometimes for selfish reasons, sometimes because you're scared, sometimes because you feel like you're not worthy of the person you're with."

Shawn froze and bowed his head. Damon, Kevin, and Malcolm looked at him.

"You feel like you'll never be good enough. Even though they tell you they love you, you just feel unworthy of the love they give you. I know that feeling well. And I know because I hurt the person who loved me most because I had my own insecurities as a man. I felt like I could never be what I should have been for my relationship. So I stepped out on it and messed up everything. And now all I can say is that I'm sorry for the pain I've caused you. I love you and I hope you still love me too. This is my song."

He sang "I'm Sorry" and for the next five and a half minutes, he professed his love for Shawn without saying his name or mentioning that he was singing about a man. And he apologized for everything he'd done wrong. Shawn couldn't hold back his tears either. He just let them roll. Damon passed him a tissue and Kevin rubbed his back. As Jamon sang his heart out, Darnell's eyes filled with angry tears because he knew who Jamon was singing about. He could feel his heart snap in two and he walked out of the club. When Jamon was done, he got a standing ovation and wiped his own tears away.

"Wow. Thank you. I told y'all it's the most personal song I've ever written."

A female audience member passed him a tissue.

"Thank you, baby," he said.

Shawn wiped his tears away and mouths the words "I love you" to Jamon. Jamon nodded and said "I love you too" before speaking back into the microphone.

"Alright, y'all, are we ready to have a good time and party?" The audience clapped. "This is one of my favorite old school joints to do. This is 'Cruising' by Smokey Robinson. Most of you probably know the D'Angelo version and this is my rendition of it. Here we go."

The band played the song and Jamon's smooth vocals made everyone rock back and forth. People got up and started dancing as the song built to its crescendo. He let the background singers get some shine by letting them do some adlibs during the song when he told the band to break it down. He did more of his original songs and sang the hit songs he wrote for other artists and people sang along. He walked around the audience so he could get closer to everyone. When he got to his mother and two brothers, he passed them the mic and it was clear music ran in the family. His mother had a wonderful opera voice and his brothers were both singers just like him. He gave a special shout out to Rell and introduced his singers and band members. He got an exciting standing ovation when he finished and saw the record execs nodding their heads and smiling as he bowed.

"Thank you, New York! Thanks for your support. I'm coming out there to hook y'all up with CD's and pictures. I love y'all! Good night!" Jamon said waving as he left the stage to change his clothes.

In another part of the club, a line had already formed at the table where Jamon and his manager were going to be selling his mixtape CDs, posters, and giving autographs. A photographer was taking pictures of people in front of one of Jamon's promo shots. It was the same close up picture of his face that was on the front door.

"We've got four meetings next week with those label guys. I have all their cards but they're eager to meet with us," Rell said to Jamon.

"That's what I'm talking about! Let's get it."

"You did it, baby. You killed them tonight!"

"I couldn't have done this without you, man. Thank you so much," Jamon said as he gave him a big hug.

"No problem, man. Let's get this money."

They walked to the table and met the adoring audience members standing in line. He spotted Shawn and his boys standing off to the side talking. He got Shawn's attention and waved him over. He hugged Shawn and said, "Come sit with me for a minute."

Shawn pulled up a chair and sat next to Jamon as he signed autographs and spoke to people who told him how they enjoyed the show. Darnell walked up and saw Shawn sitting with Jamon. He looked at both of them and stormed out. Shawn noticed Darnell's attitude and rolled his eyes. Jamon continued to talk to the fans and then he went to pose for pictures in front of his big promo shot on the wall. The photographer got some photos of him by himself and then with fans. Shawn went and stood back with his boys while he looked on as Jamon took pictures.

"Your man can sing his ass off. He killed that shit," Malcolm said.

"He really did. I knew he could sing but I didn't know he could *sang* like that," Kevin said.

"Yeah, I couldn't believe his voice. He let everybody know what was up tonight," Damon said.

Shawn blushed. "I'm so proud of him."

Shawn turned around and saw Jamon's mother.

"Hey Shawnie baby!"

"Hey, Ms. King."

She gave him a big hug. "It is so good to see you. You're looking real good, honey."

"So are you. You sounded awesome."

She leaned in close. "Thank you baby. So I don't need to ask who that song was about." Shawn blushed. "Mmm-Hmm. Well listen, you have my permission to send him right back to me if he gets out of line. I'll straighten his ass right out and make sure he's doing the right thing. I'mma get outta here cuz mama don't do crowds, honey. Good night, baby. I love you." She kissed his cheek.

"I love you too."

Jamon's brothers were behind her and they dapped and hugged Shawn. They went over to hug Jamon good night and they snapped pictures with him.

"Wait. Hold on. Shawn!" Jamon called out.

Shawn turned around. Jamon and his brothers waved Shawn over to come take pictures with them. Shawn walked over and Jamon brought Shawn next to him and the photographer snapped pictures. He put his arm around Shawn and brought him closer. For the first time in a long time, Shawn felt like he was a part of Jamon's inner circle. It didn't get any closer than family.

As the crowd began to filter out, Jamon asked Shawn to come help pack up his things from his dressing room. He followed Jamon backstage into his room and they closed the door.

"What do you need packed first?" Jamon locked the door.

"You." The look on his face drove Shawn wild. "Come here, Mr. Jones," Jamon said with a wicked smile. Shawn put his arms around Jamon's neck and Jamon held him close.

"I've been a bad boy, Mr. Jones."

"And you deserve detention."

"I might like it. Me and you in a quiet room is my kind of lesson. Teach me teacher."

"Teach you?"

Jamon started singing "Teach Me" by Musiq Soulchild. He sat down and Shawn sat on his lap facing him. Jamon looked him in his eyes and Shawn was entranced by him. For a brief moment, neither of them said anything.

"That was a beautiful song you sung."

"Thanks. I meant every word of it. I hope you know that."

Shawn nodded. Jamon kissed him deeply and started to unbuckle Shawn's pants.

"There are people out there."

"Well then, let's keep it rocking until they come knocking."

Jamon got up and put his condom on and Shawn lathered it with lube from Jamon's bag. His slid down on Jamon's dick and rode him. As he bounced up and down, they held each other close. Jamon bit his bottom lip and Shawn clenched his teeth. They felt closer and more connected than ever. As they gazed deeply into each other's eyes, they could feel the love and passion they had for one another. They never wanted it to stop. It was as if they could see right through each other.

As sweat covered both of their bodies they were so into it they could feel each other's warm breath on each other. With every thrust and grind, they became more entranced. And every time Jamon threw it at him, Shawn gave it back. Their fingers locked and their eyes never left each other. Shawn's sweat dropped onto Jamon's bald head and they went on and on and on. Shawn started to moan and squirm. Jamon pulled him close and held him tight. As he was inside of Shawn, he nibbled on Shawn's nipples which drove him wild.

"Give me that fucking nut, lil' nigga."

"Mmmm. Say it again."

"Give me that fucking nut."

"Mmmm." Shawn's body began to twist and squirm again.

"Yeah that's right, squirm nigga. I ain't never lettin' yo ass go. I ain't never gon' stop fucking you."

"Never?"

"I ain't never gon' stop fucking you."

The more Shawn's body twisted and turned in Jamon's tight grip, the more aggressive Jamon became. And the harder he cursed at him.

"Where the fuck you think you goin' boy? You ain't fucking going nowhere. I own yo ass nigga. I'm your fucking master. I control you. What's my name?"

"Jamon."

"Who the fuck am I?"

"My master."

"Who the fuck am I lil' nigga?"

"My master."

"Fuck is my name?"

"Jamon."

"Say it again."

"Jamon."

"Say my fucking name again like you mean it nigga!"

"Jamon."

"What's my fucking name?"

"Jamon."

"And who the fuck am I?"

"My master."

"That's right nigga I'm your fucking master. Don't forget that shit either, lil' nigga. You gon' forget?"

"No."

"You gon' fucking forget?"

"No....no I won't forget."

"That's right cuz I'm your fucking daddy too. I'm your fucking daddy nigga and you belong to me. I own yo ass, you hear me? You fucking hear me nigga?"

"I'm yours."

"Das right. You're mine. And I'm all yours." Jamon grabbed Shawn's dick and caressed it. It pulsated in his hand and he rubbed the tip. He knew stroking the right part of Shawn's hard dick would make him cum ropes. And he wanted an explosion. Shawn began to pant and moan from Jamon stroking his dick. He was rubbing his spot.

"You better cum big too nigga." Shawn's insides were tightening. "Come on, bust that fat ass nut for me."

Shawn couldn't even talk by this point. He was in. And the more Jamon filled his insides and stroked his dick he seemingly lost consciousness. He could feel himself getting ready but it was stronger than ever before. But it was coming so fast, he didn't stop to even wonder what was happening. It felt so good though. He could feel his insides getting tighter than they ever had. And his dick began to twitch uncontrollably. His heart rate increased and he couldn't hold it back anymore. It was coming, it was coming, it was coming and then...it happened. Shawn had the orgasm of life. He came like a volcano and his wild lava soaked Jamon like never before. He came and came and came some more. Once he snapped back to reality, he couldn't believe how much came out when he opened his eyes. There was some on him, on Jamon, on the floor, and on the wall which was at least eight feet away.

"Damn, that's all me?"

Jamon nodded as he kissed him deeply. He slowly pulled out and laid Shawn across the couch in his dressing room. He stood over Shawn with his dick in his hand.

"Gimme that," Shawn said grabbing Jamon's dick. Shawn jerked Jamon off until he too came all over him. Now they were even. And cum was everywhere. Jamon got on top of Shawn and scooped him up.

"I love you."

"I love you too."

"Come on, let's go home for round two."

They cleaned up, got dressed, and packed up his things and headed outside. People were still there and started talking to Jamon as he and Shawn exited. Shawn walked down the block to start loading Jamon's things in his waiting SUV. As Shawn closed the door, he turned around and saw Darnell standing there grilling him.

"Can I help you?"

"You know it's just a matter of time before he comes back to me. I got him last time; I can get him again."

"I guess that's why I was in VIP and you weren't."

"Man, fuck you!"

"Get the fuck outta my way," Shawn said pushing past Darnell.

"Get your fucking hands off me!" Darnell said pushing Shawn. Shawn punched Darnell in the face and Darnell threw him up against the wall they stood in front of.

"Yeah, this is what I've been waiting on! The re-match!"

"Oh shit, it's a fight!" someone yelled out.

A crowd gathered as Darnell kicked Shawn in the stomach and threw him on the ground. Shawn got up and hit Darnell with a strong three-piece to the face that made him fall down. Then they just brawled. Jamon turned around after hearing the commotion and went running towards it when he saw it was Shawn and Darnell fighting. He, Rell, and some other guys pulled them apart.

"What the fuck is wrong with y'all? I can't have a good night without no drama?"

"He started it!" Shawn yelled.

"Go home, Darnell!" Jamon said.

"No! Fuck him. What, you think this shit is over? Huh? If I can't have you, neither can he."

As everyone around him gasped, Jamon fidgeted and looked embarrassed. "Man, you don't know what you're talking about. You're drunk! Just go home!"

Darnell pulled out a gun and people started to scream and run. He aimed it at Shawn. Shawn was shocked still and Jamon looked at Darnell like he was crazy. As Darnell's finger pulled the trigger, Jamon jumped in front of Shawn. Shawn closed his eyes to brace himself. Two shots rang out and Shawn could feel himself fall to the ground with what felt like Jamon on top of him. He opened his eyes. Jamon was lying on top of him bleeding from being shot. People gathered around them and Darnell fell to his knees dropping the gun. Shawn screamed and cradled Jamon in his arms.

"Jamon! Somebody call the ambulance! Hold on, J. Stay with me. Look at me!" Shawn said as Jamon's eyes began to roll in the back of his head.

"Somebody help! Rell call an ambulance! Help! Somebody helllllllp!"

Rell took out his cell phone and called 911.

# 47

## THE HOSPITAL

M s. King frantically rushed into the hospital with her mascara running followed by her other two sons.

"Excuse me. Jamon King is my son. He was shot and brought here," she said to the front desk attendant. The attendant looked him up.

"He's in ICU." The attendant had an employee escort her and her sons to the ICU where they saw Shawn and his boys, Rell, Jamon's band members, and backup singers.

"Shawn," Ms. King said.

He raised his bowed head and ran to her and hugged her.

"Shawn what happened to my baby? How is he?"

"They won't tell me anything because I'm not a blood relative. We had to wait for you," Shawn said with tears streaming down his face.

She took him by the hand and marched to the front desk in ICU.

"I am Jamon King's mother. Can you please tell me how my son is doing?"

"I'll get the doctor for you."

As the attendant was leaving, the doctor came through the main doors.

"Doctor, this is Jamon King's mother."

The doctor approached with his hand extended. "Ms. King, I'm Dr. Pantene."

"Please tell me how my son is doing."

"Well, we had to perform emergency surgery. It was a very close call. The bullet was a quarter of an inch from his spine and could have paralyzed from the neck down but we removed it in time. He'll survive. But he will need physical therapy and we'll need to keep him here for the next few days to assess his progress."

Everyone breathed a sigh of relief. "Praise God! Thank you Lord. Is he in recovery?"

"We just moved him to a room. He's resting."

"Please let me see him."

"I can give you a few moments. But that's all."

"These are my three sons."

"I can let you in two at a time but this gentleman has been here," he said gesturing at Shawn, "and we can't..."

"Doctor, you don't understand. I *need* him to come too," she said firmly.

"Okay."

"Mom, y'all go ahead first. We'll wait out here," one of Jamon's brothers said.

The doctor escorted her and Shawn down the corridor to Jamon's room as they held hands tightly.

"He's right in here. He'll be moved to a regular room tomorrow."

"Paging Dr. Pantene. Please report to the ER," the overhead announcer said.

"I've gotta run. We'll take good care of him. I promise," Dr. Pantene said rushing off.

They walked into Jamon's dark room and were silent. He had an IV hooked up, a breathing tube down his throat, and a beeping noise from the monitor for his pulse. They just looked at him. Ms. King softly sung "The Lord's Prayer" over her son's sleeping body. She kissed his cheek and talked to him.

"I love you, son. Doctor said you're gonna be just fine. I know it because God said so too. I am so proud of the show you put on tonight. You're gonna be a big star. And I know you're gonna pull through this. Mama isn't worried at all so you be strong. We're all gonna be praying for you baby. I'm gonna stay here tonight so I'll let Shawn and your brothers say something to you. I love you, son."

She waved Shawn over and stepped back so he could have a moment. She walked over to the window and looked up at the sky and prayed. Shawn took Jamon by the hand.

"Hey, JJ. You took a bullet for me tonight. I don't know how to repay you. All I can say is I love you more than anything in this world. You're the love of my life. And I'm gonna hold you down no matter what. I want you to fight. I don't care what we've been through. I'm here no matter what. I'll be here. I love you. Know that."

He kissed Jamon on the cheek and could still smell his cologne on him. He and Ms. King walked down the hallway arm in arm.

"Shawnie, what happened?"

He painfully recapped everything that had happened.

"So Darnell is the reason why my son is in there fighting for his life." She sucked her teeth and shook her head. "I told him that boy was crazy."

"Ms. King, it's more of my fault than his. I fought Darnell in the past and he wanted a re—"

"No, it isn't. You stop that right now, you hear me?" she said firmly, cutting him off. "It is not your fault. You didn't put that gun in his hand. He picked it up himself and I am gonna make sure he pays for it. I'm glad you told me what happened. You and I are pressing charges on him because he endangered you too. After my baby gets better, we're taking care of Darnell."

"Yes ma'am," he said. They walked out to the waiting room and Shawn gathered together with the boys. They all put their arms around him in support while he covered his face and wept.

*"I just got him back. I can't lose him again. I can't! I won't. My baby is gonna make it. I know he is!"*

# 48

## BY YOUR SIDE

A week had gone by and Jamon was still in the hospital recovering. Shawn had been there every single day and spent the night with him a few times. Today, he brought Jamon a strawberry banana shake from the shake shack.

"Hey, JJ," Shawn said.

"Wassup, Mook? Oh, you done been to the shake shack?"

"Just for you."

Jamon smiled. "I don't deserve you. I been craving one of these since I woke up this morning."

"I figured." Shawn set it down next to the big bear and flower bouquet he'd brought him the day before.

"Come here." Jamon pulled him close and kissed him.

"How are you feeling?"

"Good now that you're here."

"You mean good because you got that shake." Jamon chuckled.

"Babe. I'm sorry for putting you through all of this. Everything."

"You don't need to apologize. Darnell is gonna get what's coming to him."

Jamon shook his head again. "I can't believe he did this shit."

Shawn sat down and Jamon reached for his hand to hold. Shawn held his hand. "The doctor says you'll be fine."

"Yeah, he told me. Hell of a time for this to happen. I was supposed to take meetings with the label execs this week and see who was interested."

"You can reschedule can't you?"

"I'mma have to."

Silence. "At least Darnell is locked up."

"That fool could get life in prison for all I care right now. He's fucking stupid."

"That's what your mom said."

"She never liked him."

"With good reason I see. I brought your iPod so you would have some music," Shawn said taking it from his pocket.

"When I get out of here and get better, I want us to go away."

Shawn nodded. "Me too. Where do you wanna go?"

"Somewhere far. Another country. Like Europe or something. I've been wanting to take you there since I went there on my last tour."

"We can go wherever you wanna go. We have some time to think about it."

"It's gon' be hot. Just me and you. Nobody else."

"I'd like that."

"I wanna spend the rest of my life with you." Shawn smiled.

"I wanna spend the rest of my life with you too."

"You mean it?"

"I do. If I haven't learned anything else from this ordeal, it's that I don't wanna lose you."

"Don't worry, baby. I ain't going nowhere. And I'm gonna make sure you don't ever feel left out ever again. I'm sorry you didn't feel like you were as important to me as my music. I just get in grind mode sometimes, but I'mma make sure that changes."

"And I'm gonna stay by your side. No matter what. When the industry gets to be too much, you'll always have me."

Jamon smiled and they kissed each other.

# 49

## DANCE WITH MY FATHER

Despite the heavy gray clouds in the sky, Malcolm followed the attendant through the Maple Grove cemetery in Queens. For the first time on his own, he was visiting his father's grave. He carried a bouquet of flowers. Today would have been his father's 53rd birthday. They stopped in front of his gray and black headstone that read "MARK JOHN BROWN AKA MALCOLM JOSIAH BROWN SR. Father-Husband-Brother." Malcolm thanked the attendant and stood there in silence looking at his father's grave. He set the flowers down and continued to look in silence. He felt his eyes tear up. It had been years since he had been there. And now he was there alone.

"Hey, Pop. I hope you can hear me. Happy Birthday." He took out his wallet which had a picture of his father in it. "I take this picture with me everywhere I go so I always got you with me. And I got a new tat with your name on it." Malcolm rolled up his sleeve to show his new tattoo.

"Sorry it took me so long to come visit. Never thought I would be able to come here by myself. It's hard for me. I miss you, Pop. Living my life without you ain't been easy. I gotta keep it real. I was pissed with you for getting addicted to drugs and dying on me. I needed you. Wasn't I enough for you to live for? I needed you. I needed you, Pop. I needed you to protect me. I needed you to show me things and to teach me how to be a man. And Uncle Claude." Malcolm blew air from his cheeks as he tried to find the strength to continue. "I always thought if you were around, he wouldn't have done what he did to me. I needed you, Daddy! I wanted my Daddy to be with me! And you were gone." Tears streamed from his eyes, dripping over his lips and down his chin. "But I forgive you. And I love you still." He wiped his tears away. "I got something I gotta tell you, Pop." He exhaled. "I'm gay. I used to think it had something to do with Uncle Claude touching me. Or you not being around. But Mom told me that I am just because I am. But I'm still your son and while I'm not perfect, I don't wanna do anything to shame your name."

He thought about Malik, someone he tended to think about from time to time. "I fell in love earlier this year, Pop. Actually I'm still in love with him. But I fucked it all up. Sorry for cussing but I did. He was a good dude but my selfish ways destroyed what we had. I wish I had you around to talk about it. I know you could give me some insight. Moms is cool but I needed to talk to a man about it. And I don't really have nobody older than me I can talk to about that. Well I do, but I mean an older guy like you who's been there and done that."

He sat on his father's grave and leaned against the cool headstone. "You remember how I would always ask you and Mom to make me a little brother? Well, I got three big brothers now. Damon, Shawn, and Kevin. You would love 'em Pop. They show me a lot of love. When I thought nobody cared about me or loved me except Mom, they came in my life and reminded me I was worth being loved. Even though they could never replace you, they gave me a lot of what I was missing. Watching them and being around them helped me become a better man. A man who takes care of business."

A fat cold raindrop slapped his head, followed by many more. He looked up at the shower of rain falling from the sky and stood, dusting off his pants. "I finally figured out what I wanna do with my life. I wanna do the voices for cartoons. And the voiceovers for commercials. I even started looking into it. I'm getting started soon in the city. I hope you're proud of me. I miss you." Malcolm put his hands on his father's headstone and tightly closed his eyes. "Watch over me, Pop. I love you."

\* \* \*

That evening Malcolm lay across his bed watching *True Blood*, reflecting on the day's activities while looking at his father's picture in his wallet. He felt his eyes getting heavy.

"Good night, Pop," Malcolm said to the picture.

He kissed it and put his wallet on his nightstand and drifted off to sleep. Some hours later he heard "Love TKO" by Teddy Pendergrass. He woke up to look out the window where the music was coming from. The sun was shining brightly, kids were playing on the sidewalk, people sat on their stoops laughing and talking. Everything was so bright. A silver

Rolls Royce playing the song pulled up outside of Malcolm's building and he went outside. When he reached the front door, a tall dark skinned man stepped out of the car. He wore a black suit with platinum accessories and a matching fedora. His black shoes were shiny and fly. Malcolm looked closer at the man who looked up at him and smiled. Malcolm couldn't believe his eyes.

"Wassup, Pop?" Malcolm said.

He rushed down the steps and hugged his father tight.

"How you doing, son?" Mr. Brown asked hugging him back.

"I'm good Pop. Real good. How you?"

"I'm great, son. You're looking good and my, you have gotten tall," he said looking up at his baby boy.

"Yeah, they all say I look just like you. Is this your whip?"

"Yeah all mine. You wanna go for a ride?"

"Hell yeah! Let's go. I always wanted to ride in one of these."

Mr. Brown opened the passenger side door and Malcolm got in and buckled up. His father got in and opened the sunroof, turned up "Love TKO", and lit a blunt as they pulled off. They rolled down to 125th St with the music, the bud, and in style in the Rolls Royce. It was a clear bright sunny day with nothing but white clouds in the sky.

"So your mama still looking all good, huh?"

"Most beautiful woman in the world."

"You better know it."

Malcolm looked at his father driving and could see all of their similarities. It was almost eerie how much Malcolm looked like him. Even down to their hands and their side profiles.

"125th Street never changes. The center of Harlem. I spent a lot of wild nights here," Mr. Brown said as they drove past the world famous Apollo theatre. They stopped at a red light.

"Son, I want you to know something. I love you just the way you are. You're still my boy and whether you like boys, girls, rainy days, or sunny days, you're my seed. And I love you no matter what. You just be careful because love is some crazy shit no matter who you like. I take it you know that now after your experience with Malik." His father gave him a knowing look with his eyebrows raised.

"You know about that?"

"Oh yeah. I see everything you do, son. I'm your guardian angel. I go everywhere with you. It makes me laugh because your temperament and your sexual appetite is just like mine. Good God, you're just like me in that area. But please be careful cuz times are different from when I was running the streets. Now they got diseases that'll really make your shit fall off."

"True that."

"And I want you to promise me that you'll look after your mama as she dates this dude."

"I will."

"I'm sorry I had to leave you that way. I know you feel like I let you down. I got caught up, son. Drugs are the devil. Don't you ever get addicted to no drugs you hear me? Never. Especially not cocaine or heroin. They're all bad but those were my poisons of choice and if you ever come across those, I want you to remember that's what took your old man out. I hope you can forgive me."

"I do."

Malcolm took a pull of weed and nodded his head. "So if drugs are the devil then why are we smoking bud?"

"Because this is the real shit. Ain't nobody ever died from smoking herb. This is natural. Pass that on over here." Malcolm took a pull and passed it to his father. They hit the west side highway and rode through Times Square.

"I used to bring your mother down here to see Broadway shows. We used to have so much fun when we first started going out. Your mama was a real fox. I used to love showing her off."

"I saw the pictures. She looked like a model."

"She was like an African goddess. Everyone thought she was gorgeous."

They made their way up to the 59th Street Bridge and crossed over into Queens. They rode through their old neighborhood in the Astoria houses projects.

"Wow, I ain't been around here in a long time, Pop! That's our old building right there! I'll never forget. Apartment 4D. That was home."

"That was definitely home."

Malcolm looked out the window and had so many happy memories. His father drove to the Astoria Park. "Look, there is the park you used to take me to."

"Yup. And look at that," Mr. Brown said as he pulled over and put the car in park.

"Hey, that's me!"

Malcolm saw himself as a little boy running to the park with a windbreaker jacket on. His tall and handsome father was following him wearing a slick black leather jacket and a hat. Grown up Malcolm looked at little Malcolm with a bright smile.

"Come on, Daddy!" Little Malcolm said with excitement.

"I'm right here, son," his father said.

Little Malcolm ran to get on one of the swings and his father came to push him on it. "I wanna go higher!"

"Pump your legs like I showed you. You'll get up there."

"I love you, Daddy!"

"I love you too, son."

Grown up Malcolm looked at his father.

"I love you, Pop."

"I love you too, son."

Malcolm and his father looked at themselves from what seemed like a past lifetime.

* * *

Malcolm woke up to see his mother come in his bedroom and turn off his TV.

"Mama," he said.

She jumped, startled. "Oh baby, I didn't know you were awake."

"I just woke up. I had a dream about Dad."

"Really?"

"Yeah. He was driving a Rolls Royce and we went all over New York. We even went back to the Astoria houses. It was so real. I could even smell his cologne. And the new car smell of the Rolls."

"Sounds like he was checking in on you. What did he say?"

"He apologized for getting hooked on drugs and said to be careful cuz love is crazy."

"He would know that better than anyone."

"It was crazy."

"I believe he really was visiting you, you know. You meant everything to your father. When you were born, he was so happy to have a son.

I was in the backseat with you as we came home from the hospital and he told everyone he saw, 'That's my baby boy she's holding back there.' I said, 'Well I *am* his mother. What do you think I am, his nurse?'" They laughed. "He loved you so much. I love you too."

"I love you too, Mama."

"I'll see you in the morning." she said as she closed the door. He smiled and looked up at the sky.

"Good night, Pop." He put his ipod headphones on and listened to "Love TKO" and drifted back off to sleep.

# EPILOGUE

As the pristine waters of Tahiti washed up on the island's shore, drenching his feet and legs, Shawn looked down at his pretty toes in the clear water and wiggled them. He spread his toes wide letting the water and sand get between them. He chuckled knowing that was something Jamon would have loved to see him do. The sun caressed his face and he had already turned one shade darker from enjoying the sunshine for the past few days. He felt like he was channeling Malcolm being that he had his shirt off almost the entire time he was in Tahiti, except when he went to eat. While deep in thought beneath the warm sunrays, he felt so sexy and sensual. What an eventful year it had been. Not only had he survived everything he'd experienced, he emerged stronger with a love of self he'd never had before.

*You made it Shawn. You made it through. And now life is good.*

He could feel Jamon come from behind him before wrapping his arms around him and kissing him on the neck.

"What you doing out here?"

"Just thinking."

Jamon sighed. "You're not tripping about that phone conversation, are you?"

He was referring to the disturbing phone call that Jamon had received from Darnell last night. Darnell had called him, knowing full well that the court had banned him from making any contact with Jamon. After a brief trial, Darnell had been sentenced to eight years for illegal weapons possession and aggravated assault with a deadly weapon. The court had been lenient enough to give him sixty days to turn himself in.

Yes, the conversation had Shawn bothered. Darnell had called to apologize to Jamon for shooting him. And Jamon had quickly accepted his apology and issued an apology of his own for misleading Darnell and scarring him emotionally. With the truce called between the two, Shawn wondered what would happen once Darnell was released from prison. Would he try to win Jamon's heart again? Would he try to kill Shawn again?

Jamon's sigh sounded sad. "So I guess you are still thinking about that conversation."

"Honestly, I've been thinking about a lot of things."

"So have I."

Shawn glanced over his shoulder. "What have you been thinking about?"

"Come inside. I wanna show you something." Jamon took him by the hand and led him back to their beach hut that sat on the water. Shawn was amazed at how quick Jamon's recovery process had been. After a few weeks of physical therapy, he already walked standing up straight and moved around as if he had never been shot. And the lovemaking had gotten deeper and more sensual, reaching levels neither of them had ever experienced. They had surpassed orgasms. They hit the sky together.

Once back in the bedroom of their quaint tropical villa, Jamon hit a button on his laptop, bringing up his Skype account. Genuine surprise covered Shawn's face when he saw the faces of his parents and Jamon's mother on the screen, looking at them.

"Mom, Dad, Ms. King."

"Hey babe!" Ms. Jones said as she and Shawn's father waved. Shawn quickly grabbed a shirt to cover his bare chest.

"Jamon, what's going on? Why didn't you tell me we were skyping? Got me all naked in front of everybody," Shawn said through clenched teeth as he snatched on a wife beater and hit Jamon's arm.

"Ain't no use in covering it up now; we done seen it," Ms. King said laughing.

"I don't know why he's shy now. He's been walking around the last few days just like that," Jamon said as he pulled up another Skype window with Damon, Kevin, and Malcolm looking on.

"Harlem boys, y'all there?"

"We're here. We saw Shawn and all his *nekkidness*," Kevin said as they laughed.

"Are y'all having fun?" Damon asked.

"Yeah, we are."

"Jamon, what's going on?" Shawn asked.

"Sit in this chair."

"I don't wanna sit. I wanna know what's going on."

"I'll tell you. Just sit." Shawn did as he was told and looked at Jamon impatiently. All eyes were on the both of them. Jamon took a deep breath. "You know I love you, right?"

Immediately, Shawn put two and two together and his eyes widened with shock as his mouth opened.

"Wait...are you..."

"Shhh. Let me talk."

Shawn looked at the faces of their parents and his boys who were looking on with expressions of joy.

"So you know the record deal I just signed with Sony Music is going to take me away for a few weeks, while I start recording the album, right?" Shawn rolled his eyes. *Please, don't remind me.* "And I remember you feeling like my music was drowning you out. I don't want that to happen this time—"

"Jamon, if you're about to tell me that you've decided to cancel that record deal I won't let you—"

"No, Mook, that's not it. This is a little harder than I thought it would be, but just be patient with me." Taking a moment to gather his emotions, Jamon inhaled deeply. "I'm never gonna put music before you again. You held me down, stuck by me even when I didn't deserve it, and then after doing the worst thing I could do to you, you came back and loved me even more. And when I got popped, you nursed me back to health. I've never had unconditional love like that. What I'm saying is, I don't wanna just be your friend. I don't wanna just be your roommate or your lover. I wanna be your husband." Jamon took a ring box from his pocket and opened it, revealing a shiny silver band with tiny white diamonds em-bedded inside. "Shawn Ellison Jones, will you marry me?"

Tears of joy immediately spilled from Shawn's eyes.

"Oh my God. Yes, yes, yes, I will marry you." Jamon slid the ring onto Shawn's finger and they stood to kiss. To the sound of their onlookers' applause, they cried in each other's arms and rocked back and forth in a loving embrace. Once they caught glimpse of the family watching, both of their mothers were wiping tears and the boys were smiling big.

"I'm happy for you, son. You found love in this world. Nothing is more important than that. You take care of my boy, Jamon. He's a good one," Mr. Jones said.

"Yes sir."

"I love you Jamon King."

"I love you too, Shawn Jones King." They kissed again and watched the beautiful sun set over the Atlantic Ocean.

* * *

The tension mounted in the New York City courtroom where Kevin was suing Charles for all he had done. It was eerie to see Charles now because his once beautiful body was severely burned. The only thing that wasn't charred by the fire was his face. But his hands, neck, and everything else was clearly burned. Surprise witnesses were called to the stand from Charles' past. Two men Charles dated before Kevin came forward and told their stories of how Charles was physically abusive to them as well. In a shocking twist of events, Charles younger brother Elijah showed up on the stand and told startling stories of Charles' terrible temper from when they were growing up. He even revealed a burn on his back given to him by Charles from when he was a teenager. Elijah's testimony was something that caused a divide in the Wright family, but once he found out what his brother had done to Kevin, he felt convicted to speak up.

It was a painful two weeks, but the judge and jury ruled in Kevin's favor. Not only was Charles going to jail for 66 years, but Charles was ordered to pay Kevin ten million dollars in damages and all of his legal fees. Kevin resigned from his job and enrolled in a master's degree program at the college.

Damon helped him find a fabulous sprawling condo overlooking the scenic Morningside Park in a hilltop luxury building in Harlem. With a new home, a master's degree in progress, a good therapist, his boys, and new money, Kevin was slowly putting the pieces of his shattered life back together.

* * *

Malcolm did some googling and found a reputable voiceover class to attend in the city. His teacher was very impressed by his natural comedic timing and his ability to make his voice do exactly what he wanted it to. With her instruction, he completed the course in less time than expected and re-corded one of the best voiceover demos to come out of the school. With a new lease on life, he had found his true calling and was ready to take the industry by storm and hopefully become a commercial and cartoon voice-over actor.

* * *

Damon received a call from the personal manager from a famous rapper from New York who was looking to buy a house out in Jamaica estates. The rapper wanted to be covert so his manager didn't even give Damon his name. He asked if they could meet up at Damon's office and drive out to the property for sale together. Damon nervously accepted; when he opened the door of the rapper's SUV, he couldn't believe who the rapper was. He was a multi-platinum hit-making gangsta rapper who was quite famous. Not to mention, he was gorgeous and had a beautiful smile. In person, his baby smooth skin, shiny bald head, dark beard, and bass heavy deep voice was more alluring than it was on TV. Damon couldn't help but ask why all the mystery had surrounded their meeting.

"Because I wanted to get you alone and talk to you uninterrupted. I did a little research and your name came up as one of the top realtors in the city. And after I saw what you looked like, I heard you were single and I wanted to meet you."

"You mean—you're gay?"

"I'm a lover of men."

"But I saw your reality show with your child's mother trying to work things out."

"That was for show. And they paid me well."

"Does she know you date men?"

"She knows. She also knows what will happen to her if she tells anyone my secret. But she's cool about it."

"She looked like she was crying real tears over you on the show."

"She's trying to be an actress. That reality show shit ain't real. It's all scripted."

"I see. So...what is it about this house you like?"

"It's everything I need. Out in the cut and outside of the city so I can have privacy, a big yard for my son, and lots of space so I can make it a nice home. And I want you to get the commission when I buy it. You will sell it to me won't you?"

"How much are you trying to put down?"

"I'll write you a check for the full amount today. And my credit is perfect."

Somehow, Damon managed to conceal his excitement. "Sounds good."

"Do me a favor, though."

"What's that?"

"Kiss me." After a moment of hesitation, Damon moved close and kissed him. And boy could he kiss. "I been wanting to kiss you since I saw your picture." Damon blushed.

"So what should I call you? It seems too formal if I call you—"

"Poppy. Just call me Poppy."

"Alright Poppy. Well let's go look at this house." Poppy pulled off and Damon had butterflies in his stomach as they cruised down the street.

*I wonder where this will go. I'm not gonna have any expectations. I'm just gonna live in the moment,* Damon thought to himself as Poppy got on to the Robert F. Kennedy Bridge leaving Harlem behind and heading into Queens. He sat back and enjoyed the ride and watched as the Manhattan skyline whizzed by.

L adies and Gentlemen, we have reached our final stop on this train. Hopefully, your trip to Harlem was pleasurable. Please gather your belongings and exit the train. Now you're probably wondering, will Damon finally have a man of his own? Will Shawn and Jamon really get married? Just how will Kevin rebound after all he's been through? And will Malcolm slow down his whorish exploits and finally settle down and be faithful? Find out the answers to all your questions in *Harlem Boyz II: Let's Do It Again* coming soon. Thank you for riding the Jerzee Boy Publications express service train. Have a good day!

THE END

# Discussion Questions

1. Out of all four Harlem Boyz—Damon, Shawn, Kevin, and Malcolm—who was your favorite character? Why?

2. Did you predict the fate of Shawn and Jamon's relationship?

3. If you fell in love with a married man or woman, would you stay and hope they get divorced? Or would you leave?

4. Could you date someone like Malcolm?

5. Did you have any idea Charles would be the way he was?

6. What would you have done in Kevin's situation?

7. What did you think of Malcolm's relationship with his mother, Mama Nzingha?

8. What were your thoughts on gay men before reading this book? And now?

9. If you could hang out with any one of these guys, who would it be?

10. If you could date one of these guys, who would it be and why?

11. Which storyline resonated with you the most?

12. What would you like to see happen with Damon since reconnecting with his father?

13. What would you like to see happen with Shawn and Jamon?

14. What would you like to see happen with Kevin after all he's been through and his new gains?

15. Which character do you think had the most growth?

16. Did you expect something worse to happen to Kevin?

17. What do you think Malcolm will be like after all he has experienced?

18. Do you have any idea who it is that Damon gets in the car with at the end?

19. Will you be back for the sequel?

20. If this were a movie, who would you like to see cast for the roles?

25340462R00175

Made in the USA
Charleston, SC
26 December 2013